COLLECTED FICTION

Born in Ireland, Neil Jordan is an award-winning writer
and internationally celebrated film director. He is the
author of a collection of stories, *Night in Tunisia*
(winner of the *Guardian* Fiction Prize), and three novels,
The Past, The Dream of a Beast and *Sunrise with Sea
Monster*. His films include *Angel, The Company of
Wolves, Mona Lisa, The Crying Game,* which won him
an Oscar for best screenplay in 1993, *Interview with
the Vampire* and *Michael Collins*.

Neil Jordan

COLLECTED
FICTION

VINTAGE

Published by Vintage 1997

2 4 6 8 10 9 7 5 3 1

Night in Tunisia copyright © Neil Jordan 1976
The Past copyright © Neil Jordan 1980
The Dream of a Beast copyright © Neil Jordan 1983

Night in Tunisia
First published by the Irish Writers' Cooperative, Dublin, Ireland, 1976
First published in Great Britain by Writers and Readers
Publishing Cooperative, 1979
Vintage edition 1993
The Past
First published in Great Britain by Jonathan Cape Ltd, 1980
Vintage edition 1993
The Dream of a Beast
First published in Great Britain by Chatto & Windus Ltd, 1983
Vintage edition 1993

This edition first published in Great Britain by
Vintage, 1997

Vintage
Random House, 20 Vauxhall Bridge Road, London SW1V 2SA

Random House Australia (Pty) Limited
20 Alfred Street, Milsons Point, Sydney
New South Wales 2061, Australia

Random House New Zealand Limited
18 Poland Road, Glenfield,
Auckland 10, New Zealand

Random House South Africa (Pty) Limited
Endulini, 54 Jubilee Road, Parktown 2193, South Africa

Random House UK Limited Reg. No. 954009

A CIP catalogue record for this book
is available from the British Library

ISBN 0099753618

Papers used by Random House UK Ltd are natural, recyclable products made from wood grown in sustainable forests. The manufacturing processes conform to the environmental regulations of the country of origin

Printed and bound in Great Britain by
Cox & Wyman, Reading, Berkshire

CONTENTS

NIGHT IN TUNISIA

CONTENTS

ACKNOWLEDGEMENTS

New Irish Writing, Stand, London Magazine, Best Irish Stories, ed. David Marcus (Paul Elek), Icarus, Journal of Irish Literature, St Stephens.

To Vivienne Shields

INTRODUCTION
by Sean O'Faolain

THIS IS A highly original, personal, distinctive and
interesting book. What more can one ask of any book except
that it should be written by a man who also has the gift of
words, images, feelings, responsiveness? Neil Jordan shows
all these qualities. If he keeps and develops his primal gifts –
he is quite young; barely 25 when this first collection of
stories appeared – he will become an outstanding writer. At
present he is intensely concerned with things of the mind and
spirit rather than with the social world in which most of us
spend most of our busy lives, but he is also tremendously
responsive to all the things, people, surroundings and influences that have affected him as a youth – which is precisely
how one would also describe the relationship of Joyce to his
world in *Portrait of the Artist as a Young Man*. A further
cause for special interest in Neil Jordan is that while being
thus engrossed in his locale he is in no way, as Joyce also
was not, in the least bit parochial or regionalist. In fact,
surprisingly and delightfully, the hero of the central story of
this group of stories is American jazz music, the objective
correlative of his theme is an alto saxophone and its presiding
deity is old Charlie (Bird) Parker. In harmony with the mood
of this music Jordan concentrates on the sexual growth of a
very real boy through his relationship with a very real girl,
who like himself is a life-yearner, as well as one with the
watchful father, one of the last of the old brass-men. In
the course of that tale music releases the youth to life, to
love, to selfhood. This kind of metaphor and symbol is a
new and releasing thing in Irish literature. It is a personal
language. It has no echo of the worn out, now rather boring

old language and symbolism of rural Ireland's little white-washed country cottages, her wet winding roads, her colleens driving home the cows, her old priests, the little country chapel, the patriotic songs and laments of country pubs. This young man's metaphors are songs like *The Crying Game*, *The Tennessee Waltz*, *Night in Tunisia*, a boy fingering an old piano in a dance hall, the sax wailing high, and out there beyond the tin hut where he and his father live, enclosed and alone, the dusk, the waves on the beach, the night, the girl, the world, the future.

LAST RITES

ONE WHITE-HOT Friday in June at some minutes after five o'clock a young builder's labourer crossed an iron railway overpass, just off the Harrow Road. The day was faded now and the sky was a curtain of haze, but the city still lay hard-edged and agonisingly bright in the day's undiminished heat. The labourer as he crossed the overpass took note of its regulation shade of green. He saw an old, old negro immigrant standing motionless in the shade of a red-bricked wall. Opposite the wall, in line with the overpass, he saw the Victorian facade of Kensal Rise Baths. Perhaps because of the heat, or because of a combination of the heat and his temperament, these impressions came to him with an unusual clarity; as if he had seen them in a film or in a dream and not in real, waking life. Within the hour he would take his own life. And dying, a cut-throat razor in his hand, his blood mingling with the shower-water into the colour of weak wine he would take with him to whatever vacuum lay beyond, three memories: the memory of a green-painted bridge; of an old, bowed, shadowed negro; of the sheer tiled wall of a cubicle in what had originally been the wash-houses of Kensal Rise Tontine and Workingmen's Association, in what was now Kensal Rise Baths.

The extraordinary sense of nervous anticipation the labourer experienced had long been familiar with him. And, inexplicable. He never questioned it fully. He knew he antici-pated something, approaching the baths. He knew that it wasn't quite pleasure. It was something more and less than pleasurable, a feeling of ravishing, private vindication, of exposure, of secret, solipsistic victory. Over what he never asked. But he knew. He knew as he approached the baths to wash off the dust of a week's labour, that this hour would be the week's high-point. Although during the week he never thought of it, never dwelt on its pleasures – as he did, for instance on his prolonged Saturday morning's rest – when the hour came it was as if the secret thread behind his week's existence was emerging into daylight, was exposing itself to the scrutiny of daylight, his daylight. The way the fauna of the sea-bed are exposed, when the tide goes out.

And so when he crossed the marble step at the door, when he faced the lady behind the glass counter, handing her sevenpence, accepting a ticket from her, waving his hand to refuse towel and soap, gesticulating towards the towel in his duffle-bag, each action was performed with the solemnity of an elaborate ritual, each action was a ring in the circular maze that led to the hidden purpose – the purpose he never elaborated, only felt; in his arm as he waved his hand; in his foot as he crossed the threshold. And when he walked down the corridor, with its white walls, its strange hybrid air, half unemployment exchange, half hospital ward, he was silent. As he took his place on the long oak bench, last in a line of negro, Scottish and Irish navvies his expression preserved the same immobility as theirs, his duffle-bag was kept between his feet and his rough slender hands between his knees and his eyes upon the grey cream wall in front of him. He listened to the rich, public voices of the negroes, knowing the warm colours of even their work-clothes without having to look. He listened to the odd mixture of reticence and resentment in the Irish voices. He felt the tiles beneath his feet, saw the flaking wall before him the hard oak bench beneath him, the grey-haired cockney caretaker emerging every now and then from the shower-hall to call 'Shower!', 'Bath!' and at each call the next man in the queue rising, towel and soap under one arm. So plain, so commonplace, and underneath the secret pulsing – but his face was immobile.

As each man left the queue he shifted one space forward and each time the short, crisp call issued from the cockney he turned his head to stare. And when his turn eventually came to be first in the queue and the cockney called 'Shower!'

he padded quietly through the open door. He had a slow walk that seemed a little stiff, perhaps because of the unnatural straightness of his back. He had a thin face, unremarkable but for a kind of distance in the expression; removed, glazed blue eyes; the kind of inwardness there, of immersion, that is sometimes termed stupidity.

The grey-haired cockney took his ticket from him. He nodded towards an open cubicle. The man walked slowly through the rows of white doors, under the tiled roof to the cubicle signified. It was the seventh door down.

'Espera me, Quievo!'.

'Ora, deprisa, ha?'.

He heard splashing water, hissing shower-jets, the smack of palms off wet thighs. Behind each door he knew was a naked man, held timeless and separate under an umbrella of darting water. The fact of the walls, of the similar but totally separate beings behind those walls never ceased to amaze him; quietly to excite him. And the shouts of those who communicated echoed strangely through the long, perfectly regular hall. And he knew that everything would be heightened thus now, raised into the aura of the green light.

He walked through the cubicle door and slid the hatch into place behind him. He took in his surroundings with a slow familiar glance. He knew it all, but he wanted to be a stranger to it, to see it again for the first time, always the first time: the wall, evenly gridded with white tiles, rising to a height of seven feet; the small gap between it and the ceiling; the steam coming through the gap from the cubicle next door; the jutting wall, with the full-length mirror affixed to it; behind it, enclosed by the plastic curtain, the shower. He went straight to the mirror and stood motionless before it. And the first throes of his removal began to come upon him. He looked at himself the way one would examine a flat-handled trowel, gauging its usefulness; or, idly, the way one would examine the cracks on a city pavement. He watched the way his nostrils, caked with cement-dust, dilated with his breathing. He watched the rise of his chest, the buttons of his soiled white work-shirt straining with each rise, each breath. He clenched his teeth and his fingers. Then he

9

undressed, slowly and deliberately, always remaining in full view of the full-length mirror.

After he was unclothed his frail body with its thin ribs, hard biceps and angular shoulders seemed to speak to him, through its frail passive image in the mirror. He listened and watched.

Later it would speak, lying on the floor with open wrists, still retaining its goose-pimples, to the old cockney shower-attendant and the gathered bathers, every memory behind the transfixed eyes quietly intimated, almost revealed, by the body itself. If they had looked hard enough, had eyes keen enough, they would have known that the skin wouldn't have been so white but for a Dublin childhood, bread and margarine, cramped, carbonated air. The feet with the miniature half-moon scar on the right instep would have told, eloquently, of a summer spent on Laytown Strand, of barefoot walks on a hot beach, of sharded glass and poppies of blood on the summer sand. And the bulge of muscle round the right shoulder would have testified to two years hod-carrying, just as the light, nervous lines across the forehead proclaimed the lessons of an acquisitive metropolis, the glazed eyes themselves demonstrating the failure, the lessons not learnt. All the ill-assorted group of bathers did was pull their towels more rigidly about them, noting the body's glaring pubes, imagining the hair (blonde, maybe) and the skin of the girls that first brought them to life; the first kiss and the indolent smudges of lipstick and all the subsequent kisses, never quite recovering the texture of the first. They saw the body and didn't hear the finer details – just heard that it had been born, had grown and suffered much pain and a little joy; that its dissatisfaction had been deep; and they thought of the green bridge and the red-bricked walls and understood – .

He savoured his isolation for several full minutes. He allowed the cold seep fully through him, after the heat of clothes, sunlight. He saw pale, rising goose-pimples on the mirrored flesh before him. When he was young he had been in the habit of leaving his house and walking down to a busy sea-front road and clambering down from the road to the mud-flats below. The tide would never quite reach the wall and there would be stretches of mud and stone and the long sweep of the cement wall with the five-foot high groove running through it where he could sit, and he would look at the stone, the flat mud and the dried cakes of sea-lettuce and see the tide creep over them and wonder at their impassivity, their imperviousness to feeling; their deadness. It seemed to him the ultimate blessing and he would sit so long that when he came to rise his legs, and sometimes his whole body, would be numb. He stood now till his immobility, his cold, became near-agonising. Then he walked slowly to the shower, pulled aside the plastic curtain and walked inside. The tiles had that dead wetness that he had once noticed in the beach-pebbles. He placed each foot squarely on them and saw a thin cake of soap lying in a puddle of grey water. Both were evidence of the bather here before him and he wondered vaguely what he was like; whether he had a quick, rushed shower or a slow, careful one; whether he in turn had wondered about the bather before him. And he stopped wondering, as idly as he had begun. And he turned on the water.

It came hot. He almost cried with the shock of it; a cry of pale, surprised delight. It was a pet love with him, the sudden heat and the wall of water, drumming on his crown, sealing him magically from the world outside; from the universe outside; the pleasurable biting needles of heat; the ripples of water down his hairless arms; the stalactites gathering at each fingertip; wet hair, the sounds of caught breath and thumping water. He loved the pain, the total self-absorption of it and never wondered why he loved it; as with the rest of the weekly ritual – the trudge through the muted officialdom of the bath corridors into the solitude of the shower cubicle, the total ultimate solitude of the boxed, sealed figure, three feet between it and its fellow; the contradictory joy of the first impact of heat, of the pleasurable pain.

An overseer in an asbestos works who had entered his cubicle black and who had emerged with a white, blotchy, greyish skin-hue divined the reason for the cut wrists. He looked at the tiny coagulation of wrinkles round each eye and knew that here was a surfeit of boredom; not a moody,

11

*arbitrary, adolescent boredom, but that boredom which is a
condition of life itself. He saw the way the mouth was tight
and wistful and somehow uncommunicative, even in death,
and the odour of his first contact with that boredom came
back to him. He smelt again the incongruous fish-and-chip
smells, the smells of the discarded sweet-wrappings, the metallic odour of the fun-palace, the sulphurous whiff of the
dodgem wheels; the empty, musing, poignant smell of the
seaside holiday town, for it was here that he had first met
his boredom; here that he had wandered the green carpet of
the golf-links, with the stretch of grey sky overhead, asking,
what to do with the long days and hours, turning then
towards the burrows and the long grasses and the strand,
deciding there's nothing to do, no point in doing, the sea
glimmering to the right of him like the dull metal plate the
dodgem wheels ran on. Here he had lain in a sand-bunker
for hours, his head making a slight indentation in the sand,
gazing at the mordant procession of clouds above. Here he
had first asked, what's the point, there's only point if it's fun,
it's pleasure, if there's more pleasure than pain; then thinking
of the pleasure, weighing up the pleasure in his adolescent
scales, the pleasure of the greased fish-and-chip bag warming
the fingers, of the sweet taken from the wrapper, the discarded wrapper and the fading sweetness, of the white flash
of a pubescent girl's legs, the thoughts of touch and caress,
the pain of the impossibility of both and his head digging
deeper in the sand he had seen the scales tip in favour of
pain. Ever so slightly maybe, but if it wins then what's the
point. And he had known the sheep-white clouds scudding
through the blueness and ever after thought of them as significant of the pre-ponderance of pain; and he looked now
at the white scar on the young man's instep and thought of
the white clouds and thought of the bobbing girls' skirts and
of the fact of pain – .*

The first impact had passed; his body temperature had
risen and the hot biting needles were now a running, massaging hand. And a silence had descended on him too, after
the self-immersed orgy of the driving water. He knew this
shower was all things to him, a world to him. Only here

could he see this world, hold it in balance, so he listened to what was now the quietness of rain in the cubicle, the hushed, quiet sound of dripping rain and the green rising mist through which things are seen in their true, unnatural clarity. He saw the wet, flapping shower-curtain. There was a bleak rose-pattern on it, the roses faded by years of condensation into green: green roses. He saw the black spaces between the tiles, the plug-hole with its fading, whorling rivulet of water. He saw the exterior dirt washed off himself, the caked cement-dust, the flecks of mud. He saw creases of black round his elbow-joints, a high-water mark round his neck, the more permanent, ingrained dirt. And he listened to the falling water, looked at the green roses and wondered what it would be like to see those things, hear them, doing nothing but see and hear them; nothing but the pure sound, the sheer colour reaching him; to be as passive as the mud pebble was to that tide. He took the cake of soap then from the grilled tray affixed to the wall and began to rub himself hard. Soon he would be totally, bleakly clean.

There was a dash of paint on his cheek. The negro painter he worked beside had slapped him playfully with his brush. It was disappearing now, under pressure from the soap. And with it went the world, that world, the world he inhabited, the world that left grit under the nails, dust under the eyelids. He scrubbed at the dirt of that world, at the coat of that world, the self that lived in that world, in the silence of the falling water. Soon he would be totally, bleakly clean.

The old cockney took another ticket from another bather he thought he recognised. Must have seen him last week. He crumpled the ticket in his hand, went inside his glass-fronted office and impaled it onto a six-inch nail jammed through a block of wood. He flipped a cigarette from its packet and lit it, wheezing heavily. Long hours spent in the office here, the windows running with condensation, had exaggerated a bronchial condition. He let his eyes scan the seventeen cubicles. He wondered again how many of them, coming every week for seventeen weeks, have visited each of the seventeen showers. None, most likely. Have to go where they're told, don't they. No way they can get into a different box other than the one that's empty, even if they should want to. But what are the chances, a man washing himself ten years here, that he'd do the full round? And the chances that he'd be stuck to the one? He wrinkled his eyes and coughed and rubbed the mist from the window to see more clearly.

White, now. Not the sheer white of the tiles, but a human, flaccid, pink skin-white. He stood upwards, let his arms dangle by his sides, his wrists limp. His short black hair was plastered to his crown like a tight skull-cap. He gazed at the walls of his own cubicle and wondered at the fact that there were sixteen other cubicles around him, identical to this one, which he couldn't see. A man in each, washed by the same water, all in various stages of cleanliness. And he wondered did the form in the next cubicle think of him, his neighbour, as he did. Did he reciprocate his wondering. He thought it somehow appropriate that there should be men naked, washing themselves in adjacent cubicles, each a foreign country to the other. Appropriate to what, he couldn't have said. He looked round his cubicle and wondered: what's it worth, what does it mean, this cubicle – wondered was any one of the other sixteen gazing at his cubicle and thinking, realizing as he was: nothing. He realized that he would never know.

Nothing. Or almost nothing. He looked down at his body: thin belly, thin arms, a limp member. He knew he had arrived at the point where he would masturbate. He always came to this point in different ways, with different thoughts, by different stages. But when he had reached it, he always realised that the ways had been similar, the ways had been the same way, only the phrasing different. And he began then, taking himself with both hands, caressing himself with a familiar, bleak motion, knowing that afterwards the bleakness would only be intensified after the brief distraction of feeling – in this like everything – observing the while the motion of his belly muscles, glistening under their sheen of running water. And as he felt the mechanical surge of desire run through him he heard the splashing of an anonymous body in the cubicle adjacent. The thought came to him that somebody could be watching him. But no, he thought then, almost

14

disappointed, who could, working at himself harder. He was standing when he felt an exultant muscular thrill run through him, arching his back, straining his calves upwards, each toe pressed passionately against the tiled floor.

The young Trinidadian in the next cubicle squeezed out a sachet of lemon soft shampoo and rubbed it to a lather between two brown palms. Flecks of sawdust – he was an apprentice carpenter – mingled with the snow-white foam. He pressed two handfuls of it under each bicep, ladled it across his chest and belly and rubbed it till the foam seethed and melted to the colour of dull whey, and the water swept him clean again, splashed his body back to its miraculous brown and he slapped each nipple laughingly in turn and thought of a clean body under a crisp shirt, of a night of love under a low red-lit roof, of the thumping symmetry of a reggae band.

There was one intense moment of silence. He was standing, spent, sagging. He heard:

'Hey, you rass, not finished yet?'

'How'd I be finished?'

'Well move that corpse, rassman. Move!'

He watched the seed that had spattered the tiles be swept by the shower-water, diluting its grey, ultimately vanishing into the fury of current round the plug-hole. And he remembered the curving cement wall of his childhood and the spent tide and the rocks and the dried green stretches of sea-lettuce and because the exhaustion was delicious now and bleak, because he knew there would never be anything but that exhaustion after all the fury of effort, all the expense of passion and shame, he walked through the green-rose curtain and took the cut-throat razor from his pack and went back to the shower to cut his wrists. And dying, he thought of nothing more significant than the way, the way he had come here, of the green bridge and the bowed figure under the brick wall and the facade of the Victorian bath-house, thinking: there is nothing more significant.

Of the dozen or so people who gathered to stare – as people will – none of them thought: 'Why did he do it?' All of them, pressed into a still, tight circle, staring at the shiplike body, knew intrinsically. And a middle-aged, fat and possibly simple negro phrased the thought:

'Every day the Lord send me I think I do that. And every day the Lord send me I drink bottle of wine and forget 'bout doin' that'.

They took with them three memories: the memory of a thin, almost hairless body with reddened wrists; the memory of a thin, finely-wrought razor whose bright silver was mottled in places with rust; and the memory of a spurting shower-nozzle, an irregular drip of water. And when they emerged to the world of bright afternoon streets they saw the green-painted iron bridge and the red-brick wall and knew it to be in the nature of these, too, that the body should act thus –

SEDUCTION

'YOU DON'T BELIEVE me, do you', he said, 'you don't believe anything, but I've seen her' – and he repeated it again, but I didn't have to listen this time, I could imagine it so vividly. The naked woman's clothes lying in a heap under the drop from the road where the beach was clumsy with rocks and pebbles, her fat body running on the sand at the edge of the water, the waves splashing round her thick ankles. The imagining was just like the whole summer, it throbbed with forbidden promise. I had been back in the town two days and each day we had hung around till twilight, when the hours seemed longest, when the day would extend its dying till it seemed ready to burst, the sky like a piece of stretched gauze over it, grey, melancholy, yet infinitely desirable and unknown. This year I was a little afraid of him, though he was still smaller than me. I envied and loved his pointed shoes that were turned up and scuffed white and his hair that curled and dripped with oil that did its best to contain it in a duck's tail. I loved his assurance, the nonchalant way he let the vinegar run from the chip-bag onto the breast of his off-white shirt. But I kept all this quiet knowing there were things he envied about me too. I think each of us treasured this envy, longing to know how the other had changed but disdaining to ask. We loved to talk in monosyllables conscious of the other's envy, a hidden mutual delight underneath it like blood. Both of us stayed in the same guest-house as last year. My room faced the sea, his the grounds of the convent, the basket-ball pitch with the tennis-net running through it where the nuns swung rackets with brittle, girlish laughter. We sniffed the smell of apples that came over the

17

town from the monastery orchard behind it and the smell of apples in late August meant something different to me this year, as did the twilight. Last year it would have meant an invitation to rob. I wondered did it mean the same to him. I concluded that it must, with his hair like that. But then he was tougher, more obscene.

'Look, she's coming out now'. He nodded his head sideways towards the chip-shop and I stared in through the dripping steamed glass. It looked warm inside, warm and greasy. I saw the woman coming out of the tiny corridor in which the chips were fried, leaning against the steel counter. Some older boys waiting for orders threw jibes at her. She laughed briefly, then took out a cigarette, put it in her mouth and lit it. I knew that when the cigarette came out its tip would be covered in lipstick, the way it happens in films. When she took the coins from them two gold bangles slipped down onto her fat wrist. There was something mysterious, hard and tired about her, some secret behind those layers of make-up which those older boys shared. I watched them laughing and felt the hard excitement of the twilight, the apples. And I believed him then, though I knew how much he lied. I believed him because I wanted to believe it, to imagine it, the nakedness of this fat blonde woman who looked older than her twenty-five years, who sang every Saturday night at the dance in the local hotel.

'Leanche's her name. Leanche the lion'.

'Lioness', I said, being the erudite one. He looked at me and spat.

'When'll you ever dry up'. I spat too. 'Here'. He held out the chip bag.

I took one. It was like when I came to the guesthouse and he had already been there a day. He stood in the driveway pulling leaves off the rhododendron bush as we took things off the rack of our Ford car. I looked over at him, the same as last year, but with a new sullenness in his face. I hoped my face was even more deadpan. He turned his face away when I looked but stayed still, pulling the oily leaves till the unpacking was finished. Then I went over to talk to him. He said that the town was a dump this year, that there was an

Elvis playing in the local cinema. He said that Ford cars with high backs had gone out since the ark. I asked him had his people got a car yet and he said no. But somehow it seemed worse to have a car with a high back and rusted doors than no car at all.

He said 'Come on, we'll go to the town' and we both walked to the gate, to the road that ran from the pier towards the town where every house was painted white and yellow and in summer was a guest-house.

'Let's go inside' he said, just as it was getting dark and the last of the queue filed from the chipper. 'We've no money' I said. 'Anyway, I don't believe you'. I hoped my fright didn't glare through. 'It's true', he said. 'The man in the cinema told me'. 'Did he see her' I asked. 'No, his brother did'. There was disdain in the statement that I couldn't have countered.

We pushed open the glass door, he took out a comb as he was doing so and slicked it through his hair. I went over to the yellow jukebox and pushed idly at the buttons. 'Are ye puttin' money in it son'. I heard. I turned and saw her looking at me, the ridiculously small curls of her hair tumbling round her large face. Her cheeks were red and her dress was low and her immense bosom showed white through it, matching the grease-stains on her apron. 'No' I said and began to blush to the roots, 'we just wanted to know . . .'

'Have you got the time' Jamie burst in. 'Have you eyes in your head', she countered. She raised her arm and pointed to a clock in the wall above her. Twenty past ten.

We had walked past the harbour and the chip-shop and the Great Northern Hotel that were all the same as last year. The rich hotelier's son who had left the priesthood and had gone a little mad was on the beach again, turning himself to let his stomach get the sun now that his back was brown. Jamie told me about the two Belfast sisters who wore nylons and who were protestants, how they sat in the cinema every night waiting for something. He asked me had I ever got anything off a girl that wore nylons. I asked him had he. He said nothing, but spat on the ground and stirred the spittle with the sole of his shoe. The difference in the town was bigger now, lurid, hemming us in. I borrowed his comb and slicked it through my hair but my hair refused to quiff, it fell back each time on my forehead, incorrigibly flat and sandy-coloured.

The woman in the chip-shop smiled and crooked her arm on the counter, resting her chin on her fist. The folds of fat bulged round the golden bangles. 'Anything else you'd like to know.' I felt a sudden mad urge to surpass myself, to go one better than Jamie's duck-tailed hair. 'Yeah', I began, 'do you . . .' Then I stopped. She had seemed a little like an idiot to me but something more than idiocy stopped me. 'Do I!' she said and turned her head towards me, looking at me straight in the eyes. And in the green irises underneath the clumsy mascara there was a mocking light that frightened me. I thought of the moon with a green mist around it like the Angel of Death in the Ten Commandments. I saw her cheeks and heard the wash of the sea and imagined her padding feet on the sand. And I shivered at the deeper, infinite idiocy there, the lurid idiocy that drew couples into long grass to engage in something I wasn't quite sure of. I blushed with shame, with longing to know it, but was saved by her banging hand on the silver counter. 'If you don't want chips, hop it'. 'Don't worry', said Jamie, drawing the comb through his hair. 'Don't worry', I said, listening to his hair click oilily, making for the glass door. 'I still don't believe you', I said to him outside. 'Do you want to wait up and see then'. I didn't answer. Jamie drew a series of curves that formed a naked woman in the window-dew. We both watched them drip slowly into a mess of watery smudges.

We had gone to the cinema that first night, through the yellow-emulsioned doorway into the darkness of the long hall, its windows covered with sheets of brown paper. I smelt the smells of last year, the sweaty felt brass of the seats and the dust rising from the aisle to be changed into diamonds by the cone of light above. There was a scattering of older couples there, there was Elvis on the screen, on a beach in flowered bathing-trunks, but no Belfast sisters. 'Where are they' I asked him, with the ghost of a triumphant note in my voice. He saved himself by taking out a butt, lighting it and pulling harshly on it. We drank in Elvis silently. Later the cinema projectionist put his head between both our shoulders and said 'Hey boys, you want to see the projection-room?' His breath smelt the same as last year, of cigarettes and peppermint. But this year we said no.

Later again I sat in my room and watched the strand, where two nuns were swinging tennis-rackets on a court they had scrawled on the sand. It was ten past nine and the twilight was well advanced, the balance between blue and grey almost perfect. I sat on my bed and pulled my knees to my chest, rocking softly, listening to the nuns' tinkling laughter, staring at the billows their habits made with each swing of their arms. Soon even the nuns left and the strand was empty but for the scrawled tennis-court and the marks of their high-heeled boots. But I watched on, hearing the waves break, letting the light die in the room around me, weeping for the innocence of last year.

We pressed ourselves against the wall below the road, trying to keep our feet from slipping off the large round pebbles. My father was calling my name from the drive of the guest-house. His voice seemed to echo right down the beach, seeming worried and sad. Soon even the echo died away and Jamie clambered up and peeped over the top and waved to me that no-one was there. Then we walked down the strand making a long trail of footsteps in the half-light. We settled ourselves behind an upturned boat and began to wait. We waited for hours, till Jamie's face became pinched and pale, till my teeth began to chatter. He stared at the sea and broke the teeth from his comb, one by one, scattering them at his feet. I spat in the sand and watched how my spittle rolled into tiny sandballs. The sea washed and sucked and washed and sucked but remained empty of fat women. Then Jamie began to talk, about kisses with the mouth open and closed, about the difference between the feel of a breast under and over a jumper, between nylons and short white socks. He talked for what seemed hours and after a while I stopped listening, I knew he was lying anyway. Then suddenly I noticed he had stopped talking. I didn't know how long he had stopped, but I knew it had been some time before I noticed it. I turned and saw he was hunched up, his face blank like a child's. All the teeth were broken from his comb, his hand was clutching it insensibly and he was crying softly. His hair was wild with curls, the oil was dripping onto his forehead, his lips were purple with the cold. I touched him on the elbow and when his quiet sobbing didn't stop I took off my coat and put it gingerly round his shoulders. He shivered and moved in close to me and his head touched my chest and lay there. I held him there while he slept, thinking how much smaller than me he was after all.

There was a thin rim of light round the edge of the sea when he woke. His face was pale, – though not as grey as that light, and his teeth had begun to chatter. 'What happened', he asked, shaking my coat off. 'You were asleep' I said, 'you missed it', and began a detailed account of how the woman had begun running from the pier right up past me to the end of the strand, how her breasts had bobbed as the water splashed round her thick ankles. 'Liar' he said. 'Yes' I said. Then I thought of home. 'What are we going to do?' I asked him. He rubbed his eyes with his hand and drew wet smudges across each cheek. Then he got up and began to walk towards the sea. I followed him, knowing the sea would obliterate his tears and any I might have. When he came near the water he began to run, splashing the waves round him with his feet and I ran too, but with less abandon, and when he fell face down in the water I fell too. When I could see him through the salt water he was laughing madly in a crying sort of way, ducking his head in and out of the water the way swimmers do. I got to my feet and tried to pull him up but his clothes were clinging to every bone of his thin body. Then I felt myself slipping, being pulled from the legs and I fell in the water again and I felt his arms around my waist, tightening, the way boys wrestle, but more quietly then, and I felt his body not small any longer, pressing against mine. I heard him say 'this is the way lovers do it' and felt his mouth on my neck but I didn't struggle, I knew that in the water he couldn't see my tears or see my smile.

22

SAND

THE DONKEY'S HOOVES were like his sister's fingernails, long and pointed. Except for the ends, which were splintered and rough, not fine and hard.

He was sitting on it, trying to make it move. He could feel its spine against the bone between his legs. He could feel its flanks, like two soft sweaty cushions against each knee and thigh.

He dug his heel into one of the flanks and it shifted a few feet.

'Stop kicking up sand', his sister said. She had that annoyed tone in her voice.

'Will you come for a swim if I stop', he asked.

'Oh just stop, would you'.

'No' he said.

He kicked at the donkey again, though he dreaded his sister's tongue. When she spoke she seemed to know so much that he didn't. It was like her suntan lotion, like her habit of lying by the sea with her eyes closed, on their towel. He felt that somewhere he knew as much as she, but when he came to say it he could never find the words.

'If you kick more sand at me – '

'Alright', he said. 'Alright'.

He put his hands on the donkey's neck and wondered how he could get down with some dignity, some of her dignity. He looked at the dark blue of the sea and the light blue of the sky, thinking about this. Then he heard something far away behind him. A shout. He turned on the donkey, saw someone running across the burrows, arms waving.

He clambered down quickly, without dignity. He thought

23

of tinkers. He knew most donkeys belonged to tinkers. He looked at this donkey and it was as impassive as ever, its hooves curling out of the white sand.

The figure came nearer, running with a peculiar adult single-mindedness. It wasn't an adult however, it was a boy, not much older than him. The boy had run beyond the rim of the grass now and was kicking up sand. He was totally naked. He held a boot in one hand with which every now and then he covered his genitals.

But mostly he couldn't cover them, his arms flailing as he ran. And the boy saw the naked figure, smaller than him, but stronger and much browner, jogging to a halt. He saw the open mouth panting and the eyes, wary as his were, but older and angrier than his could ever have been. The brown nakedness stopping at the waist becoming grey-white nakedness. The boot stationary now in front of the patch of hair.

'That's my donkey. Leave hold of it'.

He did so immediately. Not because he was afraid, which he was, but because he would have done anything those eyes asked. He looked at the shoe and it didn't quite hide that curl of angry hair and that sex. He looked at his sister. She was looking the other way, blushing, arched rigid in her blue swimsuit.

'I'll give you that the next time'.

A small bony fist hovered before his face. Behind it were the eyes, young as his, but with clusters of ancient wrinkles round the edges.

'Okay' he said. He tried not to sound defeated. And the tinker turned and pulled the donkey after him by the thin hair on its neck.

'Really', his sister said.

And now he blushed. The tinker was on the burrows now, pulling the donkey by the hair on its neck. His buttocks swung as he walked, two white patches against the brown of his thin body.

He felt blamed for that nakedness. He felt he could hate his sister, for blaming him.

'Really', she said. 'Some people'.

He felt the words were false, picked up from grown-ups.

24

Her body was arched forward now towards her drawn-up knees, her arms were placed across her knees and her chin was resting on her arms. Her eyelids were lowered, not quite closed, but sealing him off. He wanted to say sorry, but her eyes lay between him and his words. Then he did hate her. He hated her in a very basic way, he felt he would tear her apart, the way one tears the many wrappings off the parcel in the pass-the-parcel game, to see what's inside. He didn't know whether he'd hate what would be inside.

'Jean – ' he began, but she turned on her stomach, away from him, exposing her long back to the sun.

He heard a shout behind him and he turned, glad to escape her. He saw the tinker waving his hands some distance down in the burrows, shouting something he couldn't hear. There was something urgent about him, flailing hands against the sky. So he walked, even though he was afraid, leaving his sister with her cheek resting on her linked hands.

As he walked the tinker grew bigger and the flailing gradually stopped. There was the hot feel of the sand under his bare feet, then the feel of grass, whistling by his calves. Then the boy was in front of him, arms on his hips, waiting for him to approach. He was wearing men's trousers now, sizes too big for him.

'You want a go on the donkey'.

He nodded dumbly.

'I'll give you half an hour with the donkey for half an hour with your sister'.

The boy began to laugh at the thought, his sister and the donkey, an even swop. The tinker began to laugh too and that made the boy laugh louder, huge laughs that went right through his body and stretched his stomach-muscles tight. The tinker's laugh was softer, more knowledgeable. The boy heard this and stopped and looked into the blue eyes which wrinkled in some complicity and kept laughing. Then the boy began to laugh again, loving his laughter, the way he sometimes laughed when adults were laughing. The joke had changed into another joke, a joke he didn't understand, but that made it all the more funny.

25

Then the tinker stopped suddenly. He cupped his hands together to make a stirrup and held them out.

'Here'.

The hands were grimy and lined, skin flaking off them. The boy felt compliant. He was opening a box to let the winds out. He knew and he didn't know. He placed his left foot in the stirrup of flaking hands and swung onto the donkey and the tinker's foot kicked the donkey and the donkey ran.

He was holding its neck, fearful and exhilarated. It was running like he didn't know donkeys could run with rapid thumps of hoof off the grass, with its spine, hard as a gate, crashing off his groin. He pressed his head against its neck and could hear its breathing, angry and sullen, thumping with its hooves. His knees clutched the swollen belly and his hands, gripping each other under the neck, were wet and slimy with saliva from the open jaw. His eyes were closed and he saw in the black behind his eyelids something even blacker emerging, whorling and retreating again.

Then it stopped. He slid over its head and fell to the ground. He fell flat out, his cheek against the burrows' grass and heard his sister screaming, a clear scream, clear as silver.

The donkey's head was hanging and its sides were heaving. Between its legs a black erection dangled, heaving with its sides. The scream still echoed in the boy's mind. Clear and silver, speaking to him, like the reflection of sun on sea-water. He ran.

He ran faster than the donkey. He saw the green burrows, then the white sand, then the clear blue of his sister's swimsuit then a browned tanned back. The sand was kicking up in clumps around him as he threw himself on that back.

He felt the naked shoulders under his hand. Then he felt the shoulders twisting and a hard body pushing him downwards, something hot, hard against his stomach. Both of their fists were hitting the other's face until he was hit hard, once and twice and they both, as if by mutual decision, went quiet. He lay until he became conscious of the other's hot hard groin, then squirmed away. He looked up at his sister. Her head was in one hand and the other hand was covering the bare skin above her swimsuit. He heard a rustle of sand and heard the tinker boy getting up.

'I thought we'd made a swop'. There was a spot of blood on his wizened mouth. He bent forward as if to strike again but changed his hand's direction just as rapidly and scratched the hair behind his ear. The boy started. He grinned.

'I'd only put it through you' he said. Then he hitched up his falling trousers and walked towards the grass.

When he got there he turned.

'That's the last you'll see of my donkey', he said. Then he chuckled with infinite sarcasm. 'Unless you've got another sister'. And he turned again and walked through the grass towards the donkey.

She was crying, great breathful sobs.

'You won't – ', he asked.

'I will', she said. 'I'll tell it all – '

The boy knew, however, that she would be ashamed. He picked up her towel and her suntan lotion and began to walk. He had forgotten about his hate. He was thinking of the donkey and the tinker's flaking palms and his sister's breasts. After a while he turned.

'Stop crying, will you. Nothing happened, did it.'

His hands were wet with the donkey's saliva and to the saliva a fine film of sand was clinging. When he moved his fingers it rustled, whispered, sang.

MR SOLOMON WEPT

THE CHILD HAD rolled pennies and the dodgem wheels had smoked for half a morning when Mr Solomon took time off to stand by the strand. He stood where he was accustomed to, on the lip of the cement path that seemed designed to run right to the sea but that crumbled suddenly and inexplicably into the sand. Mr Solomon smoked a cigarette there, holding it flatly between his lips, letting the smoke drift over his thin moustache into his nostrils. His eyes rested on the lumps of rough-cast concrete half-embedded in the sand. His breath came in with a soft, scraping sound.

The sea looked warm and lazy in midday. Down the beach a marquee was being erected. Mr Solomon looked at the people on the beach, the sunbathers and the men who were unwinding the marquee canvas. He wore a brown suit with narrow legs and wide lapels, his thin face looked like it was long accustomed to viewing sunbathers, people on beaches. Mr Solomon then stopped looking at the people and looked at the sea. He took the cigarette from his mouth, inhaled and replaced it again. The sea looked dark blue to him, the colour of midnight rather than of midday. And though it looked flat and indolent and hot, its blueness was clear and sharp, a sharpness emphasised by the occasional flurry of white foam, the slight swell far out. Mr Solomon knew these to be white horses. But today they reminded him of lace, lace he imagined round a woman's throat, a swelling bosom underneath, covered in navy cloth. He had seen an advertisement for Sherry once with such a picture. He saw her just under the sea, just beneath the film of glassblue. If he lifted his eyes to the horizon again the sea became flat and indolent, and probably too hot for swimming.

Mr Solomon lifted his eyes and saw the flat sea and the flat yellow strand. He thought of the child he had left, something morose and forlorn about the way he pushed penny after penny into the metal slot. Then he looked down the strand and saw the large marquee pole being hoisted and only then realised that it was race day. And Mr Solomon remembered the note again, he remembered the nights of surprised pain, the odd gradual feeling of deadness, how before it happened it had been unthinkable and how after it happened somehow anything other than it had become unthinkable. Now he dressed the boy, shopped, the boy sat in the change booth staring at the racing page while he drank in the Northern Star over lunchtime. He remembered how his wife had left him on Race day, one year ago. How he had come to Laytown three days before the races, to catch the crowds. How on the fourth day he had gone to the caravan behind the rifle-range and found it empty, a note on the flap table. Its message was hardly legible, though simple. Gone with Chas. Won't have to hate you any more. He remembered how he had wondered who Chas was, how he had sat on the unmade bed and stared at this note that over the length of the first night assumed the significance of a train ticket into a country he had never heard of. For he had long ceased to think of her with the words love or hate, he had worked, rolled his thin cigarettes, she had totted the books while he supervised the rent, those words were like the words school or god, part of a message that wasn't important any more, a land that was far away. And now he saw the note and thought of the world that had lived for her, thought of the second May, the May behind the one that woke first beside him in the cramped white caravan, that was sitting beside the singing kettle when he woke; this was Chas's May – but it mightn't have been Chas, it could have spelt Chad – and the thought that she existed gave him a feeling of surprised pain, surprise at the May he had never known of, surprise at the loss of what he had never possessed. But after three days the pained surprise had died and a new surprise asserted itself – a surprise at how easily the unthinkable became possible. He found it was easy to cook, to tot the books, to supervise the dodgem tracks and shooting-range all in one. The boy helped him, he watched the boy from behind the glass of the change booth emptying the slot-machines. When the races finished he stayed on, found the move to another holiday-spot too much bother and unnecessary anyway, since less money would do now. Even when the season ended he didn't move, he sat in the draughty amusement hall through winter and made more than enough to keep rolling his thin cigarettes. The rusted slot-machines became a focus for the local youths with sullen faces and greased hair and he found forgetting her almost as easy a task as that of living with her had been. She had been shrewish, he told himself as her memory grew dimmer, her hair had often remained unwashed for days, she would have soon, within the year, gone to fat. Thus he killed the memory of another her neatly, he forgot the nights at the Palais in Brighton, the evenings in the holiday pubs, her platinum hair and the rich dark of the bottled Guinness (a ladies' drink then) tilted towards her laughing mouth.

But he saw the marquee pole stagger upright and suddenly remembered her as if she had died and as if the day of the Laytown Races was her anniversary. He saw the white horses whip and the marquee canvas billow round the pole and thought suddenly of the dress she had called her one good dress with its sad lace frills and the bodice of blue satin that had more restitchings than original threads. A sense of grief came over him, a feeling of quiet sadness, not wholly unpleasing. He began to think of her as if she had died, he thought of the woman who had lived with him and who indeed had died. He imagined flowers for her, dark blood-red roses and felt bleak and clean as if in celebration of her imagined death he was somehow cleansing both him and his image of her.

He lit another cigarette and turned back on the cement path. He passed a family coming from an ice-cream van a little down it, the cones in their hands already sodden. Mr Solomon watched them pass him and felt he had a secret safe, totally safe from them. He felt as if there was a hidden flame inside him, consuming him, while the exterior remained the same as ever, the smoke still drifted over the same thin lip. He passed the green corrugated hall that served as a golf-club and remembered how each year they came through she had got him to pay green fees, how they had both made an afternoon's slow crawl over nine holes. How she had longed to be someday, a proper member in a proper club. 'But we never settle down enough, do we Jimmy, 'cept in winter, when it's too wet to play . . .'

Mr Solomon walked down the cement walk away from the beach and the rising marquee and felt his grief inside him like old port, hot and mellow. He came to the tarmac road and stood, staring at the tottering facade of the amuse-ments and the dull concrete front of the Northern Star opposite. He wavered for one moment and then headed for the brass-studded door of the Northern Star, the mute lights and wood-and-brass fittings being like night to him at first until his eyes settled. He ordered a drink and gave the barman a sharp look before downing it.

'This one's for my wife', he said.

'I didn't know you had one' said the barman, who was always courteous.

'In memory of her. She died last year'.

'I'm sorry', said the barman. 'Her anniversary?'

'Died on Race day', began Mr Solomon but by this time the barman had headed off discreetly for a customer at the other end. He blinked once then finished his drink and began to feel very angry at the courteous barman. He felt the whiskey tickle down his throat, he felt something in him had been sullied by the bland courtesy, the discreet lights of the hotel bar. He left.

Outside the brightness blinded him as much as the dark-ness had before. Mr Solomon stared down the lean yellow street. It was packed with people and as he watched them, Mr Solomon began to feel for the first time a hatred towards them, en masse. He felt a malignant sameness in them. He felt they laughed, in their summer clothes. He felt they didn't know, in their summer clothes. He felt like a cog in the mechanism of holidays, of holiday towns, he felt somehow

31

slave to their bright clothes and suntans. He no longer felt she had died, he felt something had killed her, that impersonal holiday gaiety had enslaved them both, had aged him, like a slow cancerous growth, had annihilated her. He felt his grief burning inside now, like a rough Irish whiskey. He crossed the street a little faster than he normally did, though his walk was still lethargic by the street's standards. He went into the pub with the black-and-white gabled roof.

That afternoon his tale competed with the banjo-playing tinker, with the crack of beer-glasses, with the story of the roadworker's son who returned and bought out three local publicans. Mr Solomon shouted it, wept it, crowed with it, nobody listened, his thin face acquired a weasel look, a sorry look, his eyes grew more glazed and his speech more blurred, the reason for his grief grew hazy and indeterminate. By half-past four he was just drunk, all he knew was there was something somewhere to feel sorry over, profoundly sorry, somewhere a pain, though the reason for it he could no longer fathom, nor why it should be his pain particularly. Why not that Meath farmer's, with the flushed face and the tweed suit, and at this Mr Solomon grew offensive, sloppily offensive and found himself removed.

He went through the hard daylight again into the dark of the Amusement Parlour. He heard a rustle in the left-hand corner and saw the boy starting up guiltily from the peep-show machine. Mr Solomon thought of the near-naked starlets in high-heels and out-of-date hairdos and got angry again. 'I told you never to go near that', he rasped. The boy replied with a swift obscenity that shocked him silent. He could only stare, at his homemade cloth anorak, his hair clumsily quiffed, sticking out in places, his thin impenetrable face. At his son's face, new to him because he'd never seen it. He made to move towards him, only then realising how drunk he was. He saw the boy's hand draw back and an object fly from it. He raised his hand to protect his face and felt something strike his knuckles. He heard the coin ring off the cement floor and the boy's footsteps running towards the door. He ran after him drunkenly, shouting.

The boy ran towards the beach. Mr Solomon followed.

He saw the horses thunder on the beach, distorted by his drunken run. He saw the line of sand they churned up, the sheets of spray they raised when they galloped in the tide. He saw the boy running for the marquee.

Mr Solomon could hear a brass band playing. He ran till he could run no longer and then he went forward in large clumsy steps, dragging the sand as he went. The sound of the reeds and trumpets grew clearer as he walked, repeated in one poignant phrase, right down the beach. Mr Solomon came to a crowd then, pressed round the marquee and began to push his way desperately through it. He felt people like a wall against him, forcing him out. He began to moan aloud, scrabbling at the people in front of him to force his way in. He imagined the boy at the centre of that crowd, playing a clear golden trumpet. He could see the precise curve of the trumpet's mouth, the pumping keys, the boy's expressionless eyes. He began to curse, trying to wedge himself between the bodies, there was something desperate and necessary beyond them.

He felt himself lifted then, carried a small distance off and thrown in the sand. He lifted his face and wept in the sand and saw the horses churning the sea-spray into a wide area down by the edge. He heard a loud cheer, somewhere behind him.

NIGHT IN TUNISIA

THAT YEAR THEY took the green house again. She was there again, older than him and a lot more venal. He saw her on the white chairs that faced the tennis-court and again in the burrows behind the tennis-court and again still down on the fifteenth hole where the golf-course met the mouth of the Boyne. It was twilight each time he saw her and the peculiar light seemed to suspend her for an infinity, a suspended infinite silence, full of years somehow. She must have been seventeen now that he was fourteen. She was fatter, something of an exhausted woman about her and still something of the girl whom adults called mindless. It was as if a cigarette between her fingers had burnt towards the tip without her noticing. He heard people talking about her even on her first day there, he learnt that underneath her frayed blouse her wrists were marked. She was a girl about whom they would talk anyway since she lived with a father who drank, who was away for long stretches in England. Since she lived in a green corrugated-iron house. Not even a house, a chalet really, like the ones the townspeople built to house summer visitors. But she lived in it all the year round.

They took a green house too that summer, also made of corrugated iron. They took it for two months this time, since his father was playing what he said would be his last stint, since there was no more place for brassmen like him in the world of three-chord showbands. And this time the two small bedrooms were divided differently, his sister taking the small one, since she had to dress on her own now, himself and his father sharing the larger one where two years ago his sister and he had slept. Every night his father took the tenor sax and left for Mosney to play with sixteen others for older couples who remembered what the big bands of the forties sounded like. And he was left alone with his sister who talked less and less as her breasts grew bigger. With the alto saxophone which his father said he could learn when he forgot his fascination for three-chord ditties. With the guitar which he played a lot, as if in spite against the alto saxophone. And with the broken-keyed piano which he played occasionally.

When it rained on the iron roof the house sang and he was reminded of a green tin drum he used to hand when he was younger. It was as if he was inside it.

He wandered round the first three days, his sister formal and correct beside him. There was one road made of tarmac, running through all the corrugated houses towards the tennis-court. It was covered always with drifts of sand, which billowed while they walked. They passed her once, on the same side, like an exotic and dishevelled bird, her long yellow cardigan coming down to her knees, covering her dress, if she wore any. He stopped as she passed and turned to face her. Her feet kept billowing up the sand, her eyes didn't see him, they were puffy and covered in black pencil. He felt hurt. He remembered an afternoon three years ago when they had lain on the golf links, the heat, the nakedness that didn't know itself, the grass on their three backs.

'Why don't you stop her?' he asked his sister.

'Because', she answered. 'Because, because'.

He became obsessed with twilights. Between the hour after tea when his father left and the hour long after dark when his father came home he would wait for them, observe them, he would taste them as he would a sacrament. The tincture of the light fading, the blue that seemed to be sucked into a thin line beyond the sea into what the maths books called

35

infinity, the darkness falling like a stone. He would look at the long shadows of the burrows on the strand and the long shadows of the posts that held the sagging tennis-nets on the tarmac courts. He would watch his sister walking down the road under the eyes of boys that were a little older than him. And since he hung around at twilight and well into the dark he came to stand with them, on the greens behind the clubhouse, their cigarette-tips and their laughter punctuating the dark. He played all the hits on the honky-tonk piano in the clubhouse for them and this compensated for his missing years. He played and he watched, afraid to say too much, listening to their jokes and their talk about girls, becoming most venal when it centred on her.

He laughed with them, that special thin laugh that can be stopped as soon as it's begun.

There was a raft they would swim out to on the beach. His skin was light and his arms were thin and he had no Adam's apple to speak of, no hair creeping over his togs, but he would undress all the same with them and swim out. They would spend a day on it while the sun browned their backs and coaxed beads of resin from the planks. When they shifted too much splinters of wood shot through their flesh. So mostly they lay inert, on their stomachs, their occasional erections hidden beneath them, watching on the strand the parade of life.

It galled his father what he played.

'What galls me', he would say, 'is that you could be so good'.

But he felt vengeful and played them incessantly and even sang the tawdry lyrics. Some day soon, he sang, I'm going to tell the Moon about the crying game. And maybe he'll explain, he sang.

36

'Why don't you speak to her?' he asked his sister when they passed her again. It was seven o'clock and it was getting dark.

'Because' she said. 'Because I don't'.

But he turned. He saw her down the road, her yellow cardigan making a scallop round her fattening buttocks.

'Rita', he called. 'Rita'.

She turned. She looked at him blankly for a moment and then she smiled, her large pouting lips curving the invitation she gave to any boy that shouted at her.

He sat at the broken-keyed piano. The light was going down over the golf-links and his sister's paper-back novel was turned over on the wooden table. He heard her in her room, her shoes knocking off the thin wooden partition. He heard the rustling of cotton and nylon and when the rustles stopped for a moment he got up quickly from the piano and opened the door. She gave a gasp and pulled the dress from the pile at her feet to cover herself. He asked her again did she remember and she said she didn't and her face blushed with such shame that he felt sorry and closed the door again.

The sea had the movement of cloth but the texture of glass. It flowed and undulated, but shone hard and bright. He thought of cloth and glass and how to mix them. A cloth made of glass fibre or a million woven mirrors. He saw that the light of twilight was repeated or reversed at early morning.

He decided to forget about his sister and join them, the brashness they were learning, coming over the transistors, the music that cemented it. And the odd melancholy of the adulthood they were about to straddle, to ride like a Honda down a road with one white line, pointless and inevitable.

His father on his nights off took out his Selmer, old loved talisman that was even more shining than on the day he bought it. He would sit and accompany while his father stood and played – 'That Certain Feeling', 'All The Things You Are', the names that carried their age with them, the embellishments and the filled-in notes that must have been something one day but that he had played too often, that he was too old now to get out of. And to please his father he would close his eyes and play, not knowing how or what he played and his father would stop and let him play on, listening. And he would occasionally look and catch that look in his listening eyes, wry, sad and loving, his pleasure at how his son played only marred by the knowledge of how little it meant to him. And he would catch the look in his father's eyes and get annoyed and deliberately hit a bum note to spoil it. And the sadness in the eyes would outshine the wryness then and he would be sorry, but never sorry enough.

He soon learnt that they were as mistrustful of each other as he was of them and so he relaxed somewhat. He learnt to turn his silence into a pose. They listened to his playing and asked about his sister. They lay on the raft, watched women on the strand, their eyes stared so hard that the many shapes on the beach became one, indivisible. It made the sand-dunes and even the empty clubhouse redundant. Lying face down on the warm planks, the sun burning their backs with an aching langour. The blaring transistor, carried over in its plastic bag. Her on the beach, indivisible, her yellow cardigan glaring even on the hottest days. He noticed she had got fatter since he came. Under them on the warm planks the violent motions of their pricks. She who lived in the chalet all the year round.

The one bedroom and the two beds, his father's by the door, his by the window. The rippled metal walls. The moon like water on his hands, the bed beside him empty. Then the front door opening, the sound of the saxophone case laid down.

His eyes closed, his father stripping in the darkness, climbing in, long underwear and vest. The body he'd known lifelong, old and somewhat loved, but not like his Selmer, shining. They get better with age, he said about instruments. His breath scraping the air now, scraping over the wash of the sea, sleeping.

The tall thin boy put his mouth to the mouth of the french letter and blew. It expanded, huge and bulbous, with a tiny bubble at the tip.

'It's getting worked up', he said.

He had dark curling hair and dark shaven cheeks and a mass of tiny pimples where he shaved. The pimples spread from his ears downwards, as if scattered from a pepper-canister. His eyes were dark too, and always a little closed.

'We'll let it float to England', he said, 'so it can find a fanny big enough for it'.

They watched it bobbing on the waves, brought back and forwards with the wash. Then a gust of wind lifted it and carried it off, falling to skim the surface and rising again, the bubble towards the sky.

He had walked up from the beach and the french letter bound for England. He had seen her yellow cardigan on the tennis-court from a long way off, above the strand. He was watching her play now, sitting on the white wrought-iron seat, his hands between his legs.

She was standing on the one spot, dead-centre of the court, hardly looking at all at her opponent. She was hitting every ball cleanly and lazily and the sound that came from her racquet each time was that taut twang that he knew only came from a good shot. He felt that even a complete stranger would have known, from her boredom, her ease, that she lived in a holiday town with a tennis-court all the year round. The only sign of effort was the beads of sweat round her lips and the tousled blonde curls round her forehead. And every now and then when the man she was playing against managed to send a shot towards the sidelines, she didn't bother to follow it at all. She let the white ball bounce impotent towards the wire mesh.

He watched the small fat man he didn't recognise lose three balls for every ball won. He relished the spectacle of a fat man in whites being beaten by a bored teenage girl in sagging high-heels. Then he saw her throw her eyes upwards, throw her racquet down and walk from the court. The white ball rolled towards the wire mesh.

She sat beside him. She didn't look at him but she spoke as if she had known him those three years.

'You play him. I'm sick of it'.

He walked across the court and his body seemed to glow with the heat generated by the slight touch of hers. He picked up the racquet and the ball, placed his foot behind the white line and threw the ball up, his eye on it, white, skewered against the blue sky. Then it came down and he heard the resonant twang as his racquet hit it and it went spinning into the opposite court but there was no-one there to take it. He looked up and saw the fat man and her walking towards a small white car. The fat man gestured her in and she looked behind at him once before she entered.

And as the car sped off towards Mornington he swore she waved.

The car was gone down the Mornington road. He could hear the pop-pop of the tennis-balls hitting the courts and the twang of them hitting the racquets as he walked, growing fainter. He walked along the road, past the tarmac courts and past the grass courts and past the first few holes of the golf-course which angled in a T round the tennis courts. He walked past several squares of garden until he came to his. It wasn't really a garden, a square of sand and scutch. He walked through the gate and up the path where the sand had been trodden hard to the green corrugated door. He turned the handle in the door, always left open. He saw the small square room, the sand fanning across the line from the door-step, the piano with the sheet-music perched on the keys. He thought of the midday sun outside, the car with her in the passenger seat moving through it, the shoulders of the figure in the driver's seat. The shoulders hunched and fat, expressing something venal. He thought of the court, the white tennis ball looping between her body and his. Her body relaxed, vacant and easeful, moving the racquet so the ball flew where she wished. His body worried, worrying the whole court. He felt there was something wrong, the obedient ball, the running man. What had she lost to gain that ease, he wondered. He thought of all the jokes he had heard and of the act behind the jokes that none of those who told the jokes experienced. The innuendos and the charged words like the notes his father played, like the melodies his father willed him to play. The rich full twang as the ball met her racquet at the centre.

He saw the alto saxophone on top of the piano. He took it down, placed it on the table and opened the case. He looked at the keys, remembering the first lessons his father had taught him when it was newbought, months ago. The keys unpressed, mother-of-pearl on gold, spotted with dust. He took out the ligature and fixed the reed in the mouth-piece. He put it between his lips, settled his fingers and blew. The note came out harsh and childish, as if he'd never learnt. He heard a shifting movement in the inside room and knew that he'd woken his father.

He put the instrument back quickly and made for the tiny bathroom. He closed the door behind him quietly, imagining his father's grey vest rising from the bed to the light of the afternoon sun. He looked into the mirror that closed on the cabinet where the medicine things were kept. He saw his face in the mirror looking at him, frightened, quick glance. Then he saw his face taking courage and looking at him full-on, the brown eyes and the thin fragile jawline. And he began to look at his eyes as directly as they looked at him.

'You were playing', his father said, in the livingroom, in shirtsleeves, in uncombed afternoon hair, 'the alto – '

'No', he said, going for the front door, 'you were dreaming
– '.

And on the raft the fat asthmatic boy, obsessed more than
any with the theatre on the strand, talking about 'it' in
his lisping, mournful voice, smoking cigarettes that made his
breath wheeze more. He had made classifications, rigid as
calculus, meticulous as algebra. There were girls, he said,
and women, and in between them what he termed lady, the
lines of demarcation finely and inexorably drawn. Lady was
thin and sat on towels, with high-heels and suntan-lotions,
without kids. Woman was fat, with rugs and breasts that
hung or bulged, with children. Then there were girls, his age,
thin fat and middling, nyloned, short-stockinged –

He lay on his stomach on the warm wood and listened to
the fat boy talking and saw her walking down the strand.
The straggling, uncaring walk that, he decided, was none of
these or all of these at once. She was wearing flat shoes that
went down at the heels with no stockings and the familiar
cardigan that hid what could have classified her. She walked
to a spot up the beach from the raft and unrolled the bundled
towel from under her arm. Then she kicked off her shoes
and pulled off her cardigan and wriggled out of the skirt her
cardigan had hidden. She lay back on the towel in the yellow
bathing suit that was too young for her, through which her
body seemed to press like a butterfly already moulting in its
chrysalis. She took a bottle then and shook it into her palm
and began rubbing the liquid over her slack exposed body.

He listened to the fat boy talking about her – he was local
too – about her father who on his stretches home came back
drunk and bounced rocks off the tin roof, shouting 'Hewer'.
  'What does that mean', he asked.
  'Just that', said the asthmatic boy. 'Rhymes with sure'.

He looked at her again from the raft, her slack stomach bent forward, her head on her knees. He saw her head lift and turn lazily towards the raft and he stood up then, stretching his body upwards, under what he imagined was her gaze. He dived, his body imagining itself suspended in air before it hit the water. Underwater he held his breath, swam through the flux of tiny bubbles, like crotchets before his open eyes.

'What did you say she was', he asked the fat boy, swimming back to the raft.

'Hewer', said the fat boy, more loudly.

He looked towards the strand and saw her on her back, her slightly plump thighs towards the sky, her hands shielding her eyes. He swam to the side of the raft then and gripped the wood with one hand and the fat boy's ankle with the other and pulled. The fat boy came crashing into the water and went down and when his head came up, gasping for asthmatic breath, he forced it down once more, though he didn't know what whore meant.

His father was cleaning the alto when he came back.

'What does hewer mean', he asked his father.

His father stopped screwing in the ligature and looked at him, his old sideman's eyes surprised, and somewhat moral.

'A woman', he said, 'who sells her body for monetary gain'.

He stopped for a moment. He didn't understand.

'That's tautology', he said.

'What's that?' his father asked.

'It repeats', he said, and went into the toilet.

He heard the radio crackle over the sound of falling water and heard a rapid-fire succession of notes that seemed to spring from the falling water, that amazed him, so much faster than his father ever played, but slow behind it all, melancholy, like a river. He came out of the toilet and stood

43

listening with his father. Who is that, he asked his father. Then he heard the continuity announcer say the name Charlie Parker and saw his father staring at some point between the wooden table and the wooden holiday-home floor.

He played later on the piano in the clubhouse with the dud notes, all the songs, the trivial mythologies whose significance he had never questioned. It was as if he was fingering through his years and as he played he began to forget the melodies of all those goodbyes and heartaches, letting his fingers take him where they wanted to, trying to imitate that sound like a river he had just heard. It had got dark without him noticing and when finally he could just see the keys as questionmarks in the dark, he stopped. He heard a noise behind him, the noise of somebody who has been listening, but who doesn't want you to know they are there. He turned and saw her looking at him, black in the square of light coming through the door. Her eyes were on his hands that were still pressing the keys and there was a harmonic hum tiny somewhere in the air. Her eyes rose to his face, unseeing and brittle to meet his hot, tense stare. He still remembered the rough feel of the tartan blanket over them, three of them, the grass under them. But her eyes didn't, so he looked everywhere but on them, on her small pinched chin, ridiculous under her large face, on the yellow linen dress that was ragged round her throat, on her legs, almost black from so much sun. The tiny hairs on them glistened with the light behind her. He looked up then and her eyes were still on his, keeping his fingers on the keys, keeping the chord from fading.

He was out on the burrows once more, he didn't know how, and he met the thin boy. The thin boy sat down with him where they couldn't be seen and took a condom from his pocket and masturbated among the bushes. He saw how the liquid was caught by the antiseptic web, how the sand clung to it when the thin boy threw it, like it does to spittle.

He left the thin boy and walked down the beach, empty now of its glistening bodies. He looked up at the sky, from which the light was fading, like a thin silver wire. He came to where the beach faded into the mouth of a river. There was a statue there, a Virgin with thin fingers towards the sea, her feet layered with barnacles. There were fishermen looping a net round the mouth. He could see the dim line of the net they pulled and the occasional flashes of white salmon. And as the boat pulled the net towards the shore he saw how the water grew violent with flashes, how the loose shoal of silver-and-white turned into a panting, open-gilled pile. He saw the net close then, the fishermen lifting it, the water falling from it, the salmon laid bare, glutinous, clinging, wet, a little like boiled rice.

He imagined the glistening bodies that littered the beach pulled into a net like that. He imagined her among them, slapping for space, panting for air, he heard transistors blare Da Doo Run Run, he saw suntan-lotion bottles crack and splinter as the Fisher up above pulled harder. He imagined his face like a lifeguard's, dark sidelocks round his muscular jaw, a megaphone swinging from his neck, that crackled.

He saw the thin band of light had gone, just a glow off the sea now. He felt frightened, but forced himself not to run. He walked in quick rigid steps past the barnacled Virgin then and down the strand.

'Ten bob for a touch with the clothes on. A pound without'.

They were playing pontoon on the raft. He was watching the beach, the bodies thicker than salmon. When he heard the phrase he got up and kicked the dirt-cards into the water. He saw the Queen of Hearts face upwards in the foam. As they made for him he dived and swam out a few strokes.

'Cunts', he yelled from the water. 'Cunts'.

On the beach the wind blew fine dry sand along the surface, drawing it in currents, a tide of sand.

His sister laid the cups out on the table and his father ate with long pauses between mouthfuls. His father's hand paused, the bread quivering in the air, as if he were about to say something. He looked at his sister's breasts across a bowl of apples, half-grown fruits. The apples came from monks who kept an orchard. Across the fields, behind the house. He imagined a monk's hand reaching for the unplucked fruit, white against the swinging brown habit. For monks never sunbathed.

When he had finished he got up from the table and idly pressed a few notes on the piano.

'Why do you play that', his father asked. He was still at the table, between mouthfuls.

'I don't know', he said.

'What galls me', said his father, 'is that you could be good'.

He played a bit more of the idiotic tune that he didn't know why he played.

'If you'd let me teach you', his father said, 'you'd be glad later on'.

'Then why not wait till later on and teach me then'.

'Because you're young, you're at the age. You'll never learn as well as now, if you let me teach you. You'll never feel things like you do now'.

He began to play again in defiance and then stopped.

'I'll pay you', his father said.

His father woke him coming in around four. He heard his wheezing breath and his shuffling feet. He watched the grey, metal-coloured light filling the room that last night had emptied it. He thought of his father's promise to pay him. He thought of the women who sold their bodies for monetary gain. He imagined all of them on the dawn golf-course, waking in their dew-sodden clothes. He imagined fairways full of them, their monetary bodies covered with fine drops of water. Their dawn chatter like birdsong. Where was that golf-course, he wondered. He crept out of bed and into his clothes and out of the door, very quietly. He crossed the road and clambered over the wire fence that separated the road from the golf-course. He walked through several fairways, across several greens, past several fluttering pennants with the conceit in his mind all the time of her on one green, asleep and sodden, several pound notes in her closed fist. At the fourteenth green he saw that the dull metal colour had faded into morning, true morning. He began to walk back, his feet sodden from the dew.

He went in through the green corrugated door and put on a record of the man whose playing he had first heard two days ago. The man played 'Night in Tunisia', and the web of notes replaced the web that had tightened round his crown. The notes soared and fell, dispelling the world around him, tracing a series of arcs that seemed to point to a place, or if not a place, a state of mind. He closed his eyes and let the music fill him and tried to see that place. He could see a landscape of small hills, stretching to infinity, suffused in a yellow light that seemed to lap like water. He decided it was a place you were always in, yet always trying to reach, you walked towards all the time and yet never got there, as it was always beside you. He opened his eyes and wondered where Tunisia was on the Atlas. Then he stopped wondering and reached up to the piano and took down the alto saxophone and placed it on the table. He opened the case and saw it gleaming in the light, new and unplayed. He knew he was waking his father from the only sleep he ever got, but he didn't care, imagining his father's pleasure. He heard him moving in the bedroom then, and saw him come in, his hair dishevelled, putting his shirt on. His father sat then, while he stood, listening to the sounds that had dispelled the world. When it had finished his father turned down the volume

47

controls and took his fingers and placed them on the right keys and told him to blow.

He learned the first four keys that day and when his father took his own instrument and went out to his work in Butlins he worked out several more for himself. When his father came back, at two in the morning, he was still playing. He passed him in the room, neither said anything, but he could feel his father's pleasure, tangible, cogent. He played on while his father undressed in the bedroom and when he was asleep he put it down and walked out the door, across the hillocks of the golf-course onto the strand, still humid with the warmth of that incredible summer.

He forgot the raft and the games of pontoon and the thin boy's jargon. He stayed inside for days and laboriously trans-ferred every combination of notes he had known on the piano onto the metal keys. He lost his tan and the gold sheen of the instrument became quickly tarnished with sweat, the sweat that came off his fingers in the hot metal room. He fashioned his mouth round the reed till the sounds he made became like a power of speech, a speech that his mouth was the vehicle for but that sprang from the knot of his stomach, the crook of his legs.

As he played he heard voices and sometimes the door knocked. But he turned his back on the open window and the view of the golf-course. Somewhere, he thought, there's a golf-course where bodies are free, not for monetary gain –

He broke his habit twice. Once he walked across the fields to the orchard where the monks plucked fruit with white fingers. He sat on a crumbling wall and watched the dark-ening and fading shadows of the apple trees. Another night he walked back down the strand to where it faded into the river mouth. He looked at the salmonless water and imagined the lifeguard up above calling through his megaphone. He imagined childhood falling from him, coming off his palms like scales from a fish. He didn't look up, he looked down at his fingers that were forming hard coats of skin at the tips, where they touched the keys.

And then, ten days after it had started, his face in the mirror looked older to him, his skin paler, his chin more ragged, less round. His father got up at half-past three and played the opening bars of 'Embraceable You' and instead of filling in while his father played, he played while his father filled in. And then they both played, rapidly, in a kind of mutual anger, through all his favourites into that area where there are no tunes, only patterns like water, that shift and never settle.

And his father put his instrument away and put several pound notes on the table. He took them, put the case up above the piano and went out the green door.

It was five o'clock as he walked down the road by the golf-course, squinting in the sunlight. He walked down by the tennis-court onto the strand, but it was too late now and the beach was empty and there was no-one on the raft.

He walked back with the pound notes hot in his pocket and met the fat boy with two racquets under his arm. The fat boy asked him did he want to play and he said 'Yes'.

They had lobbed an endless series of balls when the fat boy said 'Did you hear?' 'Hear what', he asked and then the fat boy mentioned her name. He told him how the lifeguard had rescued her twice during the week, from a part of the beach too near the shore to drown in by accident. He hit the ball towards the fat boy and imagined her body in the lifeguard's arms, his mouth on her mouth, pushing the breath in. Then he saw her sitting on the iron-wrought seat in a green dress now, vivid against the white metal. The pound notes throbbed in his pocket, but he hadn't the courage to stop playing and go to the seat. Her eyes were following the ball as it went backwards and forwards, listless and vacant. The light gradually became grey, almost as grey as the ball, so in the end he could only tell where it fell by the sound and they missed more than half the volleys. But still she sat on the white chair, her eyes on the ball, following it forwards and back. He felt a surge of hope in himself. He would tell her about that place, he told himself, she doesn't know. When it got totally dark he would stop, he told himself, go to her. But he knew that it never gets totally dark and he just might never stop and she might never rise from the white seat.

He hit the ball way above the fat boy's head into the wire meshing. He let the racquet fall on the tarmac. He walked towards her, looking straight into her eyes so that if his courage gave out he would be forced to say something. Come over to the burrows, he would say. He would tell her about that place, but the way she raised her head, he suspected she knew it.

She raised her head and opened her mouth, her answer already there. She inhabited that place, was already there, her open mouth like it was for the lifeguard when he pressed his hand to her stomach, pushed the salt water out, then put his lips to her lips and blew.

SKIN

THE ODD FANTASIES we people our days with; she had just pierced her finger with the knife, and from between the petals of split skin blood was oozing. It was coming in one large drop, growing as it came. Till her detached face reflects in the crimson.

But in fact the knife had missed her forefinger. It had cut round the gritty root of the lopped-off stem and was now splicing the orb into tiny segments. Her eyes were running. Cracked pieces of onion spitting moisture at her, bringing tears, misting her view of the enamel sink. The sink that was, despite the distortion of tears, as solidly present as it had been yesterday.

She was absorbed in the onion's deceit; its double-take. She had peeled layer upon layer from it and was anticipating a centre. Something like a fulcrum, of which she could say: here the skin ends; here the onion begins. And instead there was this endless succession of them, each like a smaller clenched fist, fading eventually into insignificance. Embryonic cell-like tissue which gave the appearance of a core. But in fact the same layers in miniature. Ah, she sighed, almost disappointed, looking at the handful of diced onion on the draining-board. She gathered these in her hands and shook them into the bowl. She washed her hands, to dispel the damp oily feeling, the acid smell. Then she turned her back on the sink, gazed absently on the kitchen table.

She had an apron on her, something like a smock. Flowers bloomed on it, toy elephants cavorted on their hind legs. There was lace round the neck and a bow-tied string at the back and a slit-pocket across the front into which she could

51

place her hands or dry her fingers. Above it her face, which was uneventfully trim, and just a little plain. She was wearing high-heeled house slippers and an over-tight bra. Her shoulder was shifting uncomfortably because of it. When one rests one notices such things. She was resting. From the diced onions, carrots, chunks of meat, whole potatoes on the draining-board. From the black-and-white pepper tins on the shelf above it.

There were two large windows on the sink side of the room. On the wall opposite was a row of small single-paned windows, high up, near the roof. The midday sun came streaming in the large window from behind her. She saw it as a confluence of rays emanating from her. When she shifted, even her shoulder, there would be a rapid rippling of light and shadow on the table cloth. Blue light it was, reflecting the blueness of the kitchen decor. For everything was blue here, the pantry door, the dresser, the walls were painted in rich emulsion, varying from duck-egg to cobalt. And the day was a mild early September, with a sky that retained some of August's scorched vermilion. The image of the Virgin crossed her silent vacant eyes. She had raised her hand to her hair and saw the light break through her fingers. She thought of the statue in the hall; plastic hands with five plastic sunrays affixed to each; streaming towards the feet, the snake, the waterbowl. Mother of Christ.

She had been humming the first phrases of a tune. She stopped it when she returned abruptly to the sink, to the window, to the strip of lard – sparrow meat – hanging outside. She chopped the meat into neat quarters and dumped them with the vegetables into a saucepan. She placed the saucepan on a slow-burning ring. Then she began washing her hands again. The scent of onion still clung to them. Pale hands, made plump by activity, swelling a little round the wrist and round the spot where the tarnished engagement-ring pulled the flesh inwards. She massaged separately the fingers of each hand, rapidly and a little too harshly; as if she were vexed with them, trying to coax something from them. Their lost freshness.

Several inches of water in the sink; a reflection there –

two hands caressing, a peering face swimming in the mud-coloured liquid, strewn over with peel. She grabbed hold of the knife and plunged it, wiping it clean with her bare thumb and forefinger. And again came the image – blood oozing, in large crimson drops. But her finger didn't gape. The knife emerged clean.

She pulled the sink plug then, hearing the suck, scouring the residue of grit and onion-skin with her fingers. She dried her hands, walked with the towel into the living-room.

There there was a low-backed modern sofa, two older tattered armchairs and a radiogram piled with magazines. She sat in the sofa, easing herself into its cushioned supports. She fiddled with the radio dial, turned it on, heard one blare of sound and switched it off again. The silence struck her; the chirp of a sparrow outside, clinging to the strip of lard. In another minute she was restless again, leafing through the magazines, flicking impatiently over their pages.

A housewife approaching middle-age. The expected list-lessness about the features. The vacuity that suburban dwelling imposes, the same vacuity that most likely inhabited the house next door. But she was an Irish housewife, and as with the whole of Irish suburbia, she held the memory of a half-peasant background fresh and intact. Noticeable in her dealings with the local butcher. She would bargain, oblivious of the demands of propriety. She would talk about childhood with an almost religious awe, remembering the impassioned innocence of her own. And, although house-proud, rigorous tidiness made her impatient; she had a weakness for loose-ends.

And in her the need for the inner secret life still bloomed. It would come to the fore in odd moments. A fragment of a song, hummed for a bar or two, then broken off. A day-dream. She would slide into it like a suicide easing himself into an unruffled canal. She would be borne off, swaying, for a few timeless moments. She would hardly notice the return. And for occasional stark flashes, she would be seized by a frightening admixture of religious passion and guilt, bordering on a kind of painful ecstasy; the need, the capacity for religiously intense experience of living; and in consequence of the lack of this, a deep residue of guilt. At times like this she would become conscious of anything red and bloodlike, anything blue or bright, any play of light upon shade.

But if she were asked how she lived, she would have replied: happily. And if she were asked what happiness meant she wouldn't even have attempted an answer.

She found herself rummaging among the magazines searching out one she had been reading yesterday. She recalled a story in it about the habits of Swedish housewives. Certain of them who would drive from their homes between the hours of two and four in the afternoon, out to the country, and there offer themselves to men. The event would take place in a field, under a tree, in a car. And afterwards, they would straighten their clothes, return home to find the timing-clock on the oven at nought, the evening meal prepared. It had disgusted her thoroughly at first glance. But something in it had made her read to the finish. The image, perhaps, of a hidden garden, sculpted secretly out of the afternoon hours, where flowers grew with unimaginable freedom.

Now she was feeling the same compulsion. 'Weekend' was the name, she remembered, selecting one from the pile. She opened it at the centre page. A glaring headline there, in vulgar black print: 'SWEDISH HOUSEWIVE'S AFTER-NOON OF SIN'. And a picture; a woman standing by a clump of trees, in a shaded country lane. A man in the distance watching her. A parked car.

She closed it instantly. It had disgusted her again. But as she sat there, the sound of distant cars coming to her from the road, her fingers began drumming impatiently on the wooden top of the radio. Something about it drew her. The sun, the glossy green of the foliage. The man's dark predatory back. Not the cheapness, the titillating obscenity. Not that.

Then she was moving towards the front door. Her tweed walking coat was hanging in the alcove. Outside, rows of starlings laced the telegraph-wires. Motionless black spear-heads, occasionally breaking into restless wheeling flights, to return again to their rigid formations. The same expectant stasis in her, her drumming fingers, like fluttering wings. She was a starling. The sudden, unconscious burst of disquiet. The animal memory of a home more vibrant, more total than this. The origin-track; the ache for aliveness.

All the way through the hall, out the front door, her fingers drummed. As she turned the ignition-key in the dashboard the engine's purr seemed to echo this drumming.

Howth was facing her as she drove, answering her desperate need for open spaces. Slim spearlike poplars passed her on her left. Oaks gnarled and knotted to bursting-point. Ash and elder, their autumn leaves discoloured by traffic-dust. She drove mechanically. She hardly noticed the line of cars coming towards her. Only the earth to her right, a dull metal plate today. Beyond it, as if thrusting through its horizon with a giant hand, the Hill of Howth.

Her forefinger still tapping on the steering-wheel. Scrubbing vegetables had banished most of the varnish from the nail. Today she didn't notice. A car swerved into her lane and away. She had a moment's vision of herself as a bloodied doll, hanging through a sharded windscreen. She drew a full breath and held it, her lungs like a balloon pressing at her breasts.

She pulled in at a causeway that led across marshlands to the open sea. She quenched the engine and gave herself time to absorb the shock of silence. Then she opened the door, got out, her fingers drumming on the metal roof.

Sounds that could have been the unbending of grass or the scurrying of insects. The lapping hiss of tide from the marshlands, its necklace of canals. But now she was here she wasn't sure why she had come. What to do with 'this' – as if the scene before her were some kind of commodity. It was the silence. The sheer pervasiveness of it.

She ran from the car door to the edge of the causeway in an attempt at the abandonment she imagined one should feel. There was a drop there, then mudflats awaiting tide. Nothing came of it however. Only the sense of her being a standing, awkward thing among grasses that crept, tides that flowed. It didn't occur to her to fall, flatten herself with them, roughen her cheek with the ragwort and sea-grass. She began to walk.

There were ships, tankers most likely, on the rim of the sea. As she walked through the burrows she saw hares bounding. She saw the sun, weak, but still potent. She saw a single lark spiralling towards it. She saw, when she reached it, a restful strand dissolve on either side into an autumn haze. It was empty of people.

The sand rose in flurries with her steps. She had worn the wrong shoes – those high-heeled slippers. Useless, she thought, slipping them off.

The sea amazed her when she reached it. Surging, like boiling green marble. Very high too, from yesterday's spring tide. There was a swell, beginning several yards out, that reached her in ripples. Each wave seemed to rise like a solid thing, laced with white foam, subsiding into paltriness just when she felt it would engulf her. Swelling, foaming, then retreating. The sun glistening coldly off it. She felt spray on her cheek. Wet, ice-cold, the feel of church floors, green altar-rails.

She decided to risk a paddle. She glanced round her and saw nothing but a black dot, like a rummaging dog, in the distance. So she opened her coat, hitched up her skirt, unpeeled her stockings. She'd stay near the edge.

She threw them, with her slippers, to a spot she judged safe from the incoming tide. She walked in, delighted with the tiny surging ripples round her ankles. Her feet were soon blue with the cold. She remembered her circulation and vowed not to stay long. But the freshness of it! The clean salt wetness, up around her calves now! It deserved more than just an ankle-paddle. And soon she was in it up to her knees, with the rim of her skirt all sodden. The green living currents running about her legs, the rivers of puffy white foam surrounding her like a bridal wreath. She hitched up her dress then, the way young girls do, tucking it under their knickers to look like renaissance princes, and felt the cold mad abandon of wind and spray on her legs. A wave bigger than the others surged up wetting her belly and thighs, taking her breath away. The feel of it, fresh and painful, icy and burning! But it was too much, she decided. At her age, skirt tucked up in an empty sea.

She turned to the strand and saw a man there, a wet-tailed cocker-spaniel at his heels, bounding in a flurry of drops. She froze. He had seen her, she was sure of that, though his eyes were now on the dog beside him. The sight of his tan overcoat and his dark oiled hair brought a desolate panic to her. The shame, she thought, glancing wildly about for her stockings and shoes.

But the sea must have touched her core with its irrational ceaseless surging. For what she did then was to turn back, back to the sea, picking high delicate steps through its depths, thinking: He sees me. He sees my legs, my tucked-up skirt, the outlines of my waist clearly through the salt-wet fabric. He is more excited than I am, being a man. And there was this pounding, pounding through her body, saying: this is it. This is what the sea means, what it all must mean. And she stood still, the sea tickling her groin, her eyes fixed on the distant tanker, so far-off that its smokestack seemed a brush stroke on the sky, its shape that of a flat cardboard cut-out. Around it the sea's million dulled glimmering mirrors.

But she was wrong. And when she eventually turned she saw how wrong, for the man was now a retreating outline, like the boat, the dog beside him a flurrying black ball. And she thought, Ah, I was wrong about that too. And she walked towards the shore, heavy with the knowledge of days unpeeling in layers, her skirt and pants sagging with their burden of water.

HER SOUL

'I'VE LOST MY wife' the man said.

'And I've lost my soul.'

She leaned back on the banisters. The man swayed as he came down, spilling his orange-coloured drink on her dress. But the dress was patterned in broad horizontal stripes like a spinning-top and all of the stripes were some shade of orange so she didn't remark on it. She held on to the banisters swaying, wondering how it had gone so easily.

It hadn't gone the way it should have, like a silver bird flying upwards leaving the shell of her behind, of an aeroplane glinting. It had slipped out of her as if she was a glass and it was the liquid, she filled too full, it slopping down her wet side. And being insubstantial it had disappeared, melted like quick ice, not giving her a chance to grab or shout come back. Well, she thought.

The music came from the room downstairs and the ecstatic party sounds. She flattened the damp side of her heliotrope dress with her hand.

'My soul' she muttered to the grey suit and the loose necktie that was ascending the stairs.

'My undying love', he said and she wondered whether this was taunt or invitation. She was past recognition of witticisms. She looked down the stairs seeing the broad swipes of shadow and the broad swipes of light and thought how easily it could have slipped through one of them. Sidled through, sly thing that it was. Her eyes ran with the shadowed stairs, bumped with them down to the stairs-end closet. Coats hung there, etched and still. Broad folds and shadows. That's it, it slipped, she thought, like a shadow slips when the sun goes in. And every shadow and every fold of cloth became an invitation to her, a door behind which the shadow-world lay, through which one could slip and float and be insubstantial and pure, like gas released from a test-tube, not heavy and swaying like in this bright-light world. That's it, she thought.

Suddenly the shadows tottered and wheeled and the cream-white walls swung dark and bright and she thought she would be blessed with entry into that shadow-world where her soul perhaps was. But then she saw the man with the open tie above her on the stairs tapping the light-bulb.

'My soul', she said thinking it was a party and one must say something.

'My beard and whiskers', he said, tapping the bulb.

'Stop it, will you'. She covered her eyes.

'I'm sorry', he said. 'Have some'.

He held out his hand, proffering a glass. She saw a silver bracelet over the hair on the wrist, then a white cuff and a grey sleeve. At the top of the sleeve was a loose tie and a fattish white neck and brown eyes and a smiling mouth. The eyes were fixed on her left ear and the mouth smiling at something adjacent to it, over her shoulder.

And she fancied, taking the glass, that that was it. Her soul hadn't dripped or flown but had retreated to some point beyond her shoulder; that point towards which people looked, the point posited by his eyes, his eyes that had ripped it from her breast or wherever, from under the heliotrope dress where it should have lain pulsing and whole; had done so because there it was safe, there it was distant.

All the anger at the loss of her soul ran through her so strongly that she imagined she could somehow get it back, that by smashing the glass with her hand on it against the banisters it would somehow appear, reappear with the real pain and the ripped palm and the red sharded pieces of glass.

But she sipped from the glass instead, thinking she would never know, perhaps it's better gone, rolling the whisky about her palate and her tongue, wondering what to say.

OUTPATIENT

WHEN SHE CAME back she was thinner than ever. She had always been thin, but now her thinness seemed to have lost its allure, her mouth seemed extraordinarily wide, all her facial bones prominent. And when he looked at her he stopped thinking of love and began to think of necessary companionship, mature relationship and things like that. It will be better, he told her, when we get the house. And he put his arms around her on the steps and knew that he had married her for that peculiar quality of thinness that had been fashionable that year. Somewhere inside him he felt obscurely angry at her for having let her stock of beauty fade; for standing before him in the same tweed cloak in which she had left, like a thin pear topped by flat brown hair and brown eyes, an oval of skin the colour of thawed snow. He felt cheated. He also felt virtuous, accepting as he was her flawed self, and only a little ashamed. And all the while she felt his arms around her on the steps she had left and imagined the house to be rectangular, as all houses are, with rectangular rooms and a pebble-dash front. And a garden. There would have to be a garden.

They walked up the steps and up the stairs, past the many flats into their own. She heard the old woman moving round above them. She hasn't died yet, she asked him. No, he whispered, and looked shocked. He told her there was nothing to be ashamed of, that it wasn't as if she had had a breakdown, just that she needed a rest. He asked her what it was like, said that her letters hadn't told him much. She told him that she had seen the Burren and described the burnt mountain landscapes. She told him about St Brigit's

Well and described the long line of pilgrims stretching up the mountain and the faded holy pictures inside the grotto and the four crutches of the cripples who had been miraculously cured. Do you believe it, she asked him. Do you believe they were cured? Perhaps, he said, they were never really crippled, or the cure was psychosomatic. But miraculously, she asked, not miraculously? and the word sounded like a peal of trumpets in her ears, she saw the biblical walls tumbling. And he didn't answer, he looked at her quickly once, and then took her by both shoulders and stood back from her, as if complimenting her on something. It did you good, he said, and it will be better this time. Won't it?

She heard the old woman moving again and pictured her wrinkled thin head bending over the one-bar electric fire. He had let his hands drop. They were standing facing one another, neither looking. Mentally she took several steps backwards. She saw two people in a room with three white walls and one orange wall, with blue coloured armchairs, prints of old Dublin and poster reproductions. There was a hum of traffic through the window from way below. If she had seen it as an extract from a film she would have known it to be the last-but-one scene of some domestic tragedy. And she knew it wasn't going to work once more, she could see the end from the extract, but it wouldn't fail tragically, it would piffle out, with barely a whisper. For she knew that once she could look at herself as if she were another person it would not work, there would be no real pain even. And she discovered to her surprise that she thirsted for pain and reality. What was it about this house, she asked. It's a bargain, he began . . .

He watched her undress as if wondering would her thinness be the same underneath. It was, except that her belly now seemed to sag outwards. She was wearing the tight girlish underwear that always had excited him. He looked at her face as little as possible so as to remain aroused, concentrating on her thin buttocks and stark ribs. He had determined not to sleep, he had determined this should stay even if the rest failed. He decided that her sagging belly was due to her stance. He looked in her face and saw her eyes, unbearably brown and her flat hair. Come, he said.

She was amazed he wanted it. She was gratified in an automatic romantic manner till she gauged his methodic sensuality and knew he was already thinking of children. She determined to disappoint him and lay flat and rigid. She knew he was disappointed but felt the dome of a great heavy bell around her, she looking out through it, at him lying flat and white, staring at the ceiling. Help me, he said. Promise me you'll help me. I can't she said, if you don't help me. What does that mean, he asked. It means there's a space between you and me that no-one can help. No-one, he said. She didn't answer. She was composing an equation, of the sum of her need and the sum of his, of the compound of their ability to give and of the small persistent almighty minus in between. Then she pulled herself from between the covers and went out to wash. We'll go to see the house tomorrow, she heard him say and she noticed how the wretchedness of his voice a moment ago had gone. It sounded common-sense and confident, coming to her in the dark of the bathroom.

He mumbled something and turned on his side, with his back to her, when she returned to the bed. He was well into sleep. But she lay awake staring at the wastes of the ceiling, thinking, I've just come back from a place where people walk three miles to see the miraculous crutches and the rotting mass-cards and he – . Her thought stopped here, blocked by something deadening, momentous, stolid. And he what, she thought. She couldn't praise or blame or hate. She thought instead of the equation again, of the sum of his giving and the sum of hers, of their mutual spaces and the ridiculous pathetic minus round which the worlds hinged. She thought herself, rocked herself to sleep, praying for more, for the miraculous plus. She dreamed of meat. She dreamt she was love-making, rigid against his rapid orgasm and above them was hanging a butcher's half-carcass, swinging between ceiling and floor. Gigot or loin, she wondered. Each rib was curved like a delicate half-bow, white, made stark by the red meat between. She wanted to shake him, and cry out: Look at that dead meat. But it swung above her, silencing her, glowing, incandescent.

The next day he drove her to the house, positively angry now at her silences, more and more repulsed by her battered thinness. It was in a North-side suburb near Portmarnock beach. Streets rose up a hill, breezes came from the unseen sea, the salt air was belied by the system-built houses. They drove up to it and parked on the opposite side. Its facade, she saw, was a large rectangle, half red-brick, half pebble dash. What do you think, he asked. She nodded her head. You'll get nothing better under eight thou, he said. She didn't answer. She suddenly hated him for that abbreviated word. She looked at the house, itself like an abbreviated word, its shape, its texture. Why is it square, she said, why not round? I want to live in a round house, with a roof like a cone, with a roof like a witch's hat. She laughed and heard her laugh echoing strangely in the car. She saw his hands clasping and unclasping, each finger in its curve on the plastic wheel. She stopped the laugh quickly then. But the silence rang with the stopped laugh.

They walked through it and she saw her imagination verified. They walked through the hall, with its regular stairs rising upwards, into the kitchen, which gleamed bright steel. They walked out of the kitchen and up the stairs, through each bedroom and then returned to the kitchen again. What do you think, he asked. She had her back turned to him and she felt the great bell descend on her, its brass tongue falling with a threat she only dreamed of. She turned to his voice, which was tiny and distant, and saw his horror of silence in his set face. She saw her face reflected in his pupil, with enlarged thin cheekbones and a too-wide mouth. Then she longed for the tongue to clang with its trumpetlike peal as she heard him say: We'll look at the garden.

And she saw him open the kitchen door, totally without her fear. She saw through the door the green mound of Howth Head, a long stretch of sea and a thin elongated smokestack of grey cloud. She saw his square back moving towards the backdrop of waste sea and cloud. He was moving to the paltry green rim of hedge at the end, avoiding

63

the mounds of cement-coloured earth, scraping with the toe of his shoe at the resilient ground. When he reached it he turned. And she walked towards him down the calloused garden wanting to tell him that this house had nothing to do with miracles and trumpets, knowing she would not. There was a wind blowing from the sea, ruffling the hedge, his hair and her kilted skirt.

TREE

THERE WERE TWO things he could not do, one was drive
a car, the other was step out of a car. So she was driving
when she saw the tree, she had been driving all week. He
was telling her another point of interest about the crumbling
landscape round them, the landscape with more points of
historical interest per square mile than – something about a
woman who was to have a baby at midnight, but who sat
on a rock and kept the baby back till dawn, an auspicious
hour, and the rock ever after had a dent in it and was called
Brigid's –

She saw the tree from about a mile off, since the road they
were driving was very straight, rising slowly all the time,
with low slate walls that allowed a perfect, rising view. It
was late summer and the tree looked like a whitethorn tree
and she forgot about local history and remembered suddenly and clearly holidays she had taken as a child, the old
Ford Coupe driving down the country lanes and the flowering
whitethorn dotting the hedges. It would appear in regular
bursts, between yards of dull green. It would be a rich,
surprised cream colour, it would remind her of a fist opened
suddenly, the fingers splayed heavenwards. It would delight
her unutterably and her head would jerk forwards and backwards as each whitethorn passed.

Then something struck her and she stopped the car suddenly. She jerked forward and she heard his head striking the
windscreen.

'What's – ' he began, then he felt his head. She had interrupted him.

'I'm sorry', she said, 'but look at that tree'.

'There are no trees'. His fingers had searched his forehead and found a bump. He would be annoyed. 'This is a limestone landscape'.

She pointed with her finger. His eyes followed her finger and the edges of his eyelids creased as he stared.

'Well there is a tree, then'.

'It's a whitethorn tree', she said. 'It's flowering'.

'That's impossible', he said. She agreed.

The thought that it was impossible made her warm, with a childish warm delight. She felt the hairs rising on her legs. She felt the muscles in her legs glow, stiff from the accelerator. The impossible possible she thought. She knew the phrase meant nothing. She remembered an opera where a walking-stick grew flowers. She thought of death, which makes anything possible. She looked at his long teutonic face, such perfection of feature that it seemed a little deformed.

'But it's white, isn't it'.

'Then', he said, 'it couldn't be a whitethorn'.

'But it's white'.

'It's the end of August'.

She turned the key in the ignition and drove again. She thought of his slight, perfect body beside her in bed, of its recurrent attraction for her. She thought of his hatred of loud sounds, his habit of standing in the background, the shadows, yet seeming to come forward. She thought of how his weaknesses became his strengths, with a cunning that was perhaps native to his weakness. She thought of all the times they had talked it out, every conceivable mutation in their relationship, able and disable, every possible emotional variant, contempt to fear, since it's only by talking of such things that they are rendered harmless. She drove the car slowly, on the slight upward hill, the several yards to the pub they had arranged to stop at.

'It is possible'.

'What is'.

'Everything's possible'.

He asked would they go in then.

She opened her door and walked around the car and opened his door. She waited till he had lifted his good leg clear of the car, then held his arm while he balanced himself and lifted out the stiff leg.

She watched him walk across the road and marvelled again at how the stiffness gave him, if anything, a kind of brittle elegance. She saw him reach the pub door, go inside without looking back. Then she looked up the road, curving upwards and the tree off from the road, in the distance. It was still white. Unutterably white.

The pub was black after the light outside. He was sitting by the long bar, drinking a glass of beer. Beside him was another glass, and a bottle of tonic-water. Behind the bar was a woman with a dark western face, ruined by a pair of steel glasses. She was talking, obviously in answer to a question of his.

'Cornelius O'Brien lived in the lower one', she said. 'Owned more than them all put together. A great packer'.

'Packer?'

'Jury-packer' she said, as if it was a term of office.

He leant forward, his face eager with another question. She slipped into the seat beside him. She poured the tonic-water into the glass, wondering why it was he always bought her that. She must have expressed a preference for it once, but she couldn't remember when. Once she drank whiskey, she remembered, and now she drank tonic. And sometime in between she had changed.

'Why did you get me this', she interrupted.

He looked up surprised. Then smiled, a fluid smile.

'Because you always drink it'.

'Once I drank whiskey'.

The wrinkles formed in clusters round his eyes.

'I remember. Yes, Why did you stop?'

She drank it quietly, trying to remember, listening to his further question about the crumbling castles. The woman answered, speaking the way children do, using words they don't understand. She used phrases to describe the dead inhabitants of those castles that were like litanies, that had filtered through years to her, that must have once had meaning. She was cleaning a glass and her eyes looked vacant as her mouth spoke the forgotten phrases.

She stared at the ice in her tonic water. She watched it melt, slowly. She wondered about phrases, how they either retain the ghost of a meaning they once had, or grope towards a meaning they might have. Then she suddenly, vitally, remembered the taste of whiskey. Gold, and volatile, filling not the tongue but the whole mouth.

'Whitethorn', she said, loud, out of the blue, as if it were a statement.

The woman stopped cleaning the glass and looked at her. He put his hand round his glass and looked at her.

'Have you come far, then', the woman asked.

He mentioned a town a hundred miles east.

'A long way alright', the woman said. Then she glanced from him to her.

'Is it herself who drives?'

She saw his hand tighten round the glass. She remembered the taste of whiskey. She said:

'He has a bad leg. There are two things he can't do. Get out of a car, and drive a car. But otherwise everything's fine. Isn't that right John?'

He had already gone towards the door. She fumbled in her pocket to find fifty pence. She couldn't and so she left a pound.

He was standing by the door of the car.

'Why did you have to jabber on like that?'

'Why did you order me a tonic?'

'You're impossible'.

'Nothing's impossible'.

'Get in'.

She drove. He swore at her in considered, obscene phrases as she drove. She knew he would swear like that, slowly and sadistically, scraping every crevice of her womanhood, till his anger had died down. So she drove with her eyes on the blaze far up the road, like a surprised fist with its fingers towards the sky, the brilliant cream-white of a dice-cube. As she drove nearer it seemed to swim in front of her eyes, to expand, to explode, and yet still retain its compact white. She could hear their breathing as she drove, hers fast like an animal that is running, his slow, like an animal that must stand in the one place. Then the white seemed to fill her vision and she stopped. She looked at the trunk below the white and the long field between it and the road. Then she looked at him.

He was crying, and his face looked more beautiful than ever through the tears.

'I love you', he said.

'I'm leaving', she said.

'Again?' he asked.

He grabbed her, half angry, half afraid, but she had the door open already and she slipped away. She walked round the car and looked at him.

'I don't – ' she began, but her words were drowned by the sudden blast of the horn. His hand was on it, his knuckles white, his body was bent forward as if all his strength was needed to keep the horn pressed. She could hear the awful blare in her ears and could see his lips moving, saying something. She shouted at him to take his hand off and his lips moved again, saying the same something, the same three words. She made out the three words then and turned from his face and ran.

She ran to the slate wall and clambered over it, scraping her shins. She felt the grass under her feet and put her hands over her ears. She was shocked by the sudden silence, like a sudden immersion in water. She was walking, but it was as if through a mental landscape, no sound but the strange humming of her eardrums. She felt she had closed her eyes and found this field, not driven to it. She knew her feet were walking her towards the tree, but it was as if the tree was coming towards her. The landscape rising with each step and each step bringing the landscape nearer. The tree on the hill, with its white made manageable now, small, tangible, familiar. She counted her steps like a little girl does and each step misplaced her hands and rang in her ears. Then something struck her about the tree, not really white, more an off-grey colour. She took three more steps and it came nearer, with the hill behind it, and its blossoms seemed to flap. But blossoms don't flap, she thought, they are still and pristine, they burst or moult, not flap and she must have run then for it came nearer in several large leaps.

And it was there then, bare rough whitethorn with scores of tiny rags tied to each branch, pieces of handkerchief, shirttails, underwear, shift, masquerading as blossom. She thought of people wishing, tying these proxy blossoms. She thought of her and her hope that it had blossomed and them, making it blossom with their hope. She wondered again what hope meant, what impossible meant, but there was less scope to her wondering. She saw faded holy pictures nailed to the bottom of the trunk but couldn't read the pleas written on them. She took her hands from her ears to tear one off and the wail of the horn flooded her again, distant, plaintive, pleading. She tore a picture off, parts of it crumbled in her fingers, but she read 'To Brigid for favours granted, August 1949'. And the horn wailed like pain.

A LOVE

THERE WERE NO cars in Dublin when I met you again, the streets had been cleared for the funeral of the President who had died. I remembered you talking about him and I thought of how we would have two different memories of him. He was your father's generation, the best and the worst you said. I remembered your father's civil war pistol, black and very real, a cowboy gun. It was that that first attracted me, me a boy beyond the fascination of pistols but capable of being seduced by a real gun owned by a lady with real bullets – I shattered two panes in your glasshouse and the bullet stuck in the fence beyond the glass-house shaking it so it seemed to be about to fall into the sea and float with the tide to Bray Head. Then you took the gun from me saying no-one should play with guns, men or boys and put the hand that held it in your blouse, under your breast. And I looked at you, an Irish woman whose blouse folded over and was black and elegant in the middle of the day, whose blouse hid a gun besides everything else. But except that you smiled at me with a smile that meant more than all those I would just have been a kid bringing a message from his father to a loose woman. As it was you walked over the broken glass away from me and I stepped after you over the broken pieces to where the view of the sea was and you began to teach me love.

And when we met again there were no cars and the head-lines talked about love and guns and the man who had died and I wondered how different your memory of him would be from mine. It was a stupid pursuit since I had no memory of him other than from photographs and then only a big

71

nose and bulging eyes and spectacles but I knew you would be changed and I knew I was changed and I wanted to stop thinking about it.

There were no cars but there were flowers in the giant pots on O'Connell Bridge, there was a band somewhere playing slow music and there were crowds everywhere on the pavement, women mostly who remembered him as something important, women who clutched handbags to their stomachs and stared at the road where the funeral would soon pass. I could sense the air of waiting from them, they had all their lives waited, for a funeral, a husband, a child coming home, women your age, with your figure, they had loved abstractly whereas you had loved concretely with a child like me. That was the difference I told myself but it was probably only that I knew you and I didn't know them. But that had always been the difference, all women had been a mother to someone but you had been a lover to me. And I focused my eyes on the empty street with them and wondered had that difference faded.

I went into the cafe then and it smelt of Dublin, Ireland, the musty femininity of the women waiting on the kerb for the men to pass, dead, heroic, old and virginal. I sat by the plate glass window and looked at the shiny chrome expresso machine, a cloud of steam rising from it. A girl in a blue smock with an exhausted face brought me coffee and I felt for the first time that I was back somewhere. I tasted the coffee and got the cheap caffeine bite, details like that, the girl's legs, too thin so the nylons hung in folds around them. Outside I could hear the brass band coming nearer, louder like the slowed step soldiers use in funerals. I knew I was out of step, it was all militarism now, like air in a blister, under the skin, it was swelling, the militarism I had just learned of before, in the school textbooks. Then I remembered something else about him, the man who had died, he had been the centre of the school textbooks, his angular face and his thirties collar and his fist raised in a gesture of defiance towards something out there, beyond the rim of the

72

brown photograph, never defined. And I wondered whether I'd rather be out of step here or in step in London, where the passions are rational. And I felt the nostalgia of the emigrant, but it was as if I was still away, as if here in the middle of it all I was still distant, remembering, apart from it. I shook myself but couldn't get rid of the feeling. Something had happened to me since leaving, something had happened to me long before I left, but then everything changes, I told myself and some things die. So I just looked out the plate-glass window and listened to the slow brass, swelling more all the time.

Then I saw someone looking like you coming down the street towards the cafe and as that someone came nearer I saw it was you, still you, your hair had got a little greyer but still kept that luxuriant brownness, your face had got thinner and fatter, thinner round the cheekbones, fatter round the jaw and neck. You hadn't seen me yet but I couldn't get myself to rise out of the seat so you would see me, I wanted to look at you like you were a photograph. I was remembering that letter of my father's, the only letter, that said you were sick and you did look sick, in the quiet way of bad sicknesses, cancer and the like. And then you opened the glass door and the brass music grew to an orchestra and the door closed and the music faded again and still I couldn't get up. And you were standing over me.

'Neil' you said!
'Yes' I said.
'Well' you said.
'Yes' I said again.
And then you sat down beside me, I was a child who isn't saying something, the thin girl came over to take your order. We were the only two in the cafe, you were talking, I was listening to you, quite natural, ordinary things after all. We were different, I was a young adult, you were an old adult, we both fingered coffee cups, mine cold, yours hot. I tried obscurely to remember, I had been an Irish boy with greased hair and a collarless leather jacket, you had been a single

73

woman who kept a guest-house in a town called Greystones and now both of us were neither, my hair was dry and short, it came straight down my forehead and my forehead had a few lines, though people still told me sometimes that I looked sixteen, you were living in a house somewhere on the South Side, you didn't work now though the car keys you squeezed in your palm and the fur sleeves that hung dead from your wrists made you look well-off, in an extravagant, haphazard way.

Then you mentioned the dead man outside.

And somehow it began to come right. I noticed the black silk blouse under the coat, the loose and mottled skin where your neck met your breast. I remembered the nights lying in your old creaking bed that looked out on the sea, our movements like a great secret between us, silent, shocking movements, our silence a guard against my father who had the room down below, our lovemaking a quiet desecration of the holiday town, of the church at the top of the hill, of the couples you fed so properly at mealtimes, of my embarrassed adolescence, the guilt you tried to banish in me, the country, the place, the thing you tried to hit at through me you taught me to hit through you. And all the time for me there was my father lying underneath, cold most likely, and awake and I wanted him to hear the beast I was creating with you, I wanted him to hear it scratching, creaking through to him from above, for your body was like the woman he must have loved to have me, I had seen her in those brown faded photographs with a floppy hat and a cane, in a garden, like you but fatter, with a lot of clothes that came off, the coloured dresses and blouses first, then the white underclothes, dampened under the armpits, between the legs. And when you undressed on the beach and I watched you from the road, watched each thing falling in a bundle on the sand, you could have been her, you could have been anyone's mother only you were naked with a belly that drooped a little and a triangle of hair underneath it. Only that when you saw me you didn't shy from my frightened stare, you

74

smiled. That smile began it. But what perpetuated it was something outside, my mathematical father lying sleepless on his bed, your civil-war gun, rosaries, that rain-soaked politician with his fist raised, clenched. Against something. Something.

The brass band seemed much nearer now, going ahead of the same politician's cortege, ceremonial, thudding slow brass. I was watching you drinking your coffee. The brass music was cascading about you. I looked at the thin part of your face, you had no make-up on, your eyes looked almost ordinary. You were different and the same, I was different and the same, I knew that that is how things happen. And yet I'd met you because I wanted something more. We are all different threads, I told myself and once we had woven each other's threads into something like a bow. Once.

'Well'.

We were stuck on that word. Then I plunged.

'What are we going to do then, before I go back?'

'Back where?'

And I don't know whether you wanted to know, but I told you it all, about the hairdresser's in Kensal Rise, the women who tipped me pound notes if I touched their plump shoulders and told them they were too young for a blue rinse.

'Is that what you do'.

'Yes'.

And I told you about the cockney queen I shared a room with who I despised but who could be warm when –

'And don't you act now – '

And yes, I told you about the sweaty revues, revue being synonomous with theatrical sex, I told you about the empty stages where we rehearsed in our underwear and fingered each other's goosepimples, simulated copulation. Then I stopped, because you were drinking your coffee again and your unmadeup face looked sad, like an adolescent, the one I had been. And for a moment I was the experienced one, I

75

clutched the gun, under my breasts, between the sheaves of my black blouse.

'We'll go to Clare. Lisdoonvarna'.

'Why there', I asked.

'I am past my prime. They are places for people past their prime'.

And I wondered should you say 'prime' or 'primes', I thought of all the hotels and guest-houses I had never been to. I knew middle-aged people went to those places and met men and took the waters and married maybe and drank sherries looking at the Atlantic, in bars that were probably closed now for De Valera's death.

'It's Autumn and everyone there will be past their prime. I want to see the bachelors court the spinsters. I want to take the waters. I want to drive in a Morris Minor past the Burren and look at the unusual flowers'.

There was an accusation in your voice as if you were trying to tell me something, something I didn't want to hear. I thought maybe you wanted to fit yourself, label yourself and I wondered would your conformity be as bizarre as my attempts at it had been.

You talked about happiness then, a murderous happiness that followed you round like a pet dog. And I looked at you, you had pressed your unpainted lips together, the blood had gone out of them and I saw the need for happiness that had ravaged you, I wondered what deity it was that would label you old maid or spinster when you had once pressed that happiness on me. Then I heard the band outside, so loud now, and the cortege was passing and the band was playing the old nationalist tunes to a slow tempo. I felt I was watching an animal dying through the plate-glass window, an animal that was huge, murderous, contradictory and I looked up at your face, not much older really than when I had last seen you and I looked out the plate-glass window again at the funeral of the man I didn't remember, the man you would have remembered. I wondered what your memories were, your associations. And I looked at your eyes, bare and washed clean and I somehow knew.

We walked outside then and the brass music became a deafening thud. We walked slowly down the street, we couldn't talk, the music was so loud. I bought a newspaper at the corner of Abbey Street and saw a headline about the funeral that was crawling along beside us. We passed a TV sales shop where a crowd of people were staring at a white screen, staring at the death being celebrated behind them.

As I remember you I define you, I choose bits of you and like a child with a colouring-book, I fill you out. The carkeys are swinging on your finger, your forefinger and thumb choose one, insert it in the lock and your whole hand tenses in the turning. Your car is like you said, a Morris Minor. It's grey and covered in dents and the chrome is rusty. Your hand turning is reddish, sunburnt, which accentuates more its many creases. Then a man-sized watch and the sleeve of your coat where the fur has rubbed off.

Once it was desire I filled you out with, not memory. You were a blown-up photograph to me, a still from a film. I brought the youthful sullenness I learnt from the hit songs to you. I ate chips before I came to you, my fingers stank of vinegar, my breath of nicotine. And you played with me, you let me fill you out, you played Ava Gardner to my James Dean. But I chose, I was arbitrary, I took what I wanted. Your brown hair, your anxious mouth, your bare feet – on the straw bedroom mat. I took some and left the rest, I didn't know what the rest meant, I didn't know what varicose veins meant or fallen arches or lace curtains, respectability, spinsterhood. I plead guilty but ignorant, I didn't know what woman meant.

'Can you drive?'

I said no. I said I would like to, I would like to feel machinistic and free but my father never drove so no-one taught me.

'What do you mean', you asked 'Machinistic – '

And I hadn't known what I meant, I got confused, I said something about the wheel driving, following the white line. Then you were quiet for a while, whether from tactfulness or not I don't know and then –

'I wasn't made for cars'.

I didn't believe you, you had shaped this car to fit you. You drove it like it fitted you, through the city that was empty, that had put its best side out for the man who had died. The streets were clean, the buildings were respectful, they seemed to curtsy before us as you drove. Then they got thinner and thinner and we were on the dual carriageway, driving west.

'I idolised him once'.

I meant to ask you about your sickness but the words wouldn't come. So you talked while you drove, abstracted talk.

'I was taught to idolise him, everyone was. I remember standing at meetings, holding my father's hand, waving a tricolour, shouting Up Dev. My father wore a cloth cap and a trenchcoat, everyone did then'.

Your eyes were squinted towards the road as if you saw what you were remembering on it.

'His face was like a schoolteacher's. Or maybe all schoolteachers tried to look like him. You could never see his eyes clearly because of his glasses. They were the first thing you noticed after his nose'.

We were passing Monasterevin. The town looped in a semi-circle round your car.

'Have you ever been to the West?'

'No', I said.

'You'll never understand this country till you have'.

Your voice sounded older, consciously older, something valedictory in it that made me remember the night my father took you out and me with him as his fifteen years old son, mature enough for adult company, my father being a lecturer in maths and a widower, a natural partner for you who was single, who kept the guesthouse he stayed in. We went to a variety in Bray where a Scottish comedian told Irish jokes and a youth with a guitar sang Lonnie Donegan songs and two girls with a ukelele sang George Formby and kicked their legs on either side of the stand-up mike. And afterwards we went for a meal in the Royal Hotel, we ate roast beef and drank sherry. I poured your sherry with the distance he had trained me in and I sat at the far end of the table while you both talked, he at length, you with many pregnant pauses. You talked about life, about friends in public life, who you knew of through your father, who he knew of through his work, he prided himself on both his aloofness from the world and his reserved contact with it. You were beautiful and intimidating in a navy dress and shawl and while in your silences you spoke to me, me in my greased hair and the suit I was told to wear, in your conversation you spoke to him and you managed the pretending so adroitly that in the end I was fooled and I screamed at you afterwards and it took three days for our mutual secret to build up again between us, for me to hold the you I wanted in my unwashed arms, selfishly and viciously, for you to tell me again about love and irreligion, about other countries where women are young at the age of thirty-nine and boys are men at fifteen.

'Are you happy?'

'Sometimes', I said.

'You used to be. You used to be very quiet, very joyful and very sullen'.

We were passing Portlaoise, the barbed-wire towers of the prison and the red wall of the mental hospital.

'It was all in your face', you said. 'In the way your snub-nose twitched – '

And we both laughed then, it sounded stupid but we laughed and your laugh was like a peal, you could have been standing in the broken pieces of glass again, beside the glasshouse, laughing. I tightened my nose like a rabbit the way I used to do, then I flushed in embarrassment doing it and that made you laugh louder, so loud that you began coughing and had to stop the car and wipe your mouth. There was blood on the kleenex you wiped it with.

'We're different', you said.

'Yes', I said. And you looked at me and giggled again. Like someone very young. Too young. You put your arms around me and kissed my face and I stayed very quiet, feeling you again, smelling you again. Your lips opened on my cheek and I could hear a tiny whistle off your breath.

'Aren't we?'

'Yes', I said, 'We're different' and I kissed you back so you could feel how different. But you stopped me.

'Don't try and change me'.

'How could I?'

'You could', you said, 'You could change me back'.

But you were happy then, weren't you? You began to drive faster, swerving gaily to avoid pigeons. You asked me about myself and my father and I answered both as well as I could. You still coughed every now and then and once you had to stop the car, your whole body tensed as if you were in pain. Your fingers clenched the wheel, they seemed to get even thinner and the bones on the backs of your hands were thin, leading like a scallop to the fingers. But you got over it then, you began to drive, you told me not to mind you, that you were only dying, it's a common complaint and you laughed like before and I laughed with you. Then we stopped in a pub for a drink and I drank a gin while you drank a pint of stout and the barman remarked on how it's normally the other way round.

When we were driving again we saw a fat girl standing by a petrol-pump following every car that passed her with her eyes and thumb. You wanted to stop but I didn't let you, I thought she'd come between us and the laughing. So we drove on and I had a clear view of the disappointment in her large blue eyes as she fumbled with her handbag, realising the car wasn't going to stop after all. And I felt sorry for a moment but your mad peculiar gaiety filled the car again and stopped me feeling sorry.

When we came to Limerick you got quieter and I thought we were stopping since it was almost dark. But you said that you hated it there and you drove on till we came to a sign saying Lahinch and a street that was flanked by burrows and summer houses. You stopped. It was fully dark. We were on the street of a seaside town. I could see a beach at the end of the street, then sea, a different sea from the one we had left. But then all seas are the same, I thought and when we walked down to the beach and watched the tide sucking off the long strand I saw it was the same, like the one that had washed your guest-house.

I began to feel it all again, the seaside town, you beside me, wild and intractable and almost old, the bed and breakfast signs, the guesthouses. In the bars men stared at us, men that looked like weekend golfers but I didn't mind, you drank your guinness while I drank my gin, you talked about happiness so much that I had to tell you to stop.

And then we went to a guest-house and it was like yours, it had a grey granite front weeping from the seabreeze, like yours except that it was a man that signed us in, held out the guest book for us with large, country hands. You paid.

I went behind you up the stairs. Your breathing was so heavy that it sang in my ears. And then we were in the room and it was so bare, there were two beds, a wash-hand basin, a Virgin and a cinema poster, so seductively bare. You asked me to turn while you undressed. My face must have shown my surprise because before I could answer you turned. And I watched you, I saw your clothes form a little heap around your feet, I saw your shoulders that were very thin and your waist that was almost fat now and your buttocks and your legs. And your skin told me you were definitely older. When you were in your nightgown you turned.

81

'Come on', you said.

There was a knowledge burning through both of us, it was like the yearning that had been there years before, a secret, like blood. But it wasn't a yearning, it was a question and an answer. You knew that with every garment you took off you were stepping into a past self, a self that had that yearning and you could see from my face that I knew too.

'Come on', you said again.

And I took off my clothes and I wore the nakedness I had worn for you, I was a boy then, and I took off your nightdress so you could wear it too.

I didn't look at you, I put my arms around you, standing there, both of us were breathing, our chests touching. You stepped backwards towards the bed.

'Come on', you said.

And we were on the bed, the sea was breathing outside like a woman, we were moving together but I wasn't thinking of you, not you now anyway, I was thinking of you before, of the time he brought you out, the second time, the time after which something finished for me and for you and for him too maybe. He brought you to the Great Northern Hotel this time, and me, there were meal-tables there and a small space for dancing to a small three-piece band. And the meal was like before, you laughing with him and being silent every now and then and me pouring sherry for both of you, in good suit and greased hair. And when the meal was finished the reddish lights came on and the dancing began. The band played waltzes and both of you moved across the floor among other shapeless couples, you beautiful, him tall and supremely confident of something as he waltzed. And I sat there looking and saw him for the first time not as my father who wrote equations on sheets of paper into the night and knew a lot about things like sea-shells but as someone young and agile who had the same yearning for you as I had. And as I drank the sherry that you both had left I began to cry, I felt older than him, insanely older, I had the knowledge of you that made him dance so gracefully, that made that difference in him. Then I drank more sherry and saw his hands around your waist almost touching at the back and I knew people do that when they waltz but I began to hate him as I would hate someone my age. Then again I saw his eyes, distant and kind of hopeful, more hopeful than whenever he had looked at me and as I knew the yearning that was behind them I stopped my hate and felt baffled, sad, older than I could bear. The band was playing the Tennessee Waltz I remembered and I tried to catch your eye but you were looking the other way, looking strict, virginal, leonine. And then I felt the huge resentment, I couldn't do anything with it, my hands were shaking and I knew something was going to end. And you both came back and I pushed the bottle onto the floor with my hand so it would break, so nobody would know how much I had drunk, hoping it would look like an accident. But the crash was loud and everyone stared and he, my father, lost what he had had with you and went white, and shouted at me and you looked quickly at me and I felt I was a child, being chastened publicly. And later I lay in your bed with this huge resentment and hate. You were asleep when I heard him coming up the first floor landing and opening the toilet door. And I got up and you were still asleep, I took the gun from your drawer and went down and stood outside the toilet door. And when I heard the chain pull and I knew he was standing buttoning his fly I raised your civil-war gun and fired quickly four times into the door. And there were four bangs and four rapid thuds and I saw each shot wedging, hardly piercing the mahogany. And I ran upstairs knowing something had finished and I gave you the gun and cursed you quietly because it didn't work –

And then I stopped remembering, you were underneath me, I had come inside you in the room in Clare. Your arms were around my neck, hard, rigid and you said what I was remembering, 'It's finished', you said. And you kissed me tenderly and I kissed you back so you could feel how different we were. And I got from your bed quietly, you were exhausted, turning to sleep already. I lay in my own bed listening to the sea outside me, listening to your breathing. There was a luminous statue of the Virgin over you on the

83

wall and a cinema poster. It said I WAS HAPPY HERE in bold letters and showed a woman in a romantic pose looming over a matchbox version of the town we were in. Then I looked at you and saw the eiderdown rising each time you breathed and your body clenching itself every now and then as if you were dreaming of pain. And I knew it had ended but I still thought to myself, maybe tomorrow –

And tomorrow you got up and drove, you drove to the town you had told me about, where the bachelors and the spinsters come, where you take the waters. We passed the fat girl again on the road but you didn't stop. And the town was like any other holiday town only more so, with its square of hotels and its peeling wooden verandas and old-fashioned cane chairs lining the verandas.

We stopped in the square. It looked strange to me, a holiday town that's inland. I said this to you, why no sea and you said 'There's the sulphur waters'.

We walked up the street a little. A man stared. I bought a guide-book in a shop. I thought of water and holidays, why they go together. Every building seemed to imply a beach, but there was none. It was as if the sea had once been here, but retreated back to Miltown Malbay, leaving a fossil. Somewhere a front door banged.

It was saying something to us, you were saying something, saying This is it, is me, always has been, the part of me you never saw, didn't want to see. And I believed it then, I knew you had always been coupled in my mind with hotels, with cane-chairs and ball-and-claw armchairs. And I crossed the square and bought a paper and read more about the President who had died, but in small print now.

We drove out to the Spa, to a building that looked like a

Swiss hotel, but with a river that seemed to come from underneath it. You asked me did I want to come in and I said no, so you went through the two glass doors alone. I sat in the car wondering whether you drank the waters or bathed in them. A couple passed, wearing suits that must have been too hot for the weather. I shouted at them 'Do you drink the water', I shouted, 'or swim in it'. The man looked at me and threw his hands up uncomprehendingly. I watched them going through the glass doors and imagined a room with a clean tiled floor through which flowed brackish, slow water. I imagined you taking your clothes off with a lot of older men and women and I watched from the side as you dipped yourself into the spa waters among people who had the minor complaints of middle-age to wash off, who had made the act of faith in water. But then, I might have been quite wrong, maybe you sat on a wooden bench in a line with other people and drank the brackish water from a tap.

And I knew it was definitely ending anyhow and that I should forget for your sake the peculiar yearning that sprang in me when my cock sprang to attention in my tight trousers that day you put the gun between your breasts into your blouse. You called it love, I remember. And it must have been.

THE PAST

To my mother and father

ONE

CORNWALL, 1914

I

TWO POSTCARDS OF the holiday town in the south-west of England. They show the same scene which makes me think they were chosen thoughtlessly, bought together maybe in the same shop without caring a whit what the picture showed. Or bought separately, two months between them. She had forgotten, of course, what the first one displayed by the time she came round to needing the second. Both are yellow and with serrated edges, yellowest at the edges as if singed by a match. But the flame is time and the smell, far from the smell of burning, is the smell of years.

They don't show the sea or the town, just the esplanade. But from the look of it, even across years, one can't doubt that this row of dowdy four-storey houses faced the sea. And from the look of them too one can surmise a town behind this esplanade that lives off this esplanade and all year waits for the time when the canvas awnings are stretched out and the canvas deckchairs are placed in the front porches. For the houses are obviously hotels and the angular porches are so obviously looking at what in the brochures must have been a sparkling blue sea, one can be sure that the esplanade was wide and elegantly paved, that there were railings on which to lean and maybe even white iron chairs on which to sit and watch that sea, perpetually blue and be cooled by its salt breezes. And there were rows of primitive paddle-boats (they had them then?) rocking, listing on the edge of the tide, and along the strand itself a row of canvas bathing huts. Canvas! Yards and yards of it are implied, painted in those circus stripes, those warm blues, fawns and yellows, stretched over windbreakers, tautened umbrellas and Punch and Judy stands and even barrel-organs. Was it the age of canvas? For the esplanade is full, there must have been attractions galore with which to fill it – and a spa too, behind the town, backed on by the houses, with the heavy lead taps and the metal baths. Was it the age of spas? For of the people who fill the esplanade, immobile and thronging, the women are most obvious, carrying sun-umbrellas. Was there devotion to water, a suspicion of sunlight? In the postcards they look like white, straight brush-strokes, their umbrellas like brighter dabs. And behind each woman, in her shadow almost, is always the predatory form of a man. They arouse my jealousy these men, suspicious themselves of sunlight, at times each man could be each woman's shadow, so much in her shadow he is. But then the whole image is drenched in sunlight as if the shot had been over-exposed or the card bleached by its years on some green felt desk near a window, through which the sun shone. But despite the bleaching of years, the blaze of sunlight could only have come from the day itself, a hot 'salad' day, and there were more of them then for the handwritten date on the back is June the First 1914. The message scrawled underneath is peremptory, almost irrelevant. Back in two weeks, Una. This though she knew, she must have known, her stay would last more than seven months. Which brings us to the main fact the card can speak of, besides sunlight and years – that she was a compulsive liar. The second card bears the same scene, the women still encased in sunlight though the sky must have leadened in those seven months since season, even then, must have followed season. And the message too promises a two-week return. But the signature is different – Una, Michael, Rene – and behind that last name there is a coy mark of exclamation (!). Which brings us to the prime fact that this card proclaims – the birth of her child. And one third fact, perhaps subsidiary, proclaimed by the months that intervened – between the first card and the second the Archduke Ferdinand was shot in Sarajevo.

2

LILI'S HOUSE RISES four storeys, like those hotels. Lili lives in the fourth. There's a door which I put my shoulder to, then a dim staircase. There's the smell of moist brickwork, of the canal outside. Memory, she told me once, is mother to the Muses. But what do I know of all those years, of Dev and the Clare election and the Custom House fire? The ashes rose over the city, she told me, of the burnt files of each birth, marriage and death. Then they fell like summer snow, for three days. Lili walked through them, maybe held out her palms, caught the down of her birth-cert on the rim of her schoolgirl bonnet. I would petition her for memories like these. I felt a sharp angle in the banisters' curve. I saw the landing then, and Lili's room. I saw Lili, by far the oldest thing in that room. When I entered, she turned in her perpetual cane chair. She smiled.

'Una went there,' she told me, 'to have the child you want to know all about. She went there because she was pregnant, had got married because she was pregnant, one of those sublime mistakes they made then as well as now. He did the dutiful thing, though I'm sure he loved her. I can't imagine him not loving anyone and by all accounts she was a beauty then, not the blousy Republican I got to know later. They married and chose that place for their honeymoon. He was from a Redmondite family, a lawyer with that blend of innocence and relentless idealism that was admirable then, really admirable, and that took the Free State to sully it. He was the best of them, by far the best of them, he was marked out for what would happen to him later, I've heard that said,

95

having no way of knowing, my only memories of him are in the kindergarten school out near Mount Merrion, he'd come to visit us in his Free State uniform, the darling of the nuns with those glazed eyes that told you precisely how much he hated it, the heavy ridiculous belts and the shoulder pistols, he must have hated it even more than de Valera hated him, he would walk through the classroom in his wide boots, stammer while refusing the nuns' offer of tea and lift Rene on to his hip. I remember her crying once, with joy at first, and then pain at the buckle of the belt against her backside, his large hands lifting her higher to nuzzle against the shoulder pistol. Then there would be a few words of affection that only demonstrated how little they knew each other when there would be a respectful knock on the school door, the shadow of an N.C.O. outside, and he would have to leave. I learned later it had always been like that, ever since she was old enough to know him, which is the trouble with public men I suppose, especially the kind of public men we had then. But those few brief meetings were enough to convince anyone of his innate goodness, the quiet enigma of him, which I suppose she inherited. And you could see how marriage to Una, who was supposed to be a beauty then, who was pregnant by him, would have been natural to him, an extension of that undifferentiated love with which I imagine he first made her pregnant. But then I could be wrong, we could be all be wrong.

'All I can really tell you is that they went there, that she was pregnant when they went there and that they stayed nine months. The war had broken out, which would have afforded him an excuse to stay. They would come back, a married couple with a child with a respectable if somewhat fine interval between ceremony and birth. And though I would lay such duplicity at her doorstep, he must have been party to it. The only point behind all this information being the fact that Rene was a love-child – '

3

SO I EXTEND the picture on the postcard beyond the serrated edge with a line, say, of unobtrusive shrubs, not quite trees, between the esplanade and the road proper. These shrubs are in wooden boxes, bound by metal hoops, smaller than those ladies and their parasols and so invisible in that miniature scene; yet stretching down that esplanade far beyond the confines of the postcard to where the esplanade must end, to where steps must run down to the strand leading to a wharf, the upright stakes of which reflect in the water beneath, the scene most perfect, most symmetrical when the water is calm. These shrubs will grow, of course, into the palms I imagine them to be with their aching stems and stunted foliage, redolent of a more torrid climate since they are transplants, burgeoning their way into later postcards, ones that I shall never see. Though they stand now in their temperate soil and their hoop-bound boxes with just their palms flapping in the breeze for their trunks are resistant. Facing the esplanade, the wharf, the water. And behind them the road proper, the line of houses. Not just that row of regular Edwardian façades behind the postcard parasols, but a row differentiated into houses and hotels. More hotels than houses, if the town is as I imagine it, and these hotels in turn differentiated into those which drew attention to themselves and those which didn't. Among those which didn't, one moderately anonymous, intimating solid comfort on a small budget. With a canvas awning like the others and a tiled porch, the walls on either side painted blue and cream, the windows white. The paint was three summers old perhaps, bubbling under the brick. And its name, Excelsior, painted of course in gold above the first row of windows, rich between the blue below, the cream above.

The palms flap and the water waits for them. They would have pronounced the name roundly, presuming its importance. The cabbie grunts, hearing it, knowing their status. Or would they have walked, unsure of cabbies, unsure of what to tip; Irish, intimidated by the parasols, carrying their cases, their clothes too heavy for the hot day and just the palms intimating a welcome, flapping in their still boxes, whispering the confidence that they too are transplants to this imperial soil.

'Una was an actress, of the worst kind, the kind that insists on you calling them by their first name. Oonagh, Oona, Una, I stumbled over it so much at first, I didn't want to be on first name terms, damn her, I was a girl of nine or ten and hardly knew her, Mrs O'Shaughnessy struck me as much much safer. I was a wily child you see, suspicious of this mother of my friend with her large blowsy kisses and her first names. Children read adults, don't they? An atrocious voice with a loud, melodramatic presence, Una never acted anyone but herself but she had the luck to be an Irish speaker and so to meet Messrs Yeats and Fay and then gradually to be thought of as the Irish woman resplendent, though her hair was mousy and her eyes pale and her face totally devoid of those high cheekbones that were meant to be typical of the Celt. Though she had plenty of Matthew Arnold's refusal to submit to the tyranny of fact, the fact being that her stage presence was embarrassing and her refusal to submit to this being quite remarkable and, in the end, a triumph. But then to be fair I only saw her later, years later, when her figure had bloomed and when Rene and me were ten or twelve. When she met him I myself was just a blush on my mother's cheek and Una O'Shaughnessy was by all accounts, sorry to repeat myself, quite a renowned beauty. But then those were the early days of the Gaelic League and as you know yourself a certain kind of passion and what they called "nobility" and in particular an ability to speak Irish, more particularly among those who couldn't, was regarded as an adequate substitute for beauty, not to mention talent. And the kind of acting she relished when her husband met her didn't take place in theatres on legitimate stages, no, nothing as vulgar as that, it found its place in drawing-rooms before select groups of thoughtful people who would gather to look at representations or friezes from their imaginary history of Ireland. You would have the "Rape of Drogheda", say, and after hours of fuss with everyone finally seated and the whispering behind the drawing-room curtain finally stilled the same curtain would draw back to reveal, if you can picture it, a few painted flats to represent Drogheda's walls and a group of ardent young Gaelic Leaguers dressed as Cromwell's Roundheads with whatever pikes and muskets they could drum up for the occasion, all standing to one side in a balletic group, pointing their pikes and things towards a group of just as ardent young girls who represented the Maidens of Drogheda. And between them both, dead-centre of course, raised on a platform, a dais, would stand Una O'Shaughnessy, who else, dressed as Kathleen in a coat of flowing green with a petticoat of red and a symbolic chain maybe round her wrists, her face contorted into an expression of frozen pain, horror or melancholy, whichever was most appropriate. They engrossed my mother's generation, those idiotic affairs. Una, by all accounts, made quite a name from it and it's quite probable, if probability is what you're looking for, that he met her there and that her Kathleen ni Houlihan began the liaison that would lead to Rene's birth in that English town you want me to talk about and which I can't, of course, having never been there. But these idiotic affairs died a death, of course, as soon as the quite amazing discovery was made that the Roundhead youths don't really have to remain like limestone statues but can actually move and fortify their expressions of hate with violent gestures. And from there it was only one step into words, blessed words. "O my dark Rosaleen, do not sigh, do not weep, the priests are on the ocean green . . ." And thus Una became an actress. But she could never play O'Casey, despite her lineage. And why not? Because O'Casey demanded more than a green costume and a *blas*, he was music-hall and melodrama, farce and real tragedy and only a real actress could have done it. And she knew this, of course, and when *The Plough* came on she shouted her guts out from the pits with the rest of them, even though Mr Yeats shouted his apotheosis from his private box. And I know, I know, all this is beside the point, but what do I know of her pregnancy and that English town except for the fact that the child inside her would partake in none of her faults and would be called Rene – '

So heartened by the flapping palms they would have walked under the canvas awning, Una's heels striking the tiles, dragging the tufts of carpet in the hallway with her and striking again the hard oak stairs; and into a clean bedroom, with the walls cream-white, the ceiling done in necklaces of plaster; with a bed which they would find to be warm, with a film of damp.

There must have been a table with an oval scoop for an enamel basin. And the table would hold an enamel jug. All three of them white, echoing the walls and the slight curve at the pit of the jug echoing her form. The guest-book below reading 'Michael and Una O'Shaughnessy' in a young, perhaps a bold hand.

'I DO KNOW there was a spa there. With those sulphur waters that she claimed gave Rene her complexion – '

So I extend the rim of the postcard even more, down the esplanade, past the steps and the wooden pier, where the palms and hotels ended, where the watering-place was, with maybe a sulphur bath. And Michael O'Shaughnessy, as young and admirable as you said Lili, reading *The Times* in the oak-panelled lounge of the hotel room, the browns mixing finely with his light tweed suit, English in its cut, sitting only a little awkwardly on his frame, set against the strength of his cheekbones and the tousled mop of his hair. He is thinking of Redmond and Home Rule while the thin light on the oak panels slowly becomes a blaze. Later he will think of Arthur Griffith and conscription, later again of de Valera and parades. But always as an afterthought, to the sweeps of light on the oak panels as he rises and goes to the window and sees the sun and the sea making a flat mirror beneath it. And his wife meanwhile is on the promenade, for the time being without that fiery quality you saw in her, just pregnant now, her belly like a swollen pod proud before her, meeting the Cornish breezes. Una hides nothing of her shape nor of the flush of her cheeks. Her dress is bulky and white and she walks like a billowing flag of a new nation down to the wrought-iron chairs to drink three cups of that mineral water and pray that it will bring the same flush to her daughter's cheeks. She prays quietly, watching the sea, hoping as everyone does for a magic child. She rises then, her stomach swollen more with the gaseous liquid and walks back, or if the breeze is too strong, takes a hansom cab to her husband who is still by the window, watching the same sea.

Because that was the first month and it would have still been a honeymoon month and the war hadn't yet broken out or the Parliamentary party been split and their bodies just might have made those shapes on the dampish bed like those maps in which the larger island envelops the smaller one, backwards admittedly, but expressive of an act of union rather than one of buggery or rape. The play of their bodies, warranted by that honeymoon under the ceiling with the plaster necklace would have been a gift to them, would have made their differences opaque. They would have lain, counting the plaster pearls which would have led, maybe, to a plaster dimpled Cupid in the centre, they would have kept smiling at its white penis and perhaps even made jokes. It would have taken two months for their differences to emerge, the repetitive whisper of an old word that slowly becomes a roar, for her swelling stomach to take its toll with its moods, its impatience with things physical, its ancient irrationality that he feels he has met before in different guises, perplexing to him at first, then deeply disturbing, a disturbance he would have kept private, however, that would merely have given to his mouth a tight, perplexed line. His face that later became a mask, unrevealing and yet somehow like glass, transparent and still hidden from her as it would later be to masses of others. And his eyes that don't want to speak for fear of what they might say would have risen further moods in her, loud silences and even louder words. For she has taken to sitting up late, Lili, smoking cigarettes, filling the enamel basin with them while he sleeps. And from sitting up late she rises even later. He leaves the bed and dresses under the plaster boy while she sleeps, each breath like the exhalation of centuries. And the flush of a month ago is rocked in that sleep so he dresses alone, dines alone and soon can't imagine things otherwise. And the later she sits up the later she rises until she is hardly awake for two hours of daylight. Is it the fear, he wonders, that as her stomach grows larger until even her billowing skirt can't hide it she might meet someone from home who will take back news of her advanced condition? A remote possibility, since they are now well past autumn and fine weather and the resort is empty but for the old, the invalid and the local. But he suspects it, hearing her talk of that 'bunch of jackals back home'. He asks her is she afraid of the prying eye, the rumour carried across water to that country where there is only rumour and everybody is related. But she hears this slur on her native country and her voice grows shrill in its defence, her nationalism growing with her belly. His is beginning to wane. He sees a war on at last, to end all wars. He travels to London to hear Redmond speak, meets friends of his student days in khaki, thinks of signing with the Irish Guards. From a bench in Hyde Park he hears an anti-Redmondite called Bulmer Hobson and the name reminds him of seabirds and kelp and he sees the flushed, hard faces he knew back home surrounded by the black plumage of the constabulary. He hears the words Home Rule used as a taunt and the names McDonagh, Plunkett, Pearse and the words flutter like fledglings in the wind around him, a renewed attempt at the age-old flight. He spends the night in a boarding-house near St Pancras and can't sleep on the damp mattress. He sits upright on a hard chair the way he knows his wife is sitting, remembering the beat of those words against the wind, they smacked of Parnell and separatist passion, of the strident lyrics of Young Ireland, the dense labyrinths of Fenianism and gradually the war drifts from his mind and with it the thoughts of volunteering and his mind reverts to the fulcrum it has never really left. He sits through the night with the image of the hotel, the sea and his wife's two hours of daylight, static, placid and somehow irreparable. And when the day comes up again and he can see again through the window the chaotic shapes of St Pancras he rises, takes his case and leaves, having decided nothing, knowing there is no decision, what is is and what must be will be. And as he travels back he thinks of history, sees something old, tarnished and achingly human rising out of the chaos of the present with all the splendid, ancient unpredictability of a new birth. He reaches the station and the last guests from the hotel are waiting to leave by the train he has arrived on. Only the perennial eccentrics are left now, Lili, and the summer prostitutes. He walks the promenade and feels one with these eccentrics. He feels outside time, events pass round him, he is in another time, an older time, his mind, once so energetic, so logical becomes a glaze through which he sees the world scream on a distant, opaque horizon. Only the tiles of the promenade have substance, and the vertical supports of the pier, their shadows in the water. He repeats the word 'soul', he feels his fabulous bicep and wonders is it real. The sea falls away beneath him and the flapping palms and holds the sky in reverse, and does it contain, he wonders, the proper order? He sits with Una until his eyes grow heavy, then sleeps before she does. Awake at nine, slipping out from beside her unmoving body, having breakfast in the lounge downstairs, he leaves orders for the same to be brought for her whenever she wakes. He stands by the window watching the sun change the oak from brown to tan, leafing through *The Times, Manchester Guardian* and *Telegraph*, reading every inch of the small print, the tiny ads, anything that would keep his mind from the main headlines. And then he walks, Lili, to the now empty sulphur baths and drinks a ritual glass. He has become superstitious about the yellowish liquid. He looks in its swirling for a shape or a sign, a hint of the future, for the whorls of their lovemaking, a map of a world, of the past few months that are changing perhaps not only his life. Then he walks back, a little hurried, afraid to give himself more than half an hour lest she has awoken. He finds her half-awake, then slipping into sleep again. So he walks again, returns again, talks with her sporadically until she wakes fully around seven, dresses and they go downstairs to dine.

'She hid her pregnancy so well, you see, that no one noticed, my mother didn't anyway, I'm sure of that and Una must have blessed herself in thanks when the war to end all wars broke out, it could have happened for her benefit, it gave her nine months' grace. And what was more natural than that he, coming as he did from a good family of Home Rulers,

104

Redmondite in the best sense my mother always said, what could have been more natural than that he would think of enlisting and would spend months thinking about it? And so she must have blessed the Archduke Ferdinand for getting himself shot and the Kaiser Wilhelm for taking it to heart and the flower of Britain's manhood for rallying to the cause of Life, Liberty and the Rights of Small Nations. But there were rumours all the same. I heard years later from people that hardly knew Rene at all that in fact she wasn't her mother's child but was born of a liaison between her hero of a father, dead years by then, and a south of England music-hall artiste or some such figure and was being kept in trust. But take it from me, that's all nonsense, she was born of Una in your postcard paradise, she was her father's child.'

Something happens to him. He loses his will and gains it. He discovers that part of himself later to become the whole of himself, the self of indomitable will, of odd humanity and gentleness that we know, Lili, from the history books. His mind becomes glazed, he interprets this as weakness. Certain thoughts obsess him, not in the logical, forward manner in which he had been schooled, but they recur eternally, come to no conclusion, seep through his perceptions to disturb him and then vanish before he can order them. He thinks of death and the soul, of a mystical order that seems to have begun with him, that will end with him. He longs to resume his studies again, the world of books, legislature and ordered reading, a longing that he feels in his stomach at times like a knot of physical pain. But the other element saps his will, seduces him. He orders books from London and leaves the packets unopened behind the desk downstairs. He wakes one night well past midnight and is unsure whether he is awake or dreaming because instead of sitting in her chair and smoking beside him she is asleep, her six-months' stomach curving upwards, her eyelids slightly open. Her eyes are like needles underneath the lids. He raises his head and stares at the slivers of light, barely revealed under her drawn lids, the source of which is somewhere beyond her dilating nostrils and her closed mouth. With each breath she takes her head moves slightly on the pillow and the lights move too until he stares at her, hypnotised by them and the rainbows round his own lashes. Her breath rises with the sadness of death and with each wave he is carried further from those points of her eyes until he is seeing them across aeons of distance, two barely visible specks of light. It is his own death he is swimming in and the feeling of unearthly ease, of buoyancy, lulls him like a massaging hand, irresistibly. He thinks, I can return or stay here. And his will expands then like a rearing horse, mighty, more than irresistible and bears him back. She is sleeping still, with her eyes now fully closed.

Meanwhile the winter is beginning, the dry cold wind from the Azores whipping spray along the promenade, dispersing hillocks and ripples of sand over the austere tiled pathway. He leaves her around twelve, ignoring the wind. The sun is shining independently of it and but for the cold biting into the cheekbones, eyelids and fingers one could imagine the promenade crowded with its quota of summer strollers. It is empty though, as if the weak sun shines only for him. He grips his overcoat tightly around him and imagines that he feels neither wind nor cold but that just what he sees is real – the bright sunshine, like a blessing, clear and even sharper than in heat, over the pier, the iron chairs, the strand and sea, the canvas whipping round the few remaining bathing shelters. He thinks sunshine and emptiness are his element and so familiar seems the scene that he almost misses the one obtrusive shape – the girl standing in the shadow the bathing hut throws towards the sea.

He saw her from behind and then she vanished, or seemed to. He walked by the tottering structure of painted canvas and saw her again, in a discoloured fawn coat, looking at the sea. From her stillness and her pose, the way her fawn coat merged with the sand and then her head and shoulders glowed against the lime-grey sea, he knew that she had seen him. He stopped and heard the silence of his absent footsteps against the tiles. He looked at the sea with her, its washing exhausted, spent. She was in the damp part of the sand and her boots were sunk. Her hands were in the pockets of her coat and there were threads hanging from them and round the calves of her boots the stitching was split. The canvas flapped, and the palm leaves. He knew that she would turn, that her face would not surprise him. She turned and looked at him. Her eyes were resentful and hopeless. They were blue. Could he have known at that distance or could the sea have suggested the colour to him? But then even the sea was lime-grey. He knows she is one of the last of the summer prostitutes, perhaps even the last. She looks as redundant as the bathing hut or the hotel signs. He decides immediately to give her money, if not warmth.

'They've all gone, have they?' His voice surprises him in the silence.

'Who've all gone?'

Her accent is local. Perhaps he has been wrong. He stumbles for words. 'The starlings.'

She is shifting her feet in the damp sand as if she wants it to flurry, to be dry, to call the summer back.

'That sand is damp. Come up.'

'No, you come down.' And a humorous flicker crosses her face. 'The gentleman always does.'

He must climb over the railings and leap. She smiles, waiting for it. Does she notice his honeymoon shoes, scuffed after months of walking, his tweed suit now shapeless round his knees? Has she seen him walking, his aimlessness not too different from hers? She must have. He jumps and sinks to his laces in the sand. She walks to him, faintly smiling, takes his arm and leads him down the beach without a word.

'WOULD UNA HAVE talked to him incessantly about the Hungarian policy and Arthur Griffith, about Sinn Fein and shoneenism, telling him that if he enlisted he was just as guilty as any Protestant on a horse? I don't think so. She would have embodied the nation aggrieved, reclining on the bed, pillows propped around her, every long dramatic pause saying more than any tirade could have; theatrical pose and political history were inseparable for her. He would be by the window, listening. I espied them both in that pose years later, in a different room. By then he was in uniform, a dull smoky khaki, the colour of gorse. Her colour. He showed no extraordinary intelligence, not in the normal sense anyway, while she had a fast, quick mind that always outdid itself. He would have let her words seep through him, like old wine through a muslin cloth which comes out slowly, but purely, all the sediment removed. So when he later took his part among the minor heroes, she could claim he was her creation, she could put the point of his conversion in that hotel of yours. There was more, she would tell us, than Rene being born – '

She shifted in her cane chair and smiled.

'Irish, now, there's what I mean, Una could half speak it, a ridiculous *blas* she had when I remember her, but by then maybe she had forgotten most of it. Her father being an early Gaelic Leaguer, who knows she could even have gone to the school of the unruly stammerer, what was it called, St Enda's, and read the motto daily, I Care Not Though I Were to Live But One Day and One Night if Only My Fame and My Deeds Live After Me. And he though he couldn't speak a word then yet he knew it later, became dutifully impeccable, sent dispatches in both languages on the back of cigarette packets and devised a code in it which Eoin MacNeill even couldn't crack. Now why? He didn't love her, couldn't have, later anyway from what I remember of them, he saw her only on flying visits from his flying column and maybe at Christmas, holy days. So why did he take those parts of her, reproduce them so meticulously, make his own mirror of them, graft them on to his own person so perfectly that when the end came she could claim he was her creation? And if you want an answer and if you want the music of things in their proper place all you can look to is the story. She made those claims of hers in retrospect, when he was already being embalmed in the oil and the scent of the great losers, and she put the point of his conversion there, in that hotel of yours. But then she was part of the story too, she was his entry to it, both of them making it as they were telling and Rene being born – '

But Michael has pulled his boots out of the sand and has walked along the beach with the girl whose name, he discovers, is June. She is an alert and a nervous talker, she reveals large tracts of herself to him immediately and yet leaves him with the impression that beyond these tracts it would be indelicate to probe. Her teeth are small, her face is small, somewhat drawn, with large brown eyes and sallow cheeks leading to a dimpled chin. Her face has none of the definition that would give it beauty but can in certain lights be beautiful, depending on its mood and pallor. When not beautiful it could best be described as drawn and he will find, in fact, that her face is in continual motion between one aspect and the other. They walk along the strand between the dunlins and oyster-catchers and they talk about their lives. She talks of her boarding house, not along the promenade like his hotel, but in the smaller streets where the promenade becomes a road and the line of the palms ends and the spa has not yet begun. She spills out tracts of herself as if to put him at ease, punctuated now and then by a light laugh and a dry cough. She has been six months in the town, she tells him, and her sojourn in it seems as disembodied as his. But she knows more about it, she mentions names and streets and places he has never heard of, and leaves him feeling even more foreign, only native to the palms, the promenade, the pier. She talks of the war and the sea and of what she calls her 'present state'. The phrase leaves him wondering about her past one and since her accent is good and her words are redolent of governesses, a somehow childish innocence with an adult pretension towards exactitude, he wonders whether before her 'present state' she was a teacher of some kind. He feels there is something Quaker about her, in the plainness of her clothes and her air of Protestant rigour. And yet walking beside him she is as disembodied as he, as will-less, and he is given the impression of limitless time waiting to be spent. An air of decided sensuality emanates from the fawn coat, from the body it covers, which seems a little forlorn, like a boat stranded and waiting for the tide it knows will come and seep round its hull. He walks with her, wondering could he carry his own needs as honestly as she does hers. He talks of the war, the sea, the town, of everything but those private areas of his life which he knows, glancing at her whimsical brown eyes, he must never touch. He laughs at one of his own expressions – having compared the jowls of a dead dogfish that lay across their path to those of Kitchener – and finds himself surprised at the person who made the observation and the person who subsequently laughed. He can see in himself a new and lighter personality emerging, which seems to be his own creation. He cocks his mental eye askance at it, walking down the strand. They come to the pier and climb up the steps. She peels bark from the stem of a palm, he rests on the wedge of the barrel. A cold gust of wind blows up and so they move into the foyer of an old hotel and then into the lounge. It is an even less respectable hotel than his and he wonders if he had come here months ago, would it all have been quite different. They drink a pot of steaming coffee. Then they leave and walk back along the strand, she insisting that they retrace their steps in the sand, placing her feet in the prints his have made the way a child does. There is silence between them now and this silence acts on them like an inevitable suggestion, leads them up to the flapping, gaudy canvas of the hut where she saw him first. She leads him inside with her Quaker matter-of-factness to the forefront. He sees there are deckchairs stacked against one canvas wall and a bundle of straw mats. She smooths one out on the sand and with practised hands, and barely lifting her skirt, she gives herself to him.

It becomes his pattern, and not one that's to be measured in days or hours, but one that has its own rhythm. Every day he walks down the promenade and the sun is as clear as when he came there first, the sky as clear, the only difference being the gathering coldness of its light. And some days he meets her there, an average of one day out of four, but never with regularity. There would be three days in a row at times, and then not one day for a week. He comes to think of these days as 'the day' and every day he thinks, 'Today will be the day.' And yet on the days on which he doesn't meet her he is never disappointed and on the days on which he sees her from above the canvas bathing hut he is pleased but not surprised. He is coming to accept the arbitrary nature of events as if the events themselves are objects of fate, dictated by a rhythm of which he is not master but servant. He surrenders his will to the accidental with the certainty that the pattern it will reveal to him will be greater than any he can impose. He thinks of Bulmer Hobson in Hyde Park, of Lord Kitchener, the Archduke Ferdinand, and of his sleeping pregnant spouse, curled like an esker in the room he has left, and walking along the promenade, anticipating June's fawn coat behind the gaudy canvas, anticipating the texture of sand and of the bark of palms, anticipating the same canvas flapping emptily without her, he feels a remarkable freedom in his total acceptance of whatever chance dictates. And when she is there they will walk, repeat the first day's pattern, reveal no more of themselves than they did then, building instead on the tracts they have discovered, creating new selves

111

daily, as their feet create fresh prints in the same sand. They choose their personalities whimsically, act out small lives while walking. A changed inflexion, a weighted word, an 'I remember' said with a grimace, a sigh or a smile evokes a type of face, of person and of past. He tells her he is a doctor, that he has studied in the Royal University and has fled from a burdensome practice in Dublin. He tells her he is a cattle exporter from a family of Dublin merchants, the eldest in the firm, he will feed England on Irish beef for the war's duration. She tells him she is an actress, left here by a repertory company at the end of a bad summer. She tells him she is a governess, sacked by her titled employers because of an affair of the heart. He prefers the second to the first, but he accepts both, just as he accepts the quick movements of her features from liveliness to pallor. There is something blessed he suspects, in the very poverty, the elusiveness of each encounter and of their knowledge of each other. And the only measure of their permanency, of their perhaps having met in some yesterday is the straw mat in the canvas hut which from the first day she has left on the floor of the bathing hut and which no one has yet disturbed. It is like an arrow pointing to their one reality, their lovemaking. And yet it is a mat, the repository of his bliss, his belonging with her to a realm of feeling, beyond which they can never belong. Through that they meet on a plane that is as far removed from the persons they chose as are they from the sand that clings to that mat that hinders their movements. They move and are covered in sand, remove little clothing; it is cold. And each time money changes hands, money, the coinage that makes the exit from the hut more bearable, that leaves them both locked in an embrace, among just sand, sea and canvas, until their next meeting. How will I not die when it ends, they both wonder, and yet when he peels the ritual three notes from his pocketbook and when she crumples them into the pocket of her fawn coat the wonder vanishes.

He is certain that he loves her. He is just as certain that outside the curve of this sea and the soft gloom of this bathing hut his love has no meaning. She is an event outside time and yet rooted in the most sordid of times, among the most precise objects.

'Is the war going to end?' she asks.

'No,' he says, and while beyond this sand the thought would disturb him immeasurably, here it fades like a whisper.

'I love you,' she says.

'And I love you,' he repeats. And yet both of them observe scrupulously the proprieties they have established for themselves. And neither feels regret since all regret, every sorrow, was implicit between them from the start.

6

'MY MOTHER SAID that seeing both of them again was like seeing ghosts of what they had been – '

Love is the word Michael thinks of all the time, that unique syllable that takes in tongue, lips and teeth. He says it as he walks, like a hymn to the fall of his steps, he forms it silently with tongue, lips and teeth while taking newspapers from the hall stand, he hums it while reading them in the oak lounge. The syllable carries him off for hours, he sees the sun has leapt suddenly from the lintel of the window to the third pane and wonders what has happened in between. It hisses from a dentist's gas mask, silences itself in the aching stems of the palm trees, laps in the waves coloured with oil that drift in at the farther end of the beach. He hears it in the rise of Una's breathing, in the 'Ta ra, love' of the fruiterer to a housewife on the prom, on the headstones of the graves he finds where the town ends and the road limps into a stretch of moorland, In Loving Memory Of, on picture postcards, secondhand novels and the slogans of commercial companies. He watches her breathing and hums a popular ditty, 'I left my love and leaving loved her more', he sees people in their waking lives dominated by it, is amazed by the tyranny the syllable exercises and each utterance of it leads him to the one place where its utterance is unnecessary – the strand, the bathing hut.

'Standing under the long glass skylight of Pearse Station (it

114

would have been Westland Row then) like ghosts of their former selves – '

And it was through it that he could tolerate the pain of his wife's pregnancy. He had known for some time that she didn't love him and what was for him worse, that he might never love her. And so he repeated the syllable and garnered from somewhere the inescapable sense of loving that would never leave him and that now reached out to every facet of that holiday town from its slate valley roofs down to its elementary sewerage system that disgorged into the sea somewhere beyond the beach, beyond the spa and beyond the graveyard headstones.

'With the child between them, the strange spotted light you get on the platform from that crazy corridor of glass, the train still steaming on the tracks, like ghosts of their former selves, come back to the country, to the multitudinous relations, the connections everywhere, the miniature intimate city where they knew every face and every face knew them, where those who have gone away are immediately judged on what seems to have happened to them. She walked forward, left him holding the Moses basket, kissed my mother and confided to her that she would not have another child – '

The wind bellows into the canvas hut and its stripes bloom suddenly, and sag. Una's day is approaching and each of his meetings there lead him towards what seems to be a delusion but what he almost hopes might not be. She is lying flat on the hard sand and he sees his wife's condition implicit in her. He imagines her slim, starved body blooming, he moves his hand over imaginary curves, begins to treat her with elaborate precautions. He insists that she never leap from the promenade to the sand and that she always walk slowly. He wills her sex, her features on to his unborn child; her blanched face, her ash-blonde hair, her peculiar childlike

115

grace, each movement so contained and satisfying. He doesn't doubt for an instant that he will have a daughter.

'But if my mother didn't notice, there were others that did. But as usual with people and with gossips in particular, they get the sense of something out of joint but the sense they make of that sense is even more out of joint. If you know what I mean. It was on him the blame was foisted – though maybe blame isn't the right word – the mystique maybe, the question mark – it was raised over him and the child in the Moses basket he was carrying. A little back from them, by the train, coming out of the steam. They raised a question mark, but they asked the wrong question. Who's child, you see, was what they asked. They saw their Una O'Shaughnessy, already quite a minor celebrity, that kind of fame that thrives on absence and aura, and they saw this young man behind her, the intense awkwardness about him that would later become his hallmark, and their guessing centred round him. It would all later bear fruit in the rumours of Rene as the illegitimate spawn of some great lady, actress, society queen. But they didn't see the real blight. People never do – '

The palms are absolutely still one day and the sea is crystal. Once inside the hut, she asks him for money, an extraordinary amount. What for? he asks. They are both standing and his head touches the wooden laths of the roof. I must see a doctor, she tells him. He tells her that he can only withdraw an amount like that from his bank in London. This pleases her. My doctor is in London, she tells him, smiling. Outside in the ice-cold sunlight she walks towards the sea. She staggers at the edge and then vomits in to the tide. It is nothing, she tells him, it will pass.

He is going to hear Roger Casement speak, he tells his wife. The name echoes strangely round the walls, and seems to carry to the palms outside. And why do you want to know, she asks him, about rubber and blacks? Mr Casement is speaking about the war, he tells her, against the war. She can only assent.

They meet in the empty station and travel up together, shocked by the sight of each other against a background of trains, dining cars and passing fields. They realise how used they are to sea, sand and deckchairs. As if it is not they who are travelling, their persons seem to leave them and each gesture and word is looked down on from above, by both of them, from that plane where their meetings began. They arrive in London and book a room in the least shabby of the hotels around St Pancras. His London is different to hers, he realises. She is a stranger like him, but a native stranger to her own capital. They walk together to his bank in Regent Street, where they withdraw the amount she needs. He wants to accompany her then but she is withdrawn and evasive. She arranges instead a time and place where she can meet him in the evening. He watches her fawn coat, barely visible in the crush of the upper deck of a tramcar. He walks from Regent Street through a succession of squares, streets and circuses towards the club in Bloomsbury where the Casement meeting is. The sunlight glances off the fringes of the lintels, bleaching all the roofs. He arrives there to find he is an hour early and so decides to dine. He orders all four courses to while away the hour but barely touches any of them. He has no appetite for food, the word love courses through his mind like a cold wind, he sees her fawn coat on the tramcar, he sees the jug and enamel bowl beside his wife's bed. He is finishing his coffee when he hears a commotion outside and sees through the glass-panelled doors a group of men arguing with a police inspector. They have Irish accents and one of them, whom he thinks he recognises, could be the Member of Parliament for West Mayo. The commotion increases and blows are exchanged and suddenly there is a phalanx of policemen and between them is being escorted a thin man in a tweed suit with the air of a country gentleman but with a black beard, an incredibly ravaged face and burning, melancholy eyes. The man walks quietly, puts up no resistance and passes, with his escort, out of Michael's sight. He finishes his coffee, watching the arguing groups, their anger subsiding gradually now that the cause of it has gone. Is that the Casement, he wonders, who toppled Leopold of Belgium? He feels he should join that group outside but he cannot summon up the energy. He sits and watches as they disappear one by one and as the last words trail off. Then he pays his bill and rises, walks through the glass door and sees in the hallway that the notice for the meeting has been written over in a scrawled hand: 'Cancelled'. He passes into the street.

He spent the afternoon in a moving-picture palace. He remembered nothing of the story but the fact that it switched rapidly from dining-room to bedroom to garden and back. He thought of how depth and movement could be caught on a square of white. He thought of the canvas hut and the hotel bedroom, all pretence of distance between them abolished, and of the death of time.

Some years later he would see an ingenious set constructed by an American on the Abbey stage for a play in which his wife would be performing. It would be the sole performance of hers he had attended since their marriage and the last he would ever attend. The set would be built on a circular rostrum, like a merry-go-round, with a representation of the interior of a peasant cottage on one side and the Lord Viceroy's drawing-room on the other. He would watch from the back row during rehearsals, his wife standing in a shawl with a bunch of flowers by the door of the peasant cottage. And then, in a sudden transformation which always amazed him, the set would slowly slide, the cabin disappearing to be gradually replaced with the Viceroy's room, the ball-and-claw tables, the sumptuous armchairs and the rattling cabinet of drinks. And there, behind the cabinet, a little in the shade, but coming more and more into the footlights as the set righted itself would be his wife, whom at that moment he loved, in a gown of lace and black satin, holding the stem of a wine glass. And he would be reminded of both his other rooms, how many years ago he can't remember, of the two people who inhabited them, while he would watch his wife walk down from the set to discuss some obscure point of stage craft with the American designer, while he would look at his child who stood before the proscenium arch, passing

118

her hand back and forwards in front of the footlights, disturbing the dust that gathered there like diamonds. He would wonder what had happened to his other room, the canvas room, to the girl who inhabited it. He would realise that both rooms were in the end his creation. Within several days he would be shot and these memories would die with him, he having left to his daughter just his love of blonde hair, his sense of the other side of things and sense of coincidence, the cumulative history of her conception and birth.

But on the Thirty-First of January 1915 he walks back to the St Pancras hotel to find June lying on the small bed, a blanket pulled over her and her cardboard case on the ground beneath it. She is paler than he has ever seen her. She doesn't look up when he comes in, her eyes are staring at the ceiling. Did you see the doctor? he asks her. Yes, she answers and he knows something is wrong by the sound of her voice. He sits on the bed beside her and he finds that the blanket is wet around her thighs. He pulls the blanket back and finds that it and the sheets are sodden with blood. Don't worry, she tells him, there is always blood afterwards, less this time than the last. He goes to ring the maidservant but she stops him, tells him it will cause trouble, everything will be over by morning. What will be over? he asks her. Don't you know what? she replies. He says nothing, but passes his hand over her face, her breasts, her stomach under the wet blanket until he sees she is asleep. Then he sits by the window looking at the dark square, turning to look at her whenever she breathes heavily. When morning comes and the shapes of the square have emerged from the mist he turns once more and sees she is awake and looking at him, but with sleep still behind her eyes. It's over now, she says. You'd better go. And you? he asks. She shakes her head. I will stay here, she says. With friends. He goes to the bed and kisses her once and her mouth responds but her eyes close suddenly, as if their opening had been simply a dream.

On the train back he thinks of nothing but the passing fields. At the station there is a maid, who tells him his wife is in labour. And the child is born with him watching, holding the curved jug above the enamel basin which is swimming with blood and water, from which the midwife wrings towels, continually.

7

SO RENE WAS born on the First of February 1915, St Brigit's day, across from the promenade which would have been by then quite empty of umbrellas.

'But why call her Brigit when the whole point of their stay there was to hide the fact? Una reached Dublin three months later and even then she claimed the child was premature. Which was how the myth grew up of Rene's extraordinary eyes and hair, her miraculous maturity. The child they saw in that station, whom Una claimed was at the most two weeks old was in fact a three-month-old bundle of vitality. I would say she was quite a tender mite, a fragile copy of the father, with blue eyes and hair that even at that age showed its blondness. No wonder they were all amazed by this two-week-old marvel with a straight, intelligent stare and hair that didn't stick to its crown like some black secretion but stood up, half-blonde, and even dared to curl. For her first few months she was a source of constant amazement among all those who saw her, a disjointed sense of awe and misapprehension was foisted on her which was fed of course by her mother, terrified that they would discover that this wonder of hers had been conceived out of wedlock, maybe in an Amiens Street hotel after a Conradh na Gaeilge meeting. I discovered this later through a First Communion form and a senile nun who didn't notice any difference. I mean, beautiful as it is to be born on St Brigit's day, the advantages are more than outweighed by the stain of illegitimacy. Which is why they stayed in England in the first place, why they took three months to travel home. And why they arrived in Westland Row Station carrying her in a Moses basket like a two-week-old.'

Standing in the corridor of glass with the escaping steam behind him, holding the head of the wickerwork basket and his wife still half-hidden in the steam, would he have shown the germ of the person he would later become and if he did would anyone have noticed? The knot of family, cousins, friends and half-friends, they stood beyond the steam waiting for it to clear. He watched their shapes emerge, moving to embrace him.

The steam died round his boots and he carried the basket behind her. They seemed like any couple. There would have been a passing sweetness in being home, greater than their differences. He quickly ensconced himself in his father's legal practice and helped to make it one of the leading firms in the city.

And she, Lili, if I have heard you correctly, began again where she had left off and rose to become the star of a new style of theatre, peasant in emphasis, nationalist in theme. She resumed her Irish classes and acquired an enviable *blas*. Her hair, which was of that arresting blonde shade that people would later remark on in her daughter, she dyed black. The eulogies to her talents in the papers of the time (with the exception of the *Irish Times*, which was Unionist in politics) are so frequent that they are hardly worth quoting. Suffice it to say that the qualities critics found to praise in her were sociological rather than aesthetic. She was praised for her 'modesty of bearing', her 'passion of utterance', but most of all for an elusive quality which was referred to variously as her 'Irishness', her 'Gaelic splendour', her 'purity of soul', a quality which, the *Freeman's Journal* claimed, was 'representative of what is best in Irish Womanhood'. And thus, in one of those qualitative confusions which are perhaps inevitable in an emergent drama, not to mention an emergent nation, her public praised her as if she were the part itself.

122

8

SHE IS SEEN in frieze, as it were, on an impromptu stage in what looks like a drawing-room with elegant french windows. She is holding a spear and she has her head thrown back, her marvellous hair bound by what seems to be a leather cord. There are two youths on either side of her, dressed in pleated skirts which could be Grecian but for the elaborate Celtic signs emblazoned on them. And all three are staring towards what must be the cowled head of a photographer.

She is in a peasant shawl, with a flat behind her depicting the gable end of a thatched cottage. The drawing-room is larger and more sumptuous and the flats are bounded by a heavy brocade curtain, covering, I have no doubt, a set of even more splendid french windows. Her head is raised and her eyes are blazing with a kind of posed defiance. To her left is a figure with a grotesque false paunch and a large top hat bearing the legend 'John Bull'. This figure is glowering, over her shoulders, towards an equally caricaturish figure on her right who can be taken, from his goatee beard and his spiked Prussian helmet, to represent the Kaiser Wilhelm. And between them Una's fleshy arm is raised to point to a banner stiffly fluttering from the cottage's thatched gable. And the banner reads: ENGLAND'S DIFFICULTY?

And in the last photo the drawing-room has given way to the interior of a theatre and the flats and the setting are more elaborate, though the scene they depict is even more decrepit. The scene is a room in a Dublin tenement in which a young man is sitting by a typewriter, his mouth open wide, obviously declaiming something to an unseen audience, his hand ruffling his unruly hair. I have no doubt that the play is O'Casey's first, *The Shadow of a Gunman*, and that the stage is the early Abbey; that the youth is Domnall Davoren and that the line he is declaiming is Shelley's 'Ah me alas, pain, pain, ever, for ever', with which O'Casey for some reason peppered the dialogue. Behind him, peeping over his shoulder at his typewritten sheet, holding a bowl of sugar, is Una. And I have no doubt that she is meant to represent the most ideal and fragile of all of O'Casey's heroines, Minnie Powell; and that her Minnie Powell was on the plump side and definitely too old. She was thirty-three by then, and looked it.

9

THEY ARRIVED ON the Second of June 1915. In the Easter
of the next year there was a revolution. A Gaelic League
colleague of hers named Eamon de Valera held Boland's Mills
and was lucky enough to survive the subsequent rash of
executions. His pallid face, his gangling, unlikely bearing, his
tenderness for mathematics and his strict academic air had,
Lili tells me, been the butt of many of her private, rather
caustic jokes. But when the revolution (which surprised her,
Lili tells me, as much as anyone, though she later pretended
of course, that she was in on it all along) extended itself into
first months and then years of gradually accelerating chaos,
then open rebellion, she lent to it her sense of melodrama
and backstage intrigue, discovered a sudden liking for the
gaunt schoolmaster.

'And rumour had its heyday here, I mean that man who
would stamp his unlikely profile on the history of this place
as surely as South American dictators stick theirs on coins
and postage stamps, the mathematical rigour of his speech,
his actions, and her, who was fast becoming the *grande dame*
of Irish Republicanism – not that there weren't others jostling
for her place, but none of them had her advantage, she was
an actress after all, a bad one maybe, but she knew how to
upstage with all the cunning of her limited talent.'

How Michael became implicated is uncertain. Taking
briefs at first, Lili tells me, in Republican cases and later
assuming a full and active role in what would become known
as the I.R.A. Una claimed it was at her behest, Lili tells
me. I would like to imagine it was in remembrance of that
promenade, remembering the affair of the bathing shelter,

125

with the sense of holocaust, like the sea, all around them. His involvement gradually took its own momentum until by 1919 he had donned the cap and trenchcoat that characterised activists in the upper echelons of the guerrilla effort.

'Never got his name on a street. That must be to his credit. It'd sound odd, anyway. O'Shaughnessy Street – '

He took at one stage to writing verse, a practice that seemed obligatory for activists in those days. He never mastered Irish. His verse is somewhat painful to read, only memorable for the number of instances in which he refers to Kathleen, the daughter of Houlihan, as blonde-haired.

TWO

DUBLIN, 1921

I HAVE TO imagine you, Rene, since he took no photographs. Una did, but only after he had died. You were three when you went to the convent on Sion Hill Road. You had a broad face for a child, eyes that could be seen as too small, but those who knew you didn't care. You were an ordinary child in every respect and what greater blessing can one ask for, than to have an ordinary childhood?

It's just your hair that is distinctive. Curls hanging all around your forehead. Your hair is thin but has a creaminess of texture that gives each strand its own way of falling. Flat near the crown but falling all around it to a fringe of spirals, like those clumps of flowers, the stems of which droop from the centre and the petals fall to make the rim of a bell. Blonde is a shade that catches the tints of the colours around it. Your hair is cream blonde and catches most lights and the outer strands make a halo of them. To have extraordinary hair is almost as good a thing as to have an ordinary childhood.

You sat with Lili on the small benches and the Cross and Passion nuns moved among the benches like beings from another world. Their heads were framed by those great serge and linen bonnets that nodded like boxes when they spoke. It is you at the time that Lili described, when your father would walk in in his Free State uniform and lift you on to one hip and then the other, trying to avoid paining you with his shoulder strap or his shoulder pistol while the gun-carriage rattled outside and the nuns whispered like a litany their offers of tea. You would have been near six then. And your clearest memory could have been mine. Of the beech tree in the gravelled yard across from the windows of the classroom. The trunk is huge and pushes straight out of the earth and the gravel is thick around it, revealing no earth or roots to prepare one for its intrusion. It backs in its magnificence against an old granite wall. The branches nearest the wall have been sawn off to stop them crushing through the granite. So all growth of branch and foliage is towards the school, towards the window at which you would have sat, staring. It is really for you, the severed half-umbrella, the monstrous segment of tangled growth that shades half the yard. Across from it again is a small shrubbery, half-bald with grass, smoothed by generations of feet. A bell would have rung, a fragile shiver of brass notes filling the classroom around you, the nun's bonnet would have nodded towards the door and you and the class would have walked jerkily towards it and once outside you would have expended yourself in that circular burst of energy that erupts from nowhere and ends nowhere, scouring the gravel with your feet, the air filled with a patina of cries that seemed to hover above your head. Only when you had exhausted yourself would you lie by the tree. But the tree would renew spent energies, would gather a ring of small bodies around it, each newcomer jostling to rest her back against the bark. You would have won Rene, continually won, by reason of that quiet ignorance of the turmoil of others which would always have found its few square feet of bark. The bark moulded in scallops, rougher than skin is.

Your name would have brought you some attention among the Eileens, Maureens, Marys and Brids. Two thin white vowels, strangely unIrish and yet so easily pronounced, as if more Irish than the Irish names. Your father's visits would have brought you more. Most of the nuns would have baulked at the excesses of the Troubles but would have supported the Free State side and have been overcome by the mystique of your father's name. He looks a little like a statue, standing in the doorway. Two of them, though, would have refused to be impressed. One from Clare, with Republican connections, whose tight mouth whenever she passed you in the corridor would have said enough. And one old, quite beautiful creature, an avid reader of Tolstoy, who would have regarded the presence of gun-carriages in a school yard as an immoral intrusion. She is old and tall, like a long translucent insect underneath her habit. The thin bones on her hands and the shining white skin on them and her cheeks, which is all you can see of her beneath the black, seem to contain more reserves of energy than any of the younger novices. Her hands are hardly warm, they hardly linger on your hair for more than a moment; each of her movements is as brief as it can possibly be, as if her body is reserving itself for a boundless, ultimate movement. And the reserve, the iron quiet that she imposed on her life has had its recompense in the cheeks that face you at the top of the class, as smooth and pallid as those of a young, inactive boy, in the grey eyes under the black and white bonnet which reflect the impersonal rewards of a lifetime's confinement. Her presence is hypnotic, as are her maxims. 'Keep your hands,' she tells you, 'to yourself. Keep your hands from yourself.' You cannot understand the contradictions of this dictum, but through your efforts to understand them it assumes a sense of truth that is, for you, greater than words. It hints at the mystery behind movement and gesture. You say the maxim to yourself in situations that have nothing to do with hands. You know the ideal is hands folded and demure on the lap of your unfolded legs, neither to nor from yourself, and you know too that this is not the final answer which, you suspect, has nothing to do with the dimpled, fleshy hands before you. Are there other hands, you wonder, unseen ones which these real hands must train to lie at rest, ready to suddenly bloom into a gesture of giving? The hands of the soul, you think, and stare at the nun who has repeated her maxim once more and is sitting, hands unseen, at the top of the classroom. Her name is Sister Paul and it expresses that maleness which must be the ultimate goal of her sisterhood.

Lili is your seat-mate. She is pert and alive, master of the social graces of that classroom. If anyone is the favourite it is she, catching the glances of nuns with the downward flickering of her eyelids. And even now I can see the small alert girl who would have arbitrated the loves and hatreds of that class, whose clothes would have been imitated, cut of hair, colour of ribbon, style of bow. She had a lisp and the lisp becomes in her an enviable possession. She is enthralled by you and your cream-blonde hair and yet can dominate you with her quickness and her tongue, for yours was more than anything an ordinary childhood.

You sit by the window and stare at the trunk of the beech. Sister Paul's voice wavers, like a thread held in air. Lili, to see the trunk, has to lean past you. You watch the shadow of its severed umbrella blacken less and less of the yard as the morning progresses. The first break passes and the second break, until the final bell rings and you run into the yard once more and find your space against the bark and if the armoured carrier is there, you are carried off in that and if it isn't, you begin the long walk down the Trimelston Road home.

The wind sweeps down the long avenue, at one end of which there is a half-built church in a new kind of granite and cement which make the half-walls rise sheer and inhuman. How large it will be and what a God it will hold. There is a group of boys playing near nettles chanting 'Up Dev'. One of them is standing in the nettles, crying and leaping to retrieve his cap which either the wind or the other boys have flung away. You stagger with Lili through the wind. It is a spring wind and pulls the green of all the sycamores in the one way, towards the sea. There is a line of coast houses behind you and the sea, which seems hardly disturbed. You walk a few steps and turn to the sea and then face the wind again and walk. Lili is laughing and clutching her gymslip. The wind makes another sweep, you close your eyes against it and a melody suddenly courses through you like a long pendulum sweeping the tips of the sycamores in a heavenly arc. It runs its course and finishes, and just when it seems past recall it comes again, its long brass tones fortified by another one and you listen and walk while the two melodies boom through you. There is a rhythm of which each tree seems a distinct beat and the bass song, too deep for any human voice. It recurs and recurs with each sweep of the wind which pulls your slip against you, gripping your knees and thighs as if it were wet. Then it leaves you finally and the wind dies down you are relieved. You turn once more to the coast houses and the unruffled line of blue and then walk on with Lili, not saying a word. The boy has retrieved his cap and is standing near the nettles, smearing his legs with dock leaves, crying softly. Lili stops, looks at him as if she might console him, but then walks on. 'Cry-babby!' she whispers.

You walk past him, looking at his green-smeared knees. You have little that is defined or personal about you. You have not yet reached the age of reason. The melody flies and your soul waits for its return. You are like a mirror that catches other people's breath. One nun refers to you as that plump, blonde-haired girl, another talks of your slender, almost nervous quietness. You willingly become each, as if answering the demands every gaze makes on you. The most persistent attitude towards you is one of pity, touched by a warm, moral, faintly patriotic glow. You are the child whose father must rarely see her, immersed as he is in the affairs of the Free State, whose mother is busy, abstracted. Through you they see your heritage, the glow of newsprint and newspaper reports, the profusion of rumours and heated discussions beside which you must seem something of an afterthought. You grow through the very stuff of those frustrated politics. You are Lili's most treasured possession, the prize that all her classroom graces have won her; though you are most at ease when unnoticed.

Are you already choosing between these images as to which of them you will eventually become? A choice that must be unconscious, but within which must lie the birth of real decision, as those glances we throw as a child are the breeding ground for the tone of gaze as an adult. Or are you, behind the screen of your ordinary childhood, holding each of them in balance, nurturing each to take part in the eventual you? For you did become all of them. You hold your hands folded, a modest distance from your body on the classroom desk. Your knuckles are still only dimples, but from those particular dimples a particular knuckle will eventually emerge. As you walk down the Trimelston Road the sea is always in front of you, a broad flat ribbon at first and then, as the road falls, a thinner strip of blue serge until eventually, when the coast houses rise to your eyes, it finds itself a thin, irregular grey thread.

One day there is a statue in the window with fresh yellow irises arranged around it in jam jars half-full of water. The statue seems frozen in an attitude of giving. The silver nun teaches you the austere beauty of its observance, tells you that this is the First of May, the beginning of summer, Mary's month. And all those girls, more than half the class, whose first name is Mary or some Gaelicisation of it, Maureen, Maire, Mairead, bow their heads and smile.

You look at the yellow irises, flapping in their jam jars on the sill of the window, behind which the beech tree can be seen studded with green now as if the month of May has hastily flecked it with a stiff green paint brush. You can hardly isolate any one spot of green from the tentative mass but you still try, with your young girl's eyes, their imperfection of focus, their totality of concentration. The points which are in fact small buds and which in autumn will become broader leaves with the texture of beech nuts and bark resist all your attempts to isolate them, merge and separate and finally through the tiredness of your eyes become what seems to be a pulsating mist, forming a halo, the limits of which you can't define around that unlikely trunk, much like your own hair, which you also must be able to see reflected in the window-glass, and the image of your own blonde halo becomes merged with the first green pulsating of the month of May. You look from the confusion of yellow, blonde and green to the black and white frame of Sister Paul's face, who is explaining in her silver voice the intricacies of May devotions; how the name was filtered through to light on half the female population of this small nation, the class. You cannot know that your first name should have been Brigit, Mary of the Gael. Sister Paul tells you that the class will replace those flowers daily.

The narcissism that allows you to confuse the glowing strands of hair round your face with the mass of half-formed leaves on the beech tree, the yellow flags of the irises, is an innocent one and more than that, an honest one, and perhaps even more than that, a happy one; an unlooked-for gift that in later life will be the one thing friends will agree is yours, that must have shown its first contours in childhood. Later that night your nurse bathes you. Her name is Madge. She must have minded you since your mother's nights were divided between performance, rehearsal and political meeting. She takes you into your mother's room to dry you, wrapped in a towel, to the centre of that soft carpet, surrounded by the mirrors of that open wardrobe, the dressing-table and the oval, quite mysterious mirror on the wash-table with its enamel basin and swollen jug. The towel is draped around you as Madge massages your hair. Then your neck and your shoulders, and it gradually slips down as she rubs your stomach, your calves and your small feet, until you can see yourself, naked and dry in the three mirrors. Your stare has the concentration of a dream. Your body is all dimples, the dimples of your breasts, your navel, your vagina, knuckles and knees. These will grow like the pinpoints of green round the umbrella of the beech, way beyond Mary's month, into the shapes of womanhood and you suspect this and your suspicion has the texture and emotional presence of the colours green, blonde and yellow that filled you earlier, but if it is a colour its hue is unearthly since you cannot picture it, merely feel it in the emotional centre where colours move you. Madge leaves the room to get your clothes. You are most attracted towards the mirror that is out of your reach, the oval one above the wash-basin. You drag over a chair and stand on it and try to see your flesh behind the reflections of the swollen jug and the basin. Your look is scientific in its innocence. You lean forward to see yourself better behind the white curves of the jug but you can't and so you stare into the water in the basin. You are reflected there, from above. Your face looms over your own cream

135

expanse, shimmering in the water, your blonde curls sticking to your crown. You hear a gasp behind you and turn to see Madge aghast in the doorway. The chair totters and you fall, bringing basin, jug and water with you. You land in the wet pool and your elbow scrapes on the enamel curve and spurts blood. It runs down your belly and thighs, turning pink with the water. Madge runs forward with a stream of prayers and admonitions and grabs a towel and wrings it in the water and wipes your thighs and wrings it continually. She blesses herself with her other hand.

I I

IT MUST BE soon after this that you reach the age of reason which, like the age of the earlier maxims, makes the undifferentiated flow of your experience manifest and outward, placing it neatly in language and time, allowing others to say to you that you are different now from what you were then. And though you wonder how such a change could creep on you unawares, yet when you hear Sister Paul explain the metaphysics of reason to the class (though she seems to be speaking only to you) you accept that you must be different if only because you are being told so. You accept that your days and memories up to this moment are one thing and after that moment will be another. You suspect a cruelty behind this knowledge though and wonder whether if you hadn't been given it would the same be true? She tells you how up to that moment you could not sin because you were not aware of sin but how after that moment the awareness of sin that she is handing you like a gift will make it possible for you to sin. And you accept a further slice of knowledge which defines this sense of difference in you, the fact that now every action will have to be balanced and passed between the twin primaries of sin and virtue, and that between them there will be an expanse of medial tones and that, no matter how fragile this difference in tone, there will always come a point where white swings imperceptibly into black, beyond which you will be able to say, Now I have sinned. You wonder whether this sense of sin is a gift to be developed, whether you must learn to sin as you once learnt to walk. You sense that these words she is imposing on the flow of your days are somewhat arbitrary, like the words she underlines, for obscure reasons, on the hymns she chalks on the blackboard. And yet there is comfort in the language and Sister Paul has after all impressed on you that knowledge can never be useless. You toy with this new knowledge, imagining some use for it while Sister Paul continues with an image of the soul as a droplet of pure water coming from God into the world, tarnished only by the fact of its birth. And you imagine God then to be a sea, remembering the water that splashed you from the falling basin, for a droplet must come from some larger expanse and a sea is the largest expanse you can imagine; you suspect that this sea is not the sea you know, always the lowest point in the landscape, but a sea that is placed somewhere above your experience, mirroring the sea that you know, permeating you with its backwards waves. But, Sister Paul continues, as our days multiply and as we progress from the age of innocence to the age of reason (and here she pauses, implying a multitude of ages, the texture of which you cannot imagine) this droplet becomes tarnished by the grains of hours and experience and only our own efforts can wash it back to something like its original purity. And you accept this image but fortify it with your own one, of that ocean in reverse washing over every hour of your days. And there is a slanting pencil of light coming through the window, falling on your hands, which are to yourself and from yourself, shaking slightly because of the wind on the umbrella of buds outside, because between your hands and the sunlight there is the tree. And Sister Paul has continued to describe to you the sacraments that belong to the age of reason, those of Confession and Communion. She asks you to rehearse the reality. Each of you is to confess to her seatmate the actions which, in the light of reason, can be seen to be sinful. Lili confesses to you a series of misdemeanours but the air of secrecy and confidence generated by your bowed heads is such that she ends with the confession that she loves you. And you confess to her another series and end with the confession that you love her. And thus you suspect a mystery in reason, sin and in the droplet of water far more bountiful than that which Sister Paul has explained; though watching her distribute the tiny pieces of wafer which are to substitute for Communion bread, you suspect she knows more than she has explained. And feeling Lili's hand curl round yours on the wooden desk you sense that reason, far from having tarnished your droplet of water, has washed it even purer and even more, has magnified it to a point beyond which it can no longer be considered a droplet, for such is the feeling welling inside you, you suspect it would fill a whole glass. All the other details of the age of reason seem ancillary to this: the Act of Contrition which Sister Paul writes on the blackboard, the pennies of bread which she distributes, which you place on Lili's tongue and she places on yours. And when the big day comes and you wear your white dress that comes nowhere near the brilliance of the yellow irises, when the events you have rehearsed take place, your real Confession seems to you a pale imitation of your first, rehearsed one. And perhaps you realise that the form of our public acts is only a shadow of that of our private ones, that their landscapes are just reflections and like that real sea below that imaginary sea, with its piers and palms and beaches, reflections in reverse.

It's soon after that that your father collects you, dressed in civvies for once, in a tweed suit and a hat like any middle-class man, a reticent figure in the doorway whom the nuns don't recognise, whose daughter runs to him, whom he holds on his hip in the old way, where she can sit comfortably for once. He carries her through the school to the yard, her blonde hair almost matching the white flecks in his tweed and there's a car there, a young soldier at the wheel. You notice the soldier's ridiculously large cap, you stretch out and tilt it to one side. He doesn't react so you stretch out your hand again but your father stops you, lifts you over the door and places you in the front seat. Then he opens the door and steps in himself, sits you on his knee. The canvas roof of the car is rolled back. The young man drives, but instead of turning right towards home he follows the coast road, past the tall houses of Monkstown, through the sedate sea-walks of Kingstown, up towards Killiney and the large mansions with their shutters barred. Your father says little on the drive. He asks you what you did at school and like most children, you tell him nothing. There is a slight pressure from his large hand round your waist which increases as you enter the wide sweep of the Vico Road, which he remembers from the train he took with his six-month wife and his three-month daughter, the Italianate sweep of which told him more than all the brown fields and woodlands that he was home. He holds his daughter closer as the blanket of sea disappears among hedges. Her limbs have filled out and her eyes stare up at him with a knowing that is independent of him but that must have come from him. He comes to realise as the car speeds towards Bray how much she has grown, between himself and the woman he rarely sees now, miraculously filling the absence between them, garnering her own life from the chaos between theirs. And the suspicion rears in his mind again with an elusive truth, with perhaps the last truth, the suspicion in Hyde Park, in the London railway hotels, in the figure of Casement being escorted from the club between a phalanx of policemen that the events which would take hold of him, whose pattern he thought he had divined at the time, were weaving quite a different pattern, that the great hatred and passion, the stuff of politics and the movements of men, were leading him merely to this child on his jaded knee, and that without this child on his knee those movements would have been nothing and would not, he almost suspects, have taken place.

This is Bray, he tells her, you have been here before, and she accepts this information and stares, as the driver turns left off Main Street at the promenade. There is a tiled walk and railings to one side and below the railings, a beach. There is a line of hotels to the right with a striped canvas canopy over each porch. He motions the car to a halt and tells the driver, whom he calls Jack, to wait. He takes his daughter's hand and walks along the prom and the clasp of their hands is tight and warm as if they both feel, in their different ways, at home. He leads her to an ice cream stand, outside which there is a board, arrayed with postcards for sale, each postcard bearing a picture of the sea front. She shakes her head when offered an ice cream, and so they walk on, her hand bouncing off the railings as if trying to grasp the beach. He misses the canvas huts lining the sea's edge but realises they are out of fashion now, their usefulness outlived, since the stray bathers are undressing in full view of the promenade. He considers the same question as he walks, remembering the sweetness of his bathing hut, of the woman to whom he has long stopped sending postal orders. He wonders which is the greater event, his encounter with her or the war of that year, this walk along the promenade or the Treaty bother. They have reached a line of sad Edwardian façades which sweep from the town to make a right-angle with the prom and on the patch of green in front there is an old man painting. Rene stands behind the man and stares at his dabbing brush. Michael stands behind Rene. He can tell even though the picture is half-finished, even though he rarely looks at paintings, that this one won't be good. But the picture still moves him. It is of a shoreline and sea, but not the sea towards which the man is looking; his sea is a brilliant blue while the real one is dull metal, grey, and it is lit by a dazzling, garish light that could belong to Italy or Greece, but not to Bray. The naive sheen of those colours seems to come from a sea the old man carries with him. He has a shock of white hair, a high stiff collar and a grey-black suit baggy round the knees, that balance between fine cloth and shabbiness which could be termed Bohemian. His concentration on the canvas has a slight pose about it, as if he is conscious of the figure he cuts and of them watching. And sure enough, he turns to them suddenly without halting the dabbing brush and tells them in a gruff, Protestant voice that they are blocking the light. Look by all means, the painter says, but leave me my light.

The beach has finished now and the promenade has tapered into a small stony walk between the hulk of Bray Head and a rocky sealine. They veer from the walk and go up through a field to the terminal point of the chair-lift. Will we go up? he asks her while a yellow chair bears down on them, swinging on its metal rope. She nods, as any child would. We went up before, he tells her, climbing up the metal stairs and into the chair, you, your mother and I. I don't remember, she tells him, settling in beside him. You were asleep, he answers, in a straw basket. The chair lurches into motion and bears them up, the wind whistling more as it rises. He points out Greystones, the Sugarloaf, Dublin and the road of her school. She stares at the painter below on the prom. I would like to stay here, she says. But you can't, he tells her, the car must go down. I could fly, she replies, if I wished hard enough. She stands in the swaying chair, her arms stretched out. Maybe you could, he tells her, looking up. And it is there, when the chair is at its highest point and the cables begin to sag again, that he stands and holds her, he is overcome, he lifts her to his chest and gasps over and over again the same few words. You are my child, he says, the chair swaying with him standing, and hers. And you feel yourself lifted, you feel his sharp bristle at your cheek, the trunk of his chest against yours and his words that seem weeping and ageless course through you like that melody and like a child too you are embarrassed, you are even stiff, you feel his ribcage crushing you and you understand, when you find your cheek wet with what must be his tears, you understand how much of the age of reason you have reached. And the chair-lift lurches to a halt and he lifts you down and stands you on the bare Head, the grass scoured by so many sightseers, and he lifts you again on to his shoulders, your bare legs round his neck and begins to walk downwards. Always, he tells you, love your mother. And you promise you will, looking over his bobbing shoulders at the paddle-boats below.

12

THE GRANITE WALL was still there, too big really, leaving only the lip of a path along which I could walk. I came to the new gates and passed into the yard, which was covered in tarmac. The tree was sprinkled with green, it being May again, and was leaning backwards towards me, having years ago lost its battle with the wall. There were prefab huts to my right where the shrubbery should have been. There was the old building still though, and the classroom, the window glinting towards the sycamore. I rubbed my cheek against the bark. Rene climbed it on her First Communion day, for obscure reasons. She couldn't have scaled the trunk so she must have walked along the wall and stepped on to the higher branches. There is still the problem, though, of her scaling the wall. A good six feet. Did she ascend into the heaven of the branches? Upwards through the air, turning reason on its head? Her dress would have been white enough. My cheek, as hairless as hers must have been, I scraped it on the bark, moved away and knocked on the heavy wooden door. I explained who I was to the young novice who answered. She had pale skin with a red flush in each cheek, dark hair and pale blue eyes. She could well have grown into a tender, iron-willed innocent of seventy and her adopted name, when she came to take her vows, could well have been Paul. She brought me down a small corridor, talking technicalities. I told her I wanted to observe, nothing more. She opened a door on the left and led me to a classroom. It was indeed the classroom. Twenty young girls turned their faces towards me. There was a dappled green light coming through the window. I placed my back to it, stood there and

143

observed. The novice didn't teach and the girls didn't sit in their desks. They moved around on impulse, took out boxes of equipment, quite bland with freedom and self-possession. We use an open day, the novice whispered. Behind me there was a statue, wedged between two iris-filled jam jars. I tried to observe, but couldn't resist the temptation. I took one, sniffed it, placed it blandly between my leaves. The beads of water clinging to the stem smudged the ink of my notes. Take more, the novice whispered, we renew them daily. But one was enough.

Your arms around the bark and your white front stained with that green pollen. Sister Paul paces the gravel six feet below asking how you got up there. You say nothing, immune to reason. She tells you the priest is here, the other girls are assembled. The tree holds you more than you hold it, your feet wedged in its umbrella. Come down Rene, she says softly. You have your head turned, looking towards the blanket of water. She walks away across the gravel and comes back with your father. He is in his tweed suit, immaculate. He holds his hands up to you, open, waiting to receive. You don't so much fly as float down. Your white dress balloons upwards. His hands grip your waist and ease you to the gravel. Sister Paul strides towards the chapel, billowing black. Inside the girls are white, lining the oak benches. All the lace is stiff and the bonnets are tied. Their breath rises like steam, to the high coloured windows. You walk down the aisle with him, your dress smudged with the green hand. The chapel is so intimate the statues could be real. You walk past the group of adults towards the priest on the altar, knowing your mother is somewhere on your left-hand side.

He came down the Head carrying her on his shoulders, down by the rocks and grass to the promenade, where he found his driver waiting. 'Home Jack,' he said and they drove past the bandstand and the hotels and away again. Within the month he would be dead, shot on his way down Trimelston

Road to what the newspapers said was early morning Mass but to what I suspect was the Booterstown seafront. The last she would see of him would be at her Communion, and for her Communion breakfast they returned to Bray, to the Seaview Hotel. Lili accompanied them. There, on a veranda which opened out on to a garden which led to a private beach, they ate grapefruit and cocktail sausages. Lili remembers the atmosphere as 'formal'. Rene's father was disconcerting in his impulse to please.

The scrapes of butter on your plate, yellow and whorled, beaded with drops of water. You shake the drops into your palm before spreading.

It would have been a quiet breakfast. Her parents sit and watch the sea and let its sound be the only speech between them. And this is enough, strangely, for all four. For the girls the sense of occasion and the cocktail sausages are pleasure enough. And her parents had long allowed other facts compensate for what was missing. Separately, each would have chatted blithely to their daughter. Together, they must make do with silence, and the waves.

The waiters would have recognised them. The scattering of other couples with their children in Communion white would have recognised them too. For Una was at her peak in her thirtieth year on the Bray veranda, enjoying, with the fame that had long been familiar to her, a sense of lithe aristocracy. An aristocracy all the more sweet in that it was an ad hoc one, its precedents changed daily, it combined the tone of ascendancy with the moral comfort of nationalist conviction and it was unburdened, as yet, by any sense of lineage. Una's mastery was total, though her glory would be shortlived. She was an actress after all. Her husband was known to have refused several portfolios. She was Republican too, wedded to the Free State. But this, Lili tells me, only gave her the added lustre of uncertainty, allowed her to carry through the days of stolidity the romance of the days of ferment.

So I shall see Una in a dress as white as her daughter's, with a wide-brimmed hat and veil. He is in a less flamboyant, though immaculate, tweed suit. They eat quietly, listening to their daughter's chatter. And when the young waiter replenishes the grapefruit and the sausages he treats them with that mixture of deference and familiarity that their public selves project. He is Republican, this waiter, he is anti-clerical and left-wing. And yet, when back inside the kitchen he hears the old cook spit the term 'Redmondite!' into the saucepan, he turns and raises his voice in defence of the family outside with a violence that surprises him.

Lili would have her use this term. And others like it. She'd have her glorying in her activism, reacting to the split like the Republican she claimed to be. 'The one marital demand he ever made on her – that she keep her mouth shut in public.' Keeping her mouth shut, her presence felt. Swathing in her dark cape and pillbox hat through Republican functions, Gaelic League meetings, de Valera attending her opening nights. Having it both ways. Married to the one character on the Free State side with 'an ounce of popular charisma', keeping up her old politics, her taste for intrigue. 'And it is a taste, believe me, a habit; which is probably why, of all the Treaty figures, he was the least vilified.' Dropping dark hints everywhere about subtle, back-room influences on him, influences 'not wholly political'. Fulfilling both her taste for intrigue and her taste for the public stage, having and eating her cake in this conflict turned increasingly vicious, from assassination to assassination, building a mystique round him that was in the end above politics. So when the end did come, she was in a unique position, having gathered about her that last element necessary for nationalist sainthood – the odour of graveyards. And by means of a graveyard gesture, uniting her public and private self. 'Mick,' she would proclaim to the handful of mourners, 'was a Republican . . .'

Sitting with Lili, staring at the cascades of butter, piling them on to the steaming sausages and as was only natural for a girl of your age, quite uninterested in the grapefruit. The young waiter takes them away, ventures to touch your hair, glancing at your father. The old cook spits into the saucepan. Guests catch your eye and give you sixpences, much to your mother's disgust. The taste of the wafer is still in your mouth, the perspiration of the priest's finger which placed it on your tongue, and you eat maybe to forget it. Una looks at the green hand on your white where the tree stroked you.

'Why did you smudge your dress, dear?'

13

MICHAEL WAS SHOT while walking down Trimelston Road, near to a church. He was not in uniform. He died quickly for, as was explained at the inquest, enough bullets were used to stop a running bull. Rene learnt of it when driver Jack came to the door without him. The wind sang the melody, beaten out by the separate trees. It is too much to believe that he died thinking of the promenade and the bathing huts.

'For a year she was the *grande dame* of them all. But who could live up to the memories she invented for him? As time went on she gradually relapsed into what she always should have been – a mediocre actress. But she had a year of grace as the nation's widow. And that was a part. Her black cape and her veil were obligatory at High Masses, state receptions, public funerals. And opening nights. Never forget them. Rene was often with her, dressed in black too. But she couldn't just play the part, she needed a sub-plot. She made ambiguous references in public about how he died. She started hinting at plots and counter plots and counter-counter plots. She gave herself the air of knowing "certain facts" not available to "the public at large". Facts, moreover, which implicated those "in power" at the "highest level". She couldn't let it rest. I mean, everyone must have known there was a war on. She made it the done thing to give the air of being in on her secret. The ladies who copied her dress began to copy her way of standing at public functions with this removed, aggrieved, defiant air. The implication was of course that those functions had no constitutional validity, that *she* graced them with her presence, as her late husband had graced them with his life. She began to refer to him by the letter M. As M. used to say. Handy, I suppose, a bare letter is as anonymous and distant and mysterious as you want to make it, I suppose. I'd hear it in drawing-rooms, not knowing who it meant. You sense these things and you learn more of them. But it couldn't last, could it?'

The two of them in black, on the sofa that whorls like a shell behind them, that seems to have been green velvet. The edges of the print are faded again by time, like a flame. Their figures stand out in what is an oval of light, or focus, the mother's hands on her daughter's shoulders, the sofa whorling out of the frame. There seems to be dust around.

'After a year they stopped listening, didn't they? The more strident her claims became for him, I mean, the more embarrassing a figure she became. And by that time even Dev was looking for a way into the second Dail. And so she wheeled round towards the worst fate of all – that of not being taken seriously. And it often happens to public widows. It began in what she would have called the "highest circles", where the bow of deference changed to the nod of indifference, and it spread gradually, like a mild disease. In the end it hit even her audience and real parts – by which I mean theatrical ones – began to pass her by. But she never lost the indefinable air of being a figure of consequence, and as theatrical circles are more loyal than most, she kept her camp followers. Still, she found herself slowly excluded from that magic circle of rumour, clandestine meetings and Chiefs of Staff until in the end Dev himself didn't turn up at the opening night of *The Moon on the Yellow River*. Needless to say, she reacted in turn, she learnt phrases like "betrayal of the cause", "the true constitution" and when eventually Dev came to sign that book of allegiance to the King with his left hand over his eyes, she condemned him more vociferously than anyone.

But by then people had almost forgotten who she was. Una who?'

The months after the Communion breakfast are hardly memorable. The irises in the jam jars wither and before Sister Paul throws them out you filch one for your copybook, where it smudges the ink. The tree changes from green to golden and then finally empties itself and you wonder whether this is what is meant by the age of reason after all – a sense of absence. Then driver Jack comes and stands in the doorway with tears in his eyes and his cap in his hand and you see on the instant that this is one event that will distinguish this time for you. You wonder what he is going to say. Something that will have the import of your father's words over the heather in the yellow chair. You look to Sister Paul for permission to rise from your seat but she anticipates the news from Jack's cap and his tears. She ushers you instead from the room, past Jack into a parlour you have never seen before, where there are oak chairs with slender ankles, green walls and a brown, glinting piano. You wait for Jack there, and his eyes and cap.

Soon after that you were taken from the school. Your education became sporadic. You would run on the Abbey stage now and then, in minor children's parts. Your mother, at the time of Jack's news, was appearing in a St John Devlin comedy, which broke all box-office records for a week. And it was in the Green Room of that theatre, the Abbey, that the photograph was taken of you. It was the first photograph. I can see you at last, your mother's arms framing your hair, which doesn't look blonde, since the print is bad. Your dress could be satin. It seems to be wet, clinging to your knees. You are staring at what must have been the cowled head and shoulders of the photographer and except for your stare, which is remarkably direct, you seem an ordinary child.

THREE

BRAY, 1922

14

AND IT IS the spirit of that photographer that impels this book. James Vance, his passion for documentation, for capturing in a frame the shades of experience. Fascinated and maybe appalled by the wealth of his senses, did he take a puritan pleasure in sliding the print out of the acid bath, in seeing all those brash colours reduced to variations of grey? Or was the delight in the image ghosted on to the clean plate? As a boy, he hears Muybridge lecture in the Antient Concert Rooms about his plates of galloping horses and wrestling men. He holds his father's sleeve, who queries loudly the airborne legs. But James just sees horses, as real as any that galloped on the Meath estate. And devotion to the magic of such images must have seemed a worthwhile thing to the man he gradually becomes. More than a pastime and yet less than a profession, since he had money, Lili tells me and his life, without the focus of necessity, needs its point. Does he grow with a conscience, Lili, a Protestant one, large and shambling, drawing him like a magnet towards all that he is not? And James Vance was unlike most of what he saw around him. So this conscience blooms, becomes like his person which is large and shambling, often ashamed of itself, ready to retreat at the slightest rebuff. His height comes to find expression in a stoop, his conscience in a constant apologetic demeanour which Lili claims was a kind of pride. History has decreed that he is more than mere Irish after all, and while his person seems bent on destroying this distinction, his speech retains it. His accent stays with him like a bad lung. He would open a door, Lili tells me, enter a room with a movement that always seemed on the point of checking itself. It gave her what she calls her 'turgid' feeling. But it can't stop me loving him, loving his obsession with days, months and years, with time and all its alterations in the faces he loves, on the building he loves, on the country he loves, as high collars must have made way for double-breasted suits, Ringsend brick for Wall Street concrete, as the waistcoats and pampooties of Aran islanders made way for shiny overcoats and steel-tipped boots. I think of the perplexity of the eternal child, of the vanity of all his efforts, as he tries to suppress the windmills of time, change and chaos into an ordered progression of prints, a march of moments pencilled in days, months and years, the four corners of each stuck down with Cow Gum, six prints to a page in that bulky album, hard-covered and black, like a Bible. I love the hopeless faith of this documentation, I pity the lack of faith that makes it necessary. I see both of us trying to snatch from the chaos of this world the order of the next, which is why even now, so long from the end, I am tempted to call him 'father'.

His father's obsession was for paint daubed on canvas. He could be seen around this time sitting on Bray prom, near the end of his years, trading on the fact, conscious of the enigmatic figure he cuts, furiously unmoved by anyone who stared, his black suit and boots and his white hair ('Bohemian') and the sea that he painted repeatedly, if it was not the promenade walk or the hotels on the road proper. Lili preferred him infinitely and takes endless pains to disprove consanguineous similarities. It is the difference, she claims, between photography and paint –

But to get back to the photographer, what I can see is his fascination with matters technical and his huge delight in that contrivance, and in every development of it. And even given what she sees as excess of humility, I imagine him taking a hidden pride, a sly pleasure in the mechanics of that black box. He knew its powers, how it worked. He would walk down the slums on the north side and plant the legs of his tripod among the turds and rotting vegetables and give pennies to thin boys to stand in attitudes of deprivation. I suspect he gave pennies because the attitudes of deprivation look so forced: he was a bad photographer after all, the only valuable thing about his 'social' prints being the buildings behind the faces. I can almost see the copper gleaming in the thin boy's eyes. So picture him, the Protestant who had exchanged his horse for a conscience, on the Gloucester Diamond surrounded by vegetable thieves and dissolute husbands and all kinds of brassers, attempting to keep his thin kids quiet for the length of an exposure. They would have heard of the way the image magically wafts on to the coated paper. They would have gathered, from those tenements without parallel anywhere in Europe, into a respectful half-circle, a good six feet between each of them and the youth with his cowl, the magic of technology fascinating them all the more because they were so unfamiliar with it. And among those on the other hand who would have disdained that magic – as they would have, I imagine, in the Abbey's Green Room – he would have been blessed with a magic of a different kind. For as he began his theatrical prints years later, he would have then been able to claim that sure sense of solid craft, that 'know-how', that abstract concern with detail which is the tradesman's defence against the leisured, the educated, the effete.

Which is not to say that he himself wasn't leisured, educated or effete. On the contrary, by virtue of his background he could well have been all three. We have already seen his way of opening doors. If we open the door slightly wider we can see him in that house in Sydenham Villas, facing Bray Head, its left side towards the sea front where in his last years his father used to paint. The last in a series of houses they owned, all of them round Bray and its environs, the first of which bordered on Lord Meath's estate and vied with it as a house of 'quality', I can see its precise, peeling, shabby grandeur; both its inhabitants with the accents of wealth, with the bricà-brac of wealth thrown in odd corners round those rambling corridors, with everything to do with wealth except the momentum which keeps wealth going. Their ambition must have wandered, generations ago, from the sturdy concerns of their Huguenot forebears. They once owned property in Bray, a small ceramics factory, a shop in London and another in Dublin. Someone had scattered delftware round Europe from there, renowned once for its blue and green hand-painted lozenges, for its whorls and for the brittle 'ting' each rim would give when plucked with the thumbnail. But as the parsimony of fathers is changed to the patrimony of sons and the painter had inherited along with an income an impatience with the details of commerce which he handed to the photographer as an inadequacy, the shops were leased to thrifty chemists and the factory, which had shut one year now long beyond memory, stayed shut, stacked with layer upon layer of forgotten, unsold delft.

15

THE VANCE FORTUNE proves more brittle than that delft.
It lasts with the glaze of its lozenge and the scallop of its
edge intact to find its home in antique collections. But their
estate decays with the symmetry of poetry leading to the
photographer, a thin trickle of dividends and the house in
Sydenham Villas. Lili claims James was half-hypocrite, with
his assumption of the causes and tenets of the revival, that
he had 'airs below his station' which she seems to think are
even worse than airs above. But one can glimpse something
different – the thin sense of despair, the slow irony of history
that reduces the difference between his house and that of his
Papist neighbours to that of a coat of paint. He carries that
difference like his conscience, like a bad lung. I see him on
the slopes of Dublin Bay, somewhere around Killiney, in
autumn, when the eucalyptus bark is peeling, reeking with
the smell of tomcats. The sea is viscous, metal-hued. That
difference has preyed on him, it becomes an effort to walk
upright. He has read Hegel, Marx, Saint-Simon and has
glimpsed the sublime unity through his favourite, Rousseau.
The exhaustion of his background seems to lift. He sees the
tide of history, and people simply washed.

He must love that sea, he feels, he must welcome all its
movements, and among them the ebb and erosion of his
class. For who is more uniquely placed, he asks himself and
almost shouts the question at the hillside, to give themselves
freely, wholeheartedly to Nationalist Ireland? It is their very
base of privilege and the decay of that base, the one shearing
them of all self-interest, the other opening their eyes, that
gives them uniqueness. Who? he shouts this time and the

echo could shift rocks. It returns, without an answer. And so he turns and decides to accept. Typically, Lili might say. To accept the decay of his fortunes and the iniquity of them, to retain the paltry privilege he has left and to work towards the elimination of all privilege. He climbs the hill, peels off some eucalyptus bark and rubs his teeth with it. And as the flavour spreads round his mouth, draining all the moisture and as his tongue retreats from the flavour of resin, the question persists with him. He sees the neatness of his formulations, how he has followed them with his shambling rigour, only to be led back to precisely the state he was in when the formulations began. And is it simply the state, he wonders, that suits him best? Is all the agony of thought, he wonders, is it just a wheel that turns and changes nothing, however wide the circumference, always returning to where it began? The cones of eucalyptus are around his feet as he heads for the Vico Road, like odd excretions from those striped erotic trees. He kicks them aside with his high-laced boots, their heavy soles that could belong to an intelligent tradesman or a gentleman who aspires to be an artisan.

The seeds of those eucalypti were brought from Tasmania by what Victorian adventurer? A hill, weeping in a blue haze, the huge trees dipping from it, divesting themselves of bark in long fleshy stripes. The bark falling to earth at the trees' roots, steaming, each stripe like leather, malleable, even useful. And the temperament that could transplant such seeds, over continents and dips and crests of climate, to root them by this bay where the rain falls in sheets and squalls, never in vertical lines. Their odour of resin and tomcats, plucked from that torrid world to fill this grey one. I walk along the hill and chew the eucalyptus. It cleans the gums, cures colds and freshens the nasal passage. I could dive into that Italianate bay, the erotic stripes of the trees above me.

It was the old man's temperament, impatient with geography, seasons, seas, impatient with everything. His rugged Bohemianism and bad taste. His tweed trousers and laced boots that were like his son's but that scarred any number of parquet floors. His voice, that never lost the haughty gruffness bequeathed him by generations of dealing in delft.

'I like eccentrics, anyway, and Protestant eccentrics most of all. I went with her now and then, when she visited the house. "How's my fashion-cover girl?" he'd greet her in that room covered in tobacco smoke and the stench of his illness. She always bore it better than I. He had a photo of her knees in silk stockings, taken from an ad in the *Freeman's Journal*. He'd pull it out and ask to compare it with reality. She'd lift her dress and show him. He claimed he'd never seen knees so perfect, given all his years with artists' models. And knees, he claimed were the pivot of the female form. There were rumours once – this was years before Rene – of a naked girl with her back to that bay window downstairs that faced on to the street. Of him bringing the habits he'd learnt in Paris home to Bray. Rumour flew the way it flies and grew in colour as it flew and it reached the parish priest as a story of a girl from the cottages on the west side disrobing each afternoon for filthy lucre. And so the priest knocked on every door in that labyrinth of artisan dwellings, interviewed each girl only to hear each girl deny it, protesting her modesty. But what else would they do, the priest thinks, these that keep coal in their baths, but deny it? So he upped and went to Sydenham Villas. And picture it, if you can, a hot day in May maybe, he in a black overcoat, his stocky black hand knocking at the door of Number One, the old man answering, the priest humming and hawing, muttering eventually vague threats about Catholic girlhood. And so at last it dawned on old Vance and the story goes that he grabbed the priest like an errant schoolboy, dragged him into the inside room and showed him, on a satin pouf, in a room misty with tobacco smoke, a naked, dark-haired and utterly bored young woman. "There's your Adam's Rib," he shouted and propelled him back to the door. "She's not under your jurisdiction," he fulminated, loud, so the whole street could hear. "She's Jewish.'"

They come down from Dublin for three months of every summer, from the days when the railway was first built, taking villas by the bowling green, the young Jewish daughters walking on the prom, plump and olive-skinned. That's before the droves of Scots and their cheap weekends. But then the story of houses and towns is decay. From the heyday of the Jewish girls and the first Great Southern line. Would the priest have transgressed years before, would he have dared call on Vance without an invitation, without coach and four to take him up the long drive with its views to the left of the Meath estate?

'Still, the old man knew who he was. He didn't have to learn Irish, stagger into rooms with a look of pain in his face, photograph every Mick and Pat with snot on his nose and mud on his boots. You could talk to him, you could love him and not despite his being an ascendancy boor but because of it. And that's the tragedy, isn't it? James, with all his reservations, got the worst of both worlds. Brooding, you see, is always unlucky. The old man never brooded. James did – '

It begins to rain. The water falls in separate threads at first and then comes faster, closer, with no wind to impede its falling. A tropical downpour. James leans against a eucalyptus, which is useless since the leaves of that genus are tiny and form a laughable contrast to the smooth sweep of its bark. He is soon wet through, with the rain streaming from the trunks and the drops hopping from the ground and turning to spray and the spray turning to mist. The air becomes fetid, the odour more resinous, as if the moisture is clinging to it and it to the moisture. He stares across the bay and sees the sheen of the water, for once without trace of current or wind, transformed by rain into an even sheet of hammered tin. The tart taste of bark is in his mouth and his gums are hot and alive. The water pouring down the skin of the trees is unable to dim the cream-coloured stripes where the bark has peeled, and he sees those stripes as unlikely murals, scoured by some careless finger. He feels there is a life sleeping in him, being awakened now by this odour of tropica. It is as if the rain has recreated the home of this bark. There is a hill, weeping in a blue haze, the huge trees dipping from it, losing their coats in long fleshy stripes. His tastes are mathematics and photography, his sympathies Republican, his background Protestant. He has entered a Catholic marriage and his wife has not long ago died, having left him a son christened Luke. He has a self that has always merely watched, merely waited and observed and that seems about to rear now like a tapeworm, pulled by this moisture through his opened lips. He stares at that hammered sea as if waiting for a face to emerge from that multitudinous pressure of drops, quietly, unheralded, each detail sculpted aeons ago, before rain and sea started, like those faces that form themselves on his metal plates.

Would he ever see that face? The meaning we demand from the span and the whole but in particular the surface frieze of the sensual world is never forthcoming; or if it is, not in any form that comforts. If it comes it comes too late, if it speaks, it is always in retrospect and the message he wants from the grey sheet of sea and the tepid air comes only when both have been dulled by memory and by time and when quite another message is demanded. And by then, besides, the rain has stopped, the sea is quite achingly blue, it washes another shore maybe, another bay and the only fresh piece he retains is the one he in fact never saw, that edged into his picture from nowhere; that face, perhaps, or that imagined hill with its outlandish climate, its quite imaginary eucalypti. And yet it still clung to him, a dogged belief in surfaces. He would have even then liked to photograph that scene, to capture that precise balance of elements, why the rain was thus on the sea, why the trees made it mist and channelled the water in sheets and perhaps it was precisely for that reason – that tomorrow the sea might be blue and the air contain nothing but the odour of dust and sunlight. And it could all be held then and pasted in his black book on his green felt table and seen as evidence of, if nothing else, the impossibility of answers. How it was, each print would say, on *this* day, the sun hit Luke's face in such and such a manner, and he was seven then, and longer than his years. This is Benburb Street, another would say, in the great days of hand-painted signs. And so the prints accumulate, each one a document of how, of a present that becomes past as soon as it's developed and only through the future gradually reveals its secrets; the accumulation of them across the years becoming a question mark, a dogged, nagging why? And perhaps he suspected as he gathered them with that fatalism common to collectors that each one was the attempted formulation of an ultimate question and that all answers are retrospective, and so it took months and years of prints for him to even know what he was asking; that he could never hope for arrival, at the most for a judicious departure. And besides, he had a passive nature, he suppressed the general, paid obsessive attention to detail; the kind of passive nature that, when the rain stops falling round the eucalypti and the blue is out at last, walks from the thin shelter they afforded and stops thinking of them too.

16

SO WHEN JAMES Vance entered the Abbey Green Room what would your first sense of him have been? Vance, from the Huguenot Vans, by now a widower, years after his eucalyptus, one Catholic son at home in his Bray house; a grandfather inhabiting an upstairs floor who was there and gone, there and gone. He walks in with his tripod wrapped in his cape. There is his way of opening doors, dressed in corduroy and braces. The stage hands are following him, holding an arc lamp. He asks them in a low voice to put it down. You can hear him, however. People carry their worlds with them. You can sense its shape, if not its precise features. You sense the way people seem to know him and the way he seems ill at ease. You have been sitting on the long couch under the portrait of the man with the removed eyes for twenty minutes now. Una has been tying and untying your bow, placing her hands magisterially round your head, then striding round the room in her black dress. You know how the long wait is eroding the public strength of her grief. You don't mind her grief being so public. She knows this photographer who enters, everyone in the room seems to know him, exchanging those taut nods of recognition that imply acquaintance, not friendship. The stage hands hold the arc lamp with a familiar, somewhat contemptuous patience. You are mapping out the landscape, the long stretches of hill and plain, the terrain in which your mother lives. It is a different world. In the two days since your father died she has entered your life suddenly and fully. You know it will be your world now. You have met people you have never seen before who greet her as old friends, who know your name, your age, your habits. You stare calmly at the creatures of this new world. They seem to you the inhabitants of reason, obeying laws of gesture and glance which must be reason's alone. You watch each new face and how each new face greets this photographer. He is restless and embarrassed and on the edge of the picture and because of that you sense you will remember him, more foreign to that room than you are. The man with the three legs and the black cloak. Your mother stares at him, leaning back on the couch.

'This was where you took Sarah Allgood?'

'No,' he says, obviously puzzled. 'That must have been someone else.'

'Now that was a photograph – '

Her tone is peremptory, with a slight edge of malice and implies a judgment on him. You sense this but cannot know that the tone is one that the bona fide Republican would always adopt with the fellow-traveller. There has been a history of tangential encounters at political meetings and Gaelic classes so they would now nod if they met on a street. They would rarely exchange words, however. You sense your mother judges him to be insignificant but don't know why. Perhaps because of his tripod, his cape, his box, every action of his seems to you to be important. You could not have known that this would be his forty-ninth theatrical photograph, that even as he is assembling the arc lamp the figure won't leave his head, seven sevens, his idle taste for mathematics telling him there's no significance in the figure, his aesthetic sense, always quickened by the imminent flash, insisting there is. So he plugs in the lamp, and mother and daughter in their dark dresses on the satin couch are lit by a white glare. It is the picture of the diminutive girl in the black dress, the cream-blonde hair against it, her eyes shut tight, her hands gripping the couch that prints itself somehow in the base of his mind, already a negative, so intense is the light. He rubs his eyes and looks at her clutching the satin, and something more than his aesthetic sense tells him that here is significance.

'It won't do here, Mrs – '

He tries to drop the sentence casually, for he has forgotten

164

the woman's name. He can't believe himself, that name that has filled two days of headlines, the woman he knows by sight, that he surely must have talked to.

She has sensed, of course, and taken umbrage.

'Why not?'

She wants to be Sarah Allgood he thinks, turning away, mumbling something about refraction of light, pulling out the plug on the arc lamp. He is about to take refuge in more technical details when suddenly, blessedly, he remembers.

'Against a flat, Mrs O'Shaughnessy. It would hold the light better.'

She walks past him towards the door. He follows them, mother and daughter, through the foyer, through the dark aisle of the theatre towards the stage. The dust is circling and circling in what light there is. He is wondering why he moved them, what he is searching for. He places mother and daughter against one flat, then another and gets the stage hands, whose patience is nearing exhaustion, to move the arc lamp in a slow itinerary round the stage. By now he knows that his forty-ninth theatrical photograph will have some significance. The significance is already there in this girl's black dress against the barest of possible lights. But will it seep into the print, he wonders, and some impulse pulls him from flat to flat, dragging his tripod with him. From this theatre, which he had always entered like a moderate imbecile, so willing to be of service, he now brooks no complaints from its stage hands or its leading lady. When she protests now he answers with a curtness that shocks him. But it shocks her too, even out of her stance of grief and she moves with tight lips and flushed face to the next flat, the next floorboard to assume her pose once more. But each flat is too dark for him and with the black dresses of mother and daughter makes their hands and faces appear dismembered, as if in a masque or a dumb-show. He stares at them through the cone of light, alive with eddies of dust, the mother's strict image of grief and the daughter's total lack of expression. The resemblance between them that at first seemed natural, unremarkable, like mother like child, comes to seem tenuous and then non-existent. Where did that face come from, he

165

wonders, and whose replica is it? A white hand moves up from nowhere and brushes an isolated lower lip. He cannot reconcile it, the auburn of the mother with the cream of the daughter. And yet he knows the mother's hair could be dyed and her round face must once have been slender. He thinks of the third face, the dead one whose power is already mythical, and for him too, since he never met the man. Do some faces belong to our heritage of seeing, indescribable, being part of ourselves? He has seen her face before, lit with harsh stage lighting. But when he says, to the mother's annoyance, that the light there isn't what he needs either and when the group have ensconced themselves once more in the Green Room, the resemblance returns with the daylight, quite natural, ordinary after all. The girl is on the couch, the mother's hands on her shoulders, her white, plinth-like arms bordering her face. He can see the resemblance in their mutual opposites, those features that make the woman coarse make the child pretty, those cheekbones with the low forehead of the mother would have led in the daughter to ugliness, but with her tall forehead could some day turn to beauty. And the pose is natural and he cowls his head and squeezes, realising as he does so that he has lessened his demands. All he wants now is the ordinary, from her, her mother and the sofa beneath them.

She exhales to the smell of phosphorous and he raises his head from the cloth, bringing his thoughts with him, none of which she could have read. She will forget perhaps the precise balance of those moments unless she sees the print one day; and then the memories will have to do with her father, slipping like a horizon out of her vision, with her mother and the new world of which she is now a part. He will carry his memories like a penumbra, as will everyone who met her then. But then he will have the print. He takes the train home, winding just above the sea and below the slopes that hold his eucalypti.

17

HE DEVELOPED IT the next day, and a portrait of Dev, and so the blonde child's head that had moved against the black flat took its place in that pit and hoard of memories that might never be spent, together with the first smell of paint in his father's attic, the smell of waxed flowers on the altar of his first wife and the wind that whipped over the Clare election meeting, necessitating de Valera to keep one hand eternally on his soft hat. They rustled there, useless and unused, like leaves in the dry pit, waiting for the rain one day to slough them to the top. And perhaps a hint appeared in the negative of the depths which memory would lend, given time.

Three days later it appeared in the national dailies, and satisfied him. Surrounded by the black print that would be read by thousands, and the headlines 'Mother and Daughter Mourn'. And the dots the image was reduced to would have had the elusiveness of wraiths. Phot. James Vance, in smaller print.

His son, Luke, would by then have been five. Lili will tell me nothing about this man – she claims ignorance, but her silence smacks of jealousy – about his crumbling house and his thin trickle of dividends, his father ageing on the prom, his spouse four years dead. The word spouse conveys an image, a pale face, a hesitant bride in white, and love somehow absent. An Irish teacher, maybe, in the National Schools; a Catholic. James takes instruction for her sake in that faith that must have seemed awesome in its simplicity, its vulgarity and its threat that in the end each word might be seen to be fact. She promises a life to him, a union with that past, that faith from which his circumstances have removed him. It is a whim, more rootless even than his politics, but this whim bleeds into life and time and gives birth to Luke. He has bought her, using the most profound, the most suspect coinage. Her body awes him into an impotence that can only silence hers. There is a green rug, grass underneath, the sound of a river. There are the lupins and tulips, the dahlias perhaps, in the church where he marries. They have the same sweet, promising texture of those that litter the altar at her funeral. He marries at Easter and she dies at Easter. And Easter flowers I remember as stiff, coated with the stillness of beeswax, more solid than real, like the ritual purples and blacks of the Easter cloths. Its pomp, its frigid succession of colour, its hierarchic universe can only appal him, the green stamens and the broad spurts of leaves, like gushing water frozen round the dark heart of flower. Does she visit Luke from further back than memory, fold her black shawl around him each night? The boy sleeps below, the father above him. The wash of sea carries up the street to their windows. Each wave falls with a lack of finish.

18

BUT I WILL still have the Bray curate walking the Bray prom, from the sacristy behind the church on Main Street past the bowling green and the intimate brick of the railway station to the front. The wind whips his soutane there and dots the ocean with white and only the bravest of hotels have their awnings spread. Ultramontane, intellectual and too plump for his years, Father Beausang's nature is childlike and innocent rather than priestly. He has been visiting the obscure Protestant since the days of his marriage. His brief was conversion, then. If he asked what his brief is now, he couldn't answer. For the visits kept on, through marriage and bereavement and dropped all pretence towards instruction on the way. Until now they have lasted so long that the bishop finds them suspect. But yet, the curate insists, though this Protestant agnostic has not yet said yes, neither has he said no. And there is after all a Catholic child to be catered for, his needs all the more pressing since his Catholic mother died. But the truth is, he knows, as he walks along the tiles past the flapping canvas, that he has come to enjoy their conversations. Ethics, the moral law and the necessity of a credo have killed themselves as topics. Only the barest of philosophic questions are touched upon. Rather they weave themselves, one afternoon every two weeks, from initial and sincere pleasantries through the fog of current events to the two subjects that alone interest them – mathematics and photography.

Years later I will walk with him past the flowered pots on O'Connell Bridge towards the dried-up canal. He will talk about maths with the same passion as he did then, with more passion even, for by then his soutane will be flecked with snuff and dandruff, there will be an unashamed smell of alcohol on his breath and his smile will have grown wiser, more abstract and innocent, from the crooked, sad crease that you photographed. Your arm is around his shoulder in that snap, the open door of your house frames you, both of your chests puffed out, endlessly amused because both of you, photographers, were photographing each other. You did it by means of an extended puff-cord which explains the way your hand is stretched out, a minor invention in the march of the camera soon to be made redundant by the timed exposure, but one in which he would have delighted in then, bringing it to you like a child, though your delight would have been more muted, I suspect, since you were after all the professional. That smile will light again when he talks to me of mathematics and tells me that God in His essence is a mathematical symbol and that love is a figure like pi, the calculation of which never ends.

Rain begins to fall on the promenade and Father Beausang quickens his step. You see him through your bay window, hurrying towards your door. The bay window is large, with a curved sill on which it is pleasant to sit. It affords two separate views, one through the left-hand curved panes of the Villas heading downwards towards the sea and sloping towards the yellow chairs that crawl up the Head; and through the right-hand curved panes are the Villas again, rising towards Main Street. It is the window on which the Jewish model sat, naked on velvet cushions before the outraged eyes of the curate's superior. There is a table there surfaced with green felt, standing in the half-circle of the window. The light is always changing from the window so those who sit there come to know intimately the moods of street and landscape under the rain, the squalls and sheets forever falling on the bay beyond. In summer the window catches the sun for a full six hours. So summer is marked by a yellow glare and the yellow boxes of the chair lift creaking towards the summit and by the bleaching of the green felt table. The quality of that room, though hardly remarkable, must have been constant, for Lili hated it, the curate when reminded of it grew nostalgic and I, when I visited it, could see at a glance what the one hated and the other loved to remember.

The drops gleam on Father Beausang's cheeks. His eyes are damp with pleasure and rain. He slips a book out from under his soutane. Luke comes down the stairs and stands on the last step while the priest ruffles his hair. You tell Luke to bring in tea and sandwiches. Father Beausang touches your elbow and holds up the book. You read the title and smile. *Arithmetic and Mensuration* by Eamon de Valera.

Once inside the unheated room, though, the book is forgotten. The curate has made a much rarer discovery – a French mathematician whom he came across, quite by chance, in the *Proceedings of the British Academy*. He tells you his theories and the sheaves of his person seem to fall away, his eyes illuminated, straining through logic towards what he hopes is beyond. You feel quite sad, listening, anticipating his inevitable return. He relates an analysis of the process of mathematical research and discovery which, he claims, could lead the secular sciences back to the point from which they departed in the late Renaissance – to a recognition of simple illumination, Divine Wisdom. He has as yet read only accounts of these theories, has gulped them down whole in his excitement, but his sense of discovery is so real that it excites you, unwillingly, in turn. Poincaré, the curate tells you, between hurried mouthfuls of cucumber sandwich, sees mathematical research not as merely the inevitable unravelling of applied logic but as a series of leaps into the unknown, for which the light thrown by logic alone could never suffice. The logic, he claims, by which the scientist seems to proceed could never suffice for his journey. The very choice of an area of investigation eliminates an infinite number of possible choices. And progress is made in a series of intuitive steps for which logic is the language but never the instrument. And there comes a point, beyond that language, beyond the resources of intuition even, at which the material amassed simply resists analysis. The curate turns towards you, lit by the grey light from the bay window. All resources seem to fail here, he tells you, and the mind is just a filament, waiting for a current. He quotes a remark by Einstein. The problem, stated and restated interminably, harried over for months gives way suddenly, quite arbitrarily, like a shattering mirror. The mind is admitted into the realm in which scientific discovery is made. And this moment is likened by Poincaré to instantaneous illumination, a step beyond the realm of the rational, through which understanding is bestowed on the mind like a gift . . .

You turn away from the dialogue to watch the rain falling in sheets now on the prom. You can see the snout of Bray Head nudging past your window, a thin strip of the promenade resistant to the water hopping off it and the broader band of sea which accepts the rain, mottled by the squalls. The dialogue has come round to that point you had hoped it would resist. This innocent, glowing cleric is drawn to it, independent of himself. A faint disturbance rises in you, the kind of upset that could be due to bad digestion, you want to fart and blame it on the cucumber sandwiches or the inordinate amount of tea you have drunk. His excitement has carried you with it. You sense it springs from your own perplexity. But your disturbance is more than gastronomic. You remember the stiff wax flowers of her funeral, the flowers the church was drenched in at your wedding, all Catholic flowers, a display of faith in the natural object placed at the heart of the human event, an insistence that those same objects are more than themselves, are symbols of what the human event pertains to, limiting it on both sides, the flowers that brushed soundlessly the first time and that stood stiff and waxed the second. And you wonder whether the curate's drift towards that point, the point at which these memories emerge and sidle towards you like forgotten enemies, to be confronted or evaded, is just an extension of his pastoral duty. Though your Tuesday conversations haven't touched on these things for years, his very presence is a subtle reminder of them. Your discomfiture gives way to mild annoyance. Some unspoken agreement has been broken. You suspect he has been breaking it all along. You resent being reminded, through the theories of an obscure, possibly dilettante French mathematician, of your agnosticism, your perplexity and your deceased wife.

The curate moves from the window and places his hand on your arm. You aren't used to hands on your arm, you are made as uncomfortable by them as by opening doors. But all you feel through his hand is the depth of his liking for you. This is another subject that has never been broached. Even that, the pressure says, will fail us some day. You look for words to answer him, somewhere between affection and faint resentment, but you can't find them. He saves you again, as if saving is always his duty. His words are like your flowers, hedging round that miniature human event. He mentions the book he has brought.

'I wonder, can Dev enlighten us?'

The door opens as he smiles. Luke comes through. You smile, almost in gratitude.

I will have Luke open doors as quietly as James, but with the added ability to do so unnoticed. Like a good waiter, unembarrassed by silence, feeling no need to explain his presence. He has a transparent complexion at the age of eight, luminous eyes that stare all the time but rarely seek attention. The grandfather's bluster makes way for the father's reticence and for Luke's transparent quiet. The youth whom Lili met at eighteen implied just such a boy. You tried to imagine him, she tells me, as a boy: did he carry himself just that way when he was twelve, eight or ten? And the boy who possessed that odd intensity, that appalling certainty would, she says, have been an intimidating boy indeed. Her impatience with the boy's father is only matched by the rapturous approval with which she remembers the son.

So he comes in quietly to take away the tea things, knowing the discussion to be all but finished. Standing there, taking in with his eyes the rain-filled window and the two figures by it, Luke understands the embarrassment of the curate's

173

gesture, he already knows his father's dislike of hands on arms and elbows. He sees his father in the window-light and listens to the opaque mystery of their conversation, the last soft wave of dialogue, those words of more than three syllables which characterise adult conversation for him, breaking to those pleasantries which for both of them signify an ending; though Luke doesn't grasp at the pleasantries but at the fading scent of the argument, at the curate's round diction and his choice of words. The words are new to him and carry an exotic allure. He is a thin, erect child who holds himself rigidly, a little like an older man. It's only in late adolescence that he acquired the look of youth that Lili characterises as 'slender'. Now he is thin and luminous, something aged about his silence, looking at his father and the curate, catching the drift of those ultramontane words. Their use is therapeutic for the curate, for whom the realities of parish life have formed a bitter contrast with his scholastic novitiate. They remind him of St John Lateran's College in Rome, of his first love, theology, and of his present ambition, to unite the logic of belief with the logic of science. They would have carried to Luke the germ of that *summa* which every utterance implied. Standing there, waiting for the pressure of the curate's warm hand on his father's elbow to cease, for them both to turn with that sense of finality which would be the signal for him to pick up the tray with its cups and remaining sandwiches and carry them outside. And of course they turn and Father Beausang and Vance look at the tallish boy with the brown hair flat on his head, sharp stickles of a quiff on the right-hand side of his parting which lend to the luminosity of his eyes an air of constant surprise. The curate thinks of his duty towards this child of a Catholic marriage, he probes the child's features gently as if to find some air of loss, of deprivation there. He can find none, however, and so he stretches out his hand and feels the stickles of the quiff with his palm.

'I have something for you,' he says. His eyes shine. 'If your father doesn't object.'

James has his back turned, his face to the window. You

174

stare from him to the curate, whose palm has stopped
kneading your hair. He hands you the book.

'Bless you.'

He leaves, walks back out through the hall to the door and
the rain on the promenade. The odd sense of maleness in
that house, that hall, the rather bare order over everything,
like a presbytery or bachelor residence, makes him feel he's
leaving one home to go to another. The house was cleaned,
but never softened, by a combination of three maidservants.
There was a hatstand near the front doorway. And a mural,
running down the stairway, covering the left-hand wall.

It was a moving picture, Lili tells me, a sprouting forest of
the old man's mental world. He works on it in bouts and
then leaves, returns months later, having decided to change
the theme. So stories run through that wall in waves, conflict
at each end and meet in the centre. Three muscular, bare-
breasted women run downwards behind the stairway, over
the peeling plaster, towards the front door. He has given the
doll-like face of the local chemist to the one who stoops for
the apple while she runs. He has put Grecian hills behind
them, a Doric pillar, crumbling, in the left-hand foreground.
But he must have changed in the course of it, switched his
obsession, got afflicted with what Lili calls a 'bout of Irishness'. He changes the background ruins into something like
stone cottages. He adorns those hills with a necklace of low
stone walls.

And the curate moves past the bare breasts and the lesbian
contours and the Hellenic pillars and the Connemara walls.
James follows, leads him to the door. The hills at that end
melt into blue, the beginnings of a sea, Atlantic or Aegean.
The curate opens the door and walks through the rain to a
view of real sea. James watches him go. Luke clatters from
the inner room with the tray of tea things.

Luke makes his first appearance in a Moses basket surrounded by a sward of green. There is a plaid rug there and a woman kneeling on it. Of the woman one can see the bottom part of a gaberdine coat, hands placed deep in each pocket, one sleeve pulled back to reveal a thin wrist. She must be looking at the child in the basket as James must be too, with perhaps the same sense of approval. One can't tell since one can't see her face, but James approved, obviously. The shot is worse than most. He has ignored the simplest rules of composition, as if his approval blinded him to them. There is no idea even of where the basket lay, Powerscourt, Bothar-na-Breena, the Dargle Valley. It is just seen from above, with the grass around it. James ignores the woman for the child, who is lying on his back. His head seems to be attempting to turn.

19

HE WALKS OUT himself, some hours after the curate. The rain has stopped by then. Does it only stop at night? The roads are quite deserted and the chairs on the Head are glowing like yellow moths, but motionless. He walks up the road and away from the sea front and the spaces between the houses become smaller and smaller. The road no longer merits the term Villas, becomes gradually a street. He has a longish tan gaberdine coat pulled tightly round him, belted too, for the winter winds are in again after a summer of picnics and photographs, perhaps not too unlike the ones in which she appeared holding the baskets or prams, ones with large wheels that dominate the frame, as obsolete now as steam engines, graver than current ones with hoops, as on flower-baskets, covered in lace. The street has become a main one and the houses one wall of red-brick, one up, one down. He met her in the Gaelic rooms in Parnell Square, could never have met her here. The huddled square could well have housed some of those who worked on his great-grandfather's delft. There was a twig pattern with a necklace of lozenges for leaves that needed a miniature, feminine hand. A factory of women, year of Our Lord 1809, when the delft still rang across Europe, when the china dust still billowed in the workshop. Does he fall in love in memory of them, at adult Irish classes, Parnell Square? Stuttering through this rural tongue with his unfortunate *blas*, the eucalyptus chewer with the bad conscience, it is the gulf between them that attracts him as much as the person herself. There is chalk-dust in the air, without the billowing texture of the dust of china. But nevertheless the young teacher's fingers, which he wants, he needs to hold, are coated white. It is love, but always as an afterthought, the unique syllable lost among the consonants of Gaelic. Her plain dress is whitened in places as he looks at her over the row of benches through a halo of chalk. She has brown hair, blue eyes and an oval face. And when he comes to hold her chalk-whitened fingers which smudge his own in turn, his love gains the intensity of all his mental agonies. Her fingers are Irish, Catholic and youthful. He drifts towards marriage holding them, since he can do nothing else. And Eileen becomes Eileen Vance, with that unbridgeable gulf between fore and surname.

I will call it loving, though it was forgetful on his part and cruciform on hers. She doesn't so much age as contract under the pressure of that gulf. That terrible forgetfulness that never focussed on her face, that never caught the sunlight on its contours in the Dargle Valley or the Devil's Glen. He was kind, like all intelligent men, and therefore amazed when she began to weep one day on the Dublin-Bray train, where it brushes the sea just past Killiney. This child will be Catholic, she said, her curve outlined by the train window and the sea behind. Even if you won't. His amazement changed to perplexity when her weeping didn't stop. It lasted through her ninth and final month, until he could only wonder how so much weeping could rest in one person. It seemed to fill each room with an element not quite water and not quite air, but definitely liquid, through which he moved slowly and only saw her from a distance, until her weeping was augmented by her breaking waters and the pain of her delivery of their child.

Does he think of her, walking past the mock-Tudor town hall at the crossroads and out towards where the houses stop, giving way to the sweeping lawns of Lord Meath's estate? Eileen Vance. The name implies the lightness Lili sees in Luke. Her face that never slid into his frame but found itself reproduced in his only child. He walks down the road with a hesitant amble, a constant phrasing of a question too deep for an answer. He cannot but form it and so his fate is to seem wrong. He reaches out through the countryside, his body arching forwards with that curious perplexity, that gait that would probably irk anyone who passes him as much as it did Lili. No one passes him, however. Though there are footsteps behind him. And her memory is still in him, as alive as ever and just as abstract.

The footsteps behind him grow louder. He hears the clunk of metal on wood. He turns his head as he walks and sees a young man behind him, with a bicycle propped against an oak tree. The young man has a bucket and a roll of posters. He takes a brush from the bucket and pastes a sheet against the bark with one wet stroke. James stops. The youth cycles past without a word. James can make out a slogan and a bareheaded sharp profile, dampened by the paste. He walks back to it. There is a sharp aquiline nose, a rigorous mouth without a trace of humour, and a pair of wire-framed spectacles. The eyes on the poster reflect his own abstraction, and with it a quite terrifying certainty. They stare into the distance, embedded with the mathematics of vision. He watches as the damp spreads round the face. There is something foolish, horselike in the features which only adds to their allure. The corners of the mouth sweep downwards, in one clean line. James smiles. Years ago he photographed it, at a Clare election meeting. He sees those features and their certainty mould into the tree's roughness as the spreading paste weds the bark to the lettering. 'De Valera – *Clann na Poblachta*: Vote for the Republic!'

179

20

JAMES WALKS WITH Luke towards the photo with Miss Meredith, towards the tea it promises, along the railway tracks. The tracks loop around the Head, which looms over Bray and makes a gentler curve away from it.

But it is far behind them now, forgotten. James points out the marks of currents in the water, the glint of schist in the beach rocks, the banks of cirrus cloud above them. He explains the difference between flotsam and jetsam and the movement of tides. They come in view of Greystones harbour and the high houses behind it. Luke leaps from sleeper to sleeper, seems not to listen. They step down from the track and walk along the beach until the pebbles give way to clear sand and the sand rises towards the sea road.

Miss Meredith suspects that Mr Vance has intentions other than the sampling of her excellent high teas. She has the table spread when they arrive and they are the only weekend samplers. A widower who seems of her own persuasion, with one son cared for only by a housemaid. She has laid out her choicest dainties, cakes that are whorled with icing, cream puffs and apple-and-raspberry tarts. This Protestant gentleman, though, eats hardly anything, stares through the laurels at the haze above the sea. For today could be the height of summer and high teas are on the lawn, the lawn with such a riveting view of the sweep of the bay. He covers her white cloths with flower-samples after the ritual gentle-manly greeting, and talk is mostly of the weather. She has come to despair of a more active demonstration of interest. And yet there's the photo. On a day like today, with one arm around Luke and one hand touching the wrought-iron table on which lie the dainties. I feel I know the house and the way the garden looked at the sea. There is a low wall, white, that hardly reaches your calf if you are an adult but forms a barrier for a child. It makes a sharp angle round a little chink of lawn which is in turn hedged round by a large expanse of gravel, a sort of drive really, leading up to the house. There is a sign above the porch advertising teas. There is a thin row of laurel bushes parallel to the house, facing the road, and the chink of lawn is to the left of both, edging out on its own, for all the world like a small promontory jutting out to sea. For beyond the wall only the sea is visible. Your three heads outlined against the white wall and the white horses, the white metal table and the blue china, an idyllic scene as I imagine it, and perhaps you would have taken more notice of the notice she took of you had it happened oftener, but the weather so rarely allowed it. How Miss Meredith must have cursed that rain, sweeping interminably over Bray Head, knocking the boats against the Greystones harbour. But she must rest content with her picture in your album, her arm around your son, who is staring at the dainties. She is looking towards me, a rather fattish face, a closed smile in which the teeth could be biting the left-hand corner of her mouth since her lip is drawn down somewhat, slanting while smiling. Her hair is drawn back tightly like a Spanish widow's, parted in the middle and clutched behind into a bun. You could have been sitting on the low wall, your back to the sea and the white horses, over which hung the four o'clock sun.

Miss Meredith pours you another cup and asks whatever happened to the family's china. She has an immaculate cabinet upstairs, she tells you, which must get more valuable by the year. You tell her there is a store of it somewhere, down by the old factory, most of it worthless, rejects. The time is gone, you tell her, for small enterprises and small nations. Versailles, you tell her, would have taught anyone the latter and the economy of contemporary Ireland would teach anyone the former. You hold such daring opinions, Mr Vance, it's a wonder you don't publish more. There are people better able than me to articulate them, you proclaim, and proceed to tell her about the Venus's fly-trap, which interests you more. But she evades the topic of the carniverous plant and returns to your opinions, which in her normal day she would shun, but which with you she feels she must air. We are both anti-Treatyites, Mr Vance, but I have heard from opposite points of view. You are really a Republican? I would favour, you tell her, a syndicalist model along the lines of Proudhon – , Ah, Miss Meredith interrupts, but he was a Frenchman and respectable, quite a different specimen from your de Valera, who is Irish and disreputable. American, you counter. Or is it Spanish –

And your imagination wanders, as it always does when confronted with the intricacies of politics, beliefs that refuse to form themselves into any semblance of order. There is a boy leading a dray-horse down the street and the boy is barefoot and each step of the dray-horse's forelegs seems about to crush the heels of the boy, but somehow their feet move in counterpoint, a counterpoint whose rhythm you cannot pinpoint. The horse's paw-like hoof is raised whenever the boy's heel arches backwards and each time the steel hoof comes inexorably down, somehow the boy's foot just withdraws itself. Is it a logic like that, you wonder, that impels politics, one that's understood just by boys walking abstractedly, by shopkeepers, tenants and small farmers? You see de Valera's face flapping from every lamp post now, since the election is drawing even nearer, and all around you, Luke and Miss Meredith on the chink of lawn is the sound of paper flapping, his face flapping against the tarred wood because a wind is rising from the sea now, a wind that makes you aware of his face, of the time and of how cold you are. So you rise and present Miss Meredith with a coin, which she refuses, which you proffer again and which she refuses again until your annoyance at last becomes real, at which point she accepts. You know that she would rather not accept, as you know that for you not to give it would imply intimacy you don't want to allow. And so you leave this woman whom you photographed as you never did Luke's mother and you trudge across the Head again with Luke.

Father and son go back down the beach, beyond the sand, to where the pebbles make walking difficult. There is a horizontal scar where the beach ends and the land begins, above which runs the railway. As they walk this scar becomes a cliff. The pebbles he walks over accentuate his stoop. He talks about the rocks in the cliff face, the angular movement of them caused by a heave in the earth millions of years ago. The boy walks by the rock, rubbing his hands along it, seeming not to listen. The man walks behind him, looking at his boots, still talking rather forlornly. He walks carefully because of the camera swinging from his shoulder, a heavy object, like a box but for the melodeon lens.

Meanwhile grandfather is at home working at his mural, the cost of oils over his latest space having done him out of a week's tobacco. So he works at the breast of Hellas with a bad temper. How does a breast look while a woman is running? He has never encountered the problem before, or a woman like this, statuesque and yet mobile. He pulls his hand back tetchily and the brush scrapes across her jaw. He curses and is about to abandon the brush to its jar of turps when he notices something. The smudge has drawn a shadow across the jaw, lengthened it even, made it what novelists term a lantern jaw. He smiles. He sees a resemblance between his lantern-jawed Hellas and a prominent member of Cummann na mBan. He remembers the puritanism of her public statements. He chuckles, takes out his brush again and with a few strokes completes the likeness. The figure becomes recognisably Irish, a cartoon sharpness about the profile. He stands back and surveys it and feels an odd, delightful surge of power. He returns renewed to her breast, as if the brush is pulling his hand.

His son was up the Head and his own son beyond him, near the crest. And as James walked, the pace of his steps seemed to match his thoughts. He saw how walking was not a continuum but a series of leaps, how Luke's feet in the distance leapt and landed and leapt again. His own thoughts leapt with them, finding themselves always somewhere else. He thought of how he would die one day and how each moment was a step leading him to that one. He reached the crest and stood there, letting his son run on. He looked at the sea below him, and the bay and he knew suddenly that death was not just like that sea, it was that sea and the only purpose of that sea was to remind him of his death. He felt that if he were to look at death, not death in general, but his private death, if one were to cultivate it like an acquaintance, or like the habit of afternoon tea, one could place all else in relief. There was power and comfort in that thought, of the fact and moment of obliteration cultivated like a friend. His life rose before him, under a garish light. Why, he wondered, why? And the realisation came, shimmering and crimson. In the flash the curate talked about, time, how he had longed to shatter and suppress it and the end of time is death. And how acquaintance with your death would place time between your lips, like a silk ribbon, like a spouse whose mother was already your intimate. To embrace, a conquest and yet an act of love. He threw both of his arms out towards that blanket of sea so that they jerked in their sockets. He gripped it in his arms, that metaphorical sea which the real sea only stood for. It was grey, like when he smelt the eucalyptus and a fine vapour seemed to hover over it, barely there. He stumbled down the Head again. Luke! he shouted, Luke! He ran to where the chairs landed but could see only the ghost of his son below him, tiny, running down the shallow field that led to the first house. He stood there holding the metal pole, the yellow chair swaying above him.

FOUR

SANDYMOUNT, 1928

21

SOON RENE WILL appear in an ad in the *Freeman's Journal*, wearing a pair of silk stockings and low-strung shoes. Lili admits herself to be jealous for the first time, really jealous, that is. She is still after all travelling down Trimelston Road each day to the convent school, while her friend's education has come to consist of two years in Miss Conway's school of acting on Clyde Road and whatever treasures she can glean from her increasingly weighty mother who has named herself to the educational authorities as the child's official instructress. This means six-monthly visits from departmental inspectors to their Booterstown house, from which they are absent, for the most part. But when they find mother and child at home, they spend two amazed hours in the company of a thirteen-year-old who is hardly numerate at all, who can repeat Irish words with a wonderful *blas* and intonation but can hardly construct a sentence. She shows herself entranced by large sections of the *Aeneid* and without any of the rules of syntax can make wild and uncannily accurate guesses at the meanings of whole paragraphs. She can barely add, but loves the music of Euclidean geometry.

Two fattish gentlemen, each holding brief cases, mid-afternoon in a suburban drawing-room. They sit on couches covered in dust sheets. The curtains are drawn. A light bulb swings from a tasselled shade, compensates for the daylight outside. Mother and daughter seem on the point of departure or arrival, perpetually so. The girl in front of them teases out Pythagoras from the paper they've given her, as if discovering the theorem for the first time. She has crumpled the paper on algebra into a ball. The dark-haired gentleman smokes a cigarette, the fair-haired one a pipe. Signs of irritability seem to threaten their patience. They are used to the national schools, where a teacher would tremble at their every whim, where each class would be a model of discipline and order. But here they are dealing with more than a national school. There have been moves, lately, to rename the street their office sits on after this girl's father. And different rules, they know, apply to those whose names have some connection with those whose names gave names to streets. So their patience is measured as they watch her grapple with triangles. Until the mother interrupts:

'Give them O'Hussey's *Ode to the Maguire*, dear.'

And Rene stands underneath the amber light and delivers the famous ode. Her voice is unremarkable, but her stance is eloquent. And the bell-like clarity of her words must compensate for her other failings. For the inspectors sigh, with either pleasure or relief, and close their notebooks. Una gives a slight shiver, then asks her again,

'Give them Jacques's speech from *As You Like It*.'

But the best educations are always through default and Una's determination to instruct her daughter in all the principles of bad acting led, perhaps more than any one thing, to the adult Rene. Una knew by this time that her star was falling and had decided not even to catch it as it came down but to impel her daughter's upwards in its place. She had become resigned at last to the limitations of her talents and the erosion of her public appeal. People no longer said, 'Isn't that so-and-so?' as she passed, forgetting her name but reminded inexorably of a 'somebody' by her flashing black hair and her regal carriage. By now her hair was streaked with grey, her figure was ruined and the clothes she could afford to buy were fairly nondescript. The invitations still came to public ceremonies, but she neglected to attend. For she had gained a sense of humour, a certain delight in incongruity. She laughed when de Valera entered the Dail at last and signed with his left hand over his eyes, and managed to make her Republican friends laugh too. When asked about her late husband she said, 'Yes, Michael,' and gazed towards the west with her old intensity, but realised now that she enjoyed the pose. She came to see, gradually, around her thirty-fifth year, when the only work she could get was in fit-ups touting peasant melodramas round the provinces, that here was a profession and that she belonged to it. She had always mixed political and feigned passion on the stage, been known above all for her 'sincerity', her 'truth' of performance, and she had in fact spoken lines as if not on a stage under lights, in front of flats, but as if in the dusty atmosphere of a nationalist meeting. She had done what all household names do, become an emblem, intruded her real self into the theatrical field and for almost a decade it had sufficed. But then a public, tired with the concerns of her real self and its emblems, had tired of her and she found herself adrift suddenly, in a profession whose mainstay is plain artifice. And she had realised slowly, like a cured invalid learning to use his legs again, the beauty, permanence and humour of the feigned passion. As the last illusion of the *grande dame* left her she found herself among the flotsam of the feigned passion, the permanent hybrids of the profession who keep its laws and pass them on, its humours, its superstitions, its attitudes of wrist, face and hand; the ageing queens, the comedians, the soft-shoe shufflers, the young tap girls, the matrons typecast as such, the outraged suitors, the overbearing parents, the lovers, passionate, true, false and profane: all of them stagestruck. She realised her talent's home and its limitations: these were her people, she was a passable actress, Ireland was a splash of green on a canvas flat. But then, among the profession she had a strange lustre that carried her over her sense of limitation, for they, permanently stagestruck, all remembered her good days. And so she carried the reputation of a once-leading lady the way others did that of a good line in maidservants. And so found herself now, a parody of her former self, playing young heroines in an ageing figure on stages with less than three flats – a parody she enjoyed, revelled in even, carried over with gusto into her real life as slowly,

slowly, the balance was reversed and where once she had sinfully pushed the real life on to stage she now extended the rim of the stage to include her boarding-house, her turn of glance in a rural street and all the minutiae of her private life.

You had grown alongside your mother since that breakfast of butter and sausages in the Killiney hotel when the Republican waiter served you so willingly. You still remember your father's shoulder pistol and his clipped 'Home, Jack' as he lifted you into the open car on the Bray prom. Your life together since he died seemed a process of melting. There are healing graces in human affairs and you have more than your share of them. Through loving you she is reinventing him in a form she can love, expiating her former indifference. Which is perhaps why, when greeted by those who knew all three of you, in the old days, ex-lord mayors of major towns, ex-commanders of guerrilla battalions now heads of government departments, friends of his only, Free-Staters now, friends of hers only, Republicans now, all of those who knew the three of you say, 'How like him she is'. And Una can take this without any rancour. She is even glad of the comparison, she resurrects him in you in a finer form. The part of him that lives through you is after all the mythical part, one simple image of the head framed by the ridiculously large cap and the shoulder pistol. One simple attribute, that of the man of action, distracted, regretful, uneasy with his role. His memory after all has become the embodiment of how different it could have been if only . . . And so when you appear with Una at public functions or at any functions at all and people say how like him you are, they see in you this wonderful, mythical alternative, this possibility of how different it could have been . . . For you are already developing this propensity, this unconscious talent for being seen from any angle and seen differently.

At thirteen you are fattish and your hair has the same blonde look with the texture of cream that it had when you were six. Your hair and your walk distinguish you, since there's not much that's beautiful in your figure or your face. You smile a lot. There's a lot to smile about for a girl of thirteen with no school to go to. You've adapted yourself to the company of adults since your father died, which could be why your walk is so relaxed. It gives a grace to your figure that shouldn't have been there, belying all the canons of school girl beauty; as if there's a moving centre to you which your figure just follows. You always walk, even in the most high-heeled, the heaviest boots, as if you are barefoot. And all this gives you ease in adult company. You only lose it in the company of your peers, of girls of your age. They are made shy by your habits which, far from seeming adult to them, seem old-fashioned. And the too-adult child always does seem old-fashioned. You have picked up habits of speech and gesture which they associate with their more ardent teachers and the comparison leaves a distance between you and them. You are always polite, for instance, you address a remark to each member of whichever company you are in. You have no sense of exclusiveness, of secrets. You rarely whisper. Your hands are smallish – practical hands that move when you talk using gestures that are never hurried but always startling.

Rather ungainly adult clothes, blouses, skirts and dresses of your mother's, which she has taken in. Her sumptuous, evening sense reflected in every garment so you could wear a velvet dress on a spring day, a strange mixture of ill-fitting and style. Your clothes make you suspect to the mothers of those who might possibly be your friends. So you learn to keep to yourself, you walk down by the stretch of marsh where the birds nest, over the railway line, over the granite ramp to the beach. You are the girl of thirteen with the large eyes and face, the halo of blonde hair, who walks along the railway tracks, stepping on the sleepers. On the beach, among the men in long coats who prod the flotsam with sticks, the young children playing truant from school. There is a woman

191

who holds her belongings in a tied bundle, who sometimes sits by the granite wall. The wall slopes towards the beach, at an angle, to keep the tracks free of spring tides. The children and the lost elders sit there and the occasional sexual predator, generally male. You are the only adolescent girl to grace the granite. The flecks of silver and the mottles of white on the large fawn blocks reflect your hair and your eyes. It is an empty place, though never empty of people. The ramp stretches down the length of the track and yards separate those who sit on it, as if some rule of place keeps them apart; the two children looking through the sea-green bottle at the sun, the man with seven coats asleep in the spring heat, the youth with the ashplant, the high trousers and the slow eyes, following the children and the green bottle. Then there is you. The woman with the bundle intrigues you. She is wearing a grey shawl, like sackcloth. She unties the bundle slowly, unwraps yards of brown paper. You are looking directly at her, something one doesn't do on the ramp and the weekday beach. She takes from the paper an evening dress and a pair of high-heeled shoes and a hat. The hat has mock fruit on top and the sprigs are twisted. The dress is crumpled, though still glittering with sequins. She takes off her shawl, then the garment under that, indistinguishable from her shawl, and lastly a stiff, coarse vest. You can see her withered breasts exposed to the sun as she holds the sequined dress to herself. She has a dowager's hump and the ridges of her spine seem to push through her white skin. She struggles into the sequined dress and pulls it down around waist and thighs, pulling off the cloth she used as a skirt as she does so. Then she puts on the high-heels, dons the hat, turns to you with an unearthly, blissful smile.

'How do they suit me?'

You smile back in answer. You watch her stagger down the ramp, across the sand, towards the sea's edge. She stands there like a thin, twisted bird, the sequins flashing in the sunlight, more sharply than the sea. She is staring at the thread of the horizon, motionless for several minutes, then suddenly she turns and walks back.

'A bit loud, don't you think?'

You are about to reply that you don't think so at all, but you see that she has made up her mind, she's already struggling out of the dress, exposing her thin breasts again. So you smile in affirmation.

You give that sea front your occasional hours round your thirteenth year. The woman with the bundle returns with a different set of garments. Dapper old men wink at you, striding towards Blackrock. You look as odd, perhaps, as most of that ramp's inhabitants, with your handed-down clothes and your air of abstraction, though the thought would never occur to you. Dreaming is a precious thing, at thirteen, on a near-empty beach. Never, I would say, does your mind form one abstract, separated thought. You souse yourself in the mechanics of dreaming, where one thought fades and leads to another and everything turns into everything else. The same breath blows through them, blowing deep, rising to the surface, then deep again. The wind raises a thread of sand and lets it fall. You get up and walk when the mood takes you, following the sand. A man accosts you one morning, a young man, so small and perfect that he could be called dwarf. He smiles at you from the granite. He is impeccably clean, his nails are long and perfectly groomed, his hair runs back from his forehead in thin waves. His small-boned, perfect face has the delicacy of an egg. His lips are tiny, somewhat sad, but his smile breaks his face into tiny creases, exposing even white teeth. He must be amazed when you smile back for he stutters when he calls you to the ramp.

Wait with me, he tells you, for the train. His knees are drawn up and one hand rests on each. It carries an opera singer, he tells you, who will throw roses at anyone who stands and waves. Will you stand and wave? he asks. You walk a little up the ramp so that you can see the tracks. His hands flutter on his knees. Why, you ask him, will she throw out roses? Because she is famous, he tells you, she is famous, most beautiful and has a wonderful voice. If you are quick enough you can catch an armful of them. Red roses, white ones, all colours. Where will I stand? you ask. Here, he says, where she can see you. He stretches up, his small hand touches your thigh. Still, he says. His hand seems to shiver on the velvet. You obey it, don't move. Will you show me your rose, he asks? I have no rose, you tell him, I will have to wait until the train comes. But you have, he insists, flashing his sad lips into a smile. You hear footsteps behind you on the granite and his hand trembles against you. You must watch for the train, he says softly, hastily, a little girl like you. He returns the hand to his knee. When will it come? you ask him, climbing the ramp to the top. Soon, he says, catch me some roses. You see him running backwards across the sand, his neat dwarf's prints before him. Flashing his distant smile. Patience, he cries.

22

THAT IS NOT, however, to be read as your first sexual experience. Nothing but your curiosity was excited, which was perhaps fortunate, and your memory of the miniature man remains with you only because of the whiteness of his teeth and the neatness of his cuticles. You thought of nothing more significant than the train and the roses when he'd left you. The machine of adolescence had to wait to come, and the train with it.

It needed Lili to meet you on the straw-coloured ramp, to cross the sand to the sea and back again. Lili comes in the more normal hours, the afternoon hours, when the place has lost its emptiness. There are comparative crowds then, schoolgirls, like Lili, in uniform. You walk down the tracks, you clamber over the sleepers, she holds your hand with one hand, presses down her blowing skirt with the other. She hints at that machine of the age beyond reason. You feel the world of intimacies, whispers and fluttering eyes. You are surprised and embarrassed since your world of adults has kept you a child, strangely innocent, innocently mature. You have stayed blissfully unaware of these long secrets of girl-hood, which Lili seems to want to share. A blush, deep and rose-coloured, a sense of shame that she should be shamed, rises on your cheek, which makes Lili giggle and makes you blush more. The blush seeps inside, it becomes a positive warmth. 'Scarlet, like a rose,' says Lili, alluding to your cheeks and perhaps your hands do go to cover your face since her air of classroom banter increases your discomfort. You feel that this sensation welling inside you as you cover the tracks, manifesting itself in your cheeks in this glorious

195

red, is one that deserves to be talked of in more than whispers. It should be discussed, you feel, with more elaborate manners than those of the diplomatic banquet your mother once brought you to. Or it should be shouted from high places, from the windows of trains, bringing roses to places you have never heard of. You cross from the tracks and climb up on the ramp and begin to tell Lili of your miniature man. But Lili tugs your palm, whispers that you should keep your voice down. A nun is passing, and the ramp is too narrow for three. You stand with your back to the sea to allow her walk by, tall, boxed and birdlike. You recognise the face beneath the bonnet, the greying hair. You call her name, though Lili's hand goes out to stop you. And Sister Paul turns, her face changing from puzzlement to recognition to the quick smile that you remember so well, creasing the translucent skin. As she talks above the railway tracks in a voice hardly different from the one in which she introduced you to the age of reason you wonder what her name would be for this new age, the one Lili seems to hold between her lips now, like a mouthful of shamed peach. It is an age, you sense, containing truths so immense that only a discipline like hers could do it justice. Behind you the tide seeps from the creases of sand.

You came of age on a day in July. It was a Monday and the beach was wholly deserted. One nun passed, whom you looked at closely, hoping to see Sister Paul's smile. But it was a plumper face, buried under the folds of a different habit. The blocks of the ramp were so hot that you could hardly sit. You sat, though, and let their heat change into a private warmth. The tide was higher than you'd ever known it, halfway up the granite, obscuring the beach. You lay for hours in the swoon of that heat, your cheek touching the granite so that your eye travelled down from the tan of the stone, so hot that its surface seemed to dance, to the huge, perfect blue world of that sea. You knew something was happening, that time was longer than it should have been and you allowed those minutes to pass like hours, teasing every fragment of yourself out into the sensual glare of that surface. You imagined bubbles you had to burst repeatedly to find further bubbles inside them, you laid one cheek on the granite and then the other so that the sea seemed to leave its fixed position and globe above you, around you. There was a slight tremor in the granite and you sensed a train far off. You saw a tanker inching across the horizon and then the ground moved beneath you, every pore in the granite seeming to leap to your cheek and the train, going where, you wondered, came and was gone. You imagined the tide, higher than it ever should have been, flooding the ramp, water spilling over the granite on to the sleepers and tracks.

23

WOULD SHE ALWAYS connect orgasm with trains, the even sleepers stretching into the distance and the border of black rail, meeting somewhere beyond her vision where they melted in a dance of haze, or in perfect union, where the laws of perspective told her they could never meet, only appear to? Or with the train itself, the mysterious rumble in the turf causing twigs to leap, heralding the sight through the haze of distance of 'the one friendly machine'? She called it that later, when she spent more hours on it than off it. But the convivial machine roars past and the child waves and never knows whether her wave is received by the unknown face in that strip of windows, whether the memory is carried towards a far-off station, a platform, a black footbridge. And the hope of roses always, for the pure-hearted waver. She would wave her hand years later, like the child who rarely sees trains. She would think of roses blooming from the window, sprouting from the axles. She would picture the landscape towards which the train always goes, always a foreign one, a garish plain where the tracks run over pliant peat, pass a disused canal and enter a clump of fir trees. The fir trees dip in gratitude. It is the landscape into which she has never been, towards which the train heads as it thunders past her, always beyond the farthest town, never on maps. She walks along the tracks looking for that carriage the dwarf told her of, which is small, like a childhood train. The tracks pass the canal that is now solid with frogspawn which falls over the sides of its banks, clinging to the fringe of pebbles by the track's edge. It spawns even as she walks. It clings to her bare feet like the gossamer of snails and she runs lightly to avoid it, stepping from sleeper to sleeper, between the tracks. The wood of those sleepers has fallen soft with age and holds the print of each of her steps. The tracks are bright with their oxides, a glare of red she never thought rust could achieve, and they thread the crest of the bog, towards the fir trees. She is walking with her head down, following the tracks and yet not following, for each sleeper is an end in itself and with each step she takes she knows she has come. The function of tracks is to lead the train from one point to another and the tracks themselves she knows are neither arrival nor departure, just partaking a little of both. But the soft wood of the sleepers and the frogspawn always doubling itself tells her with every footfall that she is here. And seen from behind, she knows, her walk would always intimate arrival, a bundle of static moments somehow thrown through time. You are here, the tracks say to her, and she holds this message as she would a towel to her bare breasts, her head bent downwards, knowing that somewhere beyond her the tracks do indeed meet. She feels the slightest shift of her thoughts could destroy this and so she walks with a terror, a terror that she feels necessary to maintain her sense of joy. For through this landscape in which every point is the point of arrival and every step is the ultimate step, she cannot deny that she is walking and that these tracks do lead towards that clump of fir trees and pass through it, to beyond. The frogspawn leaps as if to celebrate her thoughts and rises in imitation of the fir trees until she is among them and a soft glove of pine needles covers the tracks. She is at the point, she sees, where the sides of the tracks meet, despite all the laws of perspective. And beyond where the tracks seam into one lies the train the little man told her of, glorious and aged. There is that bright red which rust could hardly manage. But it is rust, she sees as she draws nearer, a kind of passionate rust for the metal surface falls apart at her touch into puffs of the russet. And the rust seems there to highlight the forgotten roses. They spill from every crevice of the bodywork, from underneath the axle, from the cracks in the leather of the passenger seats. They are red and she is bathed in their shadow. She walks to the driver's cabin, through the brambles.

I have placed the train with the roses by a disused canal and a clump of fir trees in the Bog of Allen, a flat open plane which is traversed by rail tracks, a wasteland between town and city. You tell it to Lili on the same ramp several days later. Your face flushes, but without a hint of coyness. You revere the physical details, moreover, the gleams of mica, the bumps of granite, the heat. Lili squirms and even now squirms before me in the telling, 'Because I was a schoolgirl, yes, I may as well admit it, but there was more than that. I mean I feared for her. I sensed, you see, that my shyness was given to me, my bashfulness was learnt along with my history lessons and that was how it was, a bashfulness that, whether you like it or not, is safer and much more common than forthrightness. And if Rene hadn't learnt it – not only that, she wouldn't learn it, her reaction to every giggle of mine made me feel inconsequential, worse than a child, a retarded adult – what would happen to her when she had to confront the source of that bashfulness? If she was extraordinarily lucky, she would never have to confront it, but how many of us are that lucky? And I feared for her, you see, and that's why I blushed – or that's as much why I blushed as my shame was why, if you know what I mean. And I was right to fear and blush, I discovered, when she told me that extraordinary story about the dwarf. And then I was made conscious of the fact – as she was never – the fact that we were both thirteen. Only thirteen. And that in many ways I was older than her . . . would she ever pass thirteen . . . and so I blushed and feared for . . .'

They exchange these confidences on the hottest days the beach has encountered, two girls, sitting on the lip of the ramp. Trains pass occasionally with the speed of a long, slow exhalation. The granite dances in the haze that makes the beach's inhabitants seem removed, far-off, transfixed against the blue sky and the yellow sand. But both girls hardly notice them. They are inside the bubble of their own warmth, their own words. Lili is reminded of that day the class exchanged confessions, of the rows of desks, the irises. Rene is talking, using words that are too young and too old for her thirteen-year-old mouth. She has her legs drawn into her chin, her hands are clutching her calves, damp with perspiration. Her legs are plumpish, Lili swears. Three years later they will be on the back page of the *Freeman's Journal*. They will have slimmed by then, be still fairly short, but give a definite impression of adulthood.

'But the years passed like days on that ramp. And when we finally got up with our bums creased with all that granite, it was three years later. She was sixteen – '

24

WHILE LUKE VANCE and James stand waiting at Bray station, part of the line caves in on the way to Greystones. A wave that must have germinated far out rises like an open hand, clutches the tracks and drags them towards itself. The metal bends in the water and the sleepers scud through the foam, haloed by the spray. The Bray train knows nothing of this but exhales a welcoming shroud of steam to them, father and son. Luke carries the tripod, James the case. They walk through the steam, through the door and take their seats on the seaward side.

'She had a premonition, I suppose. The dark wings brushed off her, making her cloaks flap. You will be a professional, she told Rene, there is a photographer I know. I came with them. It will be your assignment, she told her, your money. I walked with them down O'Connell Street. Can you imagine that voluminous animal dying, being there one moment, gone the next? I can't, even now. I had lived her through her stories, secondhand ever since I'd known them. But did she know, I often wonder, was that photograph a hint that she would someday live in Rene, Rene alone? An acquaintance stopped her on O'Connell Bridge. They talked for a while, they had that tone of voice, as when you talk of the Free State – '

But what is it that delights Una as she walks towards the agency with both of them beside her? It comes to her in an unfathomable shift, a sudden, unheralded flood of happiness. She has grown heavier, but she now holds her weight like a flag, a proud flag of she knows not what nation, an imposing black cloak thrown round her shoulders fluttering with the sea breeze that meets them on the bridge. The salt brings a flush to her cheeks as it had when she walked towards that spa, past the fluttering canvas, sixteen years earlier. She knows now that she loves this street with its giant pots and its green litter bins and its aura of sea coursing through it, keeping all those flags that crowd the rooftops jerking as if they themselves remember the course of events that put them there. The only faces that turn as they walk are those surprised by the unlikely aspect of this trio and she accepts the stares with equanimity, knowing that at last they are directed not at herself but at the daughter to her left whom she guides through the afternoon crowds like a statue, a more perfect image of herself. The wide, lengthy street seems a unit to her, an image of temporal home, and homes, she knows, are for leaving. A man steps from the crowd to catch her attention and the wind flaps his fawn overcoat as it does her cloak. He talks to her like an intimate and she hardly bothers to recognise him. He talks of the state and the arms dumps. They will be there, he tells her, waiting to be resurrected should Dev take one step backwards. She remembers the old complicity, the common words and gestures, the nods of emphasis for certain names, of negation for others. He is reviving, he tells her, the Conradh classes in Parnell Square. He asks her to lend a hand. She nods, as he assumes she will, and she feels a hidden surge of delight at his mistaken assumption. She sees herself and her large cloak and the person she has always seemed facing him and another impulse makes her turn and continue her walk down that wide street thinking of everything that seems, of people in groups and nods of assent and flags jerking gracelessly from rooftops. She passes the General Post Office with its three females pointing heavenwards and the wide, wide street with its flapping banners stretches out before her as if the bricks had been laid, demolished and laid again, as if the bullet holes had scarred the angels' feet just so that she could walk finally down it, closing her hand around her daughter's elbow and lead her towards her first professional assignment.

'She was more real than she ever had been. We walked up two flights of stairs into a room that was painted black. A man put the silk stockings on Rene. He sat her on a podium in different positions. Then the door was pushed ajar in a way that was irritating, hesitant. And I saw him coming through it for the first time. Was it the door that irritated me or was it him? I can't distinguish. And the boy Luke came behind him carrying the tripod. Chalk and cheese.'

Luke stares at the legs of Rene. He wants to touch them, even then. Which of them, father or son, can I choose? James shakes hands with the voluminous Una and speaks to her in broken Irish. He looks towards her daughter through the dust of the arc lamp, rubbing his eyes. The man smooths the silk stockings.

'She wouldn't live to see her daughter's picture. We walked back down the street towards the G.P.O. and she held my arm so tight that it hurt. I turned to ask her to loosen it and I saw all the colour had gone from her face. I walked on. I was puzzled. Each of us is alone.'

The wind gathers far out in the bay, up the estuary to the bridge and coils down the street like a silk ribbon. It whips Una's skirts like a flag, she stands still, they wait for her to move again. It whips each fragment of her past into a gale, would lift her over the parapet and the angel's feet and the tips of the marble spears, make each memory sweet, each enemy a loved one. It smells of the sea, the divine pungency of salt, would lift her only to dissolve her. They wait outside the G.P.O. until she gathers enough strength to walk on.

204

'But nobody dies,' Lili whispered, 'and now you're bringing her to life again. She just left a voluminous emptiness in the Pro-Cathedral. It was emptier for all those who didn't attend. Where were they all, I wondered, from the great days? There was no mention in the papers, no photograph even. De Valera was represented by a mass-card. I sat with Rene in the pews, among the actors. We had the same black veils. James came up, without his black box this time. If there's anything I can do to help, he said. There would be something, though that would come later. Luke stood behind him, staring. I turned to see what he was staring at. It was the silk stockings, of course, which she had never taken off – '

25

IF THERE'S ANYTHING I can do – James asked her on the Pro-Cathedral steps. And as Lili said, there would be. But did he search her out or did he wait for chance to tell him to search her out? The one event occurred that made a pattern of all the other events and without that event, he must have thought, months later, all the events before it would have been random. But the event occurred and took the others, like stringless beads, pulling a sudden thread through them. So afterwards he can muse in retrospect, on Killiney Head, always his incessant walks, kicking the cones away with his high-laced boots, how each must have held the germ of the significance with which it was later blessed. And so that photograph in the Green Room led to the next in the O'Connell Street dark room, each one gaining in portent with the one that followed. And the equations lovers tease themselves with – if A had not happened, then B would never have been possible, if we had never met there, we would never – he developed gradually into a mathematics of chance, passion and happenstance. We are all small nations, he would tell her later, and our past, present and future is a moving thread. And so he had photographed her twice when he met her the third time, and the circumstances of that meeting made him clutch, for the first time, at the thread. There were flowers on the altar again, funereal ones, and the priest moved with his waxen gestures against the backdrop of the cross. He looked around him and saw actors he recognised, some of whom recognised him. He felt a slight puzzlement at the sense of occasion, even at his presence there. She had never appealed to him when alive, as an actress even, and yet dead she seemed to unite these few mourners with a sense of larger event. He remembered her husband's death and the whole streets with covered windows. Time, as it lengthens, magnifies its figures, where distance miniaturises. Where are the soldiers, he wondered, looking around him for medals strung to lapels, where are the politicians? Have all the great events happened? And yet she was larger, somehow, for their absence. Every actor there he'd photographed at one time or another. Lord, he almost prayed, open my lips. And then he saw her daughter from behind, centre of the event, the blonde hair threading through the black lace veil. He felt that the mother had left so that the daughter could be seen more clearly. He let his eyes travel upwards from her blonde and lace threads to the huge dome above, the two lesser ones on either side. He thought of a dome where each brick is the cornerstone. When his eyes travelled down again through the pantheon of saints on the wall below he saw that the mourners had risen and the actors were walking out behind her. He followed them to the steps outside and it was there, with the wind blowing down Marlborough Street, tugging at everyone's dark clothes, that he asked was there anything he could do.

There would, as Lili said, be something he could do. He saw the print with the silk stockings in the daily papers. The brand turns out to be popular. It's the girl we photographed, isn't it? Luke asks him, lifting the newspaper from the green-topped table. He nods, wondering vaguely why his son uses the plural. You must learn to use the camera, he tells Luke, who shakes his head, always uninterested. You must learn Irish then. Why? Luke asks. You must do everything, he tells him. You must succeed where I failed. He looks at his son's profile, half-lit through the grey window. Luke is tearing the print from the page. Listen, he says, you must listen. Why, Father? Luke asks, his face made translucent by the grey metal light. You are my beloved son, he says, you must be everything I am not. But you made me, Luke says, turning his face around to the light. Luke shows the cut-out square of print to the old man, who proclaims it a masterful knee. I won't be with you much longer, the old man says, standing in the doorway. For a little while, then I won't be with you. You are my father, James says, you will always be with us. You made me. You made me, says Luke, turning again from the light. The old man shuffles back upstairs to where he mixes his pigments. Up there he dreams of them both, with his shock of white hair. James walks around the table to Luke until they are both washed in the light. He takes the paper from his son's hands.

Somewhere in the mass of print that swims around the space where her knees were, there is an announcement, in the curt phrases of exhibition notices, of a benefit concert for Rene O'Shaughnessy, daughter of Una. He meets her there of course, having taken the Bray train and seen the eucalypti from below, bare in the twilight, dipping hugely from the summit towards the sea. It is a sad enough affair in a governmental hall with rows of tubular steel chairs half-empty, a wooden seat and wooden back to each. A succession of artistes take the bright-lit stage and preface each act with a few words in remembrance. He listens to the tenor voices, the duos and trios, the recitations, the scraps from Boucicault and Synge. A sense of pity floods over him, whether for himself or her he can't be sure. He watches a much younger Lili recite 'My Dark Rosaleen' and approaches Rene in the interval, flooded as always with kindness. Lili drinks tea and eats a damp biscuit and begins to learn her impatience with him. A man in a check jacket, whom Rene calls Brogan, hands her a cheque. Is it coincidence, he asks Rene, that I took two photographs of you, each one near a death? She must have smiled. You could teach my child Irish, he says, embarrassed by his impulse, if you're in need of work. Your mother I remember had a *blas*. He stumbles with the unlikely word. She smiles, watching his lips quiver. But of course, he said, you act –

During the second half he finds himself beside her. A man called MacAllister proclaims her talents from the stage. Something in the man's air irritates him. The words are too pat, the phrases too ritual, she deserves more than this paternal show of warmth. She seems everyone's favourite, though. She sits upright, like a child in class, dutifully looking towards that cone of light. When he turns he can see the tip of her profile, behind the fringe of hair. The outer strands could brush his lips. She has one leg crossing the other.

26

'FOR SHAPELIER LEGS' says the caption. The contrasts are hard, as his gaze must have been. Rene's calf swells from that phrase in a long arc away from the ankle-strap. A seam traces the line of her calf and disappears into the upper of a high-heeled shoe. Her other leg juts from the lower left-hand corner, to be crossed by the first, the one that fills the picture. This leg seems pliant, resting but not at rest, as if with a benign and wholly female tolerance of time it had been swinging for an afternoon and just stopped for the shutter to click.

FIVE

BRAY, 1933

27

LARGE HOUSES AREN'T in demand these days and so when I went to Number One Sydenham Villas at the time the auctioneer had mentioned, I found it empty. The door was half-open; it was daylight outside but not a voice came through that strip of shade. The villas stretched up to my right, none as big as the first. It had been built, I imagine, when there was nothing there but field, one imposing building on the outskirts of a miniature Bray. The street and the rest came later, each year another and a smaller house, shrinking through the decades, adopting a perspective as if time were trying to imitate space. I inched the door open and watched the strip of shadow grow. The sea boomed from the prom. I felt proud of these dimensions. Nothing smaller would have done you, father or grandfather, whichever you turn out to be. I stepped inside and I smelt his world, knowing each detail was right whether it happened or not, each fact was part of him, whether real or not. There was the hatstand with the ball-and-claw feet. My shoulder touched the door, which touched it. The feet tottered and the four whorled handles swayed. I stood there, watching it totter. The hall stretched out in front of me. There were two doors off it to the left. The wall where the old man's mural should have been was covered in paper with an orange and green rose pattern, stretching up the stairs. It was soothing, even beautiful to stand there with the hatstand banging against the door and the breeze coming in from the prom below. I felt at home in the only home there is, that of imagination verified. I walked slowly through the hall and into a large kitchen, the one room I hadn't catered for. I had quite forgotten the necessity of making meals and the fact that these three males would never have done so themselves, would have needed maidservant, char and cook. There was a range covered with a film of dust. But you can't put in everything, I thought, though Luke must have sat curled up there for hours, dreaming in the heat. I went out to the hall again and into the front room and there was a bay window with a circular sofa and a piano against the left-hand wall. There was no green felt-topped table. But it could have been removed years ago, and besides, Lili gave me that piece. I felt the floor beneath me, the walls around me, the house, valued at £30,000 in the auctioneer's brochure, needing repairs, the whole magnificence of fact. And the repairs would have been extensive. There were dark patches on the cream walls and the plaster bubbled from the ceiling and as I walked towards the bay window one of the floorboards gave way under my shoe. There was just the skeleton of how they lived there, overlaid perhaps with the décor and the knick-knacks of three generations, layers of paint and sheaves of wallpaper, decades deep. But when I lay down on the circular sofa and rested my elbow on the curved sill and stretched my legs along the damp felt I could have peeled away those generations with my eyes and left the walls the way they were then, a thin blue, I would imagine, or perhaps the palest of greens. I could see the white horses beyond the promenade and the long trail of a jet, dissolving as the daylight went. And the nose of Bray Head edged past the window, rippled and frozen in the curve of the glass. The yellow pylons were still there, and the wooden café at the top where the passengers of the chair-lift used to alight, but the yellow chairs were gone and so the cables swung now, weightless. Why are the earliest photographs touched with an irresistible melancholy and why do the faces of loved ones we never met seem as large as the prints themselves are tiny? Did everyone feel more then?

I rose from the bay window and walked back across the room. I could have been walking on a beach, placing my feet in a trail of footprints much larger than mine. It took me years to cross from bay window to door, so huge had the room become. Halfway there I heard the front door bang. The hatstand rocked again, in counterpoint to someone's footsteps. I reached the door and opened it quietly, so as not to startle a prospective buyer. I saw a figure with slightly bowed shoulders and a neck which must once have been sleek and plump but from which the flesh hung limply now like those stiff folds of cloth in ecclesiastical murals. He was wearing a black hat, flecked round the rim. He was staring at the far wall, much as I had done earlier. I spoke without thinking.

'Can the paint have survived the wallpaper?'

It was indeed the curate. He turned, not at all surprised, smiling faintly. He had aged, of course, from when I had imagined him. There were forty more years, with the thirty-one I'd given him. That he drank I could see from his face, but his eyes had stayed bright in the interval, alert with his passion for theology and maths. Had his hope survived, I wondered, not without a twinge of conscience, had he unified those disciplines I'd given him so rashly? He spoke then and I thought, yes and no.

'Will we investigate?'

His voice seemed to come from an extraordinary depth, roughened by the layers of dust it had to shake off to reach me. Most of his teeth were gone. His eyes brightened with a humorous twinkle as he reached one hand up, gripped a sagging corner of the wallpaper and ripped one strip away. We both stood back and stared at the Hellenic form, head, neck and shoulders revealed above the jagged edge. It was the face of a woman with those stiff, airborne curls, her head turned in profile, looking with benign curiosity at something hidden by the wallpaper roses. Her halo of hair, her neck and her beautiful muscular shoulders were suspended, super-imposed almost, over a landscape of low grey hills, Hellenic or Hibernian I couldn't have said. The curves and definition of those hills looked suspiciously like the background to Leonardo's 'Virgin of the Rocks', but the woman's face was all the old man's own; vibrant and childlike, primitive or

215

kitsch, I couldn't have cared less since it spoke to me. I have never made aesthetic judgments.

'He mixed his own paints, you see.'

The colours were still fresh where the plaster had bubbled with damp. They were spread thinly, evenly, with nowhere the mark of a brushstroke, as if he wanted to disguise the nature of his materials. It gave his colours the worst possible texture, the texture of a photograph, a photograph of beings who were somehow larger, whose poses were more deliberate than the landscape spread out before them; of a being, too, who had attained the grandeur of colour when the world was being photographed in black and white.

Our thoughts were interrupted by the door opening again and banging against the hatstand and the entry of two well-heeled families, everyone clutching the auctioneer's brochure. We turned abruptly from the torn wallpaper as if to dispel any possible connection between us and it and I sensed, gratefully, that we had in common mutual feeling of guilt. His was complicated by an added factor, however, since both families, despite the profanity of their staring open-mouthed at the torn wallpaper without noticing the mural, all turned to him and smiled as we walked towards the door, repeating among themselves the word 'Father'. This embarrassed him, I am glad to say, as much as it incensed me and so when we reached the open door and the view of the night sea I felt a positive bond between us. He placed his hand on my elbow as I'm sure he did to Luke, as I'm sure he did to all three of them, at first to steady himself as we went down the steps but then to confide in me, as we made our way out of the gate, with the warmth in his palm and his voice of what I felt for an instant must be a much younger man.

28

'I DIDN'T KNOW her,' he said when the wind hit us, 'but I assume it must be her. Yes, although I've never seen her I've imagined her just like that. Luke described her once across the grille, a bizarre confession, but then all confessions are bizarre, there's just the pleasure of listening, a refined pleasure, let me tell you and one that has to be nurtured. As a young priest it used to terrify me, I used to slide back the hatch at any opportunity I got, would you believe, just to let my face be seen and if possible to get a glimpse at whoever was muttering the words but of course that was just a palliative, there was no cure was what I had to realise, people ceased to come to me for after all the sinner demands and deserves the right to whisper unseen. And the only way to live with the objects of one's terror after all is to take pleasure in them, which is what I had to do. Listening sets the imagination relatively free, you see, on a leash with a hand guiding it. But there was a whole country at it then, with radios, villages would gather in the bicycle shops to hear the Saturday match and so it was a confessional state, you see, in its early days, in more ways than one since everyone had their ear bent to a speaker. And so I – '

He stopped and I felt his hand on my arm again.

'Will we walk round by the Head?'

I nodded and we turned and walked back down the prom.

'And so I, instead of building a blow-by-blow account of the hurls on Croke Park from a cracked speaker, built a picture of her from a year of rumours, from one confused confidence of Luke's and even from my philosophic discussions with James, God bless his heart, since though he never mentioned her name, his thought around that time became somehow more inclusive. She was plumper, I may tell you, in my mind's eye, plumper than we have just seen her on that wall but that, I suppose, could be attributed to the old man's faulty vision. I have seen him on the prom here, on that patch of grass which used to be bald from his stool and easel, staring at the Irish Sea and yet something more akin to the Mediterranean appearing on his canvas. But I have no doubt, have you, that what we have just seen is her – '

I had no doubt. She had an adaptable figure, Lili had told me.

'I visited the house for years before she came, and the year she came my visits stopped. It was a house without a mother, you see, and in a sense it was waiting for her, and perhaps that's why my visits had to stop. If you detect a hoarseness in my voice it is because I am close to tears even now, thinking of it. Yes, I did look forward to those visits, to tea and cucumber sandwiches and to Luke taking out the tray. James and I talked mathematics and theology, we compared notes from the current journals, he stopped taking instruction after the first year, but that didn't matter. What mattered I suppose was a young curate walking from a presbytery to this household on the Bray prom and the light coming in from the bay window. Or did that matter? Our arguments were extraordinarily intense. We would hold positions for weeks on end and then drop them suddenly on a whim, because of the weather or the colour of the bay outside. James retained a fundamentalist frame of mind, you see, despite his agnosticism, he brought an intellectual rigour to the examination of the new state to which that state could never conform. A sense of chaos however is endemic to Catholic thought and a very definite mistrust of the intellect, and that of course was endemic to me, no matter how bad a priest I later became. And so we faced each other over the gulf of our background, I could see the weeping Huguenot in him, the personage his father had lost but which must have been reborn in him by proxy as it were, from perhaps his father's father, for likenesses I have always noticed recur

218

across two generations, rarely one. And so through the years I lived his various schemes with him, you have heard about his schemes no doubt. He allied himself to A.E.'s agricultural movement at one stage, at another he bought that school in Connemara to show the Bray slum youth the west of Ireland, and later he made a foray into politics – what was it his brochure said – "to draw the current Irish dialogue into a European framework". Of course he lost his deposit, a two hundred pounds which he could ill afford, but perhaps that was better, since we all know what happened to the European framework for the current dialogue. In fact I am tempted to say that it was better that all his schemes failed, schemes like his should fail, since the execution of them could never approach the delight of their conception and their failure at least allowed him to continue scheming, which the success of any one of them would have precluded. And he returned each time, of course, to his abstract art, the one we shared, mathematics, and the one that both consumed and fed him, photography.

'So you can imagine how much I loved that house with its cucumber sandwiches, "cues" I see they are called now in the vegetable shops, and its three generations of males and perhaps it was the fact that there was no woman there that enabled me to call so often. You see, once June began my visits had to stop since the Vance family, minus grandfather of course, would take off on holiday, not your two-week holiday, but generally two to three months in the country. Of course there were invitations to visit whatever small house they had rented along the western seabord but I never took them up, no, holidays for me were at the open centre in Carnsore Point, any request to visit a whimsical Protestant family in the west of Ireland would have definitely been suspect. Was it this we shared, I wonder, this absence of femininity, because it often seemed that all our discussions in that sagging house concerned an absence which all three of them suspected might one day be filled. James's distance, the old man's brusqueness when he saw me and the day I sat in the wooden box in the church on Main Street and this figure stumbled in and talked hoarsely in a voice that was trying to disguise itself but that I recognised as Luke's, they all added up to – '

We had come to the end of the promenade tiles and the beginning of the cement path that still led along the sea but that had fields now to its left and moved upwards towards the Head. There were chunks of rock and pebbles set in the cement and he held my arm again as we walked.

'They all added up to not so much a figure but the impression one has of a figure when it – she in this case – has left the room. The smell of scent perhaps, the cigarette stubbed out on the ashtray – though of course she didn't smoke – a certain mustiness in the case of women which I as a celibate am peculiarly alive to, hanging round a chair, and above all the attitude on people's faces, the look of delayed surprise, affection or fear, retaining as they do the expressions with which they gazed on her even after she has left. Now all the words passed between us in those years, the small tensions, James's elbow, which I often grasped when excited, and good Lord, I did get excited at times, the hand with which I used to pat Luke's head when she eventually did come, in 1933, and my visits stopped – of my own accord, let me hasten to impress on you – James implored me to visit again, but I knew it was finished, we both knew and what contact I did have with them was in my presbytery or on the steps of the church or now and then on the Dublin train – when she eventually did come I could see as clearly as, if you will allow me the simile, Augustine saw his city of God, I could see that all those points in our contact over the years were signs, hints if you like, about her. And that is why when we stood in the hallway just now and I ripped back the wallpaper, I could tell that the figure painted there was her, I could say quite truthfully that I recognised her. Though as I said to you, I would have thought of her as plumper – '

We had by now come to the end of the cement walk and we turned as if with one mind and walked across the fields, upwards. We came to where the pylons for the chair-lift were and stopped. I stared up at the empty cables.

'We did well to leave that house, for how can you confine it to an auctioneer's brochure or price it at thirty thousand? Better to let it fall down, don't you think, decay in its own time, let the roof fall in and the plaster bulge and peel off the walls? But things aren't let die, are they, they're bought again and redecorated, shoved into life once more to house other families, give birth to new memories in turn, there'll be a television where the circular sofa was and maybe an electric cooker in place of the range, all to house new myths that people think will die as they do and if they were to return like us they'd be appalled to find the resilience of objects and the indestructibility of life, to learn that the end was in the beginning even as it happened, and the beginning in the end. And even that cable that you're staring at will carry another yellow chair – '

And sure enough the cable creaked as I was looking at it and began to roll. I could see the grease glistening in the moonlight and a yellow chair passed over us, swaying towards the wooden café at the top. It was approaching summer, I surmised, and some Bray businessman had revitalised the lift.

29

THE FIRST THING Rene would have noticed coming down
the Bray prom would have been that lift. She has just come
off the train and the directions the photographer scrawled
out for her lead back past the station, over the tracks and
down towards the sea front. The promenade before her is a
mile and a half long, narrowing, it seems, towards this mass
of green, neither hill nor mountain, shouldering a gaunt half
circle into the blue sea. And the yellow chairs are moving up
and down the Head again. And what crowds on the prom,
in the heat, in the middle of summer! She makes her way
between them, wearing another pair of silk stockings and of
high-heeled shoes. The heels are slightly lower now but still
sharp enough to catch in the gaps between the tiles. So she
throws her weight forward to the balls of her feet, walking
in the way she would if she were barefoot. There are the
awnings of the hotels and the porches, some makeshift for
the summer, all of striped canvas; the façades of the hotels all
facing the beach with the striped deckchairs and the circular
canvas tents. Ireland in the heat is a different country, she
told herself, imagining boxes with palms bound around with
hoops. She changes her pace to avoid the flow coming
towards her, but keeps her eyes on the yellow chairs. They
go up the Head in jerks, swaying as they move. Her father
held her on the yellow chair, showing her the vista. Home,
Jack, he said, down the promenade. The voices around her
are Scottish now, for the cycle has begun. Heat in summer
makes the strollers seem to dance, raises their feet above the
surface, blurs the tiled promenade. Perhaps they saw her
walking on air, as she saw them, inches above the melting

tiles. Or are Scots naturally incurious? The curate certainly doesn't see her, though she sees him. A figure in black on such a hot day stands out. Walking quickly, from what he doesn't yet know will be his last afternoon discourse. She smiles when she sees him; turns, hoping to catch his attention. She is as demure as with Sister Paul, wants to meet all kinds of religious. But Father Beausang's head is full of Descartes, sweltering inside his circular stove, for it's on that appropriate theme that their talks have ended. He senses an ending as he walks, and he is not sure why. Is it the sea, blurred and distended in the heat to abolish the horizon? But he hardly notices the sea. Perhaps it is his suit, which as he walks has covered his body in a film of sweat. The figures that come towards him on the promenade seem to dance in the heat. As he claimed, after she had come, it was as if he knew all along she or something like her would. And so he must sense the ending. And passing the young woman who has smiled at him with an invitation to stop, he just sees another melting figure among the strollers coming towards him and wishes the heat, anyway, would end. And she turns, after a moment standing still, looking after his figure under its creased hat, which soon melts like the other strollers. She walks on to where the hotels give way to residential houses. She stops outside the largest of them, takes her eyes from the yellow chairs and walks in.

James Vance opens the door. He sees her standing, framed by the doorway as in both of his prints. But now the sea is behind her and she is a woman. She is shifting her weight from foot to foot too, as the girl in his prints could never have done. He sees her shoes and silk stockings, like the ones he photographed, their silk perfection vanishing under a very imperfect, even shabby, skirt. She has been doing more adverts, he thinks. Perhaps he wishes she could be held static like the girl he photographed, for when she moves into the hallway to stand beside him, he stays looking at the frame of the door. The sun comes in round its edges, bleaching the sea. He will later remember how glad he was, and how ashamed to be glad, that Father Beausang had left.

He says, Come in, which is unnecessary, since she is already in, staring at the extraordinary scene that covers half the wall. He stands at the open doorway watching her against that scene, thinking how her features blend with it. The old man, sensing something, clatters from his attic to the top of the stairs and gazes at her distracted, thinking the woman of his imagination, coaxed by his mural, has at last come alive. And Luke comes from the living-room with the tea things. He is now sixteen.

30

AT FIRST SHE taught her brand of Irish at weekends but she must have felt immediately at home there, for she soon comes to flood the album, and all the vistas that were photographed without her find themselves in print again, with her in the foreground and Luke or James behind. Some rustic fencing with its border of roses which must have bloomed that summer acts as a frame for her, with Luke leaning sullenly against one of the poles and her hand on his sixteen-year-old head. And the old man finds his way in too, finally, magnificently. He is standing bolt upright on the prom, his huge white mane with a sharp quiff at the parting, from which all their quiffs sprang. He has her arm firm through his arm and is clutching it proudly, as if she were his young wife. The Head can be seen behind them and the yellow chairs, which in the print show like puffs of fawn. I can see them having walked the length of the prom, the breezes from the east that came in waves lifting his mane of hair and the hem of her skirt. She has constantly to hold down her skirt, which fills with wind, billowing like a canvas tent, while the old man entertains her with his version of time lost, tells her about the Barbados, about boarding-houses in New York and about the yards and yards of canvas he has filled with paint. Every memory recalls a bad canvas and as he recounts it it seems he dispenses with it, clears himself of the burden of looking once and for all. He shows her the bald patch of lawn where he has sat sporadically throughout the last six years, painting the scene through which he is now walking, a scene that never seemed as perfect as it is today, and as he says that he lets go her arm and tells her to walk forward so that he can see her against that backdrop of blue sea and the very edge of the prom and the cones of the canvas huts nosing upwards from the beach. He stands back on the grass so that he can look at her, narrowing his eyes which are clustered everywhere with wrinkles from the effort to focus, turning his head to one side the way painters do and certain species of seabirds, and the updraught of the wind from the beach to the edge of the prom lifts her dress violently so that she limps towards him, laughing. But he barks at her with a voice he might use for servants and tells her to stand there and forget about the wind and so she stands there, her dress billowing over her knees and watches his smile, an old man's smile at a young woman, who has for once seen a perfect pair of knees –

Technically, too, this group of prints is an immense improvement. You've forgotten your reticence in the face of objects. I can see it, that you focus with such a clarity on one that all the objects around her fall into place. You do not see it, perhaps, but Father Beausang's remarks on Poincaré have been proved correct since the intractability of the world you looked at through your shutter seems to have given way, as if a veil has been lifted. And where you caught Luke clumsily, sixteen years ago, in a Moses basket and a woman's hand comes awkwardly into the picture from the left-hand corner, now you catch the woman unashamedly, face-on, and the world falls into place behind her, just like, in fact, the landscape behind the cave in Leonardo's 'Virgin of the Rocks'. How can Bray and its environs, the Dargle valley, the eucalypti around Killiney hill and the wildness of your back garden suddenly assume this neatness, this aptness, how can this solid world suddenly know its place – a place firmly behind the people that inhabit it – when for years it has edged quite brazenly and vulgarly into your vision, the horizon always at an angle, walls, trees and the ever-present seascape always at odds with and sometimes even crushing the faces you placed alongside them? I assume you didn't notice this change, and that the pleasure you always took in your photography was for once lost in the pleasure you took in the objects you photographed.

226

There are three photographs of the chair-lift. There is Rene with Luke in two and in the third Rene with your father. In the first Luke is sitting bolt upright in the yellow chair and staring without expression towards you, towards the camera. Rene is holding a black bag on her lap, looking towards the camera with a quiet smile. The yellow chair would have been swaying slightly, for the Bray that we can see behind them in the space between Luke and Rene is somewhat blurred and because of that even more like a miniature town, a miniature world. They are both staring at me now from the print as they must have stared at you, and Luke's face seems to express some resentment towards me, as father would to son, but perhaps I am only interpreting that as resentment in the light of what I know happened later. And Rene is looking at me with a smile which seems to contain whatever is between us two.

The chair is swaying in the next snap too and this time what is blurred is Rene herself, for her head is hanging over it and Luke is pulling at her elbow in mock horror. She is at the opposite end of the car this time, for Bray Head is behind them, fragments of what could be Wicklow, Wexford, dissolving into a blur, neither sea nor land. And in the third, the old man dominates, proud as he was on the promenade. He is pointing away from the sea towards the hinterland, the Sugarloaf and Lord Meath's estate. She is leaning past him to look and he must be describing the property he owned there and giving a gleeful account of the ways he managed to get rid of it.

Again there is nothing extraordinary in her face against the town of matchboxes with the railway station in the very centre and the line coming into it from Killiney and drawing away again towards Wicklow. Neither against the quite delicate line of the mountains on the other side of the chair-lift, going down this time, does she look extraordinary, Djouce, Tunduff and the Sugarloaf behind, its small peak of granite nibbling at the blue.

Which is not to deny the pleasure you took in those photographs. Whatever the object of your pleasure, your pleasurable eye is obvious. She fills them and the perspective with which you viewed her must be one of love. As if you have tried to embrace her, she leans through the prints, almost falling out of them. And the figures around her are blurred, as if the camera was jealous.

31

I MEDITATE ON her in a way and invent her in parts as you must know by now, for the secret must be out. And if it is out, I'm not sure whether I've failed, and if it's not out, I'm not sure whether I've succeeded. Anyway, if James was jealous, and jealousy I imagine is a faded, parched colour, that precise tint that all his snaps have acquired over the years, mainly, let me say, through the accumulation of dust, he was jealous of every brick in the world he looked at, of every image because he couldn't possess it and jealousy next to love is the most loving of all emotions. He was jealous of the world because he couldn't love it as he needed to and he was also jealous of her. But his jealousy for her was of a more delicate kind and even now, in these prints, was wheeling round to the point it would eventually reach, where its bulk would become thin and eventually invisible. You can imagine then that I am also jealous, having her take the Bray train each weekend over that summer in which Father Beausang stopped his visits for good. The perspiration which the heat from the window would have induced in her, her light cotton dress, blue with perfectly round splashes of white all over and the coarse material in the seat from which every movement of hers caused dust to spring. It is a moving picture I have of her, since she holds a battered dictionary, English-Irish, turns pages and sighs continually as she reads for, as Lili tells me, she was never a great reader and the Irish lessons she gives to the Vance boy will be as bizarre and laughable as her own mastery of that language is. She is turning the pages anyway and constantly shifting from the page, to look at the procession of sea outside, sheared now and then by a thrust of beach or a stretch of heather when the tracks go inland. The insides of trains never hold for her the associations that the train viewed from just below the tracks does and so she loses her constant expectation of roses from the train windows the minute she enters. For not even the best of us can picture the outside from in and there is no way she could have seen, as they passed Killiney Head, the wheels shredding the lost strips of eucalyptus bark. But it would be unreasonable for the carriage in which she travelled and the polka-dot dress and the bristling chair not to retain the sense of those roses. And so I am jealous of every detail in any of those carriages in which she sat, all the more so since the Dublin-Bray train has been sheared of all its niceties over the years, the chairs now being movable and plastic and not even arranged in rows but fixed, backs to the wall, in a way that's more appropriate to a public bus. Bray has grown, you see. But the promenade's still there and the train that leads to it, and though it's more like a metal box than train carriages should be, it still has the bolt-marks in the floor where the seats that were more proper to it were fixed. I prefer to stand at the door with my hand on the window-sash and my cheek against the glass. That way I can see the procession of water outside, sheared by the beach, by occasional houses and stretches of green. And by the wonderfully squat governmental brick of the railway stations. Is there anything as sad as that red-brick, as the fawn, uneven granite of the platform and the tracks then, with the blue to one side? The tracks were given to private tender, but those stations must be governmental. The schoolgirls rise and leave at each and nobody gets on. And this empty carriage with its plastic chairs will become the object of someone else's envy in turn as they wonder how it was then. But my urge anyway is to possess the lost carriage in which she travelled that summer and the dress which caught her perspiration as it passed Glasthule, Killiney, Shankhill. Once past Killiney the land becomes less crowded and the tracks seem to fall gently with the land, towards the sea and towards Bray. The pages of the dictionary turning and turning, rustling even now over the plastic seats. Those lessons must have been just an excuse for the tall man who met her on hard times just after her mother's death. He felt the urge to help her and also the urge to possess. Lili thinks so, Father Beausang imagines so and I imagine so too. But then we are all faintly jealous. It is through jealousy that we draw near her and because of jealousy, perhaps, that we never reach her. I have no doubt that his first instinct was the generous one, that shambling, uncertain generosity of his that Lili remembers with distaste. The payment was fixed at ten shillings a lesson, an amount that for a man like him is never enough, since the generous urge is even more bottomless than the acquisitive one. And no doubt after the first one he increased it, slipped twice as much into the brown envelope that neither of them seemed to notice, that was left with her name on it on the table by the hatstand. That the lessons themselves were an embarrassment she never realised of course, and none of them would have dreamed of mentioning it to her. The boy suffered gladly the Saturday afternoon spent learning words from Abacus to Acclamation, since her idea was to progress through the dictionary alphabetically and she hadn't an inkling of grammar. And of course the beauty of that method was that there was never enough time, a lifetime wouldn't have sufficed, and by the end of the second Saturday they had only reached Artichoke. And so her visits became weekend ones, she would come on the Saturday morning and leave on the late train on Sunday, the extra lesson on Sunday afternoon being deemed absolutely necessary even to crack the sheen of that glorious mass of words. And of course after the third weekend, habit had set in and all four of them expected her and the current words would be repeated round the household like a litany. The old man even showed a surprising interest in Irish, the language he had hardly known existed. And habit brought its odd rituals too, the main among them being that the old man pestered her each Sunday to sit for him, and that Luke reserved for himself the right to wait for her at the station every Saturday morning and accompany her down Bray prom.

And because the last mile of the journey is over land that's falling gently the train seems to slide towards Bray where the last few schoolgirls get off. The sea disappears behind the backs of houses and then appears again. I get out of the metal carriage to where Luke used to wait on the granite platform and pass through the curved awning under which they both walked to the sun, the square and Bray.

Luke takes her elbow and leads her outside the station down a small road and past the bowling green. They turn right, through a narrow tunnel over which the same train runs farther down the coast. The curved avenue of light widens as they pass through and spills on to the beach where the light becomes fawn, blue and silver. Luke is tall now, almost as tall as his father, but with what characteristics? He neither paints nor photographs, as if the law of resistance between successive fathers and sons has come to rest in him. He has a disturbing restfulness of gesture that illuminates him in any drawing-room, never belonging to it, yet rooted to it. His father's unwillingness to open doors has given way in him to this stasis, never demanding to be more than where he is, yet disturbing whole companies with this seeming passivity. He stares from corners, fearful and self-possessed. An agoraphobic child, he has learnt to control this tendency by walking down each street with an extreme slowness, as if it were a room. And so he walks down this room that is a beach, holding her elbow for support, leading her towards the water, yet tightening his grip on her elbow as they draw near. That luminous child Lili has called him, and his eyes do stand out against the grey texture of his skin, metal-blue, like mirrors. This effeminate boy, grown tall in the way of some hot-house plants, could he have been different, I wonder, as James must have done. Could his hair have been thicker, his shoulders broader? James stares at him across the familiar gulf, all his words turn to questions, held in mid-air. Those planes of distance surround them, all angles, unbridgeable expanse.

But Luke is thin and has come to the largest expanse of all, the sea, and so holds her elbow even more tightly for support. Soon her elbow will be indistinguishable from his,

his father's. There are the voices of the Scottish holiday-makers behind them and of the Jewish girls whom his grand-father loved to paint. A small paddle-boat that has gone too far out inches its way across the ribbon of blue. A man swings a leather bag beside them, calls at it to return.

32

SOME BRAY BUSINESSMAN had revitalised the lift. Will we ascend? asked Father Beausang and sprang up the metal steps with a vitality that amazed me. You are old, I began, but he was already in the yellow chair, patting the seat beside him. I was left to pay the man with the leather bag, who pulled the lever that sent us off, swaying.

'I lied to you,' he said, 'when I said I hadn't seen her. It was the house that made me melancholy and melancholy leads me to white lies. I had seen her, of course. How could I have lived in Bray and not seen her? I passed her on the prom and I see now that it must have been her first day here. But it was more a fiction than a lie and there's a kind of truth in fiction isn't there? I was hot on the prom, wearing that ridiculous black suit that always made me feel, in summer, like Descartes sweltering inside his stove. It helped him to think, he claimed. But my black suit and the sweat that ran from my collar down my shirt never helped me to think. I always walked quickly through the heat, racing to be inside once more. Though I'm sure it was her that seemed to bounce through the crowd of Scotsmen in open-necked shirts and even gesture towards me as if wanting me to stop. But of course I didn't stop, the last thing I wanted to do was stop. It had been Descartes, I remember, with James that day and the cucumber sandwiches had upset my stomach and I had notes to write on our discussions, all of this besides being hot, so of course I couldn't stop. But if you were to ask me had I seen her, I couldn't truthfully say no. But the verb to see conjures up more than mere vision. I walked the Head too, you see, every weekend, Saturdays and

Sundays, and never a weekend passed but one or other of the Vances would sway over me in the yellow chair, almost always with her. I would hear the voices from below, the words carried off on the wind of course, so I couldn't eavesdrop. If I walked nearer the cliff, I could see them in profile. She never had much hair, I could make out that, if it was her. Nothing like the great bush of hair I always associate with beauty. All I could make out was that it was a woman and James, Luke or the painter with her in the chair. And sometimes all four. What attraction this chair had for them I couldn't make out. I mean the seaside inhabitants are never the ones to use the paddle-boats – '

We had climbed higher and the yellow chair was swaying like a train going at high speed. A gust of wind carried off his words for an instant and so I couldn't hear. Rather than stare at his mouth, opening and closing silently, I leant over the side and saw the great pylons with their feet in the earth, the clumps of purple heather and the small track along the cliffs, bordering the sea, along which he must have walked. I looked up to the right of his shoulder and saw the town flowing out from it, something like a neckscarf, and beyond it the city. I turned and saw the thin finger of the Sugarloaf and beyond it Djouce, the Three-Rock, Tunduff. The attraction of course must have been analogous to the attraction of trains. Of course none of them would have bothered to ride it but her, being a visitor, and if she associated trains with roses, what would this airborne carriage with its iron seats, its cogs and its cable clicking with dark grease mean to her? The flower that would have sprung from this would have been unimaginable. It was too high to have earth in the chair, its petals would have been silk and black, perhaps. An eminently human flower which springs from thought, the swaying chair, the wind cleansing the brow and the sensation of flight. James Vance looks at her and sees it sprouting from her mouth, her opened lips, saying something he can't hear, containing it like a pot. She sees it in Luke, in James, in the grandfather, sprouting through their stiff collars in place of their faces and its stem hidden, but threading its way, she knows, to the base of their spine. The old man's mane dips and waves with it thorny, irascible but with his barely hidden delight oozing from him like perfume. And James Vance thinks he can capture this texture of flowers as he raises his camera once more and snaps. But in the print, when it emerges, the yellow chair on which her hand rests is nothing more than metal and she just a young woman, as my priest friend says, without much hair but with an extra-ordinary texture to what hair she has –

'And when I think of it, there is no one in the town that wouldn't have seen her. The word even reached my Superior that the agnostics – Protestants – no one was ever quite sure how to categorise poor James – in the Villas had a young lady staying with them. Governess, the more discreet gossi-pers called her. Fancy-woman, said the local wits. And the mothers of the sodality claimed the old man had got himself another model. And I suppose the truth is she was a little of all three. A fiction there, with more than half a truth.'

I lied. There is the unmistakable scent of flowers from those prints. Or is it the dust that gathered in the album? Dried flowers?

'Whatever was the truth, it had all the makings of a scandal. Only if she was Catholic, of course. There had been a fuss some years before. About a model who turned out to be Jewish . . .'

The yellow chair bumped to a halt and I was thrown forward into his lap. He held me for a moment by the shoulders and smiled. I could see the moisture gathering at the corner of each eye. He turned my face towards the turf and heather, now just six feet below us.

'See,' he said, 'we've come down. And I think those two small tickets of yours entitle us to a cup of tea . . .'

He gestured towards the metal stairs. I stood up and helped him to his feet and would have helped him down the stairs, but he insisted I go first. We clambered down then, one after the other, and walked across the heather to the Eagle's Nest and two cups of tea.

33

IS IT ON the close wet texture of the sand it happens, just after high tide, or between tides when the glare is an aching yellow and the sand is hot under their bare feet? If it's Luke, he's with her in the early morning. Instead of lessons under the bay window they have walked out here; James has spent the night in Dublin, and the old man is still sleeping in his sick-bed. Luke stands in the water in his shoes. She calls him back, Luke, Luke, he is her charge after all. He walks back across the ridges, all the miniature pools, to where the sand is dry again and clings like fawn paper to his shoes. He leads her by the hand to beneath the promenade wall. The sun is hottest there, it catches the glare, sand and stone, and there is a lip to hide whoever's below from the strollers above. The sun seems moderately low over the seascape, it is morning as yet, the vapour hasn't gathered to a haze, the paddle-boats are beached, awaiting their owner's leather bag. Each line is as sharp as it could be. But lying down, the sun seems high and so lying down they make it suddenly mid-afternoon, the glare pulses in an almost clear blue and the mackerel clouds disperse. The tide from a broad board becomes a flat ribbon, the sands become hillocks of fawn, all perspectives reversed. Luke covers his body in a down of blonde sand.

And for James perhaps the canvas hut. Mid-afternoon, when the boatman's calling the paddle-boats to shore seems to fade into the haze. He is old, his face is as creased as his leather, his hands are hard and coin-coloured. The boats circle to his

237

cries. James pushes aside the flapping door and walks into the world of canvas, conical, its light filtering through the blue and yellow in alternate stripes. Rene stands in the lit cone and his mind, as tendentious as ever, registers the colours, blue and yellow, echoes of the colours outside. James makes love with words, perhaps, he uses the unique syllable with tongue, lips and teeth, he manages her first name only with difficulty, Miss O'Shaughnessy he seems happier with since he pays her, after all, to teach Luke. But what coinage could allow him to approach her, none but her own, which could hardly be named as she gives it to father or son or father and son. James's voice is muffled by the canvas there and the sand beneath his feet. The cries from the beach outside are almost louder than his, but his cries are words. The skin across her back is ridged by the imprint of her shoulder blades. There are canvas deckchairs, folded in a heap. Somewhere above him a train rumbles.

But the heather could have held all three of them. We made our way through it, mounds of it. Once again he showed himself younger than his years. I stumbled now and then but he trod on.

'And what are all scandals about but love? Love, sacred and profane, carried in words, all of them echoes of that greatest scandal of them all when the word was made flesh and the scandal was the word and the word was love. She visited them for the best part of the year until the fit-ups took her on that provincial tour. The old man died soon after and the Scots returned for their summer weekends. I walked the promenade, I sat in my rooms. I turned my mathematical inquiries to that exquisite system of triadic ambiguity that is Marian theology.'

He strode on, his boots raising clouds of dust, or was it pollen?

34

DESPITE LUKE'S FEAR of open spaces he must have ventured out that summer to a garden fête, a large open field where he seems restless even in the photograph, surrounded by upturned temporary tables and crumpled cloths. There are Jesuits in the background and among them a female figure which could be Rene. He seems like a large thin bull there, who would make of the field a pattern on a living-room wall, if he could. His hair is thin and lank so that the bristling quiff, so evident above his forehead years ago, is all but hidden. He seems to be leaning towards the camera, imploring it to release him, perhaps so that he can get back to the security of those massed Jesuits. There is accusation in his eyes. He must have been held there for an inordinate length of time so that his father could get the focus right. The space of this field in which his father has placed him appals him, but no more than the spaces of the world into which his father has thrown him. And he stands, apparently tottering forward for what seems an age before the shutter clicks, and then turns and walks stiffly, as rapidly as he can without running, towards the black mass of the Jesuits and the white tables.

He meets their crowded backs with relief, their serge shoulders, shiny rather than black from rubbing against one another. The sandwiches on the long tables have gone soft in the heat but the Jesuits keep eating them and the maids keep running for more. These maids are squat and have freckled faces and wear aprons identical in shape if not in design. They approach the Fathers with slightly bowed heads, transport the blue and white plates with banana sandwiches, but once out of earshot they clasp each others' hands, they giggle, running towards the refectory for more. The Fathers stand in groups, scattered round the white tables, round the mothers of the schoolboys. They stare at this agoraphobic boy, seeing in him perhaps a lost pupil and possibility. But he just stands there clutching the white tablecloth, inhaling the odour of Jesuit serge, looking for the small circle of massed priests among whom he hopes is Rene.

James Vance brings tripod and box down past the longest of the tables and is approached by a lay brother who fifteen years ago took minor Abbey parts. I tend the garden now, this brother tells him, I dig trenches and grow vegetables for the community meals. Do you remember that snap you took of *The Workhouse Ward* where I could be seen in the background talking to the Peeler? The priesthood is not for everyone, this lay brother tells him, and not for such as me who grew up in that profane trade.

The Superior is tall and rigid and one half of his crown is bald. Perhaps the only one of the Fathers who hasn't eaten sandwiches, he walks among the tables towards James, holds him gently by the elbow. Hopkins, he tells him, *was* a poet. Swinburne, for whom I've heard you profess such a liking, has been responsible for the most blasphemous line in the last two thousand years. He quotes softly as if his lips are trying to separate themselves from the words.

> Thou hast conquered, O pale Galilean;
>   the world has grown grey from thy breath.

The Superior's crown gleams like a mirror with perspiration. His hand is firm and irritating. We must come to some arrangement, he lowers his voice, about all school photographs . . .

A young athlete from the Sixth Form walks between the tables and the knots of priests. He is still dressed for running and perspiration and effort have stiffened his hair into a mass of blond curls. He acknowledges none of the Fathers' nods, and yet the Fathers seem not to mind. Vigour, they seem to say, and youth obey their own laws. A glow of vapour and distilled effort surrounds him. A yearly figure, the Superior whispers, for portraits of all the forms . . .

Luke walks between two maids, carrying empty plates. Take me to the house, he asks them. They walk beyond the tables, clasping their hands behind his back. One is taller than him, the other smaller. Do you all wear the same sized apron? he asks, noticing how the small one is wrapped in hers, the tall one choked by hers. No, says the tall maid, laughing, there's two sizes. Too big and too small. She has a brace and her consonants click. They cross the large field, beyond the tables. Their clasped hands separate and fall around his waist.

The sun curves gradually downwards and as the day grows cooler the Fathers disperse, Jesuit by Jesuit, from their small groups. The Sixth Form athlete walks towards the field exit arm in arm with a middle-aged, elegant lady. His mother, the lay brother whispers, shaking his head, is a saint. Our persuasions are different, the Superior muses. He tries to disguise his curiosity. The young woman who came with you, she's not a local girl?

Luke finds her in the kitchen, sitting at a wooden table, surrounded by the maids. Each maid is plucking her apron, laughing coarsely. Rene's smile seems to include each one of them. We seen you on the train, says the maid with the braces, you getting off it and us getting on –

35

A YOUNG WAITRESS brought us the tea. She walked between the small patio and the Eagle's Nest, bringing first the cups, then the tea and then the sugar and milk. It was a wooden building with a corrugated iron roof which sang whenever it rained. Luckily enough the sun had again come out so we sat outside. The whole arrangement was quite a suntrap since the Head loomed over the Eagle's Nest, shielding it from the prevailing winds, and the Eagle's Nest loomed over the patio. I asked the serving-girl had they had many trippers and she said no, that we were the first yet. Could you drink outside like this, I asked her, in the old days? I don't remember, she answered. She seemed annoyed by the question and I couldn't understand why until I realised she couldn't have been born then. Is this your first job then? I continued when she came with the milk. What's it to you? she muttered, her young eyes narrowing.

We plucked the sprigs of heather from our trousers while she poured the tea. Between the last pylon of the lift and the Eagle's Nest there was nothing but heather, two or three feet deep. We both agreed that there must have been a track there once and that a new one would appear soon when the lift caught on again.

But we sat in silence once the girl had poured the tea, he hardly touching his cup, sitting with his face to the bay and his eyes half-closed. I wondered was he tired or was our silence caused by our sudden intimacy some moments back, just when the lift stopped? Or perhaps by the young girl's annoyance? I put my face close to his but only the whites of his eyes showed through his half-opened lids; they didn't register the blue bay before them. Perhaps old priests are like old horses, I thought, they sleep at odd moments only, in postures of waking. So I put his saucer on top of his cup to keep it warm and went ahead and drank my own tea. It was scalding, though a little weak.

Time passed and clouds flitted over the heather, like heather themselves. Father Beausang stayed asleep. I sensed someone looking at me then and turned to see the serving-girl in the wooden doorway with a camera raised to her face. The camera clicked as I turned and she ran into the interior, clutching it to her breast. I rose from my seat quietly so as not to waken him and walked towards the door, and inside.

I stood just inside the doorway looking across the wooden floor and the round tables to where she sat, behind the counter. Move over, she said, you're blocking the light. I walked forward and the light flooded in behind me, which seemed to satisfy her since her air of annoyance faded and she focused on the camera in her hand with a kind of innocent concentration. Is this your first job then? I asked again, but she silenced me with a Shhh! and placed the camera on the counter where I could see it. It was an instant one I saw, streamlined and plastic with an aperture from which the print would slide out. We both watched the print slide out then and fall on to the wooden counter, as if it had a will of its own. It was a wonderful grey colour which gradually changed as if smoke was drifting across it and the gaunt shape of the pylon loomed out of the smoke and the broken shape of the coastline and the softer shapes of two figures at a table. For a terrible moment I feared that the pylon would be as it was in its heyday and the heather would be worn to a track by countless feet and the figures at the table would be those of Luke and Rene. But no, I saw my own surprised face and Father Beausang with his head towards the bay and the bay itself coloured in a glorious blue, more heightened, if anything, than the blue outside.

I ordered two more teas. Outside Father Beausang was still asleep. I would have liked to ask her who had revitalised the lift when she came up with the teas. But she was still wearing her air of youthful annoyance so I asked her instead why she took the picture. Because you, she answered, are my first customers. She gathered up the old cups and set down two new ones with a fresh pot of tea. Father Beausang woke with the disturbance. He turned his head away from the water, towards me. It's getting cooler, he said, and it was.

His eyes were fully open and looking towards the yellow chairs. They only moved, I surmised, when there was a passenger.

'So I have seen her. The whole promenade must have seen her, in one way or another. Certainly my superior, a parish priest named Cartan had heard and seen enough of her to be worried. If she were Catholic and modelled each weekend for a Protestant painter, you see, something would have to be done. I had to inquire then, discreetly, into her background. And discretion suited me especially since, as you know, I couldn't visit the house any longer. It was not only a point of delicacy with me, it was my recognition that something had ended. My function in that house had been replaced by hers. Or to put it another way, the cup that I had half-filled, flowed right over with her. If I met James on the promenade or behind a bathing shelter we would continue our discussions for the length of stroll, but meeting like that was never satisfactory. The room within bay windows was missing, you see, and the figure of Luke with his tray of sandwiches and tea, which incidentally – '

He drained his cup

' – was far, far better than this. And you can't talk mathematics walking down a promenade, surrounded by Scots. I wasn't jealous or resentful of her but I was intensely curious. I felt an odd affinity with her too. She was to take up my guardianship, after all, and I could sense from James on the promenade this air of blossoming after all those years. No matter how far our discussions had ranged, you see, their original purpose had never been quite forgotten. He was still "talking instruction", I was still waiting for the staff to blossom. And there he was, blossoming after all those years.'

244

The smell of dried flowers that comes from your prints, after, as he says, all those years. How can the photographer himself blossom? He was rarely on the prom, a little like Luke in his preference for indoors. Summer smells too aren't often redolent of flowers. From where we sat I could smell the prom below us, the burnt metal of the amusement parlours and the wet sand in particular. But what the curate saw must have been like James Vance blossoming. He is forty-seven and it's the summer of nineteen thirty-three. Your angular walk along the prom and the hesitant stoop that Lili described in you. Pliant now, and perhaps that *is* the word for it. Two miles away is the hill with eucalypti, still divesting themselves of their stripes of bark. And they don't blossom either, they drop off cones, nowhere near as elegant as their stripes of bark. You could only photograph others in flower and never flower yourself.

'I would be lying if I said I wasn't faintly jealous. But then jealousy is the most loving of all emotions.'

He turned to me and smiled.

'Next to love, that is. But while one can be jealous of what one doesn't know, one can't really love whom one doesn't know. So my most overriding emotion was – '

He smiled again

' – what I would say is yours – curiosity. And curiosity about her, happily enough, had become part of my pastoral duty. So I set about finding out about her.'

The girl had brought more tea. She replaced the pot this time, but not the cups. Are these the original tables, I wanted to ask her, of the original Eagle's Nest? But she still wore that look of youthful annoyance so I desisted. A chill was coming in now, from the sea. Father Beausang poured for both of us. Those tickets were good value, he said, with the emphasis on the 'were'. I realised then that he had not realised he'd been asleep.

245

'The one pastoral duty I've ever enjoyed. And one of the many I've failed at. I found out a lot. I went to Dublin, interviewed a young aspiring actress called – '

'Lili,' I said.

'Yes, Lili. I found out that our Rene was Catholic. I found out that if the old man painted her it was at odd moments and never unclothed. When I found out who her father was my pastoral duty stopped, since the children of the blessed are above suspicion, so to speak. But of the whole story I could only get a glimpse. Months later I heard the real fact – that she was pregnant – '

The sun had touched the Head and the light was coming down in movable fingers of infinite length, since they caressed the bay as much as they caressed us. We sat watching the shifting glory. I glanced behind me and saw the serving-girl, standing behind us. She was as awed as we were, with no camera. All three of us watched, Father Beausang with his face towards the bay. I felt the time had come. Your boss, I whispered to her. Who is he? And sure enough she smiled, her face towards the bay, and whispered a name.

SIX

THE PROVINCES, 1934

36

AND SO SHE was pregnant and waiting in Dublin to tour the country. There would be three of them soon, father, son and Rene, awaiting the arrival of the child, the father of whom no one has been able, or willing to name. And time becomes stilled for them while she grows, yet all they discover is one of its more secret rhythms. They are mastered by a unit as basic as a day, a month, a year, but of which they are only now made conscious. It must have seemed marvellously arbitrary to them, nine months, two hundred and seventy days. They think of the pregnancies of elephants and whales, butterflies and moths and feel that in an odd way they have annihilated time. They fall instead into an element of the same fluidity and texture as that expanse of water they have seen for years beyond Bray Head, that the yellow chairs have bobbed over, that Rene has watched from Trimelston Road, that other sea in which the world will immerse itself, basking like a glistening dolphin. And Rene of course holds the secret of that time. She expands on the grace of her first three photos, moves to a point for which perspectives are useless.

But before there were three of them, there would be two. There would be Luke and Rene, moving in a narrowing circle, changing town and parish hall every second or third night. For a while she takes the boys' parts, but after the first three weeks when her condition becomes obvious, an improbable boy, MacAllister, with infinite grace and tact, promotes her to female parts proper and even gives her a rise. So now she can wear dresses with bodices in place of the adolescent's doublet and hose. The female wardrobe of costumes is limited to four, which must serve for all parts from Kathleen to Cleopatra. And all sense of period is totally ignored, be it Roman, Celtic, Elizabethan or Edwardian. The past is simply the past, counterpoised with the present. And for the present there is no wardrobe whatsoever, the cast swop their working clothes as the parts demand. Sad, MacAllister would whisper with his inimitable smile. But these are the provinces, dears. And these four past costumes are of four distinct types as if woman herself, whom they feigned to represent, can be categorised in four. There is Queenly Beauty, Aged Refinement, Nurse/ Nun/ Midwife, and Youthful Innocence. Rene, through her tour, uses versions of all four, changing character and lines as her figure dictates. Lucky, as MacAllister whispers, these are the provinces.

There will be no photographs, since James doesn't reach them until near the end, and Luke's flight destroys his faith for ever in the perceivable object. And is that significant as well, I wonder, as he loses his urge at last to grasp at years, to stick his moments into albums and annotate each one. Does he too feel the annihilation of time, staring from the green felt table out of the bay window, picturing both loved ones just through disappointment and desire? Nothing will revive his faith in photographs and when his faith itself revives, it will be with a strength that needs no photographs. His camera dies, and there is only the spoken word to replace it, and memory, and imagination. And all three are frighteningly elastic, handing us as a gift that freedom that annihilates more than time, the contours of our subjects themselves.

So Luke braves the Bray train alone. He walks behind the hotels, clinging to the walls of the terraced houses, treading like water the spaces of the wide streets, past the Turkish baths and the bowling green and into the station itself. I descended the Head with Father Beausang and back down the long promenade to where the station made a wooden roof above the tracks, curved, to enclose the sea in its frame. As Luke waits the rain comes and each pointed eave contains its drop. When our train came I helped Father Beausang up the step, through the door and into the carriage of plastic seats. We moved out of Bray then and towards Shankhill, through the houses, through the green to where blue expanse was on our right and the eucalyptus slopes were on our left. I thought of Luke on the wooden seat with his neck against the shoulder of felt. The rain comes and hammers the blue into the colour of tin. The scene moves past his moving window, a succession of granite platforms leading to the largest one of all, and there he rises and walks slowly to the door and through the clouds of reassuring steam into that corridor of glass. The steam billows and fades as the train pulls towards Amiens Street and Luke negotiates the platform and the slight incline of Westland Row down to the backstage of the Ancient Concert Rooms in Rutland Street.

37

FATHER BEAUSANG SLEPT through Westland Row despite my efforts to wake him. So we got off at Amiens Street, stood together on the moving stairs and had to walk towards Lili's modest residence along the canal. The giant pots on O'Connell Bridge seemed burdened with their flowers, hanging limp in the heat like the flags that hung from each new building. He refused my offer of a taxi.

Imagined James's camera swinging forlorn from the hatstand. It seems out of place there, squat, so contained in its leather case. All the coats that have hung there for years, their folds seem to stiffen as they hang, enclosing in a kind of stillness the fluted trunk of the stand. But the camera swings when he places it there, to and fro, glancing off the surface with each return. So he listens to the stand rocking faintly and looks at the unfinished mural his father left, the Connemara landscape forming a window, a gateway into this odd expanse of hills that his father imagined to be Greece; the woman's face pinioned between both as if he could never decide quite what background she needed. He can see now that it isn't quite her, the neck is too Grecian, the cheekbones are too flushed and Irish, she has been only caught in that fringe of blonde. James leaves the hall and goes into the living-room and the camera still swings from the hatstand. He pulls out the drawer in the cabinet and takes out a sheaf of papers, deeds of inheritance, mortgages, old litigations, the whole penumbra of unfinished business left untouched now for three generations. He leafs through signatures of gentlemen and Papists, Bray burghers, certificates of birth, marriage and death until he comes to a small compact pile of invoices and inventories of stock all filled in in the fine nib and hand of a long-forgotten clerkship. The stock of the forgotten pottery he finds was numbered at seventeen hundred units, 'unit' being specified as a set complete with cups, saucers, side plates and serving bowls. Their value he finds assessed in pounds, in single numbers, the total stock having been rendered almost worthless by the influx of machine-made delft from the English midlands. The whorls and curlicues of the unknown clerk's hand remind him of the fine blue lines on the delft itself, that solid grace and attention to detail that seem to him to have walked across water to here from an unknown country. He should take the train now and get off at Killiney and stand on the moulting hill again among the stripes of eucalyptus, inhaling again that scent of resin and tomcats, the wet dust of the bay. But he doesn't, it's not yet time for him to take the train. He goes upstairs and urinates in the bowl, surrounded by the odour of fathers, of the slow drip across the years, of inheritance, colouring and temper, from father to son and father to son.

We walked from O'Connell Bridge to College Green and Clarendon Street. As we passed the brash, coloured pietà in the courtyard of the church, I stopped him and pointed at her curved plaster mouth. If the Father, I asked him, fathered His own Son and yet the Son was the Father, does that mean the Son fathered Himself? Something like annoyance crossed his face, and then a hint of a smile. I apologised for my lack of acquaintance with what I remembered he had called that exquisite system of triadic ambiguity, and tried to rephrase it. In other words, I asked, if the Son fathered Himself, did He by that very act create His own Father? He smiled fully then and pulled me on. You are leaving out, he whispered, the third corner of that exquisite triangle: the Holy Spirit.

Luke finds the front-of-house doors barred and makes his

way along the side. From somewhere he can hear brass music. He walks with his hand against the russet brick that leads him to the stage entrance. The door is open and he hears voices coming from the inside gloom. He gets the odour then and I can shiver at the precise feel of that rust crumbling dryly at the touch of her fingers and the roses as she leant close and smelt them as their bowls blew soundlessly over the leather. But it is the dust Luke smells, of an unused stage. He runs his hand along the metal bar, walking inside.

We reached Lili's house and shook hands and I watched him walk across the bridge, over the grey ribbon of canal. He seemed fatigued all of a sudden. I had promised to call him when all the questions were finished, when I came back from Clare, but looking at his slow, dark walk I realised how little promises mean to the old. He didn't turn or wave, so I rang the bell and listened for Lili's difficulty in coming down the stairs.

38

'CAN YOU IMAGINE,' said Lili, quite unnecessarily, rocking softly once more in her cane chair, 'the impact of that extraordinary boy on that group of Thespians? You know what Rene meant to them, but can you imagine how the effeminate hams fawned over him, delighted in him, loved him even? The boy was their dream, they would have had him as Ophelia in a white dress strung with real watercress and lilies. But then he'd never, no matter what the inducement, go beyond carrying sets. Besides which he would have been a terrible actor. He hung around walls even more than his father did, which might be why it suited him. He'd stand behind flats, walls within walls, and watch the open stage from there. But can you imagine that gaggle of cynical, poverty-stricken actors, dedicated to nothing but the next night, willing to sell their grandmothers for the dual ends of simple survival and the practice of what they called their "art" – can you imagine them roused to all the possibilities of innocence by a love affair between their A.S.M. and their second lady? It was a conspiracy, you see, enacted on the Free State, on that society we played to. We moved through those towns, the names of which I can hardly remember, like early Christians carrying the message. But the message was sent out in an elaborate code. After the first few shows it came out that she was pregnant. Now that's a message we couldn't have spelt out. But can you imagine the pleasure in conveying it while disguising it? The happy falsity, the artifice? We did botched-up versions of the comedies, *Measure for Measure*, *As You Like It*, we did all the old staples, *The Colleen Bawn*, *The Workhouse Ward*, *The Rising of the*

Moon, The Countess Cathleen. But no matter what story each of them told, the same story always told itself through them. Which was love, I suppose. And I can never think of that word outside a story.'

Luke, you see, has found his home. The man with the flowing mane of hair and the velvet jacket and the cigarette forever in its holder who meets him just inside the stage door reminds him of his grandfather. He withdraws his hand quickly on the handshake and orders him briskly to come inside. And Luke walks into the gloom and feels instantly, unmistakably, in the home of his emotions verified. That cluttered world of dust, spiralling from the bare yellow light bulb, all his movements constricted by the canvas flats. He finds truth in the falsity he finds there. The number of flats is limited, he notices, a few bare, timeless scenes having to serve any number of purposes. There is a living-room wall with an ornate window, and through the window a vista of beach and sea. This serves, he is told, for worlds as varied as the drawing-rooms of Sheridan to, at a push (and it is a push, MacAllister smiles), the court of the Duke of Mantua. There is a garden of course, vague enough to belong to any period, defined only by a stretch of green, a border of flowers and an arch of trellis tumbling with roses. And there is a cluster of white Doric pillars against a background of blue which must be by turn ecclesiastical, courtly, or plain Athenian.

A man in a check jacket whose name must be Brogan emerges from the gloom and Luke watches him stabilise flats, sees how to intimate an infinity of spaces from a handful of canvas rectangles and some square yards of stage. The dust is drifting from the footlights to the hanging lights and Luke stands in the cones of dust and sees Brogan carry that deeply satisfying vista of beach and sea and drawing-room window from stage left to stage right.

'It was simply a tour, like any other. I remember the trains, towns flitting past the windows. We played all the parish halls and stayed one night in each – Clones, Birr, Ballina – what do I know about names? All I know was MacAllister's grand plan which hadn't changed for donkeys' years and which was to push through the midlands, do all the seaside towns in summer and do September in Lisdoon. But don't ask me for details. I remember successions of small hills. Small crowds. Until we came to Knock. Then we all noticed.'

39

I AM LOST in the midlands but I found Knock to be a small
stretch of houses, miles from the main line, awaiting the
centenary of an apparition of the Virgin there in 1879. I
walked through it at night and found it lit by those flashing
coloured bulbs that more humble townlands reserve for the
apparition of a fun fair. Wooden stalls formed a wedge down
the centre, a positive danger to those motorists who sped
through it towards Mayo. She was there in every conceivable
pose, rows of her upon the stalls, lit now by bulbs from the
inside, now by luminous paint, in metal, in plastic and all
kinds of alloy. They ranged from the very cheap to the moderately expensive, and I chose one of the expensive ones. She
was blue and glowed from the inside and was standing on a
pedestal. Walking through the stalls I found it easy to convince myself that each one celebrated quite a different
visitation – the one of Rene, Luke and Emerald Theatrical
Productions Ltd, all of whom stopped, I surmised, at the
small wooden hall wedged behind the giant grey church
which stood some yards from where the row of stalls ended.
It would be appropriate, I thought, that every stall and every
statue sold remembered an event that the visitors and the
stallowners had quite forgotten. I knew that the urge to visit
shrines is deeper and more crass than memory. And there
was an empty touring bus by the church and it pleased me
to think of those busloads celebrating an event of which they
knew absolutely nothing, though it pained me to think that
the trains had stopped and that somewhere outside the town
was a disused pale granite station, beside a canal perhaps.
All this though my statue didn't resemble her at all. And sure

enough, when I had reached the end of the coloured lights and the street had become a country road, I came upon parallel ruts in the road through which tracks must have run. And I looked through the hedge and saw the tracks running eastwards, rusted of course, with the small pale granite station dripping under trees and beside it the canal.

Luke carries the flat with the Grecian pillars from the train on to the platform and through the dripping trees. His cheek touches the canvas. And the feel of the paint reassures him as he walks through the pines with their eternal drip. He walks from sleeper to sleeper until he reaches the road and then carries his pillars down into the church, the small wooden hall. I see him walking back then through the pines to where they all stand on the fawn platform, jaded, laughing gently. Brogan hands him flat after flat from the train, which is gently steaming. The others strut on the platform, watching the moon through the pines.

There's a notice on the lamp post which flaps, a little like a flag. Rene is to play Rosalind. Those dusty halls have bare wooden stages and the chairs are sometimes cinema chairs, joined with one long iron band against each felt back. When I ran my finger along the felt chair-backs small puffs of dust rose endlessly. The dust is a problem. It rises from the wooden stage, catches all the light. The stage itself echoes with each footstep and so Rene walks slowly on it, each movement plumbed with stillness. Most of the bulbs are burned out and so the stage is lit in pools with vacuums in between. MacAllister paces the back rows conceiving his version of the miracle through which the Duke will be exiled to a manifest Forest of Arden and the wrestling match will be a wrestling match. He is smoking and squinting and striking the felt seat impatiently when Rene walks into the inadequate lights and begins her lines. He sees her walking from the gloom to the light and notices the odd retraction of her movement. Then he sees her blonde hair and flushed cheeks in the moving eddies of dust under the lights and the dust seems to carve out a space for her, anticipating each movement, leaving a faint glow behind. MacAllister, sitting in the dark among the felt seats, realises with a sudden shock that it is the glow of her pregnancy. The lights above grip her, form a cone around her of gently wheeling dust as if they could lift her upwards but she stays on the bare boards, full and three-dimensional against the sagging curtains and the painted flats. There is a heightened flush to each of her words and every gesture she makes is somehow round, flows and yet has the glow and presence of someone standing still.

'The centre of the stage was wherever she was, just that, your eyes were drawn towards her and when she moved all the lines were made redundant. Now she wasn't an actress in the normal sense of the word, in any sense even. She had inherited all her mother's faults, but where Una had the unhappy knack of turning every part into a public speech, Rene had the gift of turning each into simply herself. She had come to it by accident and stayed with it by accident. And now this self of a sudden spilled and flowed, is the only word for it, out further than the stage and those perpetually faulty lights. A happy occurrence, you might think. But what terrified us was that every line and move of hers had nothing to do with the story in question. She was telling a different, quite simple story. Every part of her said simply: I am pregnant.

'Of course we all thought of the obvious: headlines in the provincial papers, sermons from the pulpit and theatrical riots. So when the hall was half-full as usual and there was the usual half-bored, half-ritual air of a fairground or a charity concert, we were all lit by a kind of terror backstage. What she seemed to reveal every time she moved into the footlights we were determined to conceal. And what emerged, happily, was nothing to do with our fears. From the word go that stage was heightened. The facts we knew meant nothing to the two hundred odd subscribers down there. But what the facts led to did. They didn't see her pregnant, they saw her simply resplendent. And they saw every other performance stretched to a pitch to conceal the secret. Since they couldn't glean the secret, all they could glean was the pitch, the richness. What they couldn't read of the real story made the apparent story all the more enthralling. And so when the curtain went down, if our sigh of relief was audible, the applause from the wooden hall was more than adequate to drown it.'

40

I PUT THE statue on the mantle and felt the warmth coming from it. I asked Lili what the next town was. She demurred. I saw the pines again, dark green against the moon, dripping on to the pale granite platform, the tracks wet and silver, running towards another town.

'Say it was Boyle. And if it was Boyle I've no picture of it anyway. Except maybe for a market. Yes, say there was a market and a main street with a chemist's shop and the train-station was red-bricked, if you say so. But I can see a school hall, yes a hall that was used as a church once, the real church burnt down in the Troubles. Or was it just the high windows darkened with brown paper that reminded me of churches?'

They come to Boyle, maybe, where the hands of the dealers slap the bullocks' thighs and are spat on and shaken. There is Luke and the company walking through a square with streets running from all four corners. They get dispersed of course in the mêlée of cattle, so many packed between the shop fronts that there can be no sense of an open passage. They lean to each other over the rumps of cattle and shout, unsure of which corner of the square to go towards. The ground is churned into ankle-deep mud and MacAllister is pretending impatience, his blue suit smudged by the flicking bullocks' tails and his grey hair blowing. But they are all laughing, stretching over hides and laughing, touching hands when they can and falling back when the motion of a bullock shifts them, laughing in the mud. This way, boy, MacAllister whispers to Luke, to whom the pressure of the hide is even healthier than the shoulders of priests. Luke follows him, carrying his flats towards the rectangular front of the Roscommon Arms Hotel.

'It would have been unthinkable, any other year, that he'd change his plans. But now it was unthinkable that he wouldn't.'

In the lounge of that hotel which would have had a twelve-pound salmon, dried ochre scales gleaming with resin, its mouth permanently open behind the glass, he has his maps open and Luke is somewhere near as tall as him and with the same lank hair, and between them there is even a slight familiar air. If Boyle takes two days, Mountcharles will have to be skipped, but then there is Ballina, which might even take three. And the pattern of towns and halls, memories of good nights and bad, dates on which they'll be full and empty and the logic with which he's bound them together over years slowly falls asunder and he can see, just barely, the dim outlines of the pattern that's to replace them. They must reach the sea, he knows, by mid-July and trace a thread of towns down the coast towards Clare. He plans in advance for this new element and then, looking towards Luke, who is gazing at the open salmon's mouth in the glass case, he senses that no matter how he plans, a pattern of which he can gauge perhaps nothing will establish itself. And that night in the hall, pacing, as Lili says, behind the end seats he hears Rene's lines, Well, I will forget the condition of my estate to rejoice in yours, and it strikes him that no matter how he times it, days, nights, weeks and months, there is a logic there that will draw them all from town to town at its own pace, a pace he knows nothing about and can only wait to discover. She is standing in the dark pool between the foot-lights and yet can be seen clearly with that roundness of gesture that nobody could photograph. Luke, standing behind his canvas trees, can see her clearly, the whole hall can see her, against all the laws of theatrical lighting and effect.

'And it could well have been Boyle because now that I think of it, the first of the write-ups we got was in the *Roscommon Herald*. Now that is a fact, though please don't expect a yellowing cut-out, I never was one for keeping things. But I remember that one because it was the first of the write-ups, and write-ups for those summer tours of ours were more or less unheard of. Part-time journalists for those provincial papers used to writing up silage, sprout seasons and the county hunt began to shove small columns in the pages they normally reserved for litigations, commenting on the fact that instead of one night we stayed for three, that the audiences spilled outside the stage doors, things like that. Captions like "Resplendent Rosalind", "MacAllister Breaks Through", that kind of thing. Later, Dublin critics came to write us up but that was when Rene was bigger and we had touched the edge of Clare. The first was in the *Roscommon Herald* and said that Rene's Rosalind would make Shakespeare enjoyable even to those whose reading had never gone beyond a train timetable.'

264

Chapter 41

THEY PUSH TOWARDS the sea in half-circles. The texture of the platforms changes as they circle nearer of course, and the neat flower beds of the midlands stations give way to blackthorns, all bending eastwards with the prevailing winds. Stations in the small resorts on the western seaboard, so poignant to imagine, don't, regrettably, exist. To get to Strand Hill, for instance, which Lili mentions as their first holiday venue, you have to get off near Ballisodare and the grey blocks there, I imagine, must be weeping with the salt and water in the winds and though there would be alder as well as blackthorn and the blackthorns themselves would be relatively upright there must have been a hint, perhaps just in the emptiness of the station itself and the tracks running through the scrublands, waiting for trains, of the texture of coast itself. Luke holds his flat against the wind and is pulled by it down to where the platform ends, almost on to the tracks themselves. So he has to point his canvas drawing-room straight at the wind to walk forward at all.

He hugs it with him to the two hired cars that are waiting. The drivers both wear caps and the company are standing around the doors, hugging their clothes against the wind. The wind beyond the granite walls pulls the flat again and Luke flies for a minute, the drawing-room in the air above him. He feels stretched like a bird, in one clean line, and bounces in a series of airborne steps to the company, the capped drivers and the cars.

These black Fords took over after the farthest stations ended.

265

It is the first road Luke has driven with them, from Ballisodare to the coast, and the fabric of the interior seems to come apart before his eyes, through the car window, as if the strands which held the pines and the blackthorn and the broken hills are being pulled out leaving simply fields, smooth and rolling towards the largest sea. The drivers would have known the company over a succession of years, both of them squinting through the rearview mirror, their curiosity hidden by their caps. They recognise old faces and examine new ones and have to swerve continually since their obsession with their rearview mirrors threatens to leave them in the ditch. And they come to the line of the sea then that is broken by what seems to be, just where it meets the sand, this continual surge of white, the effect of the wind on that body of water that seems to Luke to form one long wave that he imagines must surge north and south, spanning the coastline, from this small patch of cement and sand where the cars finally pull to a halt.

'And the only reason I remember Strand Hill is because of the two drivers who were brothers who took us from the train to the hotel. They seemed to wear the same cap and to be always holding it with the same hand against the wind. You see, there was always wind there, it must have been on a kind of headland, because there was more wind there than on any of those western towns that I remember, but then maybe I only remember the wind because of the two brothers and their caps. There was more wind than rain but the wind was the kind that even on the finest days seemed to saturate the air with spray. And this could be quite a relief on a hot day and on a wet day you blamed the rain anyway, not the poor innocent sea, but the effect it did have was to make the walls of all the buildings damp. Weeping granite, somebody called it, which quite catches the reality – these grey hotel fronts with large patches of damp facing the sea. And the patches of damp were, if you will allow me the simile, a little like the smears a child who has been crying draws with his palm on each cheek. There weren't many of those hotels, three or four of them, and houses scattering away from them in no apparent order. Not a conducive place, you might say, for holidays, but isn't that the mystery, how people crowd in groups into the most unlikely places, just because of the habits of people before them? And it wasn't very large either, it would sustain one night at a stretch and even at that MacAllister would be huffing in the bars about just breaking even, about the venue being an act of duty, altruism, his cultural gift to southern Sligo rather than a commercial proposition. But even there we made history in our own small way because if the town could at the most sustain one performance we managed the quite extraordinary feat of playing twice on successive nights to what must have been to a man the same audience. By then, you see, Rene was far enough gone to have outgrown the first of our costumes, the one that was always used for the young, innocent parts, the Ophelias and Columbines. Most of her Rosalind was played in what you would now call drag – you do know the play – and for that she wore breeches and a smock that would have done for anything from The Saughran to Robin Hood. It was bulky, you see, hanging loose. But the scenes where she was Rosalind, the beginning and the end ones, she had outgrown the first dress and nobody had yet thought of the possibility of her changing into the more bulky, flowing, generally bald velvet or satin things that were pulled out for any part remotely middle-aged or regal. Our Gertrude dress, in a word. It seemed starkly obvious to us of course, her in that piece of cloth that was more like a nightdress than a theatrical costume. Her figure was adaptable though, and her movement seemed to melt her condition into herself, and needless to say knowledge of the fact of pregnancy leads one to see it in every gesture, but minus that knowledge one merely sees plumpness, roundness, or in her case, grace. But we had yet to be reassured by Rene in a larger dress and the pressure of her flesh on stage seemed to be caught everywhere in the lights, there was a desirability about her shape in that dress that was erotic, and so the fear and tension, the sense of urgency and secrecy, seemed to be rising on the stage like water. Or was it, I wonder, just her presence? She seemed to

267

radiate desire and the pressure of eyes on her seemed to form a glow which made more people look in turn. But for me, I saw it as fear, fear simply of discovery, and the electricity of our combined emotions seemed to pull the play towards its end in one huge, erotic gasp. And again at the end we almost laughed with relief when the curtains went down and we heard, after a space, the sound of the clapping of hands.

'But that had been the pattern since Knock. The reason Strand Hill was so memorable, and I can see it now, is the small man with the neat white beard sitting on the veranda of the Strand Hotel. He came on the second day, was instantly recognised and instantly avoided. He was, you see, the drama critic of the *Irish Times*. His and our embarrassment were naturally extreme, since he was on what he hoped would be a quiet holiday and was obviously on quite friendly terms there with a Roscommon widow with whom he wouldn't be seen dead in Dublin. So company and critic passed one another in lounge and foyer and smiled gently as they did so as if to pretend the second-rate surroundings didn't exist, or if they did, only for the benefit and use of the other. But he must have attended on the second night because several days later we got some column-inch in the *Irish Times*. He mentioned Rene by name and what is worse traced her mother's acting history. The gist of it was, you see, that the west was somehow awake, that the dramatic genius of the first decade of the century was springing up a decade later, in the most unlikely of places – '

The dunes are reputed to be unusually high, almost curling round the nearest hotel to them, and when the drivers have unloaded their cars and Luke and Brogan have carried the properties inside they must all walk down by the dunes, past the dunes and find that their bulk has been obscuring a long sweep of beach. Despite the wind and spray there is something compelling about a long stretch of beach, like the suck and draw of the tide that hits its left side, and so they are drawn naturally into the wide sweep of empty sand, almost as if they want to inhabit it, to mar its emptiness with their figures. And the hallucinatory pull of empty sand increases if anything with penetration of the beach, since there is always another stretch to be walked across, quite virgin, with only the ridges where the sand has gathered, driven by the wind. The brothers, standing hands on caps by the open doors of their cars, can see them set out as quite a homogeneous group and as they walk down farther, scatter gradually, like pebbles thrown across the white expanse by a hand, seen in slow motion. Rene is somewhere in the centre of that group, becoming a thin, almost single thread, only recognisable by the evenness of her walk. And the crash and boom of the tide on the wet sand that coats the air with its moisture. This is their first beach of that tour of course, and the reason for their tour of course is summer and beaches and so there they must feel that they have truly begun. That the other beginnings were rehearsals for this one. The more experienced ones of course, and Lili your experience with them then was three years old, would know while they would lose sight of that sea repeatedly through the rest of that summer, that sea would be their only plumb-line. It would be to them the way it is to a car, along a rocky coastline, where it disappears out of sight, is forgotten for long stretches and is welcomed on reappearance, like an old friend or an ultimate purpose. And they will leave it for nights, weekends, even half-weeks, when the line runs more conveniently through an inland town like Ballina. But there's a perpetual return when each line reaches its end and there is the last small station, the structure of which changes continually, and the colour of the platform and indeed the nature of the platform's adornment, and on leaving the station, there are the two hired cars to be taken to the view of beach and sand and sea once more. And the older hands will take a knowing pleasure of course in recognising the drivers, in greeting them with the quiet familiarity and lack of ostentation that characterises such recurrent relationships. And all the drivers will wear hats since it was, apparently, what characterised the hired car then, in the absence of a sign, from the car owned privately. And the hats will perhaps remind Rene of the much too large and angular hat worn by that youth who waited so patiently on the Bray prom until her father told him, 'Home, Jack'. Though that first hat was military, but perhaps, like all first memories, the definition given to that hat was just like the definition given to first memories and she won't have noticed such a difference after all.

Lili, though, doesn't admit or recognise the importance of beaches, but looking at her in those breaks between her talking, I can see the memory of that series of beaches written on her face, on the threads of tiny veins across her cheeks, for all the world like the criss-cross of currents on an expanse of water seen from above and on the still fine, though parched and paper-like skin on her hands, like those dried husks of cod's roe one finds way beyond, generally, the sea's edge, transparent, that scrape gently when you touch them and that are of course covered with a fine sheen of sand, for all the world like the down of hair. Her bones now seem as delicate as those of a gull's skull, bleached, of course, and washed quite clean and when she opens her eyes to talk again they are bright, piercing and enthrallingly blue.

42

THE WALK FROM the Bray station to the Main Street passes a bowling green, a sunken lawn below sea level. It is flooded today as James passes and the black curves of three bowls can be seen, aqueous and silent. The wind which whips the bay behind him leaves that water unruffled. They greet each other at the presbytery door, both exhausted by the other's absence. James moves into the curate's parlour with relief and the décor of the small living-room brings back his ponderous, dark gestures that were once framed on Tuesdays by his own bay window. The arguments begin at once of course, although instead of Luke there is an aged greying lady in a green apron, strangely male in her angular movements, to bring in the tray with tea. James eats the tomato sandwiches and notes with affection how the flesh around Father Beausang's collar has thickened. The excitement at their renewal of acquaintance, moderate at first, fills the room, then drifts and seems about to escape them, just to return, stronger than ever. Father Beausang's eyes light with enthusiasm as he elaborates a conceit of his own, a numeral system based on trinities. James's amazement is tempered by the curate's smile, coloured once again with his old, wayward humour. No, not on the Trinity itself, he murmurs, but on a triadic base, which gives quite different, exciting results than that of your binary code. Would a society, Father Beausang muses, whose mathematics were built on a triadic code, have radically different social characteristics? Two, after all, is an oddly unsatisfying concept. With two one has the dialogue, the linear, but with three one has the conspiracy of space. And thus the triangle, perhaps even more than the circle, is the symbol of harmony;

of definition within unity rather than just unity itself. Of course such a triangle can admit of no intrusion. A new element added and it becomes a square, another and it becomes a pentagon –

Father Beausang stops and sees the world as a garden ravaged by intellect. James is staring into his cup. Father Beausang shifts forward and dust ruffles from his cassock, which blurs and haloes James's face. I kept this for you, Father Beausang whispers, I thought you would want to know. He extracts the faded cutting from the *Irish Times*. James takes the square of paper from his soft fingers, which seem reluctant to withdraw. Emerald at Strand Hill, he reads. MacAllister's Western Wonder.

They walk together past the bowling green and the submerged bowls and part at the station. The curate grips his elbow as the train draws in.

'You know I never liked him. But perhaps that was jealousy. Or the impatience that uncertain people always rise in me. But then I loved Luke. They were so alike. Did I love him too? She did. And she loved me. When he came to that hotel in Gort and Luke saw him through the glass and ran to him, I hated him. I thought it was over. But I was wrong there too. I know that three of them were necessary. Now I know that. You ask me who was the father. I say both of them were. He had been following us, you see, from sometime back in Sligo. Some place, I mean,' she thought for a moment. 'And he found us in Gort. Or was it in Lisdoon?'

As the train pulls him with an ease that must have been like a long silk ribbon, since he is not conscious of stops, station changes or of the evolutions of landscape through the window, he remembers those bowls sitting on the grass, the slight upper curve above the quiet surface and the sphere below distended and enlarged by the water that held them in its pool of green. He realises that bowls seem always at rest, even when thrown, but he has never seen bowls so much at rest as these, the spaces across which they normally spin occupied by water. And the water touching each eliminated distance, and the need for movement. He reaches Ballisodare about midday and books one of the capped drivers to take him to Strand Hill. The other driver follows close, capped and curious, since James is the only passenger.

The car wheels into the square of cement and comes to rest between the sea and hotels. They have left Strand Hill, of course. His conversation with the cloth-capped driver has told him as much. James pays and walks across the square to the hotel that looms towards the sea and weeps its granite. The few posters in the lobby tell him the same. He has forgotten the date, but no matter, those posters hang limply from their corkboard with the sense of an event that has passed. To where? he wonders. Another town, but which? He sees her round, childlike signature in the guestbook and books that room. It is a single room, he finds, with a bare, narrow bed. His eyes crinkle in disappointment or affection, imagining Luke's bed three rooms down from it. He sits on the bed and the boom of the sea comes through the window like something solid and he regrets for a moment the camera he has left swinging in Sydenham Villas. The grey light of those western seabords that seems more an echo, a reflection of light than light itself, that vanquishes the space between each stone, each hill, quickens his senses with the urge to capture it once more, to photograph. But instead he sits there with, I imagine, a growing sense of relief, drawing his eyes as near to the window as possible, and all the scenes he has taken come back with the precision of memory alone. They return fast as if pulled by the ribbon of those years, each replaced by another, the moving picture of their souls. He sees Luke age from puppy fat to sinew, he sees her move in three large leaps to womanhood and it seems to him that the only sprocket moving them is love. Their surfaces, as he views them, change and shift and never settle, but it is light, he knows now, only light that allows him to view them and the light is that of love. And the light that alone brings the booming sea outside to him floods through the glass, filling the room with its weakened cobalt, a presence itself.

'Yes, it was Gort, Gort. We were in the lounge and he saw us through the glass, coming in. He must have travelled down the coast from Sligo. Difficult, I'd say, since the tour was out of rhythm. He must have gone to each town and asked. Then searched around for the next one. And asked again.'

He reads the provincial papers but finds no ads anticipating her, only reports in retrospect, after she has passed through. He walks out on to the cement square. He sees the long stretch of sand, virgin once more, and feels their presence somewhere down that coastline. The air is wet with spray, the clouds are full again and his quest is somehow fixed, that fullness drawing him on. He knows their absence is illusory. He asks the driver to take him to the train.

'The more she grew, of course, the better he could find us. The fuss got bigger as she did, the crowds kept coming, larger each time. And the reviews. That article compounded it. The *Times* couldn't outdo the *Independent* or *Press*, I mean, and we soon had the problem of meeting all sorts of critics in the oddest places. The newspaper style then was the crushed cap and notepad and the chewed stub of pencil. You'd see them lounging in the back rows of those crowded halls, chewing and writing, chewing and writing. What was happening on the stage had almost ceased to be important. We changed the play, and they hardly noticed – '

In Ballina there is no beach, just the inlet of Killalla pointing towards the heart of the town. He finds a poster, flapping on a lamp post. He walks towards the hall in which the Emerald

Theatre Company played. The bowls move towards each other and click. The front-of-house doors are arrayed with posters sagging from their pins. He pushes the bar and walks through the door, as hesitant as ever. It is a parish hall, with frames of de Valera and the Virgin on the left-hand wall. There are rows of seats screwed to the floor which give the hall some air of theatrical purpose. The open door throws light towards the stage and a breeze must be soughing through for the dust rises from the bare boards and wheels in circles and cones.

'Summer had come. The heat grew and there was a stretch in the days. Rene's Rosalind grew with the heat. We used the white gown for her with oceans of room. We had to thread it with green. The heat in the halls was cloying, but we bore it. We weaved onwards, swelling as we went. MacAllister lost more of his hair – '

He knows they must travel by rail and that being the summer they would favour resorts. He draws a rough itinerary of the seaboard towns nearest the rail lines. He will look for signs, he thinks, that will point the way forwards. These signs will be waiting for him, to be teased out from the façades of towns, the surfaces of streets. In one square there is a Civil War statue with a stone cap staring beyond the roofs of houses. In another lies a cement road crumbling into beach and burrows. Modes of transport, he knows, can tell him a lot, the texture of each station his train pulls into and the car or buggy that draws him when his train fails. Hotels can tell him more, the shapes of window, bed and wash hand-basin, the odour of boiled cabbage lingering in the hallways. There is no hurry, he knows, for once his journey is measured in minutes no longer but in a unit of time that has its own momentum, has no need for numbers. He senses that his looking for them is as vital as his finding. He swims at each beach he comes to and is hesitant entering each stage door. He questions young girls in hotel porches about everything but her and finds himself led back to her in the most delightful way. He talks of the weather, of the holiday season, of the big house. The wave that hits his body at each new beach seems a cousin of the last one. The posters pull him onwards with a rhythm of their own. Summer golfers tell him how the wind drives each ball eastwards, how one's best bet is to slice an angle towards the sea. Young maids have quite forgotten de Valera's sweep of here in 1919. The rocks his father painted begin to seep through the landscape. School teachers tell him the history of each rath, each crumbling wall. Her posters vanish from one town and reappear in the next. Everyone is somehow related. He learns of her by proxy, in the most delightful way. She grows in the descriptions of her as he moves downwards, or is it that people raise their voices more? The rock comes to flood the landscape, pushing out the grass. He avoids large towns, since they never speak as much. The grass grows lusher, in green defiance, as the rock encroaches. There is the plenty of the season and the vegetables crowd the shop-fronts and a vat of milk spills and floods a broad street. He walks through it past a church entrance where the milk laps the feet of the Virgin's statue. They multiply themselves as he travels southwards and all roads lead to hallowed places, while seeming to lead just to other roads. He searches them out in turn, the trees copper with hammered pennies, the rivers flowing upwards, the cloths that simulate blossoms on the blackthorn branches. There are fields of rock now, intricate, ornate, more luxuriant than grass. A nun talks of her in Spanish Point on a beach where the sea meets a river. He finds she fills imaginations now and the white and pink house fronts of Milltown Malbay are dotted with posters. An election coming, a capped man told him, driving through. And beside hers, he sees, is one for de Valera. The posters thicken as he drives. The rock, having ousted all grass, gives way to grass again. The posters flap in the east wind and draw him away from beaches and he senses an end, or an arrival. He moves in a half-circle, skirting the coast. Descriptions of her grow, become personal, people talk more of her and less of those delightful incidentals such as weather. And on the train to

Gort when a woman, fluttering her eyelids in the harsh sun of the seat opposite him, talks of a chance encounter with her childhood friend, he realises what he knows now he has all along known, that she is pregnant.

'And the last few towns were those little ones in Clare. It was all her walk and her sense of poise could do to hide it, no matter what clothes she wore. We circled round those towns as if MacAllister wanted to exhaust the whole of Clare. Lisdoonvarna was to be the end, you see, the festival week, you know about it, September in Lisdoon. So he pushed his time to the limit, dicing with fate. We tried to walk as little in public as we could, was it verging on the blasphemous, I wondered. We met some nuns in Spanish Point, like awkward birds they were, clutching their habits in case the wind clutched instead, and I could have sworn they guessed. But we made it to Gort, which was the last one before Lisdoon. We drove into Gort as the sun fell over the square. I know the sun never falls but it seemed to be then, just frozen in fall, lighting the bronze hair of that anonymous man of '98, was it, and the bronze shaft of his pike. We sat in the hotel lounge watching the light travel up to the tip of that pike as the sun went down. And it was that deflected, amber light full with the dust of late summer when I looked through the glass door out to the lobby and saw the front door open a little, then stop, as if outside someone had changed his mind. Was it a premonition or was it that I recognised his way of opening doors? I remembered that day in the advertisings studio. I wasn't surprised when I saw him stooping through the doorway. Neither was Luke, who jumped up, opened the other glass door to meet him and said with a voice that could have included the whole world, Father, we are pregnant.'

SEVEN

LISDOONVARNA

43

THE GREAT SOUTHERN Railway looped a triangle then round the miraculous Burren. The main line ran from Galway southwards, through Gort and Ennis where a narrow-gauge single-track flowed off, like a seasonal tributary, towards Ennistymon, Inch and the beaches at Kilrush. The line of the coast completed the triad. And though the narrow-gauge is long out of use, as I travel with Lili on the broad one towards Gort I think of how the bare facts of landscape are softened by patterns like these. There are platforms of rock, bare scourings on the landscape, the remains of stone churches that have the grandeur of signs. There is map upon map, the excreta of years, harder now than the rock itself. So the Great Southern line followed the contours of a landscape which set the pattern of ages and the movements of people who were followed by MacAllister who was followed by Rene who was followed by James and is followed by me. De Valera sped behind them in a car, towards his election posters. Everything, James Vance learned when he entered that Gort hotel, belongs to everything else. Brigit, the *Vita Sanctorum* tells me, traced her own Clare itinerary, leaving meadows where bogs were. The train shuttles and pulls us forward, equipped with broad felt seats and neck-rests and Formica tables in between. Lili is delighted by movement. She points to the sunlight, sheared by the procession of hills. Did you notice a car, I want to ask her, speeding past the tracks bearing a gaunt frame in a gaberdine coat? But she doesn't hear. Who am I to question things? I wonder as the train pulls us through Ennis, past where the Kilrush summer track lies rusted and worm-eaten. I will follow James and alight at

Gort and the texture of the platform will be a firm ageless blue-grey, the colour of those slabs that run from here, I'm told, to Mother, that raise their grassless, earthless shoulders somewhere to my right and slope down, all cracked sweeps and crevices, to the sea. Flowers of rare beauty bloom in those crevices. I rest content with imagining them, as I must with imagining that other, innocent, narrow-gauge track and the black and gold livery of the G.S.R. engine searing like a dash of Victorian optimism through that landscape of grey rock and green to the garland of towns by the sea.

The train gathers speed and Lili's delight grows. Somewhere to my right she gave birth to the child with two fathers, father and son themselves. History headed towards that fact and seems to end in me as great gusts of air begin to shoot through the carriage carrying the odour with them, is it of decay, of limestone, of diesel or generation? Lili has opened the window, I see, and the air rushes in. I breathe in more than I should. The draught hurtles through the window to the melodeon doorway and lifts the black veil off a nun in the seat beyond us, exposing a pair of grey fluttering lashes and eyes.

I stare at the sparse grass passing in the field beyond the bare whitethorn. It would have been the end of summer when James reached Gort and the whitethorn would have been just like that, bare since the spring, and he would have watched with me the grass slowly vanish, combed from the rock to leave it grey and formless, until the train slid between blocks, small ones first, then large enough to form a platform, and the train steams into that blue-grey texture, the steam and the rock surface both absorbing the light until all around the windows, through which James can see the town appear, is this metallic glare. The train stops then and the smell of diesel fills the carriage with the grey-blue light.

'Now who would have known,' said Lili, 'when he stooped in that doorway, and Jesus when I saw his stoop the sinking feeling came on me again – I mean, I knew the average doorjamb was too small for him but why couldn't he bend from the knees and make it a little less obvious, did generations of joiners and wainrights, I mean, set about perfecting the average height of the Irish doorway just to give him an opportunity to stoop from the shoulders? But even given his permanent sense of apology to the world at large, who could have foreseen the odd marriage the three of them would make? Johnny Newham was at the bar and Ferdia O'Haodha and beyond them MacAllister and beyond him in turn me, in whom the old goat was at last taking some interest. But all three of us saw the door open a little and then close and then finally open fully and then this stooping shadow that we knew must have something to do with Luke – I mean, his length and his transparency were all there in embryo. Have you ever seen a plain mother whose features transpose themselves, item for item, to her daughter and emerge there incomparably more beautiful? Well this image of length and hesitancy that turned to beauty in his son got up to greet him and stood there, neither of them touching and yet both so much the image of the other's hesitation it was as if they were embracing. And Luke said "Father . . ." No, you couldn't have told seeing James Vance coming in the door what was to emerge. We had assumed Luke was the father. But seeing them beside one another you could sense it, scent it. The smell of that incongruous union filled the bar, I mean, like ripe apples or steaming hay – '

Walking out of the limestone station and a kind of fetid air like steam or hay did fill the streets. But then it had just rained and the last heat of the day was raising vapour from the pavements. There was the square, much as Lili described it, and not too far from the station either with a glorious stone pikeman the blue-grey of that whole county, the sun glancing the blade of his pike into fire. A cart loaded with September hay passed us and the scent of rotting stayed behind. Lili led me towards a plain hotel. The cart drove slowly round the pikeman to the westward road.

It is what all the surfaces intimated. The plate of dull metal, the sheen of blue, the shreds of eucalyptus rotting on the sloping hill. Everything turns into everything else, James realises, almost at the end of his passage through that country where everyone is related. Cousins once and twice removed, fathers, sisters, sons and brothers seem to await him in that bar which he fills now with his scent of damp hay, sweet, heady and glutinous. The scent of decay, he realises, is not far from the scent of birth. Nothing is separate.

The large wooden doors were open and led towards a foyer in which everything was wood. The jamb was low so that even I had to stoop to avoid cracking my forehead. Am I as tall, Lili? She doesn't answer, but walks briskly to the glass doors and pushes them open, squinting after the low sunlight outside.

'So though I had almost willed,' she whispered, since the lounge before us seemed to impose silence, 'his head to crack on that jamb, when he came towards us with Luke, I couldn't. There were so many things I didn't know, I realised, and one of them was that between Luke's demeanour and his there was no difference, no difference at all. My sly passion for that whey-skinned youth, which was my passion for Rene, how could it not be my passion for the kid's father with whom for all I knew Rene was more passionate than with any of them? That was one of the things I didn't know. The other was that Rene was more pregnant than even I'd calculated. She always had an adaptable figure. Did I tell you that? And when they came towards me I couldn't care which of them was father. Which of them was Luke even. And MacAllister's beam was the largest of all. Well, I'm blessed! he said, when I told him who the tall one was. And when he was introduced, he said it again: Well, I'm blessed!'

I walked from the lounge through the wooden foyer. Lili

stayed there, at the glass doors. The wooden front doors threw in an oblong cascade of light and framed the square outside, half amber sky, half blue-grey brick. The foyer narrowed and changed to a corridor which narrowed again. I knew now it was eternally simple. Each through loving each loves the other, father, son and her. Could I forget the perennial which, I wondered, hoping the rooms would provide an answer. But the wood of the corridor gave way to veneer and to a white tiled floor. I realised that I was in a recent extension, an architecture that could never have been fifty years old. So I walked back to the foyer and climbed an oaken staircase, certain that it would lead to the old rooms, so strong was the scent of generation from above. The oak curved under my hand as I went upwards and I was suddenly weak with pity for her, whom they both loved through each other. The scent grew as I ascended, and with it my pity. She had to bear all of them, I thought, as well as me. Two rows of doors stretched down the upstairs corridor. I chose one, following my nose. I edged the door open and saw white gauze curtains flapping by an open window. There was a table beneath it, with a curved jug and an oval hole which once would have held a basin. I went inside. There was a narrow bed. I stood for a while breathing the scent of clean linen. The scent changed then, as if a woman had entered behind me. I turned, but there was no one there. The room was as empty as ever. Then I saw the open window, where the exhaust from the Lisdoonvarna bus was drifting past. Nothing is distinguishable, I realised. The exhaust curled through the window like a beckoning finger. A wind brushed the curtains once more. I walked out then, down the stairs towards Lili and the waiting bus.

44

THE ROAD TWISTS and turns so much that our bus seems always to plough through the cloud of dust and diesel it has just created. It is no coincidence that every bend is the bend we have just turned and that but for the balding landscape our road would seem almost circular, just as it is no coincidence that when Rene, James and Luke ploughed through this road (and there was more dust then) de Valera followed soon after with his driver, Jack. Neither is it coincidence that what fields there were on either side were strewn now, as then, with gouts of cut, yellowing hay. For all three trips were made in September the way most trips to Lisdoonvarna are and were, and the cut hay yellowed what fields there were round the town where the unmarried gathered on verandas looking for spouses and the feeble looking for cures. It seems more than the smell of hay as we all drive forward, circuitously towards the town that I have never seen, a recreative town, Lili tells me, without the sea. But how can people holiday, I ask Lili, without beach, sea, promenade and Eagle's Nest? There were spa waters there, she told me, which compensated. And that smell of hay which grows thicker as we corkscrew forward as if we are piercing towards the generative process itself reminds de Valera of nothing so much as the yellowing water that comes from the round hole of the sulphur spring. He is familiar with all the rites of his small nation. He has memorised the precise balance of sulphur, iodine and phosphorous in the separate springs and yet all four springs are one to him, part of that healing process, the bubbling core, the well of cold health, Clare, renewal, that elusive elixir of abstention politics and national health. Rene, being driven also by a hatted driver in a car in which Lili took the front seat with her and Luke and James the back, takes the smell as the corollary to the colour of her hair and her condition. And it was, Lili swears, as if it were made for her, a kind of supplicant enticement, and every field we passed through bright only in so far as its yellow gouts of hay matched the colour of her extraordinary hair. I could feel her responding to it, her leg would tremble against mine, or was it just the antics of that extraordinary driver? He remembered us from last year, you see, and even he had heard, knew in advance, the reputation of our current tour and drove so the car leapt over that road, seemed to rise from the tarmac when we took those tangential bends and seemed to be driving round, back up our own behinds, but with a speed and lightness that made it a journey, a real journey. Her leg trembled and I drank in the smell of vegetation, cut vegetation, hay-sodden grass or falling leaves, I couldn't have distinguished, but the kind of smell created by those years of falling that made the boglands, didn't they, I could hear the crashing of mile-high trees, evergreen leaves that you couldn't see now and the vegetable matter pressed into earth, oil and peat-moss and growing and falling again, and that this whole circus left just this delicate film of hay on those stubbled fields seemed to me – well, a final affirmation if you like, that brutal machine of years and that yellow down which at times looked even more fragile than the flat, even watery, texture of her hair. But that tremor – it runs from her thigh now down to her instep – it could have been – I had no idea, as I said, how advanced.

Our bus heads for a cloud of vapour that's like an embryo of the fields that generated it and passes through it, leaving its own cloud of dust and diesel. I can see the hay is falling off the fields now and the fingers of rock are showing through, a kind of crystal greyness that makes one think at first it is a trick of light, a refraction of the blue above.

We turned a corner, Lili tells me, or rather lurched round a corner, and she was thrown against me or rather sucked

287

against me as if by a wind, and I was pressed in turn to the door. I could feel the pressure of something more than her body though, was it the heat or that cloying autumn smell, for a kind of September heat did fill the car along with everything else. But it was more than just heat, it was a pressure which could have been her weight, for as I told you her figure was adaptable and I had – we had – no idea of how far gone she was. But it was more than that too because for once James Vance seemed to sit upright behind me and had discarded his stoop and for once the driver's cap low down over his eyes didn't irritate me. It was – I hardly dare to say it, is there such a thing – the pressure of our happiness. Or hers. On me. Then the car lurched the other way and she fell away.

The windows in Dev's car are tight though as he is forced gently against the door and then forced away again with the car's movement. His face is abstract and expressionless, though somewhat kindly, eternally fixed in that gaze with which it met photographers, as if now it is anticipating a photograph. It never changes. The mouth is turned downwards without a hint of sourness, but in a contemplative moral curve, hardly departing from a straight line that is sad if anything, conscious of its need for consistency. His eyes are grey-blue, echoing the rocks that are filling the fields now as the hay falls off and the strict, wire-rimmed glasses shine with a hint of that blue that is embedded in every transparency. His glasses are misting now with the vapour which, despite the closed windows, seems to seep through every crevice of the bodywork. Or is it just the heat he generates? Does his body steam with its own logic, embodying as it does generations of effort, the doctrines of eight centuries? This steam has the smell of hay, that musty, incongruously feminine smell as if, nourished on the peat of generations of the fallen, its inherited heat rubs, steams and oxidises. He is considering a scheme for turf-fuelled power stations. The steam on his glasses gathers, forms two separate tears which drop to his cheeks, as if his eyes had shed them. The car lurches once more and approaches the town.

We turn a last corner and travel upwards for a small hill, and the unmistakable sensation that we have arrived fills the bus. The air tells us, all of us, that we are here, where some moments ago we were not, though the bus is lurching one last time. The sense of water in the air when the bus exhales to what is surely a halt in a small square ringed with hotels led to by streets which are sprinkled with hotels as I help Lili down. The bus coughs and moves on, leaves the square to the two of us. But the porous quality of the air, the patient façades of the hotels, every leaded pane of which seems to anticipate a sea where in fact there is none. Where do these winds come from, I wonder, this invisible vapour, that sense of mild bluster redolent of hay instead of brine? Every house is an informant, every shop-front seems built for a beach, and the gaunt metal frames yawning from each window, some of which hold that loose striped canvas, seem to demand a placid stretch of canvas deckchairs, their wooden struts sunk in the yellow sand. Was there a sea here once, I wonder, that rolled back, the texture of which this town wants to re-create, remembering an impossible golden age? The hotels face each other in mute pathos, the expectations of each belied by the others' presence, in mutual pretence that the others aren't there. Which one did they stay in? I am overcome by the multiplicity of choices and the porous air. All four of us sit on the white metal seats.

We walked towards a patch of green and a white metal seat. There was a black, bowed figure on it. I recognised the folds of fat round the neck and the collar flecked with dandruff. I tapped him on the shoulder and raised a small cloud of dandruff like pollen from heather. It was indeed Father Beausang. He rose and stretched his hand towards Lili, his head bending forwards, a little too eagerly. Forgive me for following, he whispered after I'd introduced them, but I couldn't

289

help myself. He squeezed my arm, as before. I took Lili's, and we walked around the square.

I picture her wearing a bulky, shapeless fawn-coloured coat. They all spill out from the cars into the empty square. She has her hands in her pockets and so drags the coat downwards, pear-shaped from her narrow shoulders. She loses James and then Luke walking past the hotel fronts. They see her among the faces and lose her again. She walks past the awnings and the leaded windows wondering will one of these roads bring her to the sea that all the façades seem to promise. She comes to the square and sees the grey shoulders of the mountains beyond it. Luke quickens his step and comes up behind her but then stops when his hand could touch her hair to call her back. He lets her walk from him. There is a patina of dust in the air and from somewhere the cries of children. A hotel door bangs. Every shop is closed. She sits on the white metal seat. Jack swings the car round one last corner and into the square. The proxy tears have vaporised again on his master's cheeks as the car circles once round her seat. There will be stuffed trout on the walls of his master's hotel and a large plaster statue in all three bedrooms, grey walls that are saved by the poignancy of the window's vista, the quiet graveness of this square and the yellowing landscape broken only by the grey mound of hills beyond. He will drive him to the spa under different conditions than in 1919 and watch him drink his yellowed sulphur water from the brass chained cup without any sense of urgency. Then drive to Spanish Point, perhaps, Quilty, Milltown Malbay and beyond. Each town square will have only the surprise of recognition for him, notable only in so far as it is so much the same. Before he hears the disyllable Home Jack. He stops the car and helps his master out and they walk towards their chosen hotel.

Old age brings a certain sweetness, said Father Beausang. What a pity James didn't experience it. I would get postcards from him from the places he went through. Knock, Strand Hill, Ballina, Quilty. I knew hardly any of them, Salthill was the West Coast to me, so you can imagine how they loomed in my imagination. Lisdoonvarna I pictured as a town of gazebos, white metal bandstands . . .

It was to be the climax of the tour, said Lili, but I must admit I can still remember our sense of anti-climax when we drove in. Other towns had been bustling, crowds lining the seawalk and the posters flapping for two weeks beforehand. Well the posters were here all right, but no crowds. Morris Minors lining the outsides of every hotel all right, but to all outward appearances, a sleepy inland town. That was what threw us, you see, the fact that it was inland. I had to remember all over again. These aren't seaside hotels, I had to remind myself, though they looked like it. These are spa hotels. So we pulled up and opened the doors and that heady vegetable scent of fullness exhaled and seemed to fill the streets. I could almost see it, like the yellow dust that rises with haymaking, drifting towards each open window saying, We are here. That it would get to them I had no doubt, on reflection. I had to remember, you see, that here it all happens indoors.

We cross the square towards the spa road. Dev strides ahead and Jack follows behind. They talk mathematics as they walk, a mutual love, even a necessity for all his personal staff. Jack's uniform becomes lined with sweat, inevitably; there is not a breath of wind and the green texture of his Free State jacket loses any semblance of freshness, that bright sycamore green conceived in the childhood of this state saturated with both dust and moisture seems aeons old now, dandruff-flecked as if seeking out and exhaling in its turn the odour of years of vegetation, falling, regeneration and decay. They discuss the combustible potential of peat turf in kilowatts, ohms and ergs. The miracles wrought by the historical Brigit occur to him, who created flames out of mud and sand in an empty grate, who transformed an arid bog into a field of yellowing hay. He makes a mental note to visit her well, Liscannor, on the heights beside Moher. He passes Rene who must have seemed the embodiment of this yellow, but of course he doesn't notice since his sight, bad at the best of times, has become clouded with her vapour, condensing into tears again on his rimless glasses.

The road curves from the town and the hotels fall away to be replaced by the borders of nodding fuschia. The scent is musk and heady and there's the hum of wasps. Your first impact with Lisdoon, Lili told me, is deceptive for it is only when you have entered your hotel, signed the guestbook and settled down in some lounge for an afternoon snifter you realise the secret life of the place. Those bent shoulders in those wood-panelled snugs don't belong, as you might think, to the usual assortment of cattle-jobbers and afternoon chemists but to bachelors in search of unwed ladies, matchmakers, fathers, uncles, cousins once removed, all treating with beautifully embarrassed civility subjects of the utmost delicacy. There's no spitting on hands and hearty jokes. Instead there are everywhere deep blushes and sweating necks under stiff collars and stifling Sunday suits. Which might account for the extraordinary humidity of the place which I noticed had grown ever since we left Gort and went round and round those yellow September fields, but which once I entered the lounge of the Spa Hotel I found what possibly might be an explanation. Ah, I thought, it's the odour of embarrassment, the sweating pores of the rite known as courting, that vaporous sign emanating from the shy and gentle rural males of the snugs and lounges towards the spotless matron who sipped tea as a rule on the sun verandas facing the street. And morning and afternoon were just a preparation for night, during which the embarrassment and humidity reached their climax in foxtrots, quicksteps, halting conversations and even hurried kisses, in the midst of whatever entertainment the town could provide. It was with some trepidation that I realised then that we were to be the entertainment for the night, we were to provide the focus for this coughing, underspoken rite and MacAllister beside me, hands shaking as he poured his mixer into his gin, I could see he realised it too. Our last night, he said to the assembled company, and then – Dublin. Would Dublin be able to hold us though, I wondered, seeing the clouds of expectation gathered round the bar and the air settling in the street outside, the opaque texture of which might, I imagined, have originated from the spa and the sulphur springs.

Dev walks towards the spa with both fists clasped tight and his thumbs rigid, a brisk walk, his long frame upright and his profile etched against the afternoon haze, tilted slightly upwards, looking forward. The line of his nose, strong and almost elegant, is what seems to pull his body forward, echoed by two deep lines falling downwards to the curve of each lip. Were there ever lines deeper than those and is it the sense of smell that pulls him forward with the profile of his nose, towards some distant future? There is something military in his clasped fists, more than military even, since his pace is easier than that of Jack who is now quite drenched in sweat and the former bright green of his uniform is stained to what is more like an earth-coloured muddy brown. Used to cars, armoured carriers and even horses, this soldier is quite unused to walking and feels himself slipping into the mists of his own perspiration, can hardly find the will to keep his eyes raised to the rapid, easy feet of his chief, whose light step straddles the past and whose profile points towards any number of possible futures. The road curves and leaves houses altogether for a moment, then rises a little and falls again and Dev can see the fields with their splashes of yellow in the distance and the circular road through which we all have come and below him, on this road, the chalet which houses the spa. I slow my pace coming down towards it. Built of wood and raised on stilts, it is striped like a boating hat, rich cream and black, and between the stilts which raise the chalet like wary legs afraid of dampening the hem of a fine striped skirt there runs a river. A house over water. I think of how apt those hotels are with their beach-like fronts.

293

But Dev is familiar, he is familiar with everything and he walks through the gates, down the avenue without losing a step.

Luke, Lili tells me, despite the day's heat and excitement, had the sets up an hour early. Bless that boy, MacAllister said, and dragged us down an hour early to rehearse. We had come to the end, we knew, of Rene's costumes and I had managed to pucker the last one, her matron's smock, into something like a gown. The hall was wedged between decrepit hotels, and there was Luke when we entered illuminated by that cloud of smoke in the yellow footlights brushing down his canvas pillars, forests and his palace façades. We went through the scenes like sleepwalkers, the lines had so gripped us through repetition that they seemed not to exist anymore, what emerged was simply speech, undefined by words. How doth, sweet coz, said Rene and I saw how well my puckering had done its job; her figure, as adaptable as ever floated from shape to shape, caught by one footlight then by the next, and was like the words, indefinable. There was yellow gel over the footlights which gave her that ripened look. But this is September, I said when MacAllister wanted to change them, and yellow's right surely, and would you believe, I turned to James Vance for confirmation. I had forgotten his stoop, his apologetics, all my irascibility. We are all persons, I simply thought, or even person. Isn't yellow right, James? I called down into the belly of the hall but he wasn't there. I turned to Rene and would have pinched her cheeks to highlight the yellow but she wasn't there either.

The roof is triangular. The water surges through the stilts and disappears. Then night was coming, says Lili. Amorous night. The humidity gathered and the chaff and the yellow had compounded the dark. It was a smell, that night, not a colour. All the sideways glances and the shy gazes and the

294

throaty whispers. I was sent to find her. I found her down here by the pools.

We walk down long halls beyond the depths of the chalet and doors lead on either side to the pools, the brass taps. The sound of dripping seems everywhere, or is it Dev's footsteps echoed by those of Jack, or James's memories, perhaps each one dripping into that pool, which now envelope everything? The yellow sulphur water he drinks from the brass cup smells almost resinous and the elegant curves which the waters make from the flowing taps streak themselves with yellow and cream like his eucalypti of years ago. Everything turns to everything else, he thinks, and every image he has slid from his acid bath reappears in the damp oozing from the limestone and the encrusted brass of the tap handles. I see those pools leading to the caverns below and the large sea and every image this town implies reproduced in that darkness which intimates every form.

Father Beausang brought a cup to his ageing lips. The messages were cryptic, he said. But how they spoke to me. I thought of James, his need for words diminishing. Of the talks we could have had. I pursued my researches into that exquisite system. Logos, the Word made Flesh, the aural connotations of the Virgin Birth. I made notes, hoping for lengthy discussions on his return.

De Valera comes to the sister pools. He compares the motive powers of water with the combustible powers of turf. He lowers his lips to one, then the other. He sees his own face reflected, his spectacles like pools themselves. The curve of his mouth loses its strictness in the water's ripple. He sucks with extraordinary power.

45

WE WALKED BACK the long road from the spa to the square of hotels. The light was fading and from the hedges the fuschias gave their last musky exhalation. I walked between her and Father Beausang through the scent on each side until the bushes gave way to the first few houses and the hotels began. Night was then down, amorous night. All the coloured bulbs swinging from the rooftops now came into their own. They glowed against the dark blue sky and obscured the stars. They caught the bare outline of the fingers of rock behind. They swung back and forwards, faintly moving orange shadows across us as if in time to the thin music that came from some hotel ballroom. Lili led us across the square to the hall of the last performance and the lilt grew louder. There was a small queue of people waiting to get in.

Do I have to tell you, she said, how packed it was? You could hear the silence and the held breaths and the close stiff bodies. The lights in the house went down. The curtain came back and the amber lights came up. Rene began her Rosalind. She said each line with an extreme quietude as if the time were there just for her. She moved from left to right in a series of still poses that were hardly movement at all. We were terrified, offstage and on. How could they not notice –

I paid for all three of us and we walked inside. There was a shabby corridor with a lady taking coats. I gave her Lili's

296

coat and got a ticket for it. Father Beausang kept his dark jacket. We walked towards the hall and the music got louder. I recognised the tune. Do you know it? I asked Father Beausang. He squeezed my elbow and whispered, the Anniversary Waltz.

Need I tell you, said Lili, that they didn't notice? They became one single eye, staring. I saw Luke behind the flat with the ducal pillars. He was reaching forward through the darkness as if always on the point of walking on stage. I saw James on the other side. He had to stoop to keep his head below the canvas. I could see the smoke of MacAllister's cigarettes. I kept thinking of the end and the nuptual dance. I was waiting for it to come and hoping it wouldn't come. It was all a dance.

We walked through a pair of swing doors and the hall spread out before us. There was a band on the stage playing the chorus of the Anniversary Waltz. Couples swept in stiff and formal quarter-circles round the floor, mainly in one direction. They wore dark suits and white collars, navy skirts and patterned blouses, orange flowers on some bosoms, grey threads in hair. Some danced, some stood around the walls. The bachelors who stood around the walls waited for the dance to end. I excused myself from Father Beausang, took Lili in my arms and swept her out on the floor. Her hand clutched mine with a thin, brittle strength and the fluidity of her steps far outdid me. I trod on her toes. I apologised. My generation, I told her, has forgotten so much.

We were quite bare, you see, on that stage. But there was a magic up here that disguised us. Her figure, as adaptable as always. Who would have known? I can remember a murmur down the hall then.

Father Beausang swept by me with a woman in blue. His small legs in their dark creases stretched upwards to accommodate her height. He was sharing some joke with her. She laughed out loud as she danced. He looked years younger, his face near hers.

I was afraid of that murmur. But it was just de Valera, I found out later. He came in late, with his driver chap.

Lili's face with its multitude of creases and its fine down of hair. It was close to mine, her eyes were closed and her mouth had that smile of neither laughter nor pleasure but of remembered things.

You bring me back, she whispered. He was so like you.

Which of them? I asked her.

Both, she said.

I swept her up a small incline and on to the stage. The band were surprised but they kept on playing. The Emerald Ceilidh Band, said the lettering on the bass drum. We danced up there, while the hall danced below. The rhythm was 3/4, simple, eternal.

So he came in, said Lili, the father of us all. I didn't see him. He took his seat like the rest of them. We waltzed towards the end.

There were shreds of curtain obscuring a proscenium arch. The footlights were weak, glinting in the metal of the organ and the electric guitar. I swept Lili past the band into the comparative darkness backstage.

Then there was applause. Quite a wind of it. Huge gusts of it, shudders. It pulled her dress against her. It must have been a wind.

298

There were tattered flats of a landscape of hills, of a blue sky, a tree. I saw the white flash of what could have been a pillar. We danced between them, stepping wide of the canvas flats.

She bowed. From the waist, like a clown or a girl.

I danced Lili out into the lights again and down on to the floor. I swept her in the longest of arcs towards Father Beausang and left her in his arms. They danced together, which was, I suspected, what they both wanted. I stood there while the couples swayed around me. I would have waved my arms, I would have orchestrated all their movements but they were all beyond me now, moving of their own accord. And it was a ladies' choice, I discovered, when a youngish woman in a tight dress said to my face: Shall we dance?

46

WE TOOK THE Ennistymon road the next day in a hired car. Lili dozed on Father Beausang's arm. His suit was crumpled and his eyes had a slow, meditative look. Tell me about Woman, I asked him. He smiled softly. Think of generation, he said, conception and birth in its scriptural shape. How man was made in God's likeness and was given by woman to eat and how paradise died and the eternal now and how man became subject to chance, accident and time. But it was man who had eaten and woman who had given, man who engendered the seed of time and woman who nurtured it. Down to Joseph, he says, down to Mary and I can see that same haze touched with ochre and the almighty sun over some Judaean field and the oozing humidity of laurel groves. And woman therefore, says Father Beausang, loved by more than man, could not but give birth to the love-child untouched by time, resplendent, immortal. I see his eyes through the rearview mirror, shining softly. Lili shifts in the crook of his arm. We travelled, says Lili, back the roads we had come the next day, a sentimental tour you might say, but she wanted to see those trains again and we hired, would you believe, a separate carriage to take the whole company on the loop around the coast. Rene's love for trains had affected all of us and out we journeyed for all the world like children with packed lunches and picnic baskets. Did it remind her and Luke and James, I wondered, of their beloved Bray express, could that account for the bliss that filled the carriage once the old porter had slammed the door in Ennistymon and the train moved forward in bumps, each one of which bumped her between them. It was our last day of course, and which of them I could call father I cannot even now fathom, both of them or neither. Her happiness rippled through the carriage and illuminated each of the seats the dust rising off the red felt covers as it was beaten out periodically by our laughing backs. And what, I ask Father Beausang, of woman now? Now as always and his words seem slurred, awaiting the second coming. Can God come twice? I ask and as the road whorls and whorls and we plough through our own clouds he gives me an inventory of signs presaging that event. Son will not know father, he tells me, and minor rail tracks will fall into disuse. Photographic images will substitute for faces, colours will reach us with the texture of smells, everything will become everything else. Jack drives de Valera towards St Brigit's Well, Liscannor, and he stands on the heights and sees the historical Clare below him and points out the lands of Turlough the Packer O'Brien who could trace his lineage to Brian, to Niall, to Moses, to Adam and thence to God. Christ O my white sun, he murmurs and blesses himself passing the four crutches, entering the grotto, surveying layer upon layer of postcards, pleas and litanies fixed to the dripping stone. Who have recourse to Thee, he reads on the first one, Mother Immaculate he reads on the one below it. He peels away year after year until the dates and pleas become illegible, the faces of the Virgins fall away at his touch and he reaches the damp surfaces, whitened by mildewed paper, of the sodden rock where the water seeps through, beyond the reach of dates and years. The moisture clouds his glasses once more and promises tears. Home, Jack, he says. Could he be called a love-child? asks Lili, shifting in the crook of her prophet's arm. Father Beausang smiles. Her happiness flowed outwards in waves, she says, in shudders that ran through the whole carriage, rattling the picnic baskets. Was it her I wondered or the small twin-cylindered engine puffing out its gouts of steam below us that seemed to answer to every ripple of hers. And MacAllister was staring with his cheek to the window blissfully waiting for the first view of ocean when I felt the water lapping round my feet, up to my ankles then over my knees, and that smell, was it hay or years or just the steam outside, and it was going through a small rocky field, I remember, coming to a level crossing that I realised the water was real, not just her happiness and I pulled the cord. Jack cruises to a halt and beeps his horn at the standing train but Dev patient as ever walks from the car through the field to the aqueous window. Father Beausang tips Lili's cheek and now I in that standing train the steam of which was hissing towards silence through those waters and that musk of generation came.

THE DREAM OF A BEAST

Kill not the Moth nor Butterfly
For the Last Judgement draweth nigh.
WILLIAM BLAKE

I

WHEN I CAME to notice it, it must have been going on for some time. I remember many things about that realisation. Small hints in the organisation of the earth and air, the city. Everyone was noticing things, remarking on things around them, but for me it was critical. Change and decay seemed to be the condition. It wasn't always like that, people would say while waiting for the white bus or circumventing the mounds of refuse that littered the pavements, but from the tone of their voices it seemed just a topic of conversation; the way once they talked about the weather, now they talked about how 'things' got worse. It was during a summer that it all quickened. There was the heat, first, that came in the beginning and then stayed. Then fools who for as long as I had known them had been complaining about wet Junes and Julys began to wonder when it would end. The pavements began to crack in places. Streets I had walked on all my life began to grow strange blooms in the crevices. The stalks would ease their way along the shop-fronts and thick, oily, unrecognisable leaves would cover the plate-glass windows. And of course the timber on the railway-lines swelled, causing the metal to buckle so that the trains were later than ever. The uncollected bins festered but after a time grew strange plants too, hiding the refuse in rare, random shrubberies. So they had plenty to complain about, no doubt about that. For my part though, I didn't mind too much. I had always liked the heat. I took to wearing a vest only, under my suit, and walking to work along the buckled tracks. Those trains that did arrive I took advantage of, but for the most part I took advantage of the walk.

But then I've always been a little simpler than those around me. By that I mean that people somehow, even friends of mine – perhaps mostly friends of mine – would find plenty of chances to laugh at me. I had never minded their laughing. I accepted it. Things they seemed to take for granted I found difficult, and vice versa. Tax-forms, for instance, I could never fill out properly, so I would put them off until the writs began to arrive. Neither has gardening ever been my strong point. But give me a set of elevations, give me a thumbnail sketch, give me a hint of a subject even and I can work wonders with it. I often wondered: had my eyes been given a different focus to most others, so that while we looked at the same scene all right we saw quite different things? And of course people laughed, they will laugh, even get indignant, as when the tea you make is weak or you burn the toast only on the one side.

So when other people noticed the heat, what I noticed were the soldiers. I often wondered if they thought they could control the heat by having more of them around. Or were people succumbing to the leaden days in ways that were alarming? They were getting younger too, with that half-shaved look that kids have in their teens. Mostly on their own, never in groups of more than two or three, you'd see them keeping guard by the tiphead shrubberies, or walking the opposite way to everyone walking home from work, as if obeying some other plan. Is there a reason for it all, I wondered, that they don't know but that those who have plotted their movements know? And my memory of the time of my first realisation is connected with one of them.

2

THERE MUST HAVE been a white bus that day. I didn't walk along the tracks anyway because I was walking up the roadway from the concrete path by the sea. I was walking up past all the gardens to my left and there was the sound of all the sprinklers hissing when I saw one of them inside the gate. He was as young as the rest, and dark-cheeked, bending over a rose tree. His khaki shirt was damp all over the back and under the arms. I could see his nostrils almost touching the petals. He is as alert as an animal, I remember thinking, or something inside me thought. There was the smell of just-cut grass. All the gardens stretched away from him, like wrapped boxes waiting to surrender the scents of their rose-trees. Then a door in a house opened and the soldier straightened himself, but not fully, for he slouched out of the garden and down the road. Underneath the rose-tree, I could see now, there was a pile of cut grass and a dog curled in it. I saw his long cheek and his glistening nostrils. They were flaring with the smell. Do they smell more keenly than mine, I wondered? Then suddenly I knew that they didn't. I was riddled with this extraordinary scent, moist and heavy, like a thousand autumns, acres of hay longing to be cut. I stared for a long time before walking to the house.

My garden curved, like a segment of fruit or a half-moon, from the gate to the front door. The house itself was square. It had been built in the days when houses were getting rarer and the ones that were built assumed ever-more-manageable forms. I walked through that curve of garden, past our roses, carrying that strange new sensation. I stopped then, just beyond the roses. I became conscious of a sound. It was a whispering, liquid and lispish, and it grew. I was carrying a briefcase, as I always do. I looked down to my left. All the gardens seemed to sing at once, a symmetrical hum of praise to that afternoon that would have been forgotten by anyone but me, and even by me, had the thing not begun. They curved away out of my vision and I imagined the last garden overhanging the sea, the same dullish hot blue that it had been for months, ivy trailing down a broken brick wall and touching the glimmering water. There must be a reason, I thought, the gardens are opening their pores. Then I walked towards the glass door, realising that the smell was cut grass and the sound was the hissing of sprinklers.

3

O F COURSE I wondered would Marianne's friends be there, talking about the heat, about the weather. I would not have been surprised to see, through the hallway and the open living-room door, the Ambroses sitting round our glass-topped table drinking weak coffee from our long, thin cups. I would have said something inconsequential I suppose, and retreated to the conservatory to think. There I could look out on the back garden and watch the shadow creep round the sundial, the broad leaves of the knee-high grass glistening in the hot light, the garden which was by now a whispering, torrid tangle of olive-green. I could think there about the changes, without panic or despair.

But there were no Ambroses and Marianne was standing alone in the dark of the hallway. She glanced up when I came in and mouthed my name with that slight diffidence in her voice which was by now familiar to me. There had once been nothing diffident in our love. Her red hair was falling around the nape of her neck, so white that it always reminded me of china. She was turning and turning on her finger her band of gold.

Matilde is sick, she said.

I touched her neck, where the hair curled round it. She withdrew slightly, and shivered.

She's been calling for you.

Marianne walked through to the living-room. I turned upstairs and saw my fleeting shape in the mirror over the first steps. I stopped and walked back down. That shadow had for some reason disturbed me. I saw my shoulder enter the left-hand corner of the mirror and stared. I hardly recognised the stranger who stared back at me. Had I not looked for so long, I wondered. I stared for a long while and concluded that I mustn't have. Certain moods of self-loathing had in the past kept me from mirrors, but never had the gap between what I remembered and what I eventually saw been so large. Marianne moved into the living-room. Matilde called my name. I left my image then, carried on up the stairs and into her room.

Matilde lay curled on the bed, her hair tracing the curve of her child's back. I touched her forehead and felt the heat there. She turned and looked at me, her eyelids seemed heavy with the weight of her long lashes. The almond green of her eyes was flecked with gold. They stared at me, knowing more about myself than I ever could. She lifted her head slightly and her lips brushed the hairs on the back of my fingers.

I was dreaming of you, she murmured.

She seemed not yet out of sleep, or feverish. I could see my reflection in her pupil, ringed and flecked with almond. I was curved there, my cheekbones and forehead were large, the rest of me retreating into the darkness of her gaze.

Read me a story.

The stories she favoured were of unicorns and mythical beasts. She would drink in every detail of those creatures, the bulging arch of their brow, the skull the skin of which is so thick it could have been scaled, the luxuriant hair along each arm and palm of hand. So I read once more of the merchant with the three daughters, the sunken ship, the sea journey to the garden and the waiting beast.

After a while her eyes closed and her breathing became a long slow murmur and the blush on her forehead faded a little. I looked out through her window and saw the sun had vanished from the fronds of grass. I made my way out there and listened to the hissing of sprinklers from neighbouring lawns. I could see the mauve haze descend on the town, somewhere beyond my garden. There was the hum of night machines beginning, taking over from the last roars of day. I touched my finger off the sundial, so hot with the day's sun that it burnt the skin. I rubbed the burnt spot, noticing how hard it was. I rubbed finger after finger then and found each of them hard. Again I wondered how long since I had done this, or had this leathern hardness suddenly appeared? I looked around for no reason other than impulse and saw Marianne in the kitchen window, staring at me. I saw what she saw then, which was me, hunched and predatory, bending over a sundial to stare back at her. Her red hair glistened and her eyes shone. I shambled towards her through olive-green growth. There was the smell of burnt meat.

The radio was crackling when I went in. Let me help you, I said to her. I took the hot plates from the oven. Again my flesh stuck to the surface, but I felt even less than before. The meat was smoking gently and the smell of flesh drifted round the room. Sit down, I said to her. The word love, which I wanted to utter, froze on my lips. When I touched her neck, just where the red hair met the white, she pulled back sharply from my hand.

We ate the vegetables first and then the meat. The voice on the radio crackled on, bringing as it always did the slight panic of the outside world. Turn it off, I asked Marianne, but she didn't want to and so it drifted on like a voice between us, making our conversation for us. What is happening, I asked her after a while. I don't know, she answered.

While I washed the things, I heard her inside, tinkering on the bass notes of the piano. It was quite late by then, since we always ate late. I walked from the kitchen into the living-room. Can I play with you, I asked her.

She made room for me around the higher notes. We played the Chaconne in D minor, in a duet form we had worked out in the first months of our love. She played the bass as smoothly as ever, almost without a thought. My fingers found it hard to stretch, though, and an awkward rhythm crept into the tune. She was annoyed, understandably. She stood up swiftly after the end of the tune and lit a cigarette. I stared at my fingers, which were still holding the white keys. I heard the note hang in the air long after it should have died. Will you come to bed, Marianne asked me.

We made love of course. I watched her undress and thought of all the words to do with this activity. My mind soon exhausted itself. I took her white throwaway pants in my fingers. She was lying under the featherdown sheet waiting for me. She turned off the light. I buried my face in her paper pants, then took off my own clothes.

There is a halo round you, she said. I looked down at myself. There was light coming through the window. Each hair on my body seemed isolated by that light like a bluish gossamer, a wrapping. It is a trick of the light, I thought. I made my way to the bed and felt her hand reaching out for mine. It rested on my arms.

Her fingers were long and bony, but soft, with the softness of her white neck. I had known them in so many ways, clutching the pillow, rubbing my cheek, scouring my back, that the fact that they felt different now didn't seem remarkable. Something was happening, I knew, with us as well as with the rest of it. She ran them down my arms and all the small hairs there sprang to attention. I touched her eyes with my fingers, which miraculously seemed to have lost all their hardness, they were like pads, responsive to her every pore. Her eyelids fluttered beneath them and so I drew my fingers down her cheeks to the bone of her jaw and down to that white neck. I leaned my face forwards and kissed her lips. My mouth seemed larger than human, able to protect hers in its clasp. I felt her tongue beating against my lips and opened them and soon I felt her saliva in mine. My mouth crawled down her body and she opened her vagina for me. Her murmurs seemed to fill the air. Her knees were bent around the small curve at the back of my head, pressing it downwards. We seemed to twine round each other as if our limbs had lost their usual shape. We made the beast with two backs then and somewhere in between our cries another cry was heard, a little more urgent. Matilde was standing in the doorway, still in her dream.

You go to her, Marianne said, turning over. I rose from the bed and took her in my arms, which seemed no longer pliant, but heavy and cumbersome in every movement. Matilde whispered parts of her dream to me as I carried her to bed.

Marianne was asleep when I got back. I looked at my

314

body in the dark and saw all the tiny hairs glistening in the moonlight. I began to dream, standing there. There was a skylight and the moon in my bedroom shifted above me, for I was a child, with face pressed to the skylight, staring down below. There were women, crossing and recrossing a parquet floor. Each woman carried a cup. The cups glistened with liquid. They entered a tiny arch and came out again with each cup empty. I inched my way down the glass to see better and for the first time noticed my shadow below, marked-out by the moon, much larger than I was. They noticed it too, for they all pressed into a circle and stared at me together, their raised faces like a large ageing daisy. The glass below me melted slowly and they each held a cup up to catch the drops. I melted in turn and an arm gathered me in a raised cup and a woman's face with two soft, feathered lips bent towards me to drink.

I awoke and the moon was outside the gauze curtain once more and Marianne was beside me, a swathe of crumpled blanket between us. Her slightly tilted nose and her upper lip jutting out from her lower looked strange, strange because once so familiar. How I would dream when we first met of that full petulant rose of her upper lip, the dreaming wistfulness it gave to her face. I would try to describe it in words, as if talking to a stranger. But no stranger could have understood.

I touched her long athlete's back and she shivered in her sleep, drew the sheets around her. She pulled away as if from a stranger. I looked at my hand on the white sheet that covered her white skin. It was much darker than it should have been. The skin was wrinkled and glistening, like the soft pad that is underneath a dog's paw. The nails were hard, thicker than they had been in the afternoon, the points curling round the tips of the fingers. There were five blisters there, from the burning of the sundial and the hot plates. I covered my hand with what was left of my end of the sheet and lay with my mouth close as it could be to her hair without waking her, my breath shifting the strands at ever longer intervals as sleep overtook me.

315

4

WHEN I AWOKE the sun was coming through the gauze curtains, cutting the air in two with a beam that hit the edges of the sheet wrapped round my legs. The dust wheeled in the beam towards the green carpeted floor. I heard the sound of the front door closing and of Matilde making her way towards school. There was the sound of clattering dishes and of the lawn sprinklers starting on their circular motion. Marianne came down the corridor and as she neared the room I wrapped myself in the sheet as a cover. I saw her in the mirror when she entered and she must have caught my glance for she turned and told me in that soft brusque voice that it was late. When she left the room again I rose. I kept my eyes from my body since sunlight is so much more revealing than nightlight. Both hands fitted through my shirt-sleeves only with extreme difficulty. I dressed fully and slowly and made my way to the kitchen.

The moods that were between us were almost richer than speech. I sat watching her eat, eating only occasionally myself. However much I loved to watch her, I knew there was nothing I could do to dispel this silence. It had its roots in things done and said and it was like ivy now, twining round me. I spoke a few words, but my voice sounded harsh and unnatural. I then rose to leave and tucked my hands round my leather case, walking backwards towards the door. She told me that the Ambroses would be dinner-guests tonight. I will come home early, I said, and talk to you. There's something I must say. Do, she answered.

But what had it been that I had intended to say, I wondered, when I passed through the gate and began the

316

walk down the long sequence of lawns. The heat had brought a mist from over the waters, it clung to the edges of the lawns and the grass borders of the pavement. There was a steady movement of people from the lawns, down the pavement, towards the city.

The sea glistened from beneath the mists and I left the crowds waiting for the trains which I knew might never appear and walked along the tracks. Wisps of haze clung to the sleepers. I walked calmly, but inside me was building an unreasonable joy. This joy was nameless, seemed to come from nowhere, but I found if I gave my thoughts to it it answered back, asking nothing of me. It frothed inside me. The leather of my briefcase seemed moulded to my palm. I brushed back my hair. My tough nails scraped off my forehead and my hair leapt apart at the bidding of my fingers. The joy abated then and became still water. I knew I must keep it as much a secret as my monstrous hands. I heard a sound behind me and leapt back as a train thundered past.

I walked through the smoking piles on the outskirts of the city till the tracks tunnelled beneath the ground. I let the sleepers guide me through the void. I emerged in a long corridor of glass with listless crowds below, waiting for trains. I made my way to the silver escalator, which had been still for some years now.

In Nassau Street the tendrils of plants swung over the railings and brushed off the crumbling brickwork. The gaps between buildings gave a view of clear blue sky. The haze was dispersing now. I knew Morgan would be sitting in the office we shared, with his green eyeshade jutting from his forehead, his sharp observant eyes fixed on the drawing-board. I feared what those eyes would notice and so stopped off at a tailor's shop. I bought a pair of gloves, there, several sizes too big for what I once had been. I fitted them on behind a tailor's dummy while the assistant busied himself with labels. They made two large white, knotted lumps of my hands, more noticeable to me, I hoped, than to anyone else.

I reached our office in Crow Street. There was a games parlour downstairs that opened out onto the street. I saw the screens glowing dimly inside, lit every now and then with flashes of white, the shadows of youths bent over them. I made my way upstairs to where Morgan sat, his eyeshade cutting his face with a half-moon of green.

Having been partners for years, we talked very little. Whether we didn't need to or didn't want to had become unimportant, since it was comforting just to know each other's movements, to be allowed room in another's presence, to work in alternative rooms and make coffee on alternate days. We liked each other, and I rarely heard Morgan complain about the heat. From his window he could see the wide street spill over to the giant building opposite where the paper-sellers would crowd with each new edition calling the days' news. He would talk about the quality of coffee I made, about the crossword puzzles and the state of trains, but he would never question, senses of panic and unease were unknown to him. He did the elevations, the line-drawings, the fine-pencilled work. I would do the colours, the story-boards, the broad sketches.

He told me a woman had called, and would call again later. I walked past him and picked up, besides the acrid smell of his sharpened pencils, the smell of something quite different. As I entered my room it seemed to follow me, or I followed it. I knew that smell, though I hadn't met it before.

I had been given details over the phone. She represented a perfume firm who wanted to advertise a thing called musk. She had described the associations she wanted the odour to carry in the minds of the public. It was to be feminine, seductive, yet to carry a hint of threat, like an aroused woman surrounded by a threat she cannot touch, feel or even see. So I had sketched a long rectangular drawing, almost Cinemascope in shape. On the left-hand side was a white, porcelain bath. There were ornate brass taps, a female leg crooked between them, dangling over the floor, the rest of the body beyond the picture's confines. A fine-boned hand was soaping the leg. Water trickled over the arch of the foot and gathered in drops at the perfect heel. The floor was patterned in black and white tiles, of which I'd forced the perspective a little, so the lines seemed to run like a web to the farthest wall. The dripping water from heel to floor then carried your eye over the chequerboard tiles to an open door and a corridor outside. On the open door was a gilt mirror. Full-length, turned in such a way that the bather couldn't see it, it reflected the corridor outside. And there I had sketched in a marble table, a telephone, a discarded bathrobe just thrown on the carpeted floor. There was an empty space, in the vague outline of a figure. That was to be the threat, awaiting definition.

It was odd to see my work on the boards, a product of yesterday's thoughts. I was different now, and found myself looking at it with a certain nostalgia. That threat, which seemed to be one thing yesterday, would be quite another today. I took my pen in my swollen hands and began to draw. Soon the pain of bending my massive fingers eased and the lines came. The lines of that fallen bathrobe seemed to clash with anything vertical and so I knew he would be prone, whatever else he was. I lined in a sinuous passive object almost touching the robe. The shape became bunched like a fist and the nails sunk into the carpet went deep, like claws. Hardly human, the curves of that bunched fist went backwards, always close to the floor, more a stretching leg than an arm. It began to rise then, with all the majesty and sureness of a sphinx. There was a torso there, waiting to emerge. I sat there, feeling it grow. It was all sensation, no line could have drawn its image. My back rippled and arched, there was a scent everywhere. There was the sound of a door opening.

She was wearing a hat, with a black fringe of lace round it. There was a small smile on her lips which showed that one upper tooth was cracked and angled inwards slightly. She walked slowly through the room, leaving that scent in the air behind her. I stayed at my board with my pen in my hands and my hands between my knees. I glanced at her every now and then. She had mumbled a word or two of greeting, hardly listening for an answer. She traced an arc round my things, picking up a sketch here and there and an odd finished drawing, the way professionals do, tilting her head as if to assess it, but already I knew her interest was

319

more than professional. I find it difficult to explain how I knew this; my hands began to feel damp, as if they were sweating copiously under the bandages. Most of all it was the scent, which seemed to hang in the air like figures of eight. I felt that creature in my drawing in the empty shape in the corridor begin to grow, like a growing-pain. I could not yet see the form it would take, but I knew now that I would recognise it when it came, as I recognised that scent, which carried the name musk.

She pulled over the swivel chair and sat down beside me.

This is it, then, she said, looking at my drawing.

I said it was as yet only an idea. My voice sounded strange to me. Not so much hoarse as furred. I told myself I should not be embarrassed. But that scent, when she was close, was overpowering.

We need something extraordinary, she whispered. Things are so bad, firms are on the line. They want me to bring them a miracle.

I said nothing. I was a professional after all, not a miracle-worker. But I felt the pressure of something extraordinary, too extraordinary to be talked of. I felt a throbbing, like a pain, in my back, beginning in my left shoulder-blade, then creeping its way round my ribs. There was a knot of fur in my throat.

She changed from talk of the picture to talk of herself. I listened while she told her story. She came from the country intending to be a nurse but found all the hospitals over-staffed. I could see what a wonderful nurse she would have made. She had beautifully long bones in her arms and hands that folded with this restfulness. Her hair was auburn under the black lace and would have swung around her face as she bent over each bed and, together with those hands, would have given the bandaged heads a sense of heavenly reassurance. She told me how she wandered from job to job, mostly on the fringes of artistic worlds. Her tall figure and her auburn hair were considered a suitable adjunct to galleries and theatre foyers. She felt outside the events that went on there and yet people seemed to think, she told me, that she

320

embodied their essence. Her present job had been foisted upon her out of the same misapprehension.

She had finished her story. Her odalisque eyes were wide open on mine all the time she spoke. They were by no means beautiful, but they gripped me. I fell into the dream again, with the daylight all around me, I saw a long, golden stretch of desert. Nothing moved except occasional flurries of sand which rose in tiny whorls, as if filling vacuums in the air. The sand was sculpted in hillocks, which could have been the length of miles or the length of a fingernail. My eyes sped over these stretches, the outlines hardly varying till the expanse was broken by a jagged rectangular shape, pure black, sinking at an angle into the sand. It was marble, porphyry, or some alloy of glass. Inside I could glimpse a face, barely visible in that blackness of ice, hair frozen in statuesque, perpetual disarray. I had never seen the face before. One of the teeth was cracked.

She saw the half-drawn shape by the bathrobe as some kind of beast. I told her that was the obvious form for such a threat to take, but what kind of beast? She mused about it for a while, and began to enumerate species. I stopped her, telling her it was unwise to presume, one must let it assume a form of its own, one that we could never anticipate. She suggested a visit to the zoo tomorrow, to muse further. I agreed. She left then, tipping my arm every so slightly, as if to impart some hidden message, or to imply some secret we shared.

I drew a few more lines. Soon my arms became extraordinarily heavy. My head was swimming with images. I let the pencil fall, let my arms hang by my sides and breathed deeply. Slowly and inexorably, the rush of joy built up. It was like a gathering wind. I sat there with my back slightly bent, my hands dangling and swinging gently as if to the sound of late afternoon traffic outside, the smell of musk in the air. The windows were rattling with the wind and beneath all sounds I could hear the deepest one, the one that was at the base of all sounds. I had never heard it before, but recognised it instantly. It came from below the building, from the earth itself. As if the roots of being stretched down, so deep down like a tuning-fork, and sang with an eternal hum.

Morgan must have come in then, for my interest was diverted and the joy slowly subsided. He had taken off his eyeshade, the first of the signals of his imminent return home. I rose from my chair. My arms felt light once more. Outside, night was coming down on the full street.

5

NIGHT HAD BEGUN to fall with a disturbing swiftness. Without any of the change from summer to autumn, around 1800 the sky would begin its wheel from cobalt to blue, and down in the streets faces, buildings and vegetable growths would be lit with a strange, lurid glare. It was the glare of changing, of heightened shadows, it threw darkened shadows under the eyes of passers-by. There was this yellow, febrile glow until the night lights took over.

The hot air seemed to enclose the crowds in a continuous bubble of movement. They arched their bodies, embraced, queued, made talk and love against the peeling brick. They seemed to glory, for a few brief moments, in the heat, in the sense of lost time and future. Their brightly coloured shirts and skirts moved towards me, the women indistinguishable from the men.

Morgan turned left at the river. I could see the bands of youths gathered outside the game halls. I could hear the buzzing of innumerable machines. I crossed the bridge. The crowds always seemed about to engulf me but clove apart as I approached. I suddenly felt older than any of them, older than anyone I could possibly have met. My steps became halting, my neck scraped off the collar of my suit with the roughness of what felt again like the pad beneath a dog's paw.

I found myself outside the station. The artificial palm fronds which passed me on the escalator seemed limp with the day's heat. Inside on the platform the crowds were there again, waiting for the train's arrival. The eaves on the corridor of glass above each held a drop of moisture which grew to fullness only to fall and be imperceptibly replaced by another. It seemed so much like rain, but I knew that to be an impossibility. And sure enough I saw a man in a blue uniform standing between the tracks holding the nozzle of a hose and sending a high arc of spray over the glass skylight and the artificial fronds alike. Walking on sleepers when the light is gone is foolhardy, I knew, so I stood in the shadows waiting for the train. The spray cleared the grime from the glass above and made the light and shade harsher. The man walked past me with his arc of water, dragging the pipe behind him in an arc of black.

The hall filled up with steam then and glass was obscured by billows of smoke behind which liquid flashes still managed to glint. In the shadows of the palm frond I rubbed my cheek with my left hand. I saw a series of tiny flakes twirl towards the ground, displaying a rainbow of colours in the half-light. I saw the crowds press from the platform into bunches round each door. I moved out from the shadows and pressed my way amongst them. I held my face down. I was disturbed at the thought of what it might reveal to them. Knowing how each one of us assumes that what is seen of him by others is not what he knows to be the truth but a mask, I felt a sudden terror that the whole of me was about to be laid bare. Whatever adjunct of our persons it is that maintains this demeanour, it was slowly leaving me, I realised that now. The skin of my person was being shed to usher in a new season, a new age. It would peel off me slowly and inexorably as if pulled by a giant hand.

My main concern, though, was that others should not see what I knew now to be the case. I pressed myself behind the last backs at the door nearest to me. I have always been considerate of others. My urge to spare their feelings will drive me to outlandish lengths. So I took my place some distance from the doorway, my face to the wall. When the train lurched forwards, our bodies swung to one side, then the other. The last of the evening light bled in both windows.

The movement slowly lulled us all. I felt the cramped space between windows easing a little. I let my eyes take in the shapes around me. Bowed shoulders and heads led in waves

324

to the window opposite. The angular city drifted by the glass, then gave way to the tips and heads of the outskirts and behind them a steady thread of blue sea. This blue slowly came to fill the window and to outline, and darken by contrast, the face that was nearest it. It belonged to an ageing lady. She had cascades of lines round her eyes and a fullness round the cheekbones that softened these with warmth. As the blue sea faded from the window a white, rich light slowly filled her face. She was remembering, I sensed. Her eyes were creased with those tiny wrinkles and had the wistfulness of everything that is best in humans. I knew I would either meet her again, or had seen her before. Then slowly recognition dawned. She was my mother.

6

I TWISTED MY body so I faced the opposite window. I heard a loud rending sound and several heads turned. I kept my face down, but from the corner of my eye could see that she had noticed nothing, she was in a world of remembrance all of her own. I remembered the poplar trees at the end of our garden and the plaid rug she spread beneath me. I looked down at my right arm and then my left. My sleeve had split below the elbow and the bandage was now in shreds. The change had spread to my wrist and then must have raced in a sudden surge towards the knot of muscle in my forearm. She would roll up the sleeves of her dress to let me count the freckles on her skin. I knew she lived upon the route but had never seen her take the train before. I would count the freckles till my eyes swam. My weekly visits had become an embarrassment of late with the gloom that swept over me in waves. I thought of how she must have missed me. In one full moment I felt how much I had missed her. My longing to touch her seemed to fill the carriage like a soaking cloud, like steam. A strange warmth rose from the whole of my body. I felt a dry rustle on my forearms and heard a soft fall on the floor, as if innumerable flakes were drifting downwards. I imagined them on the metal, in an untidy pile. They would be swept away on the return journey, perhaps by that porter with the water-spray. He would drown these shards of me without a thought.

I saw my mother's expression changing. From her window she could obviously see the platform approaching. The train halted and she left, with several others. There was more room, but I stayed pressed in the shadows. I imagined her walking down the blue-lit street towards the house I grew up in. I wondered would the time ever be right to call. I suspected it might not be.

My platform crept through that window, the train halted, I walked up the concrete steps. The liquid blue lay like a shroud over the tracks, the undergrowth beyond them and the rows of houses above. I walked, trailing my torn sleeve and bandage behind me.

The sprinklers were uttering their last whispers. Small piles of grass lay gathered beneath each rosebush. A dog barked from the third garden. A door opened and then closed again. I saw a car outside our house, with sounds coming from it. They were bright, chattering voices, so brisk and hopeful that for a moment I imagined they belonged to the Ambroses themselves. But as I drew nearer I heard the metallic crackles of the airwaves and saw the red light of the radio flashing on the dash-board.

7

THE FRONT DOOR was open. I heard voices coming from
the kitchen. I walked quietly past, up the stairs and into the
bathroom. My cheeks had begun to discolour in blotches,
the skin ridged and bumped along them, puckered with holes.
I put plasters over each one and I wrapped a long white
bandage over my forearm, which was by now unrecognisable. Everything had changed or would change, I knew, and
this knowledge made my efforts to hide it even more pathetic,
and yet I pressed on with them. Such is the persistence of the
human, I thought, and made my way downstairs again.

The voices seemed involved, like those on the car radio, in
some common human drama. James's was the loudest and
yet I could not distinguish the words. I heard a sound that
was like an insect's hum for his, with an odd, irregular
climax. I heard a more plaintive note for Marianne. Mary's
sound I could not hear at all. I saw all three of them turning
towards me when I entered. James rose and the hum became
more and more irregular as if the insect was beating its wings
fiercely, to escape. I avoided shaking his hand. I noticed for
the first time how awkward his bones were, how he was all
bumps and angles under his sleek black suit. His temple lobes
were too long and his nose too sharp. Mary turned and
smiled but her eyes were wide open in a stare that seemed
as if it would never lose its amazement. Her pupils throbbed
with the beating of her heart. Marianne looked up momen-
tarily and smiled. Then the fringe of her hair covered her
face as she held out a plate to me.

I heard all three sounds start at once, in conversation.
There was tongue on the plate before me. I ate slowly, some-

thing of the flavour of the creature disagreed with me. James's hum throbbed on, swinging round towards me now and then like a pendulum. I heard the sound of Marianne's voice answering for me. It was soft, conch-like, falling like a wave, as if to protect me. I continued to eat. The soft threads of tongue on my own tongue made me feel as if somehow what I ate was myself. I looked up and saw Mary's eyes fall.

James hummed and rose an interval or two, then soared up an octave. Was it because I could not distinguish the words that I felt the need to talk? Or did his tone enrage me to the point of utterance? I knew I had embarrassed them, I knew it was all wrong, but I felt the need to tell them about the joy. You could not believe the joy of what has happened, I said to them, though everything may point to its opposite. Let me describe to you that unreasonable beauty that fills up my soul, unreasonable only because so unexpected . . .

I stopped when I saw my words were not helping any. There was absolute silence for a moment, then the sound of the tongue on James's plate being rent and lifted to his mouth. Then the sounds of conversation began again. They were coloured this time with a deep blush, as if with shame for something that had happened.

I rose with difficulty and excused myself. I crossed the long distance to the living-room door. The silence kept on. I closed the door behind me then and made my way across the hallway. I could hear the sounds raising themselves again. I went into the music-room. I looked at my bandages, which were now stained in places with a dull, rust-coloured liquid. I suspected I was sweating. I sat down at the piano and began to play. Though my fingers were cramped by the swathes I did get through, slowly and haltingly, the first part of the Chaconne. The long, full bass notes seemed to throb through the piano's frame, to mine, to the floor itself. I thought of the question, as I played, of why music soothes the restless soul.

I heard the sound of voices at the doorway, then Marianne's footsteps back along the hall and the sound of a dinner evening ending. I stopped, I had lost the urge to play. I saw the liquid had seeped from my fingers on to the keys, staining the white ones with irregular threads. It made highlights on the black ones too. It looked like weakened syrup, but I suspected it might taste of salt. It was not at all unpleasant. I heard Marianne's footsteps up the stairway and the sound then of large, heavy rustling from upstairs. I followed, soon after.

The weight of my form must have shifted towards my head and torso, for walking up the stairs I had to grab the rails every now and then to stop myself falling backwards. The house was silent now but for a rustling of bedclothes somewhere and the tiny hum of Matilde's breath. I stood on the landing, listening to the new quality of this silence. Slowly it came to me that silence was not what for years I had supposed it to be, the absence of sound. It was the absence, I knew now, of the foreground sounds so the background sounds could be heard. These sounds were like breath – like the breath of this house, of the movement of the air inside it, of the creatures who lived in it. They seemed to wheel around me till I heard a piece of furniture being pulled somewhere, too much in the foreground, and the spell was dispersed.

I knew I must wash myself before the next move. Now was not the time to approach Marianne, and when that time came cleanliness would be essential. The bathroom, like that of most of our neighbours, was our pride and joy. The taps were gleaming silver, with handles and spigots elaborately wrought, with an elegant adjustable arm fixed to one side, holding a shower nozzle. The spray that came from this was fine and hard, with a lever at its base which changed the water gradually from cold to the sharpest heat. I thought of the countless times I had stood beneath it, in a different season, and the water had stroked me with its heat, washed away all the grass cuttings till Marianne sometimes joined me, her hair bundled beneath a cellophane cap, closing her eyes with pleasure and pain at the heat and her mouth puckering as she did so, waiting to be kissed. I would kiss her and let the water palm us both and her eyes would open as much as they could under the streams, her spare lashes looking like drowned kittens, her fingers, each one, edged into the ribs on my sides. The kiss would last until the hot water ran out and it would be a test of each other's endurance to wait through the cold till it came back, for the heat came in cycles.

So I remembered as I undid my hands how it was she who taught me to be excessively clean and how there are some lessons one should never unlearn. Now my hand was not my own, I saw the ridges and tufts of flesh come clear of the bandages, the hair matted with liquid and the muscles like scallops leading up to the forearm. I peeled off the other hand and the rest of my sodden clothes and ran the bath as I did so. The shower water would be riddled with memories; I thought I was wise to bathe in preference but discovered my mistake when the enamel filled enough to still the liquid and my reflection became clear. I had come to accept that I was not myself but had no conception of the enormity of the disparity between me and the being who confronted me. He was arresting, without a doubt, his forehead was tall, his nose broad and somewhat pushed in as if some afternoon, years ago, it had been broken in a fall. His hair was luxuriant and thick and swept back in clumps from his crown. His eyes were almond-shaped, fronted by even bushes of hair, white round the edges of the almond, streaked a little with red, then amber, gathering into black. Beneath his neck, which was ridged with two angular tendons, was a sharp V, then a scalloped expanse which swept in sharply then to his stomach which in turn swept in towards a tiny whorl. Beyond his stomach my vision was blocked by the edge of the bath but that was enough to see what a piece of work I had become. I stepped into the steaming water and dispelled my image with ripples. I found my changeable limbs floated with a strange bouyancy and took no stock at all of the heat. It filled them with ease, dispersed all thoughts of strangeness from me, everything found its place. How natural it seemed to loll in that water, to turn and face the air again and turn again. The steam rose in the darkness like versions of myself and the lapping water seemed to echo round the lawns. I held it in my monstrous hands and let it drip down to the whorl on my stomach, where it gathered till it spilled over my flat sides. I couldn't have noticed the

331

door opening, for I saw a shape in the corner of my vision then, a white shape, and it seemed to have been there some time. It was Matilde, in her nightgown. By her wide-open eyes, I knew she was still in her dream. Her dreams of beasts were never nightmares, for her stare had all the fascination of a child for an object of wonder. Her eyes travelled down the length of this body that jutted in and out of water, that filled her dream, that perhaps even was her dream. A knotted hand clutched the edge of the bath and she blew soft air out of her lips to ruffle it. I raised both hands and turned her then in the direction of the door. She walked out that way as silently as she had come.

I heard the rustle of her bedclothes and her turning over to sleep. I raised myself from the water and hammered the bath with the droplets that fell from me. I searched for a towel in the dark, but could not find one. I walked outside into the hallway and lay down in the thick carpet, letting it absorb the moisture. I turned on my back, then on my front, stared back towards the bathroom door. It was open. The gilt mirror fixed to the doorway held the reflection of the bath, but none of myself.

Within minutes I was dry. I rose and walked down towards the bedroom. The corridor seemed shrunk, as if the angles had become forced in upon each other. Through the bedroom door I could see the moon behind the gauze curtains. Marianne was asleep on the bed, the blankets rolled tightly about her. She had thrown two blankets on to the floor at her feet. I reached out my hand to touch her shoulder, but saw its texture against her white skin and withdrew it again. I rolled myself in the blankets at her feet.

8

WHEN I AWOKE Marianne was above me. She had thrown more blankets down, whether because of the excessive heat, or from the impulse to cover my shape, I tried not think. I had all the appearance of sleep and so didn't move when she threw one leg over my shoulder to stretch for her stockings. I watched her cover herself with pants and then sheath each leg with nylon and saw her breasts vanish under a brassiere. She raised both hands in the air and drew on a flower-patterned blouse. She slipped her feet into two white high-heeled shoes, then drew her heels back sharply, grazing my cheek with a metal tip. She wrapped a kilt around her and walked from the room.

I lay on. I had awoken, but my dream was still with me. The moon shone through opulent French windows on to a parquet floor. The resinous gleam from the floor was similar to that over which the women had traced their circles. I was suspended from above, swinging inches above that gleam. The hairs of my cheeks brushed off the varnish. My eyes followed the rope which bound me, a vertical climb up to a creaking pulley, then a long sagging angle away. My eyes followed the rope down that angle to the floor, where it was knotted round the heel of a high-heeled shoe. There was a leg in the shoe which gave it weight and substance, immensity even, and yet strangely fine proportions with its line of ankle moving smoothly to the swell of calf. I swung my body on the rope. I rocked myself in ever-widening arcs towards that heel. I held out my arms to grip at the ankle but could never quite reach. Then the foot walked off abruptly, as if its owner was tired of waiting. I was swept quickly to the ceiling. I shattered the skylight through to the moon.

Marianne came in again. She unwrapped the tartan kilt from around herself and pulled on a skirt instead. When she had gone, I pulled the blankets down. My body responded only slowly to my efforts to move. My veins seemed sluggish and all my muscles seemed grossly overstretched. I made it over to the wardrobe and sought out my largest suit. This was a dress-suit, with adjustable buttons for waistcoat, jacket and trousers. I found a white starched shirt-front which I tied around my neck, since none of my shirts, I knew, would cover me. The problem of shoes I solved by slitting the sides so wide that my feet could splay through the opening. I then tore one shirt into strips for use as bandages, since my stock had quite run out. I waited then till I heard Matilde leave for school, then made my way downstairs.

Marianne was sitting with her face to the window. There was coffee across the table from her, with a bowl for me. I sat and ate as quietly as possible. She didn't turn or speak. Her red hair fell away in strands from her cheekbones. Her mouth expressed both hurt and horror, but most of all a kind of outrage. When I had finished the bowl I got up to leave. She turned her face towards me as I was at the door. There were tears rolling down each cheek.

She asked me how I could do this to her. I replied that it was not me that was doing it. Again the sound of my voice made me not want to say anything further. She said she would like to kiss me, but could not bring herself to. Will I kiss you then, I asked. When she nodded, I walked towards her. My shadow reached her first. I bent down and brought my lips to her cheek. Her tears moistened my lips and brought them some relief. I stood up then and thanked her, and made my way to the door. I didn't look back.

Such is the complexity of the human, I thought, as I made my way to the station. My appearance attracted attention, but I kept my eyes rigidly ahead. Anger, pity, love, hate, the names we give to our emotions signify a separateness, a purity that is rarely in fact the case. She had stared with anger, pity, love and hate. I walked, again, along the buckling tracks. The sea was leaden today, like a pit of salt, with only a little mist. The fronds of the artificial palms, when I came to them, were still fresh and erect after their night watering. Morgan's eyeshades touched the drawing-board in greeting when I entered.

I sat down to work. I began with tiny details, put the major questions quite out of my mind, and as often happens when that is the case, the details themselves began to answer the questions. I filled in the highlights and shadows of the enamel bath. This led me to her leg, which I lit with an almost porcelain finish. The shadow fell from an unseen light-source, cutting an angle between the side of the bath and the carpeted floor. I followed the tuft of carpet the way one does a wheatfield, with a series of vertical strokes nearest the eye, followed by a ruffled expanse. The sun was falling on the left-hand side of my face. I rubbed my cheek occasionally, because of the itching of the heat, causing a shower of flakes to litter the page, which I each time duly blew away. And in this way I was led to the figure. He extended himself from the tufts of carpet, with a shape that was indeed sphinx-like, two noble paws pressed deep into the pile. Sphinx though seemed too common a name for the creature he was becoming. I teased my mind as I drew with names for him, but any others that occurred seemed equally inadequate.

I had him half-sketched when I suddenly broke off. I found myself exhausted without knowing how or why. The sun had nearly crossed my drawing board which was, I surmised, more than two hours' journey. I remembered my appointment. I rubbed my face and snowed the drawing once more. I went to Morgan's room, but he was out. His room was eerily silent, as if he had never been there. I decided to walk.

I wrapped my bandages round my hands, arranged my shirt-front so it covered the widest possible area and ruffled any further flakes from my hair and face. I then borrowed Morgan's eyeshade, the shadow of which I hoped would be more than enough to cover my visage. Then I ventured out.

9

HOW LONG WAS it since I had walked between morning
and night? The city seemed to curl under the sun like a
scalded leech. The shadows were tall and black, the pavements white and empty. I crossed Westmoreland Street alone,
the only movement the rustling in the patches under the
walls. Is the world to be left to me, I wondered, and such as
me? A statue of hot bronze pointed nowhere, his finger
warped by the years of sunshine. I walked through the
sleeping city, blinded by the glare, meeting no one. I came to
the river, which had narrowed to a trickle in its caked bed.
I walked beside it up by Parkgate Street. The Wellington
Monument jabbed towards the white haze, I passed through
the parched Hollow towards that long avenue, whose perspectives seemed to beckon towards splendours unseen. I saw
then, after some time, a shape approaching out of the melting
tarmac. I heard the clip-clop of hooves and readied myself
to spring into the bushes, in case I met horse and rider. But
no, it was a deer which walked down towards me and
stopped some feet away, as I did, to stare. I noted the grace
of his rectangular jaw, the dapples that led from it to his
sprouting horns. Do you see things differently from me, I felt
like asking, are your perspectives wider than mine, have you
two planes of vision to carry everywhere you go? Whether I
thought this or phrased it, he seemed to hear, for his lower
jaw moved at odds with his upper and he bounded past me,
in two neat, langorous leaps, as if inviting me to imitate him.
I merely watched him, though, disappear into the city haze.

As I walked on, the shape in front of me defined itself. I
could see a glittering white façade with two proud pillars

and the whorling fingers of a wrought-iron gate between. Walking further, more pillars defined themselves, white ones, stretching in pleasing harmonies from the façade of the house. It slowly dawned on me that it was the presidential palace. Then the memories came. They flooded in on me, like the dreams, the avenue was full of them. I leaned against a slim tall tree, with no foliage at all except for an umbrella at the top. I saw my mother, walking towards it. She was wearing a narrow pleated jacket, with a flowered skirt. She was walking down the avenue, holding my hand. I was pulling her towards the hedge beyond. She wished to view the palace from behind the gates, but I wanted to see – what was it I wanted to see? The zoo, I realised. And I stepped out from under my tree-trunk, remembering. Enclosed by those hedges, I remembered, the animals would leap at that tall barbed wire, lining the path to the presidential palace.

I crossed the avenue and walked along the hedge. I heard a few mournful snarls, as if of creatures woken for the first time in years. I came to a turnstile and walked through. The Swiss-style cottage was still there, but now it gave out no afternoon teas. The wires were everywhere covered in ivy, the bars were twined in eglantine, honeysuckle and in thick trembling vines that lined the roofs of the cages. I walked through the empty zoo and heard a few parakeets squawk, I saw the flash of a pink flamingo rising from a pool, I saw a treetop swarming with small green monkeys, but all the great animals seemed vanished. I felt a sudden wash of disappointment and realised then that I had come here to find my beast's prototype. He was no cousin of those chattering monkeys or those squawking birds. I came to a pool then and saw a ripple break the covering of thick green slime. A seal's shape curled out of it, its back speckled, even coated in this weight of green. His glistening, troubled eyes made me feel more akin to him. Then he dived and left the surface unbroken once more.

I was walking through a tunnel of vines when I heard footsteps. I bent beneath the hanging branches, as fearful as before. The gardens were free now, to animals as to humans, and yet my fear kept me cowed. There was the dusty odour of evergreen leaves. Then another scent crept through it, the scent of quite a different place. I ventured out to those approaching footsteps and recognised her walk.

She was carrying a black handbag, swinging on the crook of her arm. She did not seem to be aware of it. She was wearing a fawn hat which made a circle of shadow round her face. I swear I could smell the perfume from where I was. Her high heels clacked and clacked as she walked nearer, her eyes searched around constantly. She was on time, I gathered, as I must have been. When I stepped out in front of her path, she didn't show fear or surprise, only a familiar gladness.

I took her arm without any hesitation. We walked through the vines and out the other side, where once there was a reptiliary. The shed skins of its old inhabitants lay scattered about, colourless and wafer-thin. Her heels clattered off the tiled floor. She told me more about her life, but asked no questions at all about mine. Why I found this so comforting, I wasn't sure, but walking round the glass cases, my arm fell about her waist and hers around mine. We came to the exit sign and walked through, finding ourselves on a long green lawn. Even under the rolls of bandage and under her cotton dress, I could feel the bones of her hips and the movement of her skin above them. We sat down on the lawn.

Take it off, she said, pulling off my eyeshade.

Don't you mind, I asked, feeling drops of sweat fall down my outlandish forehead. She had a matter-of-fact air, however, that made such questions seem redundant.

You look tired, she said.

I was tired. She took my head between her hands and laid it on her lap. She stroked my forehead and my matted hair then, while talking in a deep, hypnotic voice about the project and herself. While she talked, although my back was to her, I could see the limpid shapes of her eyes before me. She talked of the complaints of everybody around her, of the hundreds of minor dissatisfactions they gave voice to daily. She herself, she told me, felt a dissatisfaction that was deep, but that she knew would never end, so what was the point in voicing it? She told me how heat appealed to her, she could wear light cotton dresses and always kept a colourful supply of wide-brimmed hats for going out in the sun. She told me how her life to others seemed to follow no shape, since she never worried or guarded against the diminishing future. But she said that the fact was that while she did accept most of what happened to her, she would have a premonition of important events some time before they occurred, as if to prepare her for them, so she could take advantage of them. She had felt that when she first heard the name musk.

I turned my head and looked up into her face. I put my hand on her knee as I did so. Take it off, she said, and began to unroll my bandages. I protested, but she whispered, in this persistent voice, that it could do no harm. She unwound it and unwound it till the first hairs began to appear between the white, and then the huge fist was exposed. She put my hand on her knee then and wrapped my elongated fingers round it. I felt her whole knee in the cup of my hand.

She told me more about herself. I could see long machines cutting corn in swathes as she talked. She talked of herself as if she were describing an acquaintance she had known for years, but never well enough. There was a girl, I gathered, before the woman. The thought that we all had some past was becoming difficult for me. But looking at her I could see her face diminish into the other she must have been. She stretched out her leg so that her knee straightened under my fist. Some bright green-coloured birds flew out of the cedars. I felt her knee change shape once more as she bent her long leg at an angle under my chin and began to talk about the beauty. My voice sounded deeper than ever and so I turned my head to see if it had alarmed her. What I found was her eyes staring wide at me in a way that left no doubt that each was understood. I told her about the sounds I had discovered beneath the surface of things, the hum from the girders, the mauve twilight. As the surface of everything becomes more loathsome, I said, thinking of the thing I was, the beauty seems to come from nowhere, a thing in itself.

She leaned towards me and again I knew I had been understood. But the pleasure of that thought brought an anxiety with it, as to whether she had been. She took my face in her

339

hands, she was smiling. How long was it, I wondered, since I had felt uncalloused skin against my own? The beauty came in a rush. Joy was the word I thought of, joy I knew then was that word for when beauty was not only seen or heard, but felt from inside. The sound of it was all around me. Her eyes were the brown of burnt heather, with tiny flecks of gold in the dark. They glowed as she bent her head down towards me and rested her lips on mine.

The green birds must have flapped closer, because I heard their cries, one after the other so that they became a throaty purr. How I admired her boldness, in meeting my lips which must have changed beyond recognition. The rest of me must have learnt a new suppleness, however, for while still lying on her lap I managed to turn and raise her above me in the same embrace. Can I describe the garment that wrapped round the top of her legs? She murmured again and smiled, and again I thought of her descriptions of herself as not herself. She gave a small cry as of a bird released and all the green parrots flew into the air at once. Her limbs wrapped round me, each one seemed interchangeable, always with the same texture, and I knew then that I had a soul for she met it, embraced it and breathed on it with her own. We lay there, brute and beauty, a small curtain of pollen seeming to fall on us as if cast off from the blue skein above. There was a dry flowered smell.

It was some time before we rose. My soul had twisted itself into a knot that it would keep, for ever, I thought. We walked back through the arboured tunnel. Her heels clicked once more against the path. She told me that the insides of her legs were wet. She rested her hand on the crook of my arm. Behind us tiny animals followed, unseen, only present by the noises they made, small whisperings and rustlings as if to celebrate the hour that had passed. We agreed to revisit the reptile parlour, then to go for the time being on our separate ways.

Even as we walked through the shattered awning, I was made aware of further changes, by the minute. The skins of dead reptiles hung off the vines and as we walked beneath we set them swinging, collapsing the remaining panes into shivers of crystal. How wise of that genus, I remarked to her, to cast off a surface with each new season. She rubbed her nail up and down my forearm and told me more about her childhood.

I listened as she talked about books, how an unlettered farm girl would remove them from a large tea chest beneath her father's workbench and phrase to herself the long words, few of which she understood. They seemed a secret knowledge to her, and when she came to work in galleries, her surprise at the fact that others shared it was only matched by their surprise at the freshness her childhood knowledge had retained. Several times I tried to answer but found my voice retreating once more to the deep cavern of my throat. As the words went, then panic came that the essence of that hour we had spent was vanishing, shedding itself in turn. She turned to me suddenly, as if noticing this, on instinct. It is time to go, she said.

Before leaving she wrapped me carefully once more. We left by different entrances. I walked back down the long avenue and knew that each change that happened was reflected in that bowl-like essence that lay somewhere beneath the skin. The avenue was empty of people, the shadows slept at the feet of the trees, long and somehow full of ease. My feet moved over the grass, faster and then faster, I felt abandoned beneath those trees and dared to move out into the open fields. I saw a mark on my wrist and made out a number, in stately blue ink, barely smudged. She had written it there. Everything would be for the best I felt, having no knowledge of what awaited me.

IO

TRAVELLING IN THE mauve light at the irregular time that
I did, the train was quite empty. The city barely rippled in
that light, the soldiers had left it, the water lay still to my
right like a sheet of well-tempered glass. My vision was
obscured with a fringe of hairs to the left and right of the
oval it had become. I sensed this was caused by the growth
round my temples. But it leant a charm to that seascape,
fringed by rainbows that threw into relief that gunmetal blue.
Then all the light bled from the carriage, my shadow came
to match the tint of the metal floor. I felt suddenly darker.
The train lurched on its sweep forwards, as if dragging me
towards some armageddon.

And small gusts of spray blew over me when I came to the
gardens. There was wind at last. I thought of the conversations that wind would make around evening tables. There
was a slow dull pain in the palm of my hand. I looked down
and saw that my fingers were curled like clams. I had mislaid
my briefcase.

The front door was ajar. I made my way through the
house. I could hear Matilde or Marianne or both moving
round upstairs but I didn't call. I felt they had heard me.
Something moved me through the house and out of the
French windows on to the lawn. I stood by the sundial amid
the mounds of cut grass. I felt Marianne's eyes approach the
window upstairs but didn't turn or look. I tried to imagine
what she must see below her, but no effort on my part could
make that leap. Sure of what I felt like, all images of what I
looked like were beyond me. Was I rotund, I wondered, did
these luxuriant clumps of hair spill out from the crevices of

342

what served as my garments, intimating the chaos inside? Or was the hair in fact quite sparse, did the flakes that I left behind me like gossamer cover my cheeks, my fingers, every centimetre of available flesh that wasn't hidden by cloth? I remembered that my skin at times had made her uncomfortable. Did she remember that now, I wondered, and then realised how futile it was. All I could gauge was that whatever creature was filling her gaze had his left hand placed upon the disc of the sundial, the two largest fingers supporting the weight of his leaning body. I didn't dare return it. All I could bear was to call her name, my eyes fixed on the digits of the sundial, and wait for a reply.

I must have waited a long time for her voice, because when I became aware of my surroundings once more I was encircled by a halo of tiny insects. They hovered over the dial's copper surface, then up along my forearm, into a lulling, shifting crown around my head. The light that came through their penumbra was green, that strange pea-green aura I remembered from the first days of spring. Their combined hum was like the murmuring of angels. Their eyes were bright and green, and to my huge blue the magnificent swathes of their wings reduced to just that transparent glimmer. I remembered a glen, and her red hair surrounded by them, her long fingers flicking them from her face. I took my fingers from the sundial and began to walk back towards the house. They followed me, like a retinue all of my own, but then they thinned as they approached the French windows, as if their proper home was outside. I entered the house with some sense of loss.

There was no meal in the kitchen. Once more I waited. I stood by the range feeling that to impose myself any further might be a mistake. I sensed a presence and heard a footfall behind the door, but could only see the door's gentle swing and the ghost of a shadow on the floor.

Have I become repugnant to you, I wanted to ask, as gently as the tilt of that door. But I feared the sound of my voice. So I waited to see would she enter, of her own accord.

The shadow departed and the footsteps retreated up the stairs. I kept my silence for a moment, and then thought of

Matilde. The longing to say goodnight made me move once more. I crossed tile after tile of the kitchen floor. The scalloped shape of the soles of my shoes no longer suited my posture. I would have thrown them off and walked barefoot, but felt that would have worsened things. I pushed open the kitchen door and felt the resistance of tiles change to the softness of carpet. As I reached the bannisters there was a rustling above. I heard her voice.

Don't come up, she pleaded, Matilde's not asleep.

Please, my darling, I said, but the words sounded like heavy drops of oil, don't be afraid. I want to kiss her goodnight. I would have said more but I could feel her fear rush down the stairs towards me like a wall of water. I could by no means blame her, but that fear served to goad me even more.

Matilde, I called, hoping I could pronounce at least that. Marianne's sob answered me from above.

Come up then.

The top of the stairs was bathed in light. Marianne was there, a spiked baking tin in her fist.

Say goodnight from the doorway, she said.

Your voice, I tried to say, sounds as foreign as mine must be. Again the words curled beyond speech. I walked up slowly. She kept her metallic shield thrust towards me. I placed my palm against the spikes. The landing seemed unnaturally narrow. I followed her covered hand to a door.

Goodnight Matilde. I attempted the syllables slowly. The broad *a* reminded me of a field of grass and the *ilde* made me think of a thin bird flying directly upwards. I tried to picture both of these as I phrased her name, the thin bird flying directly upwards out of the sea of grass. To raise the timbre of my voice I contracted all of my throat muscles.

I heard no reply. I drew as quiet and deep a breath as I could and began again. Before I reached the first consonant, however, I felt a blow from behind. The metallic spikes scraped me like a claw, I fell headlong, I heard a door slam and a key turn in a lock with a short reverberant click.

344

I I

THE HOUSE FELL into its evening mood, that mood of
which one might remark how quiet it is. On the contrary, it
was a harvest of sounds. I lay with my cheek on the carpet
and listened. I knew now that I was not in Matilde's bedroom
but in my own, or, to use the terminology of the past, our
own. My fingers touched off a gossamer substance which
seemed for a moment or so to be castaways of mine but
which I discovered, as I pulled it towards my lips, to be a
long silk stocking. I drew it through my lips and the smell
of her skin came to me with a strength that it never had had
before. I recognised the odour of the drops she added to her
bath. Woman and the world that word implied seemed as
strange a bestiary to me as the world I had become. I listened
to the sounds and tasted the memories that smell brought to
me. The moon was swelling into the rectangle of the window.
I was in a bar with oak and gold-coloured fittings, waiting
for her entrance. There was a door adjoining which led to a
dancehall, and dancers surrounded me, some awaiting their
partners, others already joined. I stood a little on my own,
as if to express the pride I felt, knowing that when I held her
in my arms I would want no other. I glimpsed myself in the
bar-room mirror, quiet, saturnine, but above all, proud. They
surrounded me in couples but none would be as beautiful as
she. Then she came in, wearing what she called her dis-
graceful dress. It was white, glittering with spangles, slashed
all over with half-moons that showed her flesh. The dark silk
of this stocking glowed beneath it, flashed black as she moved
towards me and one leg parted her dress's sheath. We kissed
at the bar, before the mirror, and moved towards the dance-

hall; even before we had approached it our movements blended into dance. We wove through those thousand couples and that perfume was our own.

The memory of that perfume was easier than her name. One by one the lawn sprinklers stopped their hissing. The insects that had thrived on the long heat beat against the window-pane, lit by the globule of blue light that the moon had become. The perfume waned and ebbed in my senses through the chorus that I once thought of as silence. My arms were tough as beetle-hide beneath me on the carpet. My lids were heavy but took a long time to close. Slowly, though, that chorus changed from bluish to black and I fell asleep.

12

THERE WERE CURTAINS of dark like curtains of silk, the blackest furthest away. There was one lone hair on an expanse of tan, which swathed off from me like a desert. At its base the earth swelled a little like a pore, then sucked inwards. And as I stood there it grew. Grew so much that it bent away near its tip, under pressure from its own weight. A tiny drop formed there, fell away and splashed at my feet. I began to walk over that undulating surface, through the curtains of dark. What had seemed darkest from some way off melted, as I approached, into the hue of what I had left behind. There were no humans in this landscape, though all about me was the aura of humanity. The darkness dispersed as I walked towards it, then formed again in the middle distance. I felt I would meet a woman here. Another smooth basilisk grew some way off, soaring from its pore beyond my field of vision. Around it grew neighbours, too smooth to be a forest, too separate to be a field. A drop splashed beside me, so large that it wet my ankles. Then another fell and another, so much so that the water rose to my waist, surged in a current and drew me away. Its colour I would have registered as blue, had the light been clear enough. I hardly swam, I was borne with it over that landscape that sank under its even progression. There were threads of hair beneath me, stroking my body like moss or water weed would, but of a more silken texture, long, flowing with the water, as if each strand was endless. I dared to put my feet down and felt the fleshly surface. I walked to a bank and raised myself up. The water ran below me now, the hair wafted with the flow. There was a woman some yards beyond me, on the bank. Two great webbed feet caressed the woman, her hair made fury with the water. All above me was the beating of wings. A white neck curled from the sky as if on a sudden impulse, its predatory beak turned this way and that. Was it the sight of me, I wondered, that made the sound of wings more furious, that caused those feet to rise, that white neck to coil about that woman, bearing her upwards? Her hair dragged itself from the yards of water and soared, whipping my face with droplets before it was gone. The bank from which she'd risen flooded with water, forming a pool. I made my way to it and bent. I saw my monstrous head reflected there, ringed by a circle of eggs. Were they the swan's, or the woman's, I wondered and lifted one of them out. The heat of my unruly paw was anathema to it, for the droplets of water began to sizzle and steam and a crack sped across the white surface. The sheaves of egg fell away and a cherub stood there, creaking its downy wings. One by one the other eggs split and the cherubs beat their way to the ceiling. They settled into niches in the plasterwork. There was the sound of falling water.

13

WHEN LIGHT FINALLY spread over the contours around
me and the clusters of colour gathered at each eyelid I found
I was on the floor no longer. The bed was beneath me and
the sheet was crammed into a ball, shredded in parts where
my fingers had clutched it too ardently. There was a sound
in the air which I could not immediately divine. I got to my
feet and it was all around me, a steady thudding like the feet
of many children. I went to the window where the light was.
My eyes were unsteady as yet but when I pulled back the
gauze curtain and gazed out on the unfamiliar, I saw it all.
It was raining.

The water came in straight threads, the darkest ones furthest from my gaze. Had I dreamed that liquid, I wondered,
from the constant sky. But I saw that in the gardens all about
me the sprinklers had stopped, and gathered that others must
hear it too. There was moisture in the air, that scent of
dryness had vanished. My bandages clung like a mask.

There was the sound of a table being laid downstairs. I
was not at all hungry. I squatted, held my knees close to my
chin and listened to the downpour. Each echo that came from
downstairs was different now, muffled by the falling water.
Towards evening I heard music and the sounds of guests. I
rocked backwards and forwards by the window. There was
a rhythm to the falling water to which I responded. A kind
of sleep came.

I dreamt I was in the room downstairs. A metronome
ticked from the piano, with the sound of dripping water. I
played, keeping my fingers on the black notes. Marianne
stood above me. Matilde danced, in her confirmation dress,

349

the white frills spreading as she turned. The liquid beat spilled over the piano though and soon my hands began to sweat. My bound fingers stretched for the notes, so that Bach was slowed to their shape. I knew it was going badly. Can we not try it again, I asked Marianne, but the russet stain was creeping from the black notes to the white, making them indistinguishable. The liquid thud from the mahogany frame began to wilt then, to melt into a gurgle. Matilde turned bravely but the wafer-like stiffness of her confirmation dress became sodden in turn. It hampered her movements, it clung round her knees like whipped cream. She twirled and twirled, but could not defeat it. Her tears made matters worse and soon her Crimplene elegance was plain grey, clinging to her sides. The greyness oozed from the keys, the same as the colour that bound me, and soon music, room and all of us were buried in its path. I saw their hair, twined just above that matter, in the shape of a fleur de lys. It bound and unbound itself as if in final parting, then too went under.

14

THE RAINS MERGED day into night and night into day again. The dull throbbing and the whispering of rivulets outside and the distant cascades of trains enveloped me. A light fungus grew on the walls, a furred coating of gossamer. I would loll against this vegetable surface, my breath wreathing the room in billows of steam which dripped in tears from the ceiling. So my room wept at intervals and the carpet vanished beneath a film of grey. My lungs, like sodden sponges, inhaled their own moisture. At intervals a plate was pushed through the door. I ate, but hardly noticed the textures. Each dish grew a web of its own. I slept and woke and slept again, lulled by those watering noises. My limbs ceased to concern me. There was a kind of peace in this moisturous world and I wondered once how it was regarded by the world outside. Morgan's eyeshade would be dispensable, I gathered, since the hard sunlight was no more. The streets would have changed from a dusty tan to a shimmering grey. I dreamed that perhaps my condition might have lessened. Then the rains stopped and I knew that I could dream no more.

15

THERE WAS A calm, willow-green evening light. All the
drops had finished but their liquid echo lasted for some time.
Old sounds gained precedence, old but fresh because so long
unheard. There was the crackle of burning fat from below.
A plate clattered. Then came the hissing of sprinklers, like
barely-discernible strings.

I rose, very slowly. My limbs stretched at their coverings,
having grown in the interval. I knew there would be no
reversal. Certain tendons felt like wads of bunched steel. I
walked to the doorway. It was locked as before but I gouged
round the keyhole with my nail. The wood splintered easily,
the door swung open. Now that crackle of fat sounded louder
and the pall of singed flesh slowly filled the room. But
stronger than that was the pall of memory. I heard the front
door open, the sound of voices, of entering guests. The door
closed again and the voices fell to a murmur, broken by the
occasional soft ringing of glass. I stepped on to the carpet. I
thought of my appearance, but looked in no mirror, as
mindful of my own terror as I was of theirs. The landing,
which had once been planes and angles, throbbed as I walked
through it, the ceiling seemed to congeal beyond me into a
closed mouth and yet raised itself as I came forwards, as if
parting its lips to let me through. The stairs whorled below
me in turn. I followed the glimmer at the end of them,
through which the sounds seemed to emanate. My fingers
gripped the rail and my new hands left palm marks on the
cedar wood. There was the door then, tall, soft-cornered and
ringed with light. I stopped, listening to the voices. I meant
to enter, but knelt first on the carpet and put my eye to the

keyhole of light. I saw the dim shapes of figures round a table. Then the handle turned, the door fell from me and I collapsed inside.

There were kitchen tiles by my cheek once more. I saw the foot of Marianne, the long black heel rising to her ankle, and her hand, clutching the doorknob and her face, far above me. Her voice was raised, but the words I could not distinguish. I understand your anger, I said, I have become an embarrassment to you, I can see that clearly. But from my prone position on the tiles those words didn't sound like words. My darling, I tried again, perhaps it's better that I leave. Through the curve of her shoe's instep I could see that table, the dinner-lamp hanging low and the Ambrose couple, male and female, staring towards me with curved, craned heads. Marianne's foot rose and fell again, nearer now to my eyes. I inched backwards away from it as I felt I should. It rose again and the heel sang off the tiles. I gathered myself on to all fours. Do you remember that evening we danced, I began, but that heel numbed me into silence. I craned my head round and stared up at her face, which seemed larger than a full evening moon after wet weather. Should I go, I mouthed and the eyes, though they didn't seem to hear me, seemed pregnant with the word Yes. I backed away and sidled round the doorway, still longing for a contradiction. But the heel clacked off the doorway and the doorway clacked shut. I heard the rustle, the regretful whisper of the key turning. I raised my weighty palm to that door and gouged some words on the cedar. Goodbye.

16

THE DARK HAD brushed all the gardens outside. Each lawn
swam with what the rain had left and the cuttings of grass
lay like moss upon the surface. I walked. I was watched only
by the moon, which shone silver above me, swollen, as
though it could contain any number of dreams. When I
reached the tracks a few restful stars had joined it. The
sleepers had swollen into giant sponges and between the lines
of track, glowing dully with the rust it had gathered, a steady
stream of water ran. I found night so much more comforting
than day, each shape seemed like a disguise, each shadow a
mask. A reptile slid down towards me through the waters,
passing under my legs to the sleepers behind me. The city,
when I reached it, gleamed with the metal of new rain. I
walked along the river, glistening at last, laced with ropes of
fungus and the pads of lilies. The bridge barely curved above
its growth. It seemed now hardly necessary, the river at points
spawned a bridge of its own, vegetable and massy, beneath
which it remembered its liquid state. There was the steady
moan of travelling water and a film of moisture followed its
curve to the bay, and beyond to dimness. My feet padded
over the metal bridge and their muffled echo seemed to come
from beyond. A fish leapt clear of the lilies, gripped a moth
in its jaws and plunged downwards once more. I walked,
with no knowledge of where I was heading. Somewhere, I
felt there was a place for me. And the bridge led me, as
it only could, to the empty street alongside. There was a
cobblestone archway ahead. A tangle of foliage hung from
above. Through the olive-green leaves I saw an edifice

glowing. I brushed the leaves apart with my arms and walked on towards it.

17

AS WITH CREATURES whose bone structures enclose their flesh, ants, crabs and armadillos, lending support from without rather than within, so the girders of this structure bound the planes of concrete and glass. It was square-shaped, beetling over the tiny streets around. It threw more a mood than a shadow on its environs. Not a soul walked on the pavements around it and the mists, which were now dispersing elsewhere, seemed to cling to the brickwork for comfort. How had I not noticed it, I wondered, in what I was at last beginning to think of as my former life. I had the dim memory of waiting under that Dutch-style façade beyond for a cream-coloured bus. How long must that have been, I wondered, and how long did this immensity take to build and under what conditions of secrecy? It was a seat of some power, I sensed. The surface of the brick was smooth, even metallic, and it tingled gently under the pads of my fingers as if to give just a whisper of the power within. The mists rose to my waist, close to the wall. I walked along it, feeling that tremulous whisper. I reached a corner. It was sharp, seemed dropped like a plumb-line from the stars. I could then see large steps and a concrete patio leading to the miniature street. The dimensions of that street, once so snug and human, now seemed absurd. This giant that scraped the stars had winnowed any purpose it might have once had. There were vast globes on the patio that lit it from the front. The building rose beyond their beam though, and vanished into gloom. The steps rose to plate-glass doors, higher than any human frame. They would have sufficed even for me.

I walked back beyond the corner to the girder-point. I removed the bandages from my palms and I began to climb.

Soon the mist was below me, and the patio, and the street. My cloths unwrapped as I rose. They made white flags in the breeze beneath me. Then even the clouds dispersed and the moon rolled yellow next to the clean line of brick. My shadow came with it, darkening the streets. The stars pricked the sky all over, the moon ladled over them and the wind whipped round my loosened limbs. It tore at my bandages, set them free then in one long roll from my waist. I had come to the end of the girder. There was a parapet above me. I paused, clinging with both hands to an overhang.

The last piece of white unravelled from my calf. I let loose one hand and grabbed the cloth with it, swinging freely. I was naked, I realised, but observed by nothing but the moon and stars; for one moment my body sang. I hung on, and each tendon felt at home. I looked up at the moon and whispered a sigh of thanks. The stars glowed brighter for a moment. I heard the wind and the furling of cloth. I let my eyes follow the bandage, which billowed in a long white arc, drawn into a curve by the high wind and tracing figures to the ground below me.

It was no longer empty. A small boy stood there. His hand was stretched in the air for the white end. It hung above him, moving back and forth. I considered what he would have seen and felt proud of myself, his eyes watching. He had the calm concentration of all children. I let the bandage go, as a message or gift, and swung myself in one movement over the parapet.

I thought of wheat fields at night, their yellow tips gleaming as the full sweep of the night sky came into my vision. All the stars had cleared themselves of mist for me, like hard bright cornheads waiting to be gathered. I balanced on that parapet without much difficulty. My toes gripped the edge while my heels still hung over the void. There was humming in the air. It had two pitches, bassy below and thin and wavering above. Did it come from those stars or this building, I wondered. I let my eyes fall with it from the wheatfields to what lay at my feet.

The roof was of plain cement with a spiral staircase jutting out into the skyline. Many yards away, near the opposite parapet, was a rain trough. I stepped down on to the roof and felt the cement beneath my feet.

The staircase was made of thin steel which sang when I plucked it. It made a dark half-segment through the roof. I climbed down, into the building below.

I found a long, low-roofed storeroom. There was a rolled carpet against the wall. Through the slim rectangular windows the wheaten stars could be seen. I crawled inside the cylinder of carpet and was soon asleep.

18

MY DREAMS WERE of humans. I was smooth once more, my hair was cut close to my temples, I was wearing a suit I had never seen, it is tighter in fashion than in my day I remember saying. Absolutely unfamiliar with myself, like one who has drifted off and been suddenly woken in mid-afternoon, I knew obscurely that what I carried under my elbow, pressed to my side, was a brief of some kind. I walked down a long corridor with flowers on the floor, there were sweeps of light coming through successive windows. When I came to the fourth door I knew that this was where my assignation was, though there was no indication that doors down the long corridor beyond were any different. I knocked, heard no answer but entered anyway.

She was standing by the window with some beads on the high-frocked dress which gave her figure the repose it had always promised. She was twisting the beads in her fingers. She did not look up when I entered, allowing me to see to the full what a woman she had become. The creature I had left, so small, so unformed, with those long ribbons of years ahead of her, had emerged, both bound and unwrapped by them, the child I barely knew so changed as to be almost hidden and quite another creature revealed.

Matilde.

She turned when I called her name. Like those exotic birds in whom, by reason of acquaintance with their more prosaic cousins, we recognise some characteristics, I could see in that long neck, in that tiny ruffle which seemed to spread from it to the crown of her short cropped hair, some ghost of her childhood movements.

She came towards me and kissed me. The kiss was a brief one, but in the quick withdrawal of her face from mine I sensed a torrent of emotion. I looked into her eyes and saw them at once angry and pleading for kindness. I knew then she was in love, she had been in love and felt mishandled. I felt pity, but even more, a sense of great misplacement that her body had touched another's, her soul had met another's. She called me by a name then, not my own, and it dawned on me that she was in love with me.

She asked me to reconsider my feelings. She told me no one but me could fill her life, now or for a long time to come; perhaps for ever. My coldness she could not understand, but she could live with it if I were to give even a hint of my former affection. Nobody could have been like me, she whispered, during those moments.

I wondered what I had done, how I had met her, how I had kept my identity secret. But the light that came through the great plate-glass window from what seemed to be a workaday, silver-lined city outside imposed its own order on my words, my movements. I felt the great ageful wash of guilt, I must have known, obscurely, in the pit of the consciousness with which I performed whatever acts I had performed, who and what I was. It inhibited my words even more. She was bathed in that light, so proud and vulnerable, shifting backwards and forwards, her tall comely shape like a product of it, so statuesque and proud, waiting for words I could never utter now I knew who I once was, what I later was, to her. At last she took my silence with finality. She became as shapely, as functional as that light.

The light surrounding her was oblong and tall, suiting her proportions. Then the light changed and all the angles softened and I was staring now at a circular orb as rich as morning. There were rainbows in front of my eyes and the multitudinous curve of those hairs once more. Like sedge-grasses or rushes sweeping down a dune, they glistened with pinpoints of moisture as if Morning herself had bestowed them upon her, sucked through that invisible line between light and dark. I knew then it was my arm, on which my large head was resting. The long funnel of carpet was up there, a mouth of light. The morning sun filled it almost totally, distorted only by the grime on the plate-glass window. I stared at this sun for a long time. It as golden as ever, but no longer an orb. It was blessedly elliptical, as if the lenses of my new eyes had given it depth. Then the sun was eclipsed by a shape that entered its curve abruptly and hung there, wavering slightly, its edges blurred. Was it cherub or flying creature, I wondered, hovering just beyond the edges of that plate-glass; until it spoke then, and in a boy's voice.

I brought you your things, sir.

The voice was high-pitched and eager, with a slight hint of the Americas. I wondered what being would call such as me sir. I dragged myself towards the light. His face withdrew somewhat, then approached again. A hand stretched.

I kept these for you. The way you climbed that building was really something.

His hand was firm and surprisingly strong. It grasped mine until I clambered out. I rose to my full height and stretched myself. I could feel his eyes on me constantly, admiring and awestruck. I almost shared his wonder at my movements. The air was cut in half with the light which slanted in one rigid plane, darkened my upper half and lightened my lower. There was a plain white marble block by the window. I sat on it, my knees became half-orbs of grey. The marble was cool, chalk-smelling. I placed my chin in the palm of my hand and looked up from the repose of myself to his face.

I kept them for you, he repeated. They're as good as new.

He held the bandages in his tiny hands. The first stirrings of haze began in the city behind him. The bandages were amber-coloured; last night's rain had sullied all the white. He held them out as if presenting a gift. And when I took them from him I felt the mood of my last self rise like steam off them, they carried an odour like the juices of a thousand memories, if memories could have been crushed like grapes or rose petals. I let them drop to the floor and a cloud of dust rose from them, as if they were unwilling to say goodbye.

Is there anything you'd like? he asked.

I had been reluctant to speak, remembering the loathing

that my voice once produced. But I trusted in his trust of me. I told him slowly and carefully that yes, I did feel hungry.

What do you eat?

And I realised for the first time that I was not sure. I had the memory of what had once been a tongue shredded on a plate, and of murmuring voices. Had I not eaten since then? I told the boy I was not sure. He described, his eyes wide open and eager, the various kinds of foods that he could get me. His father grew sweetcorn in the basement, where the heat from the immense boiler that he stoked let them grow to 'that size' – and he stretched out his arms. There were leftovers from the office canteen. He could even get me whole dinners, at a pinch.

I imagined the broad green leaves of the sweetcorn and so asked him for that. He ran to the door then, but stopped there and turned. He stared at me. His brown eyes seemed almost embarrassed.

Is there something wrong? The timbre of my voice was by now like whole forests. His eyes flashed towards me and away.

I want to see you walk.

So I rose from the marble block and took his hand in mine and walked to the plate-glass window. Every tendon seemed to stretch like never before. The light filled me when I reached it. I let go of his hand and pressed both arms against the glass. The glass, which transmitted such heat, was itself like ice. My forearms blazed with colour. I turned to see was he happy, but he was gone.

I felt the light come through me. I walked up to the spiral staircase and climbed outside.

19

THE CITY HAD grown its coating of haze, so thick that the skyline imitated a horizon, an even murky blue, but for the largest buildings which soared above it. Periodic gusts of hot winds spread across it, dragging me now in one direction, now in the other. I was drawn towards the cement pool and there saw myself again, with wonder now and a touch of delight. The water was miraculously still, maybe four feet deep. I was fawn in colour, strange elegant angles like curlicues whorled where my elbows were. Underneath the tawny sheen my limbs seemed translucent, changed into some strange alloy, gelatin perhaps, opaque where the bones might have been. I could have stretched for an age. I slid into the water then and assumed its element. Threads of gold flowed out from me, shifting with the ripples. I rolled my head under and around and came to the surface again, dreaming of that hair again that flowed towards a bank. Two great webbed feet were splayed above it. There was the sound of flapping wings, the sky was muddied by white and the feet slowly rose, underneath the bales of beating feathers. A large egg rocked there, backwards and forwards. A line streaked across its surface, then a regular crack which grew, emitted small bursts of chalk dust. The sides of egg split, two wings struggled to light and a Phoenix head above them, a jabbing, mareotic beak turned this way and that. It grew to fullness then flew, again the flapping bales of feather drew the webbed feet upwards. The fragments of shell tumbled into the water and hissed there, bubbling gently. Something green floated among them. I gripped it between two fingers. It was a head of corn.

The boy stood by the pool's edge, his thin arms folded round a host of green corn-tips. He smiled and I saw for the first time a gap between his teeth. I slid from the water to the pool's edge. I ate the corn slowly and he ate one too, as if to share the moment with me. I peeled the broad green leaves which the wind whipped away over the parapet into the haze beyond. He told me how the corn struggles through its envelope of green and only throws it off when it attains perfect ripeness. Has that happened to you, he asked. I answered that I could not be sure.

He told me then how his brown complexion came from stoking the enormous stoves which powered the building which his father, the boilerman, kept under his charge. He had stoked them for six years, and was now aged twelve. He asked me my story and I told him of the changes, the bandaged dinner-parties and the escape into the night. He nodded, and seemed to understand. I remembered Marianne and Matilde, and standing by the sundial underneath the fencing, and my cheeks moistened with tears. I felt a pain where my heart should have been and my shoulders began to heave with uncontrollable sobs. He put his hands on my temples and laid my head on his minute shoulder. He told me of dreams he had of changes, that his father was in fact a king who lorded over quite a different building in a large suite, serviced by a glittering lift.

Will nothing bring you back? he asked.

I told him I was not sure. He spoke to me then of wizards, of magic potions and maiden kisses. He kissed me on the fingers, as if to see could that effect a cure, and his eyes took some time to change from hope to disappointment. Then he confided in me that his disappointment would perhaps have been greater if I had changed back since nothing could be as splendid as what I was now.

There was a rumble in the building then and the liquid in the pool broke into ripples. That sound started up, both high and low at the same time. They were the boilers, he told me, starting up for the day. He would be needed to run errands and stoke them. Was there anything else I needed?

And I remembered her then. Like a clear liquid that one

drinks with very special meals, the taste brought back that perfume, that dark hat moving among the drawing boards, those long knees in the reptile house. We had both shared the changes. My longing to see her was as sharp for a moment, as brutal, as all that had happened. I held my pliant wrist, remembering the bandage she had written on. I told him there was a number, written on the bandages down by the carpet-roll, could he ring it and tell her I was here.

I saw him run across the large empty slabs below, the white bandage streaming after him. He stopped at the edge of the street to roll it in a ball, but it unwound when he ran on again, trailing through the morning crowds. I sat on the parapet, feeling somewhere that I should think of things, but my thoughts resisted any shape. Each minute brought a mood of its own to which I succumbed.

So morning passed in a series of changes. Every moment presented a different vista. The winds blew in one and died down in the next. The sun kept its heat but moved perceptibly, bringing all its shadows with it. All the creatures of the air seemed to cling to the shadows and move with them too. Towards noon they settled as if the heat had lulled them at last and they knew that the shadows, decreasing since daybreak, could only grow. The pool steamed gently. I began to walk. I paced around my rectangular home and the creatures rose in flurries with each step. They seemed to anticipate each of my movements and cleared the warm concrete under my feet before each of my footfalls. I paced the concrete for what seemed an age. Each brick was infested with life. More creatures whispered from the crevices in the parapet. I stared over the edge at that great sweep of concrete and glass, and that whisper became a roar.

There was the sound of footsteps and I turned as she emerged from the spiral staircase. The wind came from below now and tugged at her dress and the straw basket she was carrying. The boy came out behind her. He stood watching as she walked towards me past the pool. I stood with my back to the parapet. She had a flowered dress. A stick of bread jutted from the basket. I went to move but none of my muscles would answer. The wind lifted her dress in gusts like

365

the bowl of a hyacinth over the stems of black stocking which covered her knees. I felt strangely transparent under her gaze, as if she could see as she approached every cranny of me, down to that strange heart of mine still woven into a bowl from that afternoon of animals.

My darling –

She held out her hand and touched mine. Slowly the whole of me rose to attention. The boy stared from behind her. Her only expression was a smile.

You are different again.

She drew me down beside her to tell me about the world. The company Musk had gone bankrupt, the product vanished without trace. And Morgan? I asked. She had called three days in succession, she told me, found the office closed and then transformed into a manicure salon. Do things change so fast out there? I asked. Everything, she answered.

I thought of Morgan and how our years together would vanish without trace. The wind lifted her hair and transformed it utterly.

Can I embrace you? I asked her.

When she smiled in reply I put my arms around her, felt how they stretched with ease down below her spine to the tops of her thighs. She stroked my back, which seemed to mould itself into her hand's movement. I could picture the shape it assumed, a scallop, ridged to its base by her five long fingers. She drew one finger from the hollow of my temple down the long plane of my cheek and buried it in the golden strands of my torso. I lifted her in both hands, one beneath the small of her back and the other behind her knees, and walked with her to the parapet. She laid her cheek on the concrete and her eyes followed each one of my movements. Behind the flame of her hair the city steamed in its haze. My largeness was apt at last, my three fingers stretched the fabric of her dress, they exuded a warmth that filled her eyes, I was nothing that I had ever known or imagined. I carried her to the pool and dipped her slowly just beneath its surface. The green corn leaves floated everywhere, clinging to her body as I lay with one arm stretched on the bank, the other rippling the water. She made a crown of thick dark olive with the leaves. And as she played with me I changed, the hair of my forearm became sleek and shining, my fingers bunched like the feet of cattle. She nudged against my ear and drew one arm around me, wrapping the long strands of my tail about her neck. The boy made a wide fan of the corn-leaves and beat the air repeatedly to cool her. We played all afternoon under the boy's slow, quiet eyes. They filled with our delight and delighted us in turn. I saw a band of gold glistening in the water. I brought it to the surface and saw it was a wedding-ring. Long, slow tears coursed down my face then. She brushed them clear with her hands, but they kept on coming. And as if they understood my need, they held me while I wept, filling the pool to its brim, tears spilling over the sides. By evening, the whole parapet was wet.

She left with the last of the light. It held on barely, very barely, while she travelled down the core of the building. I saw her make that short, hesitant run across the piazza below and on to the empty street. The darkness slowly filled the air behind her, as if only my gaze had been willing it back. The way the inky blue of Matilde's palette gradually merged with and swamped the pink, that way the night invaded each yard of street as she passed over it.

20

THE MOON THEN came up and spread its own brand of light, and its image in the water was rippled by the wind. I was content to lie and measure its ascent and observe the gradual appearance of the stars. The spiral staircase became etched with silver. In my naivety, my joy, I had neglected to ask either of them about what lay below. That anonymous hum which even now persisted seemed to imply any number of worlds. I made my way to the staircase, swung myself on to the whorl of metal and crept downwards. I saw the concrete room and remembered my bedding in that roll of carpet. Below that again I found a hall of wires. They spread in all directions, all shapes and colours, from the tiniest to cables the circumference of my torso. The humming, so anonymous above, had grown a certain depth down here, as if each wire carried its own note, from the thinnest soprano to the basso-profundo of the thick-set cables. I thought of the music of insects, so ravishingly conveyed to me that garden afternoon. Each sound then had seemed bred of chance; no graph, no logical architecture, could have determined the glorious chaos of that chorus. But here, purpose seemed to reign. The wires sang in unison, with a constancy that had an end in view, an end I could only guess at.

The end must have been in that building, or perhaps the building itself was an end. With this in mind I made my way across the hall of wires to what had the appearance of a lift-shaft. The array of white buttons was discoloured with age. Too small for the pads of my fingers; I had to press them at random several all at once. I saw hawsers glisten through the metal grid, I heard the clicking of grease and the whir of a motor. And then the trellised box of the lift rose towards me.

We sank downwards through the building, the lift and I. Those dim halls rose to my vision and away again, each much like the one before. The buttons I had pressed must have determined our passage, because we stopped, unaccountably, in a felt-lined corridor without much distinction. I stepped through the trellised doors. I was half-mindful of going forward, half-mindful of going back again, when the doors slid closed. The lift whined and the light on the panel sank downwards.

I walked forwards. There were doors off this corridor, with rooms leading to more doors. What I had assumed to be devoid of life I soon found to be a bestiary. A deep-piled room seethed with mice. A moth watched me from a filing-cabinet. His eyes, full of the wisdom of ages and the fierceness of his few hours here, seemed to require my attention. My ears swelled with a sensation I could hardly feel as sound, let alone speech, and yet I felt from his quivering wings the urge to converse. I brushed him on to my palm. His glance seemed to harden – with disdain, it seemed – and his wings beat their way skew-wise towards the doorway.

I followed. His uneven flight, irritating but somehow alluring, drew me down stairways, passages, lit only by the fierceness of his glare. We were now in low-roofed concrete tunnels, similar in texture to the ones I had left, far above. He blundered into walls and cables, but somehow always kept ahead of me. Then that jagged flutter changed to a spiral of panic. I heard an unearthly trill, like the vibration of a toughened tongue in a mouth of bright leather. I turned and saw the scythe-like wings of a bat swoop by me, then change its flight into those jagged arpeggios the moth was now weaving. They traced each other in counterpoint for a moment and it seemed a second cry rang out with the bat's, a cry that was soft, like the sound pollen would make brushing off a wing, but yet a cry with more pain in it than any I had heard. Their paths merged into one then, the bat's mouth opened, then closed, and the bat flew on alone.

The corridor seemed like a tomb to me afterwards. That

ashy cry seemed to echo down it, bringing tears to my eyes which made the walls glow. I made my way to the corridor's end, hoping for a lift or concrete stairs. The tunnelled walls curved and were lit by a glow that seemed brighter than the rainbows of my tears. It was yellowish, it flickered, there was a rhythmic, scraping sound. I heard voices then, one old and masterful, the other young. I came to the corner and saw the boy in the distance shovelling coal into a furnace. The heap he shovelled from was replenished from a source unseen. His shovelling was too tender to keep his heap down to size; it kept growing until it almost engulfed him. He was goaded on by shouts, coarse and violent. Then a dark-skinned figure in dungarees appeared, shovelled furiously with him for a moment, sent him spinning towards the furnace with a blow and left again, admonishing him to work faster.

21

WHEN THE BOY appeared the next morning with his arms full of cornheads and that glad expression on his face, I didn't mention what I had seen. I breakfasted on the corn and watched the leaves whirl over the city on the early-morning wind. Even that wind seemed to partake of the savagery of last night's events. The mists slowly disappeared, revealing the tiny beads of the morning crowds. I bathed in the pool and as he washed each sinew, I noticed weals on his body where before I had been aware only of that dusky tan. I questioned him on the rules of the building, though. He told me that he worked by night, and by day the building fed upon the heat he had generated. The corridors were peopled by secretarial ranks and the whirr of office machines took over from the more ancient machines of the night. I asked him was he tired by day and he told me that he was, but the pleasure of my presence kept him awake. I told him that once my presence brought very little pleasure, to man or to beast, and he answered that he could not imagine how this could have been so. After a time he slept in my water-logged arms. I wrapped myself round him, to accommodate his dreams.

I awoke to find her standing above me. It must have been early afternoon. I whispered at her to be silent and placed him beneath the shade of the parapet. We became lovers once more, then many many times. The concrete bubbled with our perspirations and we took to the pool for refreshment. She floated there, staring into the sky as I told her of the bat and the helpless moth. She told me that life had its own laws, different for each species. Does one law not rule us all? I asked her. How can it, she answered, or else we would have seen it. I asked her was there a law for me, as distinct as those for the bat and the moth. If there were, she asked me, would you obey it?

I had ceased to think of thoughts as thoughts, for the effort to separate them from the clouds of sensation that germinated them was mostly beyond me. Now, however, I pulled at this thought, I needed it clear, abstract and separate so as to find an answer. Her head played around my armpit then gradually fell asleep. I remembered dimly a tale of a beast who cried to the world to reveal him his destiny, to send him a mate. If there was a law for the bat, for the moth, for the woman, there must be a law for me, a law as succinct and precise as those laws I obeyed when walking past the whispering gardens each day to work. But how to find out this law, and the destiny it implied? But then, it occurred to me, walking by those gardens, along the torrid tracks, I had been no more aware of what law I obeyed than I was now, obeying no law at all. If asked then, was there a pattern, a plan, I would have said no, categorically no. So law, if law there was, revealed itself in retrospect, like a sad bride coming to her wedding too late to partake in it.

My efforts at thought exhausted me and these fancies gradually sank into that well of sensation from which they had emerged. The darkness seeped around me, like a torpor brought on by my mood. It was indeed night. She still slept in the niche of my arm. I lifted her head and placed it at my navel, and curled around each of her limbs to make her sleeping easier. The wind ruffled her tangled clothing and set the down along her cheekbones alight. I thought about what laws bound us and she opened her eyes then, as if in answer to that thought. Her lids parted slowly to reveal my curved reflection in her pupils. I stared at myself for a time, for perhaps too long a time, seeing me, seeing her, seeing me in her. Only when her eyes were fully open did I become aware of her expression. She took a sharp intake of breath. The horror filled her limpid eyes as the night had filled mine. She drew backwards. I raised my hands to clutch her, too roughly. Please, I whispered. It's the night, she said, you're different.

No, I cried. She was standing now, walking backwards towards the staircase. You should never have let me sleep, she whispered. The dark moulded her like a curtain, her hair glowed like sullen rust. I can't help my fear, she whispered, you should never have let me sleep. Her hand searched for the metal staircase. No, I whispered again, but my whisper gathered like a roar. She ran from that wall of sound. Some-where above me, stars began to fall.

22

I LAY FOR a long time. The darkness weighed on me. Who would remember the extraordinary length of her legs, I wondered, who would delight in that softness of skin at the joint of her knee, if not me? The changes came with such rapidity. Was the air never to be still, I wondered, from one moment to the next? To whom could she tell those stories, of the large tractors swathing through the meadows, of the young girl walking through the dewsoaked stubble? And even now the pace of my grief was such that I could feel it entwining me in a skin of its own. She had seen something, I remembered, something that caused the fear, and I rose slowly to my feet and staggered to the water. All I saw there was a shadow, like some more essential shade of dark than that which surrounded me. And I managed the thought that even what she had seen was now part of the past. Yet the desire to see what she had persisted. I made for the building below, searching out a mirror.

The lift was made of trellised bars of metal. None of its surfaces conveyed the ghost of a reflection. I pressed the buttons for some level below. I heard the whine of the motor, and with it a sound that was not a sound, that was above sound, that was a sensation, around my skull, my cheek-bones, like the needle-points of a sandstorm. I raised my hands to my cheeks to locate it. Then this sound took shape, flowed into vowels and syllables, into sentences. It spoke.

You operate this lift, it said, like someone remembering what it was to travel in it. And yet you look like –

What do I look like? I asked. I closed my eyes. The voice began again.

You take your texture from whatever surface you inhabit. In this lift you belong to that odour of grease, hawsers and trellised metal. Outside it, I would have no idea.

I opened my eyes. I saw opposite me, clinging to the bars, a bat. His eyes were bright with reason. I remembered the arpeggios of fear and the death of the moth. That leatherish mouth didn't move, and yet his voice sang all around me.

Can you fly? he asked.

I shook my head.

Each animal function, he told me, has its sister emotion. Loathing, he said, has been your companion for some time.

He moved his head and seemed to smile. Do you wish to fly?

I nodded.

Take us up, then.

I pressed the buttons. He stared as we swayed upwards once more, a stare full of brightness, whimsy, intelligence.

23

HE CLUNG TO the matted hair on my arm as I walked from the staircase. I placed him on the parapet. His sightless eyes turned in their sockets. I could feel his voice again, prodding me like gorse. Forget wings, he told me. Watch!

He moved both arms as if stroking the air, stepped off the parapet and plummeted like a dead weight. I cried out in alarm, but saw his fall, of a sudden, transform into a graceful curve. It became a figure of eight and slowly drew him upwards once more. He hovered above me for a moment, full of cries.

Wings are quite useless, he said, mere symbols of our activity. Birds, being vainer than my species, love to proclaim their importance, cover themselves in feathers and tails they can fan. But all one needs to fly with is desire.

And I thought of how swallows always reveal themselves in spring like small threads of longing and as the heat grows they become rushes of memory, filling the air with their curlicues, never touching ground, symbols indeed of desire.

Do you desire? he asked me.

I had hardly thought before I flew. The parapet swung above me and the piazza grew larger, swum before my eyes till I left it behind and moved in a long curve down Dame Street, barely at the level of the second windows, piercing the rim of that layer of heat that the night hadn't yet dispersed. I took the breeze on my left side at Nassau Street and swept down that channel of air. Some instinct drew me towards the river. I felt his voice all around me again and glanced up to see him at my shoulder, his wings dipping easily and gracefully with my infant movements.

Lead the way, he whispered, so I swung him down the steaming river and then left, face above the railway tracks, under the long glass awning, through those arcs of spray that splashed on the night trains. We kept close to the rails as sleeper after sleeper sped below us, each like a resinous wall. I smelt the odour of cut grass then and rose and skimmed above garden after garden till at length I came to one where the blades had not been cut and recognised it as mine. I headed over the tips of the nodding grasses, barely able to see through the pollen. There was an immense triangle jutting from a metal plinth. I hovered over the heiroglyphs on the disc below and saw how the moon's cast upon time was at variance with the sun's. I saw a large ball of light somewhere up ahead. I left the sundial and made my way through the grasses once more. The ball of light beckoned through the clouds of pollen and then the air suddenly froze. I beat myself against it, but to no avail, the light was there, but sealed behind it, impenetrable. I had almost exhausted myself when I recognised the frozen air to be glass, the ball of light a flickering bulb. I slid downwards. A large jewelled palm wiped moisture off the pane. Through the swathe that was cut in it I could see a glass, half-filled with liquid and the same hand lifting it to the crescent space between lips. I was indeed home. I watched Marianne for what seemed an age, from below. In my absence her lips had changed from deep cherry to rust, her hair had been shorn tight, the corners of her eyes had grown two black triangles. Two fingers indented themselves on her cheek and the dome of another's head descended for another's lips to meet hers. I recognised James.

There was a letting-go and a sensation of ice sliding past my cheek. I fell down among the grasses below. Her lips, though larger to me than ever, were still those lips I remembered. Down among those roots of green I could still picture the kiss, too long, far too long for the desire that had carried me here. I tried to beat myself upwards but not a whisper of movement ensued.

I felt the air stroking my face then in soft hushes, and his voice sang round me once more.

You know now why bats are what they are, poised between

strutting and flight. To fly cleanly you must learn pure desire, a desire that has no object. Any attachment to things of the world leaves you earthbound once more.

I held a pure blade of grass between my palms and imagined pure desire. I could picture nothing, and soon nothing was all I pictured. Slowly, very slowly, the memories left me. The house, the hissing sprinklers, the sundial. That window was the last memory to go, and the kiss drifted away like whorling water, and I rose, to hover inches over the lawn. He chirped with a pleasure that made me soar. Soon the house became a tiny dot in the palette of the blue earth below us.

24

THE CITY SANK, like a glass bead into a muddied pool. The air was pure above it, with the ethereal blue of a wedding-gown. He seemed not to move, but yet was all movement, rising above me. Desire, he said, when purified, becomes desire no longer. I felt his voice and soared with the certainty. Loathing, when purified, becomes loathing no longer. I felt all affirmation and drifted towards him, his eyes glowing sightless in the gloom. Through blindness, his voice sang out, we cultivate the vision, through sensation we reach it and yet what we reach we still cannot see. He drifted around me like a thread of silk. Yet the feeling, he whispered, is our only road there, so can we doubt that the feeling is all?

He drew his limbs about him and let himself fall. I fell to his pace, just above him. The air thickened and the streets billowed out below. There is a city, he whispered, to whose shape all cities aspire. And when the sheaves of our city fall away, we shall reach it. When will that be? I asked him. Tomorrow, he sang. He curled his furred body and sped downwards.

25

I STOOD ALONE on the parapet under the moon. Alarth –
for that was his name – had vanished into the depths of the
lifeshaft. The streets were empty and silver, like a dream that
was now dreaming itself. I slid down from the parapet and
walked towards the trough. I saw my face there, as limpid
and clear as the moon beside it. Each breath I took was like
a sliver of lost time. I inhaled and seemed to drink in hours.
To each beginning there was an end, I knew, and each change
hurried it nearer. I walked down the staircase to the comfort
of the lift. I pressed the buttons and felt the gradual slide
downwards. The cables of the lift swung, shifting their curves
as they did so. I thought of the gardens, through the long
heat and the rain, of Marianne's face with its triangles of
black. That change, so miniature, had brought an ache to
me as large as that the chaos of myself had brought to her.
There was a law, I now knew, and its resolution would come
to be. I pressed the buttons with the stumps of my arms. The
door slid back and a corridor faced me, like all the others.
There was no moonlight here to illuminate my way, but the
discs of my eyes soon accepted the black and the dark became
light of its own. A swarm of midges hovered round a door.
I entered, and saw a room in the chaos that work had left
behind. There were paper cups, the rinds of cheeses and a
bottle of mineral water. There were drawing-boards ranged
against the walls and across the slope of one of them a figure
lay sleeping. I recognised the crescent of the green eyeshade
and moved myself closer. Beneath the dull green shadow I
saw Morgan's face, his lips immobile, a day or two's growth
on his chin. He had vanished when she called, she had told

me, and must have found different employment. I saw draw-ings crumpled beneath his head, those buildings of concrete and glass that had come to litter the city, half-finished. Con-ceived by nobody, it was generally imagined, and built in the owlish hours. Yet their source was here, in these immeasur-able rooms. Spanning the wall behind was a miniature of the city as it once had been. I looked at those squares in their measured movement towards the river, their proportions so human, yet so perfect to the eye. I saw the park, etched out in strokes of green, the zoological gardens at its centre. I remembered the textures of pavements under my feet, of grass round my ankles, the doorways that once stared at my child's eyes, the balanced stone of their arches and the fan-lights of glass. I saw drops splashing on Morgan's clenched hand and drew my lips down to taste the salt of my tears. The hand shifted then, the fingers stretched and touched my movable skin.

It is you, he said, after a moment's pause.

I nodded. His reddened eyes flashed under their arc of green.

What is it like, he asked, to be away from it all?

I shook my head. If I could have spoken I would have asked him not to talk, reminded him of our days without words in adjacent rooms. He rubbed his eyes and gestured round the room.

Each afternoon, he said, I draw the city for them. And each morning my instructions change.

Who are they, I would have asked.

I work for them now, he added. He gripped a paper cup and began rubbing it to shreds.

Do you remember the time, he asked, when we used to work until five and walk down the river to our separate trains?

Yes, I said. The word came out round and true.

I sleep here now, he told me. I wake and I work and I sleep again. I keep the shutters down so that the light is the same.

I asked him would he mind if I pulled them back. He shook his head slowly and watched me as I did so.

A horse walked down the street below, moved sideways to avoid a bollard. A large poppy filled the window of a haberdashery.

I stretched out one arm and touched his green eyeshade. My palm, like a mucous membrane, let his face glow through it.

Is it fair, he asked me, to have given us the memory of what was and the desire of what could be when we must suffer what is?

I heard the gravel of dust in his voice, I saw smudges of graphite on his fingers. I phrased his name slowly. Morgan.

He looked up. I felt the wind of his despair. I rose slowly till my thighs were level with his face. Goodbye now, he whispered. He stepped forwards with me and opened the window. I heard it close behind me as I sank through the gloom outside.

The horse was walking slowly, his dark grace etched against the sweep of College Green. I felt tired, I had lost even the memory of desire. I sank into the poppy in the haberdasher's window. I clung to the pistil and the petals billowed round me, settling gradually into a pillow of red.

26

I AWOKE TO the sounds of people. My arms were curled round that thrust of pistil with the dewdrop at the tip. The morning sun had stiffened the petals, the red pollen covered me as if their lips had bunched into a kiss. The early crowds passed by, but as I stretched my limbs groups of them gathered to stare. I drew myself upwards, bending the pistil towards me. The dewdrop fell on my face. They murmured as they watched, about portents and signs. Two soldiers pushed to the front. The pistil slipped from my hands then, I rolled down the petal and came to rest at their feet.

A man in the livery of a hotel commissionaire called on me to stand. One khaki leg prodded me, gently, but not without authority. Whom do you belong to, a voice above me asked.

I saw a small face thrusting through the thighs about me, a pair of arms full of cornheads. I gestured, but was unwilling to speak. Is he yours, the same voice asked, when he made it to my side. The boy nodded, with childlike pride and vigour. He pressed a cornhead into my hands.

I ate, and listened. You must keep him inside, one of the soldiers said, phrasing the words carefully, as one does with a child. The boy nodded, took my hand and led me forwards.

The crowd parted in front of us, but followed from behind. The commissionaire protested from amongst them. The soldier reached forward and the boy began to run. I ran too, over the grass above the paving-stones, and as the crowd followed faster, I gathered him in my arms and lost them.

We wove our way through the desultory streets. We came to a hotel with a park beside it. There was a waterless fountain there. We climbed into its stone flower and feasted on the cornheads. Soon the petals were littered with green.

27

HE TOLD ME he had searched for me through the depths of the building. He had waited for her, but she had never arrived. I told him I had flown, guided by a feeling that was nothing but itself. I had seen the city become a dot on the landscape and a blade of grass become a tower of green.

He told me then of Jack, who had planted a stalk that made a ladder to the skies, of how the story never told him what Jack found there. I would dearly love to fly, he said, turning his face to me. We will wait till evening, I told him, till that magic hour when our desires can picture the image that retreats from us. Will you fly to her? he asked, but I didn't reply.

All day we waited, while the sun moved the shadows through the empty grass. Some shadows walked and stopped by the fountain, gazing at us before walking on once more. He told me how the shadows thrown by the fires he stoked reminded him of the lives other boys must lead, lives he would never know anything about. Sleeping, never far from his father's calloused hands, he had longed for a friend, but could never picture what that friend might be like. A siren wailed in the distance and the city's hum rose like a final breath. What is happening? he asked, and curled his fingers round me. Nothing, I answered. Be calm.

Towards afternoon I must have slept. I imagined a moth fluttering towards the sun, the dust on its wings crackling with the heat, the flame spurring him on to his own extinction. When I awoke the mauve light had softened the shadows and given each colour a life of its own. It was evening.

The boy stood on the stone petal staring at the sky. I swung my way towards him, wrapped one arm around his torso and flew. I held his face close to mine to see the passing wonders echoed in his eyes. I bore him round at random and my desire became delight. The rush of wind drew my hair around him in a silken cloak. We flew together, out by the southern suburbs. We went far up into those realms of pure air where the rose-coloured clouds hung over the city I had loved like a brooding mushroom. The winds were fresh and keen up there. The air was aquamarine. I could see the lines of the bay very dimly, and another line too, between the metal green I knew to be the sea and the brownish mass that was the city. I sped down towards it and found not one line but two, both of which crossed at intervals, in slender figures of eight. It was the railway-track, which traced the curve of the bay. I had heard tell of these tracks, but had never yet seen them. His eyes were alert to every passing shape, as if the shadows his flaming coals threw had taken on true life. This side of the city was foreign to me, with its multitude of cramped, cracked villas tumbling towards the sea. I bore us closer to the land and found the houses gave way to a slope of trees. Though there was foliage at the tops, the trunks were quite bare and so I whipped between them, grazing the peeling bark like a swallow. The dance of those trees I apprehended without thought as I threaded my way through them and crept upwards again. We burst through the foliage and the odour there – thicker than steel wool, richer than pollen – brought to mind the one I had last held this close. I thought of musk once more. The mountainside sang of it and told me my desire had an object. The slope became a cliff, wreathed in fog. The fog bled downwards and I followed to the sea where our reflections rippled with our movement. Then there was fog no more and tracks beneath us. We passed scattered villas, imitative of a style I could not now remember. They led to a bridge, and a station beyond.

I felt the panic of a desire that had led me truly. I traced a large arc over the eaves of the station. There was a line of pleasure-parlours by a crumbling promenade. In one of them a yellow light glimmered.

28

SHE WAS STANDING by the dodgems in a blue smock. There were blotches on her face and runnels of hair along her arms. The changes, she told me, were so rapid that each day was a source of sometimes wonder, sometimes terror, sometimes both. She had longed to see me, but had been unwilling to approach, since she felt the need of a partner to delight in them. Could you now? she asked, and came towards me, the pits and shallows of her face raised in expectation. Yes, I said, but the word that emerged did not seem affirmative. So, she said, I must find another. She brushed my translucent face with her bunched fingers. Business was even worse, she told me, in the realms of entertainment than in the realm of perfume. Her friends had shunned her, she told me, seeing her as a sign, of a happening they would never allude to or define. And yet I am glad, she said. Tell me why I am glad. The fact, I told her, is a relief from its anticipation. And the feeling is all. She drew her swollen lips into a smile. Once more, she understood. A soldier entered then, his head bent low, his hands thrust deep into his khakis. You must leave now, she whispered. She drew her smock around her face and walked towards him.

We slipped through the shadows, the boy and I. I drew him over the awning in one sad curve. The soldier parted her tresses below us. She sighed with anticipated pleasure. We hovered above them, like uninvited guests, until I drew him towards the sea once more.

THE WATERS WERE calm, a long shallow pit of salt. All hint of reflection had now vanished. They were graced by a thin pall of mist.

You cannot blame her, the boy said. His voice bounced over the waters.

No, I replied. I sank with him to just above that mist.

She loved you, he said. But only for a time.

His wisdom was comforting. I fell with him into the sea and held him there, buoyed by an excess of salt.

He remarked on how it tasted like tears. I agreed with him. We let the sea carry us, and the night.

WHEN DAY CAME up, we saw that the city with its crumbling cubes was far behind us. The waters steamed gently. The liquid rose in a diaphanous haze and left behind pure crystals of salt. They stayed poised beneath the surface like a thousand eyes. I twined myself into a vessel beneath him and moved us forwards with my broad fingers. He told me of the mermaid who had ventured on land and to whom each footstep was like the thrust of a blade. Soon my arms became covered in a crystal sheen.

The sun moved slowly on the waters. At its pinnacle the haze was such that it multiplied itself. I swam on. The boy wondered whether the sun moved backwards out here. But no, it was merely the illusion of haze.

I felt little need to speak. The sound of the water, oddly reverberant in the ever-present vapour, made speech enough. The boy talked as the spirit moved him. He had strands of my hair wrapped around his fists, in excitement or anticipation. Then night came down and the light gave way quite unobtrusively.

WE MUST HAVE slept, for I awoke to moonlight and a
sense of turbulence. The sea all about us was calm, however,
and the moon was brilliant in the absence of haze. The boy
still slept. I heard a prodding all around me which merged
into a voice. I saw Alarth winging towards me across the
waters. Come, come, he whispered. A winged fish broke
the surface, twisted silver under the moonlight and enveloped
him in its maw. Then a white flash filled the air from the city
we had left. It was paler than any white that had been and
was followed by others, each paler again till the white seemed
permanent. Then the sounds came, all the sounds at once,
from the deepest to the thinnest in a circular boom, they
sang towards us in waves, and hard on their heels the waters
followed. I covered the boy and was dragged by the mountain
of water.

Wнат саме was not quite daylight and not quite night. The waters were calm and strewn with debris and cut grass. I had twined myself into a pouch round the boy. Far behind us that cloud, shaped like a phoenix, glowed with that terrible mauve. I stroked my fingers and moved us towards a promontory beyond.

A marble arm lay on the whitened sand. The boy was sick, I knew. His translucent lips tried to speak, but couldn't. I rose with him from the waters and made my way across that sand. There were the marks of feet. A fish twined its way round a clump of seagrass, its gills moving easily. I followed the webbed footprints.

When the time came that I knew the boy was dying, I wrapped myself fully round him, assumed him into myself. We both walked onwards, though my steps were weary with the knowledge that I would never see his face again. I remembered the cornheads, but felt no need for food. After a time those footprints were joined by others.

Each knew where to go, with no need of direction. With the mareotic sea far behind me, I took their advice. Many, many footprints later I came to a pool. The boy in me drew me to its surface. I put my lips to it and drank and felt his satisfaction. When the rippling caused by my lips had settled, I saw a reflection there, no less terrible than mine. A hand rubbed white sand away from a mouth. It was like mine in its shape and texture. Her hair, unmistakably female, was a whey-coloured fan in the constant wind. I raised my head and the boy inside me leapt. Her lips moved slowly and creased themselves upwards. My lips moved too. I recognised Marianne.

33

WE SPOKE FOR a while, by the pool. Once accustomed to each other's voices, we both walked together, following the footprints before us. We had similar memories of the mareotic lake. She told me of a fish that walked and of a tree that shed its covering of scales. Matilde, she told me, was inside her now. I put my arms down to her waist and felt her. The boy kicked with pleasure at the touch.

Once a large beast flew above us and her hand gripped mine. We followed the footprints, but met no others. Soon the sands gave way to a vista of grass. The labour of our feet was lessened then, that soft cushion drew us onwards. The footprints had ceased, but we followed our own path. We crossed a hill and found a landscape of tall poplars. Planted years ago, it seemed to speak of quieter times. If things lead us to anything, she said to me, they surely lead us to realisation. Each happening bears a message, as surely as those poplars speak of whoever planted them. She curled her fingers round my hand once more and I saw the translucence was slowly fading, being replaced by something like a tan. The line of poplars led us to a signpost reading: HOPE ETERNAL. The arrow had wound itself into a circle, though, the point of which pressed into its rear. There was a garden up ahead. The gates were unattended and the grasses wild. The sundial seemed bleached by an eternity of light and the sprinklers moved so slowly that they whispered. Can I kiss you, she asked and I answered yes, in a voice that had become like hers. She had to tilt her head to reach my lips which I found were once more soft. The kiss was long, long enough for the sun to cross the dial, for the moon to traverse it and for the sun to rise once more. I saw the globes of her eyes and in my visage reflected there saw something as human as surprise.